Cheers for

Karma Girl

"Sexy, laugh-out-loud fun. A big thumb̲ ⸺ d me laughing and che̲ ⸺ ⸺ avens

"A zippy prose sty̲ ⸺ e the usual run of paran̲ ⸺ *̲eekly*

"One of the most ⸺ ̲, ̲ ̲ just plain fun books I have read all year." —*Romance Reviews Today*

"A laugh-out-loud roller-coaster ride of pure escapist entertainment! . . . Ms. Estep has a gift for storytelling and showcases it beautifully." —*Fresh Fiction*

"Too funny to put down. The adventures of Carmen Cole will have you laughing, cheering, and rapidly turning the pages until the end." —*BookLoons*

"A very entertaining paranormal romance with many humorous scenes . . . highly recommended."
—*ParaNormal Romance*

"Deftly written . . . like no other book that one has read before." —*Love Romances & More*

"Secret identities and superpowers take on a delightful and humorous twist in Estep's exciting debut . . . Fun and sexy . . . [an] impressive talent." —*Romantic Times* (4 stars)

Karma GIRL

Jennifer Estep

BERKLEY SENSATION, NEW YORK

THE BERKLEY PUBLISHING GROUP
Published by the Penguin Group
Penguin Group (USA) Inc.
375 Hudson Street, New York, New York 10014, USA
Penguin Group (Canada), 90 Eglinton Avenue East, Suite 700, Toronto, Ontario M4P 2Y3, Canada
(a division of Pearson Penguin Canada Inc.)
Penguin Books Ltd., 80 Strand, London WC2R 0RL, England
Penguin Group Ireland, 25 St. Stephen's Green, Dublin 2, Ireland (a division of Penguin Books Ltd.)
Penguin Group (Australia), 250 Camberwell Road, Camberwell, Victoria 3124, Australia
(a division of Pearson Australia Group Pty. Ltd.)
Penguin Books India Pvt. Ltd., 11 Community Centre, Panchsheel Park, New Delhi—110 017, India
Penguin Group (NZ), 67 Apollo Drive, Rosedale, North Shore 0632, New Zealand
(a division of Pearson New Zealand Ltd.)
Penguin Books (South Africa) (Pty.) Ltd., 24 Sturdee Avenue, Rosebank, Johannesburg 2196,
South Africa

Penguin Books Ltd., Registered Offices: 80 Strand, London WC2R 0RL, England

This is a work of fiction. Names, characters, places, and incidents either are the product of the author's imagination or are used fictitiously, and any resemblance to actual persons, living or dead, business establishments, events, or locales is entirely coincidental. The publisher does not have any control over and does not assume any responsibility for author or third-party websites or their content.

KARMA GIRL

A Berkley Sensation Book / published by arrangement with the author

PRINTING HISTORY
Berkley trade edition / May 2007
Berkley Sensation mass-market edition / July 2008

Copyright © 2007 by Jennifer Estep.
Excerpt from *Hot Mama* copyright © 2007 by Jennifer Estep.
Cover illustration by Aleta Rafton.
Cover design by Judith Lagerman.
Interior text design by Kristin del Rosario.

ISBN: 978-0-425-22282-9

BERKLEY® SENSATION
Berkley Sensation Books are published by The Berkley Publishing Group
a division of Penguin Group (USA) Inc.,
375 Hudson Street, New York, New York 10014.
BERKLEY SENSATION and the "B" design are trademarks of Penguin Group (USA) Inc.

PRINTED IN THE UNITED STATES OF AMERICA

10   9   8   7   6   5   4   3   2   1

To my mom. Thanks for taking me to the library all those Saturdays. You've given me more than you will ever know.

And to my grandma. Thanks for just being you and for making the best fried chicken and biscuits in the world.

I love you both more than words can say.

ACKNOWLEDGMENTS

This book would not have been possible without the help of many, many people.

First of all, thanks to my super agent Kelly Harms, who believed in the book from the beginning and patiently held my hand through this whole process. Many thanks go to my fantastic editor, Cindy Hwang, for also believing and for being so nice and easy to work with. I appreciate you both more than you know.

Thanks to everyone who read and commented on the rough drafts. You all helped make the book better.

To all the comic book writers and artists out there, I hope you will enjoy my work as much as I have yours.

Many thanks to the Saturday Night Gaming Gang, for giving me countless hours of fun and laughs.

And, finally, to Andre, who introduced me to the wild and wacky world of gaming. Here's to you.

KARMA GIRL

PART ONE

Beginnings

★ 1 ★

My wedding day.

It was supposed to be the happiest day of my life. A time of joy and celebration and new beginnings. The day every girl dreams of from the time she's old enough to play dress-up in her mother's clothes.

It wasn't that sort of day at all.

I stalked up and down the narrow hotel room. My hellish high-heeled shoes poked holes in the thick carpet and rubbed hot blisters on my aching feet. My white tulle dress rustled with every step I took.

Something was wrong. Very wrong.

I'd had the feeling for weeks now that something just wasn't quite right between me and my fiancé, Matt Marion. He'd been distant lately, distracted. We'd been together over two years now, and I loved Matt with all my heart. But his odd behavior was enough to make the most trusting woman suspicious. I'd asked Matt many times if anything was wrong, if he had cold feet and wanted to postpone the wedding, but he'd assured me repeatedly that everything was fine.

Matt had been working lots of overtime at his construction job and had all sorts of unexplained bruises and scratches on his body. He'd blamed his frequent absences and injuries on work, but I couldn't quite shake this feeling, this cold sense of dread deep down in my stomach. Doubts whispered in my mind. I'd learned long ago to listen to my inner voice. Following my instincts was the reason I'd become the top investigative reporter at the *Beginnings Bugle*, the town newspaper.

I wasn't about to ignore my instincts now. I couldn't get married with this doubt hanging over me. I had to ask Matt one more time what was bothering him.

I slipped out of my hotel room and made my way to the elevator. It had been Matt's idea to get married at the Forever Inn, the most romantic hotel in all of Beginnings, Tennessee. Weddings took place on a daily basis at the four-star hotel, and no one batted an eye when I crowded into the elevator in my billowing dress and sparkling diamond tiara.

I rode up to the next floor and walked to Matt's room. It was bad luck—bad *karma*—for the bride and groom to see each other before the wedding, but I had to talk to Matt. My inner voice wouldn't shut up until I did.

I raised my hand to knock. A low, muffled moan escaped through the thick wooden door. Was Matt hurt? I frowned and put my key, the one I had in case of an emergency, in the lock. The door opened, and I stepped inside.

"Yes, Yes, YES!!!!" a woman screamed out from deeper in the room.

Oh. That's what that sound was. Someone was having a little afternoon delight. Good for them. I turned to give the enthusiastic couple their privacy when reality hit me.

Why was someone having sex in Matt's room? He should

have been in there, getting ready for his wedding, which was only thirty minutes away. His wedding to *me*.

I froze. A ball of ice formed in the pit of my stomach. I wasn't going to like what I was about to see, I just knew it, but I couldn't stop myself from looking. I tiptoed up to the doorframe, still hidden from view, and peeked into the bedroom.

Karen Crush, my best friend since the fourth grade, was straddling Matt, my oh-so-faithful fiancé. Karen's pale blue bridesmaid's dress bunched around her waist, exposing her lean legs. Matt's pants pooled around his ankles. A lacy thong sat crumpled beside the bed, along with some other pieces of blue and red fabric.

Karen flipped her black curls over her shoulder and threw her head back in pure bliss. The ecstatic look on Matt's face told me he was thoroughly enjoying himself as well. The bastard.

My world spun around. I felt as though someone had stabbed me in the chest with a butcher knife. Twice. Hot tears welled up in my eyes and trickled down my face. My knees shook. My legs threatened to buckle. Now, I knew what had been so wrong. Why Matt had been so distant. This one moment, this horrible sight, made it all so clear. So painfully clear. Love, friendship, humanity in general. My faith in those was now gone. Obliterated by the two people I loved most in the world.

Matt and Karen let out more cries of pleasure, oblivious to me. To my pain.

The sounds shattered my heart into a thousand sharp, jagged pieces. Each one cut me like a razor. I wanted to run out the door, to cry my eyes out, to sob and scream until I was hoarse from both. But a flash of bright blue underneath Matt's unbuttoned shirt caught my eye. I squinted through my cascading tears. It looked like . . . spandex.

Spandex?

"Oooh, I love it when you kiss my neck like that." A giggle escaped from Karen's perfect, heart-shaped lips.

I loved it when Matt kissed my neck like that too. Anger bubbled up in my chest like a volcano about to explode. I swiped away the rest of my hot tears and straightened my spine. I wasn't going to run away. Not from the two of them. Not until I had some answers.

Karen ran her hands down Matt's broad chest. Her long nails zipped along the fabric like scissors. She ripped his shirt open the rest of the way, revealing a blue spandex suit with a giant red *M* in the middle of it.

My mouth dropped open.

"Oh, baby. You drive me crazy!" Matt yanked Karen's dress down to her waist, exposing the lingerie-like red bustier she wore beneath. A yellow *C* stretched across her heaving chest.

I couldn't believe what I was seeing. But it was real—I would have known those costumes anywhere. Molten lava flowed through my veins, burning away everything but my all-consuming rage. My bubbling volcano of anger erupted with a scream of epic proportions. "Sonofabitch!"

Matt and Karen froze. Their heads snapped around to the doorway. Matt swallowed, his Adam's apple bobbing up and down. Karen's eyes widened. For an instant, I wondered what they were more upset about—that someone had caught them cheating or discovered their other precious secret. I didn't care either way. They'd both betrayed me.

My anger roared back, stronger than before, and I marched into the room. My hands balled into fists. My body rattled with rage. Even my wedding dress twitched with fury.

"Carmen! I . . . I can explain—"

I threw my hand up, cutting off Matt's pitiful attempt. "You're the Machinator?"

Matt sighed. He ran his fingers—the ones that weren't latched on to my best friend's exposed ass—through his blond hair. "I didn't want you to find out this way, Carmen."

"Oh no? When *were* you going to tell me you're Beginnings' own personal superhero? After we said *I do*? Maybe on our first anniversary? Or perhaps when our kids were in college? Or maybe right after you told me about sleeping with my best friend. On our *wedding day*."

"It's not his fault, Carmie," Karen said, her brown eyes big and earnest. "He wanted to tell you. We both did. About everything."

Carmie? I glared at my former best friend. She still had the nerve to call me that childish nickname even when she had her legs wrapped around my fiancé like he was a racehorse and she was a jockey. The bitch. I wanted to rip her limb from limb. After I finished with Matt. "And you're his archenemy, Crusher? The ubervillain of Beginnings?"

Karen nodded.

I rubbed my fingers over my throbbing temples. It was all too much to take in.

Sure, every town in the world had its own personal superhero, someone who showed up whenever the train ran off the tracks and wouldn't stop. Or whenever there was a natural disaster that threatened to kill hundreds of people. Or even whenever little Timmy fell down a well and needed rescuing. Naturally, every town also had its own personal ubervillain, someone who wanted to rule supreme.

Beginnings was no different. We had the Machinator, a man who could control mechanical objects with his mind. The town's ubervillain was Crusher, a woman of unbelievable strength who could break metal bars with her teeth and crush diamonds in her hand. The two were constantly at odds, with Crusher continually coming up with some wild scheme to either (a) take over Beginnings, (b) kill the Machinator, or (c) both. Usually, the Machinator would be put in grave danger before miraculously escaping to foil Crusher's latest scheme. But Crusher always got away, or soon broke out of whatever high-security, supposedly inescapable ubervillain prison the authorities stuck her in. She'd come back to Beginnings, and the cycle would repeat itself, ad nauseam.

And the whole time, I'd never known the two of them were my fiancé and my best friend.

Never even suspected. Never had the slightest clue.

I'd been such a complete, total fool.

Some reporter I was. All the classic signs had been there. Matt's many bruises and injuries, his late nights and odd hours. Karen's long, strange absences from town and uncanny ability to open any jar, despite her petite size. The pieces clicked together in my mind like a jigsaw puzzle. The two of them must have spent hours laughing at my stupidity and naïveté and trusting nature. When they weren't having hot, superhero sex, that is.

My fiancé and best friend sleeping together and hiding their secret identities from me. I didn't know which betrayal hurt worse. Or which one made me angrier.

"How long has this been going on? I would think given your . . . extracurricular activities that sleeping together would be out of the question." I spat out the words. They left a foul, bitter taste in my mouth.

"Well, it's actually a funny story." Matt laughed in a vain effort to lighten the mood.

I crossed my arms over my chest, and his halfhearted chuckle died on his lips. Too bad he didn't follow suit.

"Anyway, we were down at the old abandoned mill a

couple of months ago, doing the usual epic battle, you know, explosions and danger and stuff, when Crusher, er, Karen, reached out and grabbed me. All this radioactive waste was leaking everywhere, and it was making us both feel really strange, and we just sort of kissed and . . ."

His voice trailed off under my red-hot glare. If I had the ability to shoot lasers out of my eyes, the two of them would have been extra-crispy by now. Too bad I didn't have my own superpower.

Matt still sat on the bed, Karen straddling him. They made no move to disengage body parts or hide their costumes. I knew at once they were actually relieved I had caught them, not only doing the nasty but exposing their secret identities as well. Relief filled their treacherous eyes, and tension oozed from their pores as if a weight had been lifted off their shoulders. They were happy they'd just ruined my life with their lies and deceit and betrayal. It made me ill.

I took a step back. I had to get away from them. From both of them. My heart couldn't take any more. I whirled around to dash out of the room.

My high heels snagged on the thick carpet, and I went down in a pile of white tulle. My tiara slipped off my head and rolled across the floor, and my hair tumbled out of its pearl-studded clips. I struggled to stand, and my eyes fell on a bag full of disposable cameras on the floor. They, too, had been Matt's idea. We would use disposable cameras at the wedding so guests could take their own photos, and we could save the expense of a photographer. Except now they would go to waste.

Or would they? The volcano of anger inside me cooled and congealed into a large, black lump of hate. Matt and Karen had had their fun at my expense. Now, I was going to do something about it. Something to even the score.

The pieces of my broken heart twisted in my chest. Something to hurt them like they'd hurt me. Only worse.

I got to my feet, dusted myself off, and stalked over to the camera bag. Something crunched under the toes of my torturous shoes. I looked down. I'd just smashed my cubic zirconium tiara to bits. It, too, was fake, just like everything else in my life.

I snatched a plastic camera out of the bag.

"What are you doing?" Karen asked.

"Just giving the two of you what you so richly deserve." I squinted at the traitorous, spandex-wearing pair through the viewfinder. "Say cheese."

The next day, the headline in the *Beginnings Bugle* screamed MACHINATOR UNMASKED! CRUSHER UNCOVERED! IDENTITIES REVEALED! *Find out the truth behind town's superhero, villain. Story and photos by Carmen Cole.*

My story described in honest, if painful and humiliating detail, how I had uncovered the pair's real identities. A photo of Karen and Matt, their spandex suits visible beneath their rumpled clothes, stretched across the front page of the newspaper. When they'd realized I was taking pictures of them, they'd tried to talk me out of it. Fools. They should have saved their breath. I would never listen to a word they said. Never again.

When asking nicely hadn't worked, Karen had tried to stop me, tried to yank the camera out of my hands and squeeze it to bits. But Matt, being the valiant, noble, oh-so-faithful superhero he was, intervened. As I'd coolly backed out of that hotel room, they were rolling around on the floor, punching and kicking each other. I wasn't sure if they were fighting or engaged in some sort of kinky, rough form of foreplay. Perhaps it was all the same to the superhero-and-villain set.

Not even stopping to change out of my wedding gown, I'd gone straight to the *Bugle* and told the editors what I had. It had been one of the most embarrassing, mortifying, downright degrading things I'd ever done, but I squared my shoulders and held my chin up. Page One had been cleared.

I'd spent the rest of the day at the newspaper, digging up all the information I could on Matt and Karen, aka the Machinator and Crusher. Matt's supposed accidents at work always occurred the day the Machinator engaged in some big battle. Karen's long absences and sudden arrivals in town coincided perfectly with Crusher's stints upstate. Dates, times, places, injuries. It was all there. How stupid, how blind I'd been. I was ashamed to call myself a journalist.

When I didn't show up for the wedding, Matt's mother called the paper. I told her everything.

She didn't speak for a moment. "What about the flowers? And all the food? Everything's already been paid for. I can't eat a hundred chickens by myself."

"Didn't you hear me, Matilda? I just told you that your son is a superhero."

"Oh, I know that. Who do you think makes his costumes?"

"And did you know about him and Karen too?"

"My boy is special. He gets tons of fan mail. You didn't think he'd be happy with just one woman, did you?"

I hung up on her. The old bat. She'd never liked me anyway.

An hour later, the local news blared onto the television set. Matt and Karen had made quite a mess at the Forever Inn, and part of the historic building had collapsed. Some things just aren't made to last forever. Or to withstand a superhero-ubervillain battle. I sent a photographer to get pictures.

A couple of friends called, trying to get me to calm down and give Matt a chance to explain. I told them to have fun eating Matilda's precious, already-paid-for chicken and went back to work.

The next morning, the *Bugle* sold out in minutes. The press guys came back in to print an extra ten thousand copies. Phones rang off the hook, as the wire services and national media picked up the story. The *Bugle*'s stock soared. Management had never been happier. As for Karen and Matt, the two of them vanished once the story broke. No one could find them, or their alter egos.

I collected as many copies of the newspaper as I could and posted them all over my tiny cubicle. Everyone and his brother stopped by my desk to congratulate me on the big scoop. The publisher himself even came out of his office to give me an *atta-girl* speech. A few of the sports guys cracked jokes about how I'd gotten the story, but a heated look from me sent them scurrying for cover. I was in no mood to be made fun of.

After spending almost twenty-four hours at the newspaper, I went home. I opened the door to my apartment, tossed my keys onto a nearby table, and flipped on the lights. Piles of cardboard boxes greeted me. After our honeymoon in Hawaii, I was supposed to have moved in with Matt, and most of my things had already been packed away.

My thoughts turned to Matt. Where was he? Had he seen the story? Was he sorry he'd lied to me? Or was he with Karen? Picking up where they'd left off?

Had he ever really loved me?

My eyes traced over the boxes. Hearts and other silly cartoon figures wearing lacy veils and diamond rings decorated the cardboard. The jagged pieces of my heart scraped against each other. The wedding, the honeymoon, the happily ever after. All gone. A few tears leaked out of my eyes, but I smacked them away. I'd done my crying on the way to the newspaper. I wouldn't do any more.

I dug through one of the boxes, found some wrinkled sweats, and walked into the bedroom. I caught a glimpse of myself in the mirror over the dresser. My auburn hair stuck out at funny angles. Dark purple circles ringed my eyes. Hurt and anger burned in the blue depths. I looked more than a little crazy. I felt that way too.

To top it off, I still wore my wedding dress, although I'd chucked the unbearable shoes hours ago. I smoothed down the ruined gown. The wear and tear of the day had turned the snow-white fabric a bland beige. The diamond in my engagement ring sparkled in the dim light. I'd been so happy the night Matt had given it to me. So sure of my love for him, and his for me. Now the ring just reminded me of broken promises, shattered dreams, and my own blind stupidity.

I yanked the ring off my finger, marched over to the dresser, and pulled open a door on my jewelry box. I stared at the ring a moment, then stuffed it in the back of the drawer, and shut it. I turned a key, locking it away.

I won't be fooled again, I vowed. *Not by anyone. Never again.*

From that day forward, I was on a mission.

A mission to unmask every single superhero and ubervillain in the entire world. Oh, I wouldn't get around to all of them, but I was determined to out as many as I could, as fast as I could.

No one would be deceived as I had been. No woman would come home to find her boyfriend slipping into a neon pink codpiece. No man would be puzzled over why his wife had a strange collection of whips and an odd affinity for black leather. No mother would wonder why her son could never be on time for anything. Not if I could help it.

I started out small. After work and on the weekends, I traveled to neighboring towns and cities on my crusades, learning all I could about their respective superheroes and ubervillains. I looked at their Web sites and promotional materials. Read their poorly written autobiographies and rambling manifestos. Even bought a few plastic action figures for research purposes. Naturally, all of the super-heroes and ubervillains had colorful names like Killer and Slasher and Halitosis Hal. The only things more flamboyant than their names and personalities were their costumes. The two groups never met a skin-tight, spandex outfit studded with rhinestones they didn't love.

All the superheroes and villains had strange, sometimes frightening powers, like the ability to move objects with their minds or shoot red-hot flames out of their fingertips. Since the goals of the heroes and villains were at odds, they often engaged in long, lengthy battles that destroyed bridges, overpasses, and municipal buildings. Some of the bigger cities had several superheroes and ubervillains all battling it out for supremacy and leveling skyscrapers right and left. And they all wore masks to hide their true identities and thus avoid paying for the public property they decimated on a weekly basis.

I had plenty of time to spend on my mission. My dad had died in a car crash when I was a kid, while my mom passed away from breast cancer a few years ago. I didn't have any other family, and Karen had been my only real friend. Everyone else had been Matt's friend before they were mine. They all drifted away like smoke after my story came out. In a week, I went from the belle of the ball to an outcast. I preferred it that way. There was no one left to lie to me, no one left to hurt me.

I perused police reports, scouted out battle sites, and examined torn bits of masks and costumes. I worked up flowcharts of people kidnapped and saved by villains and heroes. I even recorded powers and weaknesses and costumes and symbols in a color-coded journal. I'd always had a knack for organization and a good memory, and both helped me immeasurably as I sifted through mountains of raw data.

In the end, it was ridiculously easy. There was always someone the superhero saved over and over and over again, whether it was a wannabe girlfriend or a boyfriend or a kindly widowed aunt. All you had to do was find that special person and see who was closest to them. Then, bada-bing, bada-boom, you found your superhero.

As for the ubervillains, their hunger for money and power tripped them up. Most villains had buckets of cash gotten in less-than-legal ways and were often involved in shady land development deals.

Accidents involving radioactive materials also raised a big red flag, since radioactive waste was a great way for heroes and villains to get their powers. So were magic rings, bites from rabid or otherwise altered animals, and the old-fashioned, natural, genetic mutation.

I soon learned that I had a knack for uncovering secret identities. All you had to do was dig long enough and hard enough and deep enough, and you'd uncover that one piece of information that would solve the riddle. I'd find a scrap of evidence, something seemingly inconsequential, and everything would fall into place. The dots connected. The picture cleared. I'd always loved puzzles, from crosswords to jumbles to word searches. Uncovering the identities of superheroes and ubervillains was the ultimate human jig-saw puzzle. And I was rapidly becoming a master.

Six months after my botched wedding, I left the *Beginnings Bugle* for a larger newspaper that wanted me to uncover the identities of the resident superhero and ubervillain. Three months later, the Kilted Scotsman and the Blue Berserker woke to find their faces splattered all over the front page. The public found out what the Scotsman really wore under his kilt, while the Berserker went, well, a little berserk over the whole thing.

A few months later, I went on to another newspaper.

And then another . . .
And another . . .
And another . . .

I left a trail of unmasked superheroes and ubervillains in my wake. Of course, not everyone was happy about my private vendetta, my endless exposés. The superheroes begged me to stop my activities or retract my stories, while the ubervillains tried to bribe or threaten me. But nothing could match the righteous fervor that had awakened in me. Not threats, not money, and especially not tearful pleas.

Nothing satisfied me more than a good unmasking.

Three years after my first superhero unmasking, I hit the jackpot.

The editors at *The Exposé* in Bigtime, New York, hired me to uncover the identities of the Fearless Five, a group of superheroes, and their enemies, the Terrible Triad.

The Fearless Five and the Terrible Triad were legends, not just in Bigtime, but throughout the world. They had the strongest powers. They waged the biggest battles. They engaged in the most amazing escapes and the most elaborate schemes. They were the crème de la crème of superheroes and ubervillains.

What made the puzzle so tempting, so intriguing, was the fact that little was known about any of them. Oh, countless stories had chronicled their escapades, but no one had a clue as to their real identities. They would be tough puzzles to solve, but I was up to the task.

After all, I was Carmen Cole, reporter extraordinaire.

The job proved harder than expected. I worked for three months and came up with nothing. Nada. Zip. Zilch. Zero. I started with the superheroes like I always did, because they were easier to unmask. Ubervillains were naturally more conniving and not shy about killing people to keep them quiet. But the Fearless Five had covered their tracks well. I pored over police reports and mocked up flowcharts galore, but nothing linked the heroes to anyone. They were ghosts who showed up, battled evil, and saved the world before bedtime.

Then, one day, I got a break. A kid called in and said he saw a man in a tuxedo transform into Tornado, a member of the Fearless Five. Such tips were not uncommon, and most of the reporters at *The Exposé* hung up on the crackpot callers. Not me. I visited the kid, who gave me a description of the man in the tux. I had a sketch artist work with the kid, then took the drawing and compared it to the men I thought might be Tornado. I narrowed my list down to three suspects, then dug deeper until I unmasked my superhero.

Tornado was Travis Teague, a wealthy businessman specializing in wind power. How clichéd. But I was sure. I could feel it deep down in the pit of my stomach. A couple of weeks later, I verified my suspicion by capturing Teague turning into Tornado through the use of a hidden camera. My inner voice crowed with pride and victory. I notched another superhero exposé on my belt.

Carmen 1, Fearless Five 0.

The day the story ran, the entire newsroom gathered around to toast me with champagne and pizza. Even the newspaper's publisher, Morgana Madison, attended. In a way. She took in the rowdy scene from the windows of her office, which overlooked the newsroom. She was always up there, overseeing her massive media empire, while we slaved away earning her more millions.

I spotted the publisher and raised my glass. Morgana smiled and raised her own glass in response. Superhero exposés were terribly good for the bottom line, and there was nothing Morgana Madison cared about more than that. She was in the newspaper business to make money, and she didn't hide her ambition.

Normally, I would have waited until I'd uncovered all the heroes' and villains' identities and written one big exposé about everyone, but my editors insisted we run the story about Travis aka Tornado Teague right away. I went along with the plan. I was, after all, the golden child. I'd uncover the others' identities soon enough.

Now, I was reaping the rewards of my clever brilliance, and so was everybody else. Everyone except Henry Harris, the newspaper's technology reporter. He was the only person not joining in the festivities. Instead of drinking, he crouched at his desk near the back of the newsroom and stared at his computer screen. His fingers stabbed the keyboard with rapid strokes. Henry was a bit of an odd duck, with his nose always glued to his computer or buried in some book about the latest, greatest, technological advances. I liked him, though. He was nice, polite, and always helped me unfreeze my computer when it freaked out.

I grabbed an extra glass of champagne, strolled over, and plopped it down on his desk.

Henry blinked like an owl. "Oh thanks, Carmen. I didn't realize it was time for the toast already. I guess I just lost track of things."

"No problem, Henry. Come on, join the rest of us. We've got free booze and pizza, courtesy of the company."

"Well, I really should finish this story—"

I pulled Henry out of his chair and into the middle of the newsroom. I wasn't going to take no for an answer.

This was one of the best days of my life, and everybody was going to share in it, whether they liked it or not.

"Speech! Speech!" one of the junior reporters shouted.

"Yeah, Carmen. Tell us why you do the things you do," someone else asked.

"It's like . . . karma," I said, espousing my unmasking philosophy, which everyone had heard many, many times before. "We all know that villains cheat and steal and lie, but the heroes do it too. They lie to their friends and families. They make excuses and let down those closest to them time after time. That's bad karma. One day, all that lying is bound to catch up with them. I just make sure it happens sooner rather than later. What goes around comes around. It's karma."

"Hear, hear," Henry said in a quiet voice.

I clinked champagne glasses with Henry and the rest of my drunken colleagues. I'd never felt so exhilarated in my entire life. I was floating, flying, soaring. I was on top of the world. Now that I'd unmasked Tornado, the rest of the Fearless Five would soon follow. After that, I'd tackle the Terrible Triad.

My phone rang, jarring me out of my smug, self-satisfied reverie. "Carmen Cole."

"Carmen, it's Chief Newman," a deep Irish voice rumbled in my ear.

"Hey, Chief. What's up? Calling to congratulate me?"

I'd spent many hours going through files with Bigtime's chief of police, and the two of us had developed a good working relationship. The chief also wanted to learn the identities of the Fearless Five and the Terrible Triad. Both groups had destroyed their fair share of Bigtime, and Newman wanted them to foot the bill for the cleanup and repairs. Not to mention all the unpaid parking tickets they'd accumulated with their souped-up supercars and vans.

"Not exactly." He paused. "I've got some bad news, Carmen. It's about Travis Teague. He's dead, Carmen. He committed suicide."

My champagne glass slipped from my fingers. It shattered on the floor.

★ 3 ★

Six months later

I swirled champagne around in my cut-crystal glass. Bubbles rose up in the golden liquid, then fizzed out.

Just like my life.

After Travis Teague committed suicide by throwing himself out of his office on the thirtieth floor of Teague Towers, my star hadn't just fallen, it had been snuffed out like a candle. Unmasking was good for business. Having Tornado, one of the most beloved superheroes in the world, commit suicide because you unmasked him was not. I got numerous death threats, not only from Tornado's fellow superheroes, but also from the general public. People crossed the street to avoid walking past me. Restaurant waiters refused to serve me. Kids gathered in front of my apartment building and threw rocks whenever I stuck my head outside. People hated me with a passion heretofore reserved only for heretics and lawyers.

I accepted the abuse. I deserved it. My guilt over Tornado's death knew no bounds. I barely ate. I hardly slept.

On the rare occasion I did drift off, nightmares plagued my feverish dreams. All I'd wanted was to tell the truth, to reveal the people behind the masks. But things had gone terribly wrong. Instead, my own bad karma had bitten me on the ass, and Travis Teague had paid the ultimate price for my smug, stupid arrogance.

After his suicide, the only thing I wanted was to hole up in my apartment and never come out again. However, the editors at *The Exposé* wouldn't let me slip quietly into the good night. Hell, they wouldn't even fire me outright. Oh no. The newspaper's cross-town rival, *The Chronicle*, would get too much mileage and glee out of that. Instead of axing me, the editors at *The Exposé* devised a fate worse than death—they reassigned me to the society beat.

I trudged to function after boring function, chatting up old, rich ladies and their spoiled, horse-faced daughters. I learned more about shoes and designer dresses and accessories in the last six months than I had in my entire life. Not to mention plastic surgery, liposuction, and prenuptial agreements.

I lived a sort of half-life at the newspaper. I came in, schlepped out to the latest debutante ball or charity function on the schedule, schlepped back, wrote a story, e-mailed it to the society editor, and left. The only one who even acknowledged my presence was Henry Harris and that was only when his nose wasn't mashed against his computer screen.

Tonight, I was attending the opening of yet another art gallery. I'd been on the scene over an hour and had done all the usual things—chatted with the artist whose work was on display, gotten some quotes from the owner, taken notes about the latest in designer fashion. Now, I sipped flat champagne and tried to find someone who would say something moderately interesting about the opening. Sandra, the other reporter who reluctantly worked the society beat, had come in, gotten a few quotes, and left after ten minutes. Not me. I might not care about who was wearing what, or who was sleeping with whom, but that wasn't going to stop me from doing the best job possible. I still had a little pride left. It was the *only* thing I had left.

Out of the corner of my eye, I spotted Sam Sloane, one of the wealthiest men and most eligible bachelors in all of Bigtime.

"Mr. Sloane! Mr. Sloane!" I waved.

Sam Sloane gave me a look that would have frozen ice. He walked right by me, his eyes fixed straight ahead. I sighed. Two months ago, my editor had ordered me to get an exclusive interview with Sloane, the owner of *The Chronicle*. I couldn't understand why my editor wanted a story on Sloane, given his legendary business battles with Morgana Madison. The two hated each other with a passion, as did the staffs of their respective newspapers. Reporters and editors at *The Chronicle* and *The Exposé* always tried to one-up each other, just like Sloane and Morgana with their corporate shenanigans. Morgana barely tolerated Sloane's name being mentioned in passing on the society page. She'd blow a gasket if we did a whole story on him. Perhaps my editor just wanted to get me fired.

Not that it really mattered. The assignment was impossible. Sloane never talked to anyone with the media, not even the reporters at his own newspaper. His conversation was reserved for the latest supermodel hanging on his arm. Unless I morphed into a six-foot-tall, blond Amazon with a tiny waist, fake boobs, and questionable morals, I wasn't getting anywhere near Sam Sloane.

Even then, I would have a hard time fighting my way through the throngs of women that flocked around the billionaire. In addition to being richer than a sultan, Sam

Sloane had dark good looks and a killer smile. Even I had to admit that a tuxedo never looked better on a man. Sloane was also supposed to be quite the charmer. Or so I'd been told. He'd never done more than stare coldly at me the few times he deigned to acknowledge my presence.

After another hour of flat champagne, moldy Brie, and stale crackers, I left the gallery and took a taxi downtown to the gigantic skyscraper that housed *The Exposé*. The glass-and-chrome building never failed to take my breath away. With its winking blue lights and glittering facade, it was even more impressive in the dark night. Only *The Chronicle*'s building, a gleaming skyscraper a few blocks away, rivaled *The Exposé*'s height and beauty.

I rode the elevator up to the one-hundredth floor, where the reporters and editors worked. I walked the length of the newsroom, or the gauntlet, to the very back wall. I'd once had a desk right in the middle of the newsroom, where the golden girls and boys lorded over their beats like queens and kings. After the Tornado fiasco, I'd been shuffled to the back, along with the other rejects who hung on to their jobs like spinach stuck in your teeth.

I reached my desk, a tiny metal affair on four shaky feet, sank into my uncomfortable chair, and smacked on my computer.

"How's it going, Carmen?" Henry Harris asked from his own desk a few feet away.

"Fine, Henry. The usual. Another night, another opening, another glass of flat champagne."

The black man smiled and went back to his computer. He pushed up the sleeves of his plaid sweater vest, adjusted his polka-dot bow tie, and started typing. The faint light emanating from the humming monitor made his glasses gleam and highlighted the smooth planes of his face. Henry was just shy of thirty, but he looked much younger, despite the old-fashioned clothes he always wore.

For the next hour, I tuned out the world, including the giggles and whispers of the golden girls and boys. I wrote a glowing story about the gallery opening, describing the scene in detail and adding in quotes from all the pertinent power players. I threw in some tidbits about the resident fashionistas and their outfits, shoes, and accessories, and sent my story to the society editor. I picked up one of the Rubik's Cubes that littered my desk and fiddled with it, sliding the rows of colors back and forth. A few minutes later, my computer pinged with a new e-mail from the editor.

Fine. You can leave now.

Ah, short and sweet like always. I gathered up my things and headed toward the elevator.

"Later, Henry."

He gave me a distracted little wave. His dark eyes never left his computer screen. I often wondered whether Henry ate or if he just subsisted on data bytes alone. I'd put money on the data bytes.

I rode down to the bottom floor, pushed through the heavy revolving doors, and stepped onto the street. It had rained while I'd been inside, and a damp, glossy sheen covered the sidewalk. Heavy clouds blanketed the night sky, and the metallic scent of more impending rain tickled my nose. No taxis cruised by, so I decided to walk home. It wasn't far.

"Hey, baby! How about a little fun tonight?" a low voice called out from a dark doorway.

"Get lost, creep," I snapped and kept walking.

My hand slipped into my purse, where I kept my pepper spray. Since Tornado's suicide and the various death threats that had come my way, I'd started taking self-defense classes.

Oh, the superheroes would never make good on their threats to injure me. Their moral compasses wouldn't allow them to harm normal folks, not even a low-down, good-for-nothing reporter like me. No, it was regular people, the ones who called me nasty names and left dead fish outside my apartment, that I worried about.

Shoes squeaked on the slick sidewalk, and I glanced over my shoulder. Two men dressed in pinstriped suits lumbered along behind me, even though it was after midnight and all the downtown office buildings were closed. This wasn't terribly unusual, as many Bigtime businessmen worked long, hard hours. But the flat, dead look in their eyes made me walk a little bit faster. Cold dread curled up in my stomach. My fist closed around the pepper spray.

I squinted, trying to make out the numbers on a nearby street sign. The subway was only two blocks away. Cops patrolled the underground tunnels all hours of the night and day, watching for purse snatchers and muggers. It would be safer down there. I picked up my pace. My feet snapped against the concrete like rubber bands. The footsteps behind me quickened, and I lunged out onto the street. A black sedan skidded to a halt in front of me. I jumped back onto the sidewalk.

"Hey!" I smacked the car's hood with my purse. "Watch where you're going!"

Something sharp pricked me. I yelped. One of the two men in suits shoved a syringe deeper into my arm. A strange, blue liquid glowed inside the glass tube. I yanked the pepper spray out of my purse and gave the goon a face full of it.

"You bitch!" he screamed and stumbled back.

I whirled around and gave the other goon the same treatment. He, too, cursed and stumbled away. The black sedan sat silent, its occupants enjoying the show. I tugged the empty syringe out of my arm and threw it down. The glass shattered. Blue liquid hissed onto the concrete, and white steam rose up from the strange substance.

My inner voice shrieked with fear. I was in serious trouble. I had to get away from these people, but everything seemed so strange. The world wouldn't stay still. It kept spinning round and round and round like a carousel. I took a step forward. Two more blocks. I could make it two more blocks.

I took another step forward. Dizziness hit me like a tidal wave. I pitched to the ground, and darkness overcame me.

★ 4 ★

I lost all sense of time and space. I was in a car, a car I didn't want to be in, with some dangerous men. What they wanted with me and where they were taking me, I couldn't imagine, but I didn't feel frightened. A blue haze bathed my fear, softening it. Voices and bits of conversation floated in and out of my drugged mind.

"Can't believe she got you two fools with pepper spray . . ."

"Not our fault . . ."

"Didn't know . . ."

"Thought she'd go down quicker . . ."

I lapsed into unconsciousness once more.

Something hard and cold pressed against my cheek, so cold that it burned. I jerked my head up. A million needles stabbed my jumbled brain. The hot pricking traveled from my head down my spine and into my limbs. A groan of pain escaped my numb, cold, chapped lips.

"Well, well. Look who's awake. Rise and shine, Lois Lane."

Cold, rough hands hauled me up. The room spun around, and I struggled to focus. I found myself face-to-face with one of my kidnappers. His beady eyes were bloodshot, and his nose was red and runny. I studied him, memorizing every detail of his flat face, his clothes, his mannerisms. I wanted to give the police an accurate description of my kidnapper, if somehow I got out of this alive.

We were in a small, empty, concrete room with only one door. I thought about distances and angles and running.

"Jimmy!" the man yelled. "We've got a live one."

The second man entered the room and grabbed my arm. I studied him as well. They dragged me outside. The sudden motion made me sick. I took deep breaths and tried not to vomit. *Focus, focus!* I had to be sharp, be strong. That was the only way I was going to get out of this mess.

I forced my mind away from the stabbing needles and throbbing headache and concentrated on my surroundings. We stood in an enormous factory or plant of some kind. A long, winding assembly line snaked over pipes, under catwalks, and around huge vats. Fog puffed up from the silver canisters. But what caught my attention was the ice—it covered everything, from the concrete floor to the metal pipes high overhead. The temperature hovered around the freezing mark. My ragged breath frosted in the air.

The two men half dragged, half carried me up a flight of stairs. I tried to dig my heels into the ground, but they skidded along the frozen floor like a pair of ice skates.

"I wish Frost had picked another place to do his experiments," the second man grumbled after slipping on the icy incline.

"Quiet!" the first man hissed. "Or he'll put the deep freeze on you."

My own insides froze with fear. I knew who Frost was. The ubervillain was a member of the Terrible Triad, along with Scorpion and Malefica. If my head didn't feel like a marching band had taken up residence inside, I might have been able to give my two kidnappers the slip. But I was no match for Frost or any other member of the Triad, even on their worst, most inept day. My inner voice let out a small, plaintive wail. This was not going to end well.

The goons dragged me through a dark hallway. We emerged onto a platform overlooking part of the factory. Ice and frost and metal stretched out as far as I could see. The two men stopped. I hung between them like a rag doll.

I cocked my head. A faint sound echoed in the distance. I concentrated. The sound came again, then again. It took me a moment, but I recognized it. The distinctive *click-click-clack* of high-heel shoes rang out through the factory, getting louder and closer with every step. My doom approached.

Malefica, the leader of the Terrible Triad, strolled into view. Skin-tight, bloodred leather hugged her perfect figure from head to toe. A black leather whip looped around her impossibly thin waist, while a black *M* strained to cover her impressive chest. A black-and-red mask obscured her face, while a red cowl hid her hair from sight. A scarlet cape and strappy sandals completed the fashionably evil ensemble.

"Ah. I see our guest has arrived. We've been expecting you, haven't we, boys?"

Frost and Scorpion stepped out of the shadows. I gasped.

Frost was a tall, skinny man clad in an ice blue suit. A shock of white-blond hair stood straight up on his head, and his eyes glowed with a vivid, blue flame. With bulging, rippling muscles, very wide shoulders, and a shaved head, Scorpion was the polar opposite of Frost. He wore black from head to toe and looked as solid as cement.

And so I found myself face-to-face with every superhero's worst nightmare—the Terrible Triad. I swallowed.

"Leave us," Malefica barked to the two hired hands.

The men dropped my arms and scurried away like rats. I wobbled and tried to remain upright.

Malefica's ruby red lips curved into a smile. "Carmen Cole. It's an honor. I've been a fan of your work for some time now."

My inner voice muttered. Somehow, I managed to speak. "Sorry, I can't say the same."

"Aren't you the feisty one? Pity."

Malefica backhanded me. The sound cracked like thunder. The woman worked out, that was for sure. I hit the ground like a sack of potatoes. The needles returned, worse than before. My head felt like it was going to explode into a million, pulpy pieces. I bit back a groan of pain. I was nothing, less than nothing, to the Triad. I would likely be dead within the next five minutes, but I vowed not to show weakness in front of them. *I would not!* My scraps of pride wouldn't let me.

I stared at the scarlet sandal tapping in front of my aching face and burning brain. It was the only way I could take my mind off the searing pain rippling up and down my body. Plus, I found it odd and somewhat funny how big and clownlike Malefica's feet were in proportion to the rest of her lithe body.

"Nice sandals," I croaked. "Bulluci's fall collection?"

"Good eye," Malefica said. "Now get up. We have things to discuss."

I slowly, slowly staggered to my feet, held my head in my hands, and tried to keep the world from careening out of control. I wasn't very successful. Unconcerned, Malefica sashayed away, her shoes *click-click-clack*ing on the iced-over floor. Every footstep made my head ache even more. I limped along behind her. Frost and Scorpion brought up the rear, making me the middle of an ubervillain sandwich. Terrific.

Malefica twisted and turned her way through the factory until we reached an office. I stepped over the threshold and blinked. It was a room fit for a queen. Wingback chairs and an enormous love seat sat on one side of the room, while a huge, canopied bed took up the other section. A mahogany desk piled high with papers crouched next to a tall liquor cabinet. Flames blazed in a marble fireplace, and sinfully thick carpet covered the floor. It was the plushest ubervillain lair money could buy. Despite my fear of imminent, painful death, I made mental notes, not only of the room, but also of the objects in it. Not that the police would believe I'd been kidnapped by ubervillains, but a girl had to try.

"Sit."

I did as I was told. There was no point in being stubborn. Besides, I wasn't sure how much longer I could stand. It was hard to remain upright when your knees shook like leaves in a tornado.

Malefica strolled over to the liquor cabinet. She plucked some crystal glasses and a bottle of amber-colored liquid out of the dark depths.

"Would you like something to drink?"

"No," I said, even though my throat was as dry as a sandbox.

"Are you sure? It's Brighton's Best."

I recognized the reference from my months on the society beat. That was a fifteen-thousand-dollar bottle of Scotch that Malefica was holding. "No. I'm not much of a drinker."

"Pity."

Malefica poured a couple of fingers' worth of Scotch into a crystal tumbler. Frost and Scorpion settled themselves on the love seat.

My inner voice whispered. Suddenly, I knew that Malefica and her companions weren't going to kill me. Not tonight. They'd gone to too much trouble to bring me here when they could have just murdered me on the sidewalk. They wanted something from me. More cold dread filled my stomach. But what could it be?

Malefica reclined in the leather chair behind the desk. She took a long pull on her drink then set it aside. Unless I missed my guess, the glass was a Hilustar tumbler. The crystal cups went for five thousand bucks a pop, making them a pricey way to quench your thirst. Then again, it would be terribly gauche to drink fifteen-thousand-dollar Scotch from a plastic cup.

"The reason you're not dead by now is that my associates and I have a job for you." Malefica's voice reminded me of a purring, pleased cat. I hated cats.

My instincts had been right once again. Maybe I would live through this yet. "A job? What sort of job?"

"A very special job, one that only you can do."

I raised an eyebrow.

Malefica tapped her long, scarlet nails together. "We want you to uncover the identity of Striker, the leader of the Fearless Five."

Laughter bubbled up inside me like fizzy champagne. I tried to stop it, as it wasn't very polite or good for your health to guffaw at an ubervillain when she was trying to cow you into doing her bidding. But the cork popped, and it spewed out anyway. I laughed.

And laughed . . .

And laughed . . .

And laughed some more.

Malefica pressed her scarlet lips into a thin, hard line. Her green eyes narrowed.

"I'm sorry. But you're kidding, right?" I wiped away my tears of hysterical mirth.

"She's quite serious," Frost said in a, well, frosty sort of voice.

"You unmasked Tornado. What could be so hard about Striker?" Scorpion growled. He cracked a few of his massive knuckles. The sounds echoed through the room like gunshots. "He's not really so tough once you beat on him a little."

I stared at the mountain of a man. "Tornado was sloppy; he made a mistake. Striker doesn't make mistakes. The guy's a ghost. I researched him for months and months and found nothing. No habits, no hobbies, no girlfriends or boyfriends, no widowed aunts who need rescuing over and over again. He's untraceable."

"Well, I'm afraid you're just going to have to find a way to track him down," Malefica said. "Or else."

I rolled my eyes. Ubervillains. Always so dramatic. My inner voice snickered, and a little bit of my courage returned. "Or else what? You'll kill me until I'm dead, dead, dead? Sorry, you'll have to be more creative. I've heard that one before."

Malefica smiled. Chills zipped down my spine.

"Ah. Smart girl. I knew you'd ask. Let's go for a walk."

Malefica led the way to a large platform that overlooked another series of huge, metal vats. A bank of computers winked at one end of the room. Four large, glass tubes with wires and electrodes attached to them crouched next to the electronic equipment. Blue and green and red liquid dripped and bubbled and gurgled in beakers on top of a workbench. All sorts of odd-shaped gadgets and doodads and gewgaws covered another table. It was Dr. Frankenstein's laboratory come to life. What the hell was the Triad up to?

Malefica pointed to the vats below us. "See those? Frost has concocted a special sort of . . . what did you so scientifically call it?"

"Radioactive, ice-cold goo," Frost said. "Actually, it's called freezeterium, a special chemical that produces some rather interesting effects in clinical trials."

Malefica waved her hand. "You know how your scientific blathering bores me. Let's move on."

We walked down a flight of stairs. A row of cages sat on the floor next to the bottom of the vats. Animals stirred at the crunch of our shoes on the icy floor.

"Go ahead," Malefica said. "Get a good look."

I crept up to the first cage. A large wolf crouched inside. I edged closer. The creature rose to its feet, and I realized it was twice the size of a normal wolf. It turned around, and I gasped. It was a wolf, and yet not a wolf.

It had probably been a wolf at some time in its life, but the creature was now a thing of nightmares. Long, jagged tusks jutted out from its enormous mouth. Ice blue eyes the size of saucers stared at me. The creature yawned, revealing a long, black tongue and row upon row of razor-sharp teeth, teeth that could rip a man to shreds in an instant. My gaze traveled downward. The creature's fur was the color of new snow, but huge, ugly, black talons curved out from its paws.

"Keep going," Malefica ordered.

I swallowed a mouthful of bile. Sweat froze on my fore-head. I tiptoed down the row of cages. Nightmare after nightmare greeted me from behind the metal bars.

"What are these things?"

"Wolves, mostly. A few foxes, the odd squirrel or two. The bears all died," Frost replied in a cold, clinical voice. "The creatures have all been given varying doses of freeze-terium, with a variety of outcomes, as you can see."

At the sound of Frost's voice, the animals leapt forward. They snarled and clawed at the bars on their cages. I jumped back. The animals' rage, their absolute hatred for Frost, and their shame at being transformed into such monstrosities hit me like an ice-cold wave. My stomach flipped over.

"See how my pets love me?" he cooed.

"What are you trying to do?" I whispered.

"I'm seeing what effect freezeterium has upon various animals before I begin conducting human trials."

"Human trials? Why?"

Frost gave me patronizing look. "It's what I do."

"Frost fancies himself a scientist. He wants to create his own little army of snow-bunny soldiers," Malefica explained.

"I *am* a scientist," Frost sniffed. "It's not my fault the academic community refuses to acknowledge my brilliance."

Malefica put a hand around my shoulder and led me away from the cages. I shuddered at her touch. Her perfume worked its way up my nose and down my throat. It was a sweet, cloying scent that made me want to retch.

The ubervillain steered me back up the stairs to the glass tubes and computers. I'd always known the Triad was the worst of the worst, but the depths of their depravity stunned me. Experimenting on helpless animals, planning to do the same to humans. Hot, sour vomit rose in my throat. Somehow, I forced it down. I would get through this. I would. Then, I would find a way to stop these vile people.

Yeah, right. As if I had a chance against three of the world's most powerful ubervillains. Right now, I would settle for just getting out of this alive.

"So you see, our proposition is really quite simple," Malefica purred in a pleased tone. "You will discover Striker's identity, or else Frost will drop you into the radioactive goo until you come out looking like one of his little pets. Only worse, I imagine. After all, his project is still in the experimental stages."

"I see." I forced the words out from my stiff, frozen lips. "Why me?"

"Because you have the best success rate. You've unmasked thirteen heroes and villains in a little over three years. Nobody else has even come close to that number. You seem to have a gift for it. Maybe that's your superpower." Malefica laughed at her bad joke. Her peals of merriment rang like a dirge for the dead in my head.

"You have one month from tomorrow. When the month is up, go to Laurel Park in Bigtime. There's a bench at the far edge of the park next to a wooden swing set. Be there at midnight. Do you know where that is?"

I knew the park well. It was one of my favorite places to go for a walk. "Yes."

"Good. Then our business is concluded." Malefica's green eyes grew dark and sinister. "One more thing. Should you discover Striker's identity before the month is out, don't even think about going to him—or any other superhero—for help. They can't protect you from us. I imagine they would turn you down anyway, as much trouble as you've caused them."

She was right. No superhero in his right mind would

have anything to do with me, unless the fate of the world was at stake. I didn't think saving my own miserable neck would measure up to that high standard. Without super-powers and a safe place to hide for the next fifty or so years, the ubervillains would eventually get me, unless I did exactly what they said, when they said it. Malefica and the others were alarmingly persistent about taking their revenge. More than one of the Triad's flunkies had spilled his guts about the group's latest world-domination scheme and disappeared into witness protection, only to wash up in the marina a couple of days later—missing several vital organs. It might not be tomorrow, or next week, or even next month, but the ubervillains would find me, corner me, and finish me off in the most drawn-out, painful manner possible if I crossed them in any way, shape, or form.

"We'll be keeping tabs on you, Miss Cole, so don't think about trying to leave town," Malefica continued. "There's nowhere you can hide. Ubervillains are surprisingly unselfish about sharing information when it comes to people who've done them wrong. But if by some miracle, we can't find you, well, we'll just have to take our anger out on someone else. Perhaps Henry Harris, that technology reporter at the newspaper. You seem to be fond of him. So, think carefully before you do anything rash."

I closed my eyes. I was trapped, caught like a fly in a spider's sticky web.

Malefica snapped her fingers. Something pricked my arm. Then, mercifully, I passed out.

★ 5 ★

Sometime later, the black sedan slid to a halt. The door opened, and two sets of arms pushed me out. I hit the ground with a dull thud. My purse sailed out after me. The car sped off, its tires squealing. I coughed on exhaust fumes and pulled myself up. A low groan escaped my dry, cracked lips. Every part of my body ached, from the top of my throbbing head to the bottoms of my tired feet. I squinted. When the world came into focus, I realized I was in the alley next to my apartment building. Well, at least my kidnappers had been considerate enough to bring me back home after a night of hell. I grabbed my purse and staggered down the alley and around to the entrance.

"Rough night?" the doorman inquired in a bored tone.

"You could say that," I muttered.

I rode the elevator up to my apartment, locked the door behind me, and collapsed on the couch.

* * *

I snuggled deeper into the groove on the soft couch. What a crazy dream I'd been having. Being kidnapped and taken to the Terrible Triad's secret lair. Seeing mutated creatures and vats of radioactive goo. I'd been reading too many comic books.

Sunlight warmed my face and told me it was well into the afternoon. Time to get ready for another night on the society circuit. I yawned and raised my arms over my head, stopping in mid-stretch. Needles of pain pricked their way up and down my body. My eyes popped open, and I eased up. I still had on the little black dress I'd worn to the gallery opening last night. Rips and tears dotted the jagged fabric, along with a variety of smudges and stains. I held out my arm. Two purple bruises marked the spots where I'd been jabbed with needles and injected with who-knew-what.

It hadn't been a dream.

"Oh, bloody hell!"

Panic flooded my body. I jumped up off the couch, my eyes fixed on the door. I had to get out of my apartment. I had to get as far away from Bigtime as fast as I could.

I took a step forward. My foot snagged on one of the legs of the coffee table, and I fell down for about the tenth time in the last twelve hours. I smacked into the floor, and the world went black for a moment. Silver stars exploded in front of my face.

The fall knocked a little bit of the panic out of me. I took deep breaths to slow my heart, which wanted to gallop up my throat and out of my body. I wrinkled my nose. The sour stench of stale beer, mold, and rotting garbage clung to me like a second skin. I smelled like I'd been sleeping in an alley all night. It wasn't pleasant, but it brought me back to my senses. First things first. If I was going to panic, I at least wanted to be clean doing it.

After taking a long, hot shower, popping a couple aspirin, and eating massive amounts of chocolate, I felt a little calmer. But only a little. My temples pulsed and throbbed with every beat of my heart. My arm ached from the injections. A hard ball of fear sat in my stomach like a lead weight.

I picked up a Rubik's Cube from my bookcase. I twisted and turned the pieces around and paced the length of my apartment, trying to puzzle out my next move.

My first option was, of course, to do exactly as Malefica had told me. Uncover Striker's identity and report to the park in a month's time. There were several problems with this option. First of all, I'd seen the Triad's indifference to life up close and personal. If I gave them Striker's identity, I knew they would kill him.

Then, I would have another superhero's blood on my hands. I didn't want that. I'd never wanted that. I had only wanted . . . what? Truth? Justice? The American Way? But that was a question for another day.

And I knew it wouldn't end with Striker. Malefica and the others would make me uncover the identities of the remaining members of the Fearless Five. The Triad would come back to me again and again, until they had eliminated every superhero who stood in their way. Or got bored and killed me.

No, that option was out. I clicked a row of colors into place and kept pacing.

My second option was to find a way to get a message to Striker or another member of the Fearless Five and tell them of Malefica's plan. But I didn't know how to contact them, other than running an ad in *The Exposé* that said, *Help! Crazy ubervillains want me to expose your secret identities or they'll throw me in a vat of radioactive goo.*

Even if I did get a message to the Fearless Five, it didn't

mean they would respond. They might think it was an elaborate trick. Or worse, they just might let Malefica have her way with me. After what I had done to Tornado, I couldn't really blame them for that.

I slid another set of colors into place.

My third option was to hightail it out of town and retire to some deserted island. But I didn't have enough money to disappear, and even if I did, sooner or later the Triad would find me, just like Malefica said they would. In my own way, I was as recognizable as the most popular superhero. But without the skin-tight spandex, leather whips, and flowing capes.

Another row of colors lined up.

But there was another option. I could try to uncover Malefica's identity, then go public with it. Hopefully, Malefica would be too busy with the Fearless Five, various law enforcement agencies, and the IRS to worry about killing me. Then again, she would probably make it a point to personally thank me for unmasking her.

I frowned and undid some of the combinations on the Rubik's Cube that I'd gotten wrong. I kept pacing.

No, that wouldn't work either. I'd been working on Malefica's identity for three months before Tornado's suicide and had come up with less than zero. There was no way I'd ever uncover her identity in a month's time. Besides, the superheroes always led me to the ubervillains, not the other way around. It was practically a rule, like putting the edges of a jigsaw puzzle together before you started working on the inside.

I stopped pacing.

The superheroes always led me to the ubervillains, not the other way around.

Perhaps . . .

Maybe . . .

Possibly . . .

What if I uncovered Striker's identity first, then let him lead me to Malefica? Superheroes and ubervillains were always connected, whether they were family, friends, lovers, business associates, or even business rivals. I'd seen it time and time again. The Kilted Scotsman and the Blue Berserker had been best friends, the Joking Juggler and the Serious Samurai had been business partners, Matt and Karen had been lovers. The connection between heroes and villains was like a weird sort of karma. One always followed the other around, like a dog chasing its own tail. The harder they tried to fight each other, the closer together they became.

If I could discover Striker's identity, I just might uncover Malefica's as well. I would then give Striker Malefica's true identity and hope I could slip away in the ruckus that would follow. It was my best hope, my only hope of getting out of this mess alive—and without fur. And perhaps by uncovering Malefica's identity, I could earn a little redemption and ease the heavy blanket of guilt smothering me. Or at least receive forgiveness from the rest of the Fearless Five. Maybe even boost my karma a little bit. It was all I could do.

I snapped the final row of colors into place. For one brief moment, the puzzle seemed to be solved.

I opened a closet door, a door I had shut six months ago. I reached into the dark depths and pulled out a heavy cardboard box. The word *Superheroes* walked up one side of the cardboard, while *Ubervillains* ran down the other. Crudely drawn puzzle pieces and smiley faces wearing masks and capes and pointy boots took up the space in between.

I let out a long breath. I'd vowed never to open this box, this gigantic can of worms, ever again. Ah well. In the end, all promises were made to be broken. Matt had taught me that. The familiar pain of his betrayal pricked me, but I shoved the feeling aside.

I yanked the lid off the box. I was back in the game. For better or worse.

I dug out my color-coded binder. The five-inch-thick book contained all the information I'd ever collected on superheroes and ubervillains. I flipped to the sections on the Fearless Five and the Terrible Triad. I'd spent so much time investigating the two groups that most of the information was permanently ingrained in my brain. Still, it wouldn't hurt to get a refresher on their powers, costume colors, and hobbies. You never knew what small bit of information would be the key to solving the big mystery.

FEARLESS FIVE: Members are Striker, Fiera, Mr. Sage, Hermit, and Tornado.

STRIKER: Male. Wears black leather suit with gray accents. Special abilities include above-average strength, unbelievable reflexes and agility, and the power to regenerate, or heal wounds rapidly. Uses two swords that return to his hand when called back.

FIERA: Female. Wears red-and-orange catsuit. Outfit and general body type are remarkably similar to Malefica's (see below). Special abilities include creating, controlling, and manipulating fire. Also has incredible strength.

MR. SAGE: Male. Wears green-and-white outfit. Special abilities include telekinesis, or the ability to

move objects with his mind, and some psychic
abilities, like telepathy and premonition.

HERMIT: Gender unknown. Costume unknown.
Never or very rarely participates in battle. Seems
mostly to provide technical support. Not known
if he/she has superpowers.

TORNADO: Male. Wears silver outfit. Special abilities
include creating, controlling, and manipulating
air and wind.

Underneath a variety of other information about Tornado, I'd written my last entry six months ago—
TORNADO IS TRAVIS TEAGUE. GOTCHA!

I wrestled with my guilt over Tornado's death. It was a black demon that would never let me be. My guilt was just like karma; it always came back around. But I had a job to do, and no time for regrets. I pushed aside my troubled feelings, then moved on to the villains.

TERRIBLE TRIAD: Members are Malefica,
Frost, and Scorpion.

MALEFICA: Female. Wears skin-tight, red leather catsuit. Outfit seems more designed to accentuate
her tiny waist and large chest rather than for prac-
ticality in battle (see Fiera above). Special abilities
include telekinesis, which she uses to fly. Has psychic abilities as well, including a strong gift for
premonition.

FROST: Male. Wears ice blue outfit. Special abilities
include creating, controlling, and manipulating
ice. Rumored to be incredibly intelligent.

SCORPION: Male. Wears black leather. Special abilities include incredible strength, agility, and regeneration. Can also poison victims by scratching them with his talon-like fingernails.

Once I'd brought myself up to speed, I put out feelers to my old contacts. I called and e-mailed everyone I'd ever gotten a hot superhero-sighting tip from. I also set up a meeting with a less-than-upright citizen who had clued me in on criminal activity in the past. She might know of something that would interest Striker and the rest of the Fearless Five. Finally, I called Chief Newman and set up an appointment to look at mug shots. It was doubtful I would find my kidnappers in the thousands of photos at the station, but I had to try.

My life depended on it.

I slid into one of my many little black dresses, put on my nightly war paint, er, makeup, and headed downtown to the police station.

I threaded my way through the crowd of detectives eating candy bars and headed for the chief's office. I spoke to the secretary, and a moment later, Chief Sean Newman stuck his head outside. Something like surprise flickered in his blue eyes. I hadn't come around the station much since Tornado's suicide, due to my own guilt and the way the detectives stared at me, as if they'd like to shoot me on the spot.

"Carmen, how nice to see you again," the chief rumbled in his deep Irish brogue. "Come in, come in."

I entered the chief's office, which was as neat as always. Every paper, pen, and paper clip rested in its own little organized tray, waiting to be plucked up and used. Even the crystal paperweights and framed photos lined up in a tidy row.

I sat down in a chair in front of the chief's gray metal desk and explained the events of the previous night, leaving out a few pertinent details, like Malefica's job for me and Frost's desire to turn me into an icicle. I couldn't tell Chief Newman the truth, not with Malefica's dire threats hanging over my head. I couldn't stand it if he or Henry or anyone else got hurt because of me. My karma was bad enough already. I didn't need to make it worse.

"Two men drugged you and tried to get you into a car, but you used your pepper spray and got away?" The chief stared at me, his face lined with worry.

"That's right. I think they were just a couple of guys, drunk most likely, painting the town red and upset over the whole Tornado incident. Still, I thought I'd take a look at the books."

"I think you need to do more than that," Chief Newman said. "I think you need a guard, Carmen, somebody to watch over you."

"No!" I shouted.

The chief raised a bushy eyebrow at me.

I fumbled for a reason to refuse. "I wouldn't be able to do my . . . job with somebody following me around. Besides, your detectives have much more important things to do than look after me. Murders, robberies, rapes, that sort of thing."

"Well, I can't make you accept protection," the chief said. "Still, you need to be careful, Carmen. There are a lot of folks who are still upset over Travis Teague's suicide. Who knows what some of them might do to you?"

Visions of giant vats of radioactive goo and horribly mutated animals flashed through my mind. *If you only knew*. The chief frowned, as if he could sense my dark thoughts.

"I'll be fine," I said in a too-bright voice. "I've got pepper spray and six months' worth of self-defense classes under my belt. What more does a girl need?"

I spent the next hour flipping through book after book after book of mug shots. My two kidnappers were nowhere to be found. Frustrated, I slammed the last book shut, thanked the chief for his time, and headed out.

I opened the door to the station and immediately stepped back. A guy dressed in black tumbled inside. He slid across the tile floor and landed with a loud thump against the information desk. An old woman followed him in. She wore a flowered dress, support hose, sensible shoes, and a string of pearls the size of Wilma Flintstone's. She looked like your typical grandmother, except for the flowered, purple mask that covered her face and the capelike flow to her white angora sweater. She held a diamond-topped walking stick in her right hand. A large handbag hung off her left arm. Ah, Granny Cane was in the house.

A cop stepped forward and helped the guy to his feet.

"Another mugger, Granny?" the cop asked, slapping some cuffs on the dazed man.

"Yep," the superhero crowed. "Tried to take my purse down on Thirteenth Street. I showed him who was boss, though." She smacked her walking stick against her left palm and launched into her story about how she had whacked the thief into submission.

I skirted around the three of them and headed outside. I didn't give the seventy-something superhero a second glance. Granny Cane had been stopping would-be thieves from preying on the elderly for twenty years now. You'd think that Bigtime's criminals would wise up and not try to rob an old woman wearing a purple mask. But no. Every other week, some scumbag tried to take Granny Cane's purse and got soundly beaten with her walking stick for his trouble.

I scurried across town to attend the latest, greatest society function, this time a fashion show by designer-to-the-stars Fiona Fine. Fiona was a real rags-to-riches story, having burst upon the fashion scene as a penniless college student and clawed her way to the top. Unlike most designers, Fiona had managed to stay there, although I couldn't see why.

She used all sorts of bold colors, canary yellows and blazing oranges and lime greens that made my head ache. Even worse, Fiona adorned said colors with feathers and faux furs and glittering rhinestones. She would have been the perfect person to design costumes for Vegas showgirls. She had gaudy and over-the-top down pat. Not to mention the fact Fiona's clothes flattered only supermodels and other women with perfectly skeletal bodies and amazingly full chests.

"Fiona! Fiona!" I shouted over the crush of people surrounding the designer. "How about a comment on your new collection?"

At the sound of my voice, Fiona turned. She was a perfectly tall woman with perfectly long, flowing blond hair and perfectly blue eyes. Fiona was so perfect she could have modeled her own clothes and looked fabulous, even if she designed potato sacks. Though she wore a dress that reminded me of an eggplant with ruffles, Fiona still looked, well, perfect.

"My collection is fabulous, as always." Fiona's blue eyes rolled over me. "Unlike your dress. Where did you get it, the Salvation Army?" she snickered.

My cheeks flamed. There was nothing wrong with my dress. I was always neat and clean, and I ironed all my clothes regularly. Hell, I even ironed my sheets on occasion.

So what if I wore a little black dress to every event? So what if I was more comfortable in jeans, sneakers, and a grungy T-shirt than anything else? I didn't have thousands to burn on clothes the way the jet-set crowd did.

Anger bubbled up in my chest. In the last day, I'd been kidnapped, drugged, and threatened. Now, some spoiled, snotty, rich-bitch designer was taking potshots at my wardrobe and reminding me yet again that I didn't belong among the glitz and glamour. I might have to write about these people, but I didn't have to take their insults.

"No, not the Salvation Army." I straightened my shoulders. "I got it at Oodles o' Stuff downtown during the big clearance sale. It's actually from your last collection, when you were going through your black, depressed phase. Remember that one? Pity you didn't stay in it. It was so much classier than your typical crayon-colored creations."

Fiona gasped. I stalked through the crowd, grabbed a glass of champagne, and gulped it down. Everyone stared at me, even Sam Sloane and his latest supermodel. I chugged down another glass of champagne.

Fiona shot me heated, *why-don't-you-drop-dead-bitch* looks the rest of the night, but I didn't care. I stayed another hour to show people I wouldn't be insulted by the likes of Fiona Fine and went back to the office. Although I wanted to write a less-than-flattering story about Fiona, her enormous ego, and horrible clothes, I typed up a bland, harmless little bit of fluff. I had to concentrate all my energy on finding Striker. I didn't have time to get into pissy catfights with Fiona Fine. The woman hated me. I didn't really care why.

I turned in my story, waited for the short-but-sweet

response from my editor, and packed up my things. Rapid typing caught my attention. Henry hunched over his keyboard. My inner voice whispered. A thought occurred to me, another way I might uncover Striker and Malefica's identities. I stopped at the black man's desk, which was a haphazard mess of papers and wires and odd, electronic devices.

"Henry, could you do me a favor?"

He peered at me through his glasses. The thick lenses made his dark eyes seem twice their natural size. "Sure, what's up?"

"Could you get me a list of the fifty richest men and women in Bigtime, along with their major assets, stock holdings, and companies?" I asked. "I need it for something I'm working on."

"Oh, sure. No problem. Something for the society section?"

"You might say that."

I'd long suspected there were more than a few superheroes and ubervillains hiding among the high-society, rich-as-sin crowd I covered. After all, heroes and villains needed vast amounts of money to pay for their high-tech toys and construct their secret, state-of-the-art underground lairs. Following the money trail had led me to more than one hero and villain. But if someone was leading a double life on the Bigtime social scene, he or she hid it well. Everyone on the society circuit seemed about as deep and interesting as a champagne flute.

"Can you give it to me by tomorrow?" I could have compiled the information myself, but it would have taken hours of digging through databases and stock reports and the like at the library, precious hours I didn't have. Plus, Henry was a real whiz at things like that. He could type a few buttons and find all the information I needed in a matter of minutes.

"Well, I have some other things I'm working on right now. I can get it to you by the end of the week, or the beginning of next," Henry said.

I tapped my foot. I needed the list right now, or tomorrow at the very latest. I needed as much information as I could get as quickly as I could get it in order to uncover Striker's identity. I didn't have time to wait around. Unlike some people in Bigtime, I wasn't a psychic or a miracle worker or even a mind reader. Not even close.

Still, it wasn't Henry's fault I was in this mess. I had nobody to blame but myself. I made my lips smile. "Thanks, Henry. This week or next will be fine. Take your time."

I left the gleaming skyscraper that housed *The Exposé* behind, took a right, and started walking. I glanced at my watch. I'd have to hustle to make it to the meeting with my contact.

"Hey, hey, hot mama! Looking for some action?" a voice called out from a dark doorway.

It was the same male pig who harassed me every night. "Forget it, loser," I growled. The guy *so* needed to get a life.

A few blocks later, I reached Paradise Park in the heart of downtown Bigtime. With a zoo, carousel, carnival rides, and concession stands galore, the park was one of the major attractions in the city. Thousands of people visited it each day, and the park never closed, not even on Christmas. Even now on a late September night, faint music and squeals of laughter rose up from the Ferris wheel and merry-go-round. The smell of hot popcorn and greasy funnel cakes permeated the cool air. I walked past the fun and games, making my way to a fountain in the far corner of the park. I sat down next to a pair of frolicking nymphs that spat water out of their mouths every few seconds.

Twenty minutes later, I checked my faux silver watch for the umpteenth time. It was nearing midnight. Lulu should have been here by now, but the only people I'd seen had been a few sweaty joggers and the occasional homeless person looking for a place to curl up for the night. I'd given one of the hobos twenty bucks and sent him on his way.

Suddenly, the hairs on the back of my neck stood straight up. My inner voice chirped. I didn't have enhanced senses, but I knew someone was watching me. A small hum sounded above the bubbling water, confirming my suspicion.

"You're late," I said.

A woman in a wheelchair zoomed out of the shadows. She shrugged. "Traffic. Cars won't stop for anybody these days. Some guy on Broadway almost mowed me down. Big mistake. I got his license plate number. Tomorrow, his credit will be toast."

I turned to look at Lulu. She was a skinny Asian girl about twenty-five with a pretty, heart-shaped face. Neon blue streaks gleamed in her short, spiky, black hair. She looked fairly harmless and innocent, but Lulu knew everybody who was anybody in Bigtime. Information was her game, and she played it very well. Lulu was one of the best computer whizzes and hackers in the business. She had her own little empire of information trading and corporate espionage that netted her millions, as evidenced by the elaborate, motorized wheelchair she sat in and the Bulluci fleece pullover jacket she wore that cost more than my first car.

I had met Lulu Lo while doing a story on Yee-haw!, a therapeutic riding center that helped paralyzed and injured kids and adults. At first, I'd thought that Lulu was just another one of the program's clients. Then, I'd started digging around and discovered the center was financed almost entirely by her. Further investigation revealed Lulu's extracurricular activities weren't exactly legal. Despite the dubious nature of its financing, my story focused on all the good the program did. Lulu had gotten some legitimate contributions from the article, and since then, we'd developed a tit-for-tat relationship. Lulu gave me the lowdown on what was happening around town, and every couple of months I did another glowing feature about the program's latest success story.

"What can I do for you, Sister Carmen? You sounded rather frantic on the phone. Not like your usual cool self at all."

Lulu always called me *Sister Carmen*. She had since the first day we'd met. I didn't really know why. I'd asked her about it one time, and she'd mumbled something about us being in the ubervillain fight together. Like sisters. I didn't understand what she meant, but I didn't mind the odd nickname. After all, Lulu was the closest thing I had to a friend these days, besides Henry.

"I want information on Striker and the rest of the Fearless Five. Do you know anything? Are any of the gangs in town up to something that might catch their interest?"

Lula's dark eyes narrowed. "Why do you ask?"

"Let's just say I'm getting back in the game." I liked Lulu, but I wasn't about to tell her my troubles. You couldn't trust anybody, not even your fiancé or best friend. A needle of pain pierced my heart. "Do you know anything?"

"There have been some rumors that the Five, or the Four these days, haven't been too happy about the Southside crew that's been smuggling drugs into the city. Word on the street is Striker is looking to take them out."

Lulu pulled a small laptop computer out of a bag attached to her chair. She fired it up and began to type. Invoices and spreadsheets flashed across the screen faster than I could blink. At times like these, Lulu reminded me of a prettier, female version of Henry Harris. One with much better taste in clothes.

"Hmmm, looks like you're in luck, Sister Carmen. The Southside crew has a shipment coming in tomorrow night. I'd lay even money on Striker and his friends being there. I'll e-mail you the time and location."

"Thanks, Lulu. I appreciate it." I got to my feet.

"What are you planning to do? Going to expose Striker and the rest of the Fearless Five?"

"Something like that," I said in a vague tone. "Is that a problem?"

"No, no, no. I don't judge. I merely facilitate. And instigate on occasion." Lulu grinned. "Playing it close to the vest, huh? I can respect that. Will I see you at the annual benefit? We're joining forces with the police department this year. All the big power players will be there. Can you imagine me chatting up the chief of police?"

"I'm sure you'll do a great job, and I'll be there to cover every detail," I promised.

Lulu dropped her almond-shaped eyes to her computer. Her fingers pounded on the keyboard, and she hunched over the laptop just like Henry. My inner voice whispered.

"Lulu, are you seeing anybody right now?"

The Asian girl's face grew guarded. "No. Why? You got some loser you want to foist off on me? Some hillbilly cousin from Tennessee who's missing his teeth?"

I gave her a sour look.

"What?" Lulu asked in a defensive tone. "I know how things work down in the South. I've seen *Deliverance*."

I dug a piece of paper out of my purse and scribbled down Henry's work number. "Give this guy a call. I think you two would really hit it off. You're both computer nerds."

"I prefer the term *information engineer*," Lulu retorted. "You're worse than my mom trying to fix me up."

"Just give him a call. Tell him I gave you his number. This guy works with me. He writes a computer column. I'm sure you'll like him."

And I was sure. The two of them had so much in common. They could talk about data bytes and hard drives for days and days and never come up for air, before getting around to the good stuff like networks and wireless connections and firewalls.

I gave Lulu the paper. The Asian girl reluctantly took it and slid it into her computer bag.

"Thanks for the info, Lulu. Now, if you'll excuse me, I've got a superhero to stalk."

★ 6 ★

I spent most of the next day at the Bigtime Public Library, tracking down every newspaper story, magazine article, and research paper ever written on the Fearless Five. I roamed through the stacks of books, and a strange feeling of déjà vu swept over me. The last time I'd done this, I'd been hot on the trail of Tornado, aka Travis Teague. He committed suicide as a result. What would Striker do when I discovered his true identity?

I pushed away my guilty thoughts. I wasn't here by choice. Malefica and her vats of radioactive goo were making me do this. But I'd turn the tables on her. I'd track down Striker, then use him to lead me to her. The Fearless Five would take care of the rest. It would all work out right this time. It had to. For the sake of my conscience, heart, and general well-being.

Truth be told, wandering through the library was a pleasant way to pass the day. It was one of my favorite places in all of Bigtime. The library took up its own square city block in the middle of the downtown district. The stone building housed hundreds of thousands of books, magazines, newspapers, and more. Overstuffed chairs and sofas sat throughout the library's many floors, inviting people to relax and read the day away in some cozy, secluded corner. Floor-to-ceiling glass windows overlooked an open-air garden that crouched in the center of the library's block.

I made copies of every story I found, no matter how inconsequential or trivial it seemed. Of course, I'd done this same thing when I'd first arrived in town, but I'd thrown most of the papers away after Travis's death. By the time I finished, I had several reams of paper to go through, the Bigtime Public Library was a couple hundred dollars richer, and another thousand acres of the Brazilian rain forest had been decimated. All in a day's work.

I stuffed the papers in a large trash bag and ignored the strange, suspicious looks from the library's older patrons. When everything was sacked away, I checked my e-mail from one of the library's computers. A note from Lulu waited in my inbox.

Delivery and show set for midnight. Address is 1313 Good Intentions Lane. Suggested viewing from top of adjacent building. Doorman/escort expecting you. Code word is Striker. Be careful. L.

I sent back a brief reply. *Thanks for the info. See you at the benefit. Carmen.*

I logged off. Then, I hoisted the heavy sack of papers over my shoulder like Santa Claus carrying a bag full of Christmas toys and left the library.

Six blocks down the street, I hit a wall of people. Up ahead, flames and smoke boiled out of a high-rise office building. Soot and ash floated like confetti in the breeze. Policemen had the area cordoned off. They directed traffic down side streets, blew silver whistles, and shouted garbled information at the crowd through bullhorns. Firemen perched on ladders and hosed the building with powerful jets of water, but the liquid streams didn't have any effect on the hungry flames. An explosion roared out. Glass zipped through the air like shotgun pellets. People screamed and shouted and ducked for cover.

"There go the last of the windows," an old man said. He sat on a nearby stoop staring at the commotion. "The fire just started about ten minutes ago, but half the building's already gone."

His companion, a woman with a tight, white bun and wrinkled face, tapped her chin. "So who do you think will show this time?"

"I'd put even money on the Fearless Five."

"Nah," she replied. "Swifte works this part of downtown. Besides, he's faster."

"Care to make a little friendly wager?"

She smiled. "Of course."

"I'll take that action," a college kid with a bulging backpack chimed in.

"Me too."

"Count me in."

Other bystanders fished out their wallets. Soon, the stoop had blossomed into a mini-betting parlor, and the man had a stack of cash three inches thick.

I gave the old guy five bucks on the Fearless Five. Who knew? If they showed up, maybe I could just follow them back to their supersecret lair and abandon all my boring research. Yeah right. My karma could never be that good.

I stood there with the rest of the crowd, gawking. A woman darted past one of the policemen.

"My baby! My baby!" the woman screamed, pointing at the burning building.

"Baby?" the old man asked. "In that big high-rise?"

The old woman nodded. "Yep. There's a day-care center inside for all the moms who work in the building. Everyone else got out already. I guess the kid got overlooked in the rush."

A policeman struggled with the woman, trying to shove her back behind the barricade. Suddenly, a multicolored blur zipped by. Swifte stopped. I blinked. One minute he wasn't there, the next he was.

Swifte was a lean man dressed in an iridescent white spandex suit. Red, orange, yellow, green, blue, indigo, violet. All the colors of the rainbow flashed in his opalesque costume. Swifte claimed he could travel faster than the speed of light. I rather doubted it, but he was quicker than anyone else in Bigtime.

"Told you," the old woman said, elbowing the man.

Groans and grumbles went up from the losers, including me. Five bucks down the superhero drain.

Swifte zoomed over to the frantic woman and grabbed her hand. "Have no fear, good lady. I'll save your baby."

He turned his good side to the Superhero News Network and other TV news cameras set up on the street and let them get some footage before dashing into the building. Seven seconds later, Swifte sped back out, cradling a small infant in his arms. Once he got clear of the blazing building, the superhero slowed down to normal walking speed to make sure the cameras caught every single moment of his daring rescue. Swifte was one of the superheroes who loved the attention. He was never too busy to stop to chat with fans or pose for a photo. He even kept a daily blog on his Web site of his latest victories. He worked the press like a pro.

Swifte handed the tiny tot over to the grateful mother. People cheered and clapped and stomped their feet. Swifte put his hands on his hips, sucked in his chest, and stuck out his chin. Behind him, the building continued to burn. It was the perfect superhero pose.

Superheroes. Always so dramatic.

I trudged home with my heavy cargo and spent the rest of the day sorting through and organizing the papers. The number of articles written about the Fearless Five amazed me, as did the sorts of things published in so-called respectable, scholarly journals. I found stories on everything from the superheroes' powers to their hobbies to their favorite sports teams. A couple of professors with way too much time on their hands had written journal articles about the superheroes' costumes and what the colors signified about each person's inner child. Academics. Sheesh.

Fiera was the most frequently mentioned member of the Fearless Five, and her impressive attributes were the most frequently mentioned thing about her. I flipped through glossy photo after glossy photo of Fiera in all her flaming glory. Long legs, small waist, huge breasts, a fiery cascade of silken hair, smoldering eyes. She looked like a Barbie doll somebody had poured gasoline on and lit up. She was smokin' hot. Literally. It was no wonder I couldn't get a date to save my life. Every male in Bigtime from fanboys to professional journalists sang Fiera's praises in their stories. Drool practically dripped off the pages. She even had her own pinup calendar, with the proceeds going to a charity to help burn victims. Naturally.

Tornado was second on the most-written-about list, with the articles being of two different sorts—before and after death. Before his death, Tornado had been a whirl-wind of energy and exuberance. Most of the articles dealt with his work with charities for victims of natural disasters and appearances as a guest meteorologist on various weather channels. However, in the last six months the articles almost exclusively dealt with Tornado's real identity as Travis Teague and his sudden, unexpected suicide. I stared at a picture of Travis taken a month before his death. He looked straight into the camera, his brown eyes boring into mine. A smile curved his lips. He looked so happy, so carefree. Now, he was dead because of me. A giant fist of guilt squeezed my heart. I put the article aside. I couldn't bear to look at it.

Mr. Sage came in third in the popularity contest. He dispensed wise, moderate advice to the down-and-out and lovelorn in a number of self-help and humor columns in various publications. He also appeared at several events, reading people's futures to raise money for various Bigtime charities.

Striker rarely appeared in print, except to growl at nosy reporters who had gotten too close to a battle scene.

I could only find a few passing references to Hermit, including one that referred to him or her as the *greatest technological wizard ever*.

By the time I finished, I had five stacks of papers, one for each superhero. I put the Striker stack on top of the coffee table and shoved the others under the sofa. Time to go see if I could spot the man, the hero, the legend in person.

I threw on some jeans, a T-shirt, and a black fleece jacket. I pulled my auburn hair into a short ponytail and grabbed my pepper spray and stun gun. I also locked and loaded the tranquilizer dart gun I'd purchased a few months ago and tucked it in the back of my jeans. Despite its name, Good Intentions Lane wasn't in the best part of town.

I took a taxi to the specified location, arriving about thirty minutes early. Good Intentions Lane squatted about ten miles past the wrong side of the tracks. The street looked like a war zone or the epicenter of the most violent superhero-ubervillain battle ever. Abandoned buildings covered in graffiti and gang symbols lined the street. Broken windows and busted-down doors grinned like dark, gaping maws. A few fires smoldered in overflowing trashcans that dotted the cracked sidewalks. Flickering traffic lights swung in the breeze.

"You sure you want to get out here, miss?" the taxi driver asked. "This doesn't look like the safest place to be."

"Unfortunately, I must take the road less traveled. I'm afraid that I have promises to keep, and miles to go before I sleep," I quipped.

The driver gave me a funny look, like I was a few sandwiches short of a picnic. Maybe I was, quoting Robert Frost at a time like this. I paid the man and got out of the taxi. The driver put his foot to the floor, and the yellow car sped away into the dark night. What a gentleman.

I looked up and down the street. Nothing moved or stirred in the night, except the foot-long rats that made their homes in the deserted buildings and alleyways. I put my hand in my jacket pocket, clutched my pepper spray and stun gun, and walked down the lonely street. Garbage and empty fast-food cartons crunched under my feet. I moved as fast as I could. I checked the address Lulu had e-mailed me and jogged up the steps to a rickety-looking building, the only one on the whole block that still had a door attached to it.

My knuckles cracked against the steel door, shattering the chilling silence. I fought the urge to duck for cover.

"What's the word?" a low male voice asked from the other side.

"The word is *Striker*," I replied.

Several locks clicked, and the door creaked open. A short, fat, Asian man glared at me. Suspicion darkened his eyes.

"You here for the show?" he asked. "You're early."

"You betcha. I brought popcorn and soda and everything. I always come early to get the best seat in the house."

The man frowned, failing to see the humor in my joke. Most people did. He turned and walked deeper into the building. I followed him, keeping a tight grip on my stun gun. Graffiti scrawled across the walls, and worn-out mattresses covered the floor. The whole building reeked of greasy French fries, wet dogs, and human excrement. I wrinkled my nose.

We worked our way up a couple flights of rotted stairs to the top of the building. The man unlocked a metal door and held it open.

"This goes to the roof. Enjoy. I'll be waiting downstairs to let you out when the show's over." He turned and disappeared back down the hall.

A wave of fear and doubt washed over me. What was I doing here in a strange building in a bad part of town in the middle of the night? I was going to get myself killed— or worse. Surely, there had to be an easier way, a safer way, to uncover Striker's identity. Visions of my body covered in fur with eyes the size of golf balls danced through my head. I swallowed. I didn't have time to be overly concerned with my safety. Besides, if I got killed, I would cheat Malefica out of the chance to turn me into a monster. There was a small glimmer of satisfaction in that thought.

I squared my shoulders, stepped through the door, and climbed up another flight of stairs. I emerged on the roof and gulped in the cool night air, trying to get the building's sickening stench out of my nose and mouth. The fresh air also helped settle my jangled nerves. A breeze ruffled my hair. The moon shone like a huge lantern in the night sky and bathed everything in a silvery glow. Stars twinkled like fireflies far above. There was plenty of light for the lens of my night-vision digital camera, which meant I wouldn't have to use a telltale flash. Good.

I walked to the side of the roof that overlooked the street. Silence. Even the rats were quiet and still for once. I dug a tape recorder out of my purse. It was no larger than a deck of cards, but it could pick up sound three hundred feet away. Henry had given the gizmo a rare five-star rating in his technology column. I switched it on and set the device on the three-foot-high wall that ringed the roof. I grabbed my digital camera out of my purse and flipped it on. It, too, was small but powerful.

My tools of the trade ready, I sat on the ledge, leaned against the side of a chimney that jutted up from the roof, and settled down to wait.

Thirty minutes later, a pair of headlights popped on at the far end of Good Intentions Lane. Midnight. Right on schedule. Another set of headlights lit up at the opposite end of the street, and the two cars flashed their lights several times in some sort of code. The vehicles crept toward each other.

I sat up, camera in hand.

The cars stopped, and several men of varying ages and ethnicities emerged. One group favored designer business suits and glossy wingtips, while the others opted for sweatshirts, pricey sneakers, and baggy pants. Drugs brought people together no matter what their socioeconomic backgrounds might be. How comforting.

Both parties hauled thick, metal briefcases out of their

respective vehicles and put them on the hoods, which faced each other.

"You got the stuff?"

"If you've got the money."

Voices floated up to me, and the briefcases snapped open. The one on the designer suit side brimmed over with the aforementioned money, while the other on the sweatshirt side contained large white packets of what I assumed was heroin, cocaine, or some other nasty, illegal substance. I snapped a few pictures with my superduper night vision lens. Even if Striker didn't show, Chief Newman would find the photos interesting.

The money and drugs exchanged hands. Once the deal was done and the briefcases safely stowed away, the men relaxed. They joked and talked and laughed about bitches, basketball, and various other topics.

I scanned the street and the surrounding alleys. Nothing. I bit back a growl of frustration. Striker wasn't going to show. I had come down to Drugs R Us and put myself in danger for nothing, not to mention wasted precious hours I could have spent researching Striker and his cohorts. For once, Lulu's information had been wrong.

I switched off the tape recorder and glanced over the edge of the roof. Both groups drifted back to their respective vehicles. The party was breaking up. I turned to go.

Suddenly, I stopped. A feeling swept over me, and I knew, just knew, I shouldn't leave yet. I listened to that inner feeling, that voice whispering in the back of my mind. It had never let me down before. I flipped my tape recorder back on and resumed my position.

I squinted and peered into the shadows. A flash of silver caught my eye, then vanished. My heart sped up. Had it come from that alley over there? Or the one a building over—

A sword sailed through the air, landing in the rear tire of one of the cars. It wobbled back and forth, and the tire hissed and flattened. As quickly as it had appeared, the sword flew out of the tire and back into the shadows. Moments later, the process repeated itself, this time on the other car.

Striker had arrived.

I fumbled for my digital camera. I set it to video mode and leaned over the roof, almost falling off in the process. A few loose bits of bricks slid off the edge and plummeted to the street below, but the gangbangers were too preoccupied to notice.

Shouts rose up from inside the two vehicles. Doors popped open, and men poured out. Now, they sported guns instead of briefcases. Evidently, semiautomatic pistols and multiple clips fit perfectly into the pocket of a designer suit these days.

But no more swords appeared. No superheroes swooped into sight. The men stood still. Their excited breath spurted out in huffs and puffs. They crouched next to their cars for several minutes in a silent standoff with someone they couldn't see. The men stared into the shadows and waited for the next attack, while I watched from above, my camera capturing every slow, agonizing second.

After five minutes, the men began to grumble. They exchanged glares and shrugs and dropped their guns to their sides.

Suddenly, a black figure sprang from the shadows.

He landed in between the two cars. The headlights spotlighted him, and I got my first good look at Striker in the flesh. My mouth went dry. He was tall with a lean figure and perfectly sculpted muscles in all the right places. Twin swords rose above his shoulders, held in place by some kind of scabbard built into his black leather suit. A black-

and-gray mask covered his face, while the *F5* insignia stretched across his chest. His black hair glistened like onyx under the bright headlights.

Striker lifted his head. I gasped at the sight of his eyes. They were gray, a shimmering, ethereal sort of gray that made me think of moonlight and the stars far above. But there was a fire in his eyes, a fire that could sear your very soul with its heat. I shivered.

Striker moved. His two swords flashed like liquid quicksilver. He ran through the men like a lawnmower chugging through dry grass. Fists met flesh and cracked bones. Swords sliced through gun barrels like they were made of paper. Bodies flew through the air and landed with dull thuds on the street.

In less than a minute, it was over. Striker stood alone. A dozen gang members littered the ground around him, taking their rightful place with the rest of the garbage. The men cried and moaned and whined in pain. Those that could crawled away. Those that couldn't hugged their knees to their chest and prayed for mercy. Striker stood still in the midst of the chaos.

I switched from video to camera mode. I shot picture after picture of the superhero. I couldn't stop myself. Something about him was so impressive, so mesmerizing, so captivating. I couldn't look away, and I didn't want to. My camera clicked and whirred with each frame.

Striker cocked his head. I stopped. Surely, he couldn't hear my camera over the whimpers of the men. Why, he'd have to have the most amazing hearing in the world to do that—

Striker's head snapped up. He stared right at me with those searing, piercing, gray eyes. I froze. My heart slammed against my ribs. He frowned.

Uh-oh.

The superhero's eyes narrowed to slits. They glittered like diamonds in the dark night. My breath caught in my throat. He recognized me. How could he not? After all, I was the woman who'd driven his friend to commit suicide. Guilt tightened my chest.

I started to duck behind the wall, to hunker down and cower, to do something, anything to hide from Striker's piercing eyes. But my inner voice chattered, and I stopped. Oh, what the hell. He'd find out I was tracking him sooner or later. Who knew, it might make my job easier in the end.

So I waved at him.

★ 7 ★

Striker was not amused. His gray eyes glowed with anger, and his gloved hands clenched into fists. He stepped over one of the weeping gang members and started toward the building. A vision of myself shish-kebabed on his swords flashed through my mind.

Striker stopped and cocked his head. A moment later, the thin wail of a siren sliced through the air, and flashing red lights appeared at the far end of Good Intentions Lane. Striker stared at the oncoming police cars, then up at me. Debating. He turned and melted back into the shadows like the ghost he was. A long, tense breath escaped from my lips. I didn't know what I would have done if he'd come up here and confronted me. Quivered with fear and begged for mercy, most likely. And probably ogled the sexy superhero. I shook my head. Why the hell would I be thinking about ogling—

The door to the roof banged open. I shrieked and fumbled for my stun gun. The short Asian man stuck his head out.

"The cops are coming. Let's go!"

I didn't need any encouragement. I shoved my camera and tape recorder into my purse. The Asian man held the door open, and I pounded down the stairs after him. He led me through the halls and out a back door that opened up onto the opposite side of the building from Striker and the approaching cops. We cut through a dilapidated parking lot. Weeds and crushed beer cans crackled under our feet.

"This way! This way!" he hissed. "The subway's only three blocks ahead."

He might have been short and fat, but the man ran like a whole gang of ubervillains was after him. Maybe they were.

I struggled to keep up. My purse slapped against my thigh like a lead weight. My lungs burned. My heart pounded. A stitch embedded itself in my side.

Just when I thought I couldn't run another step, the man slowed. A cracked subway sign flickered up ahead, and a set of graffiti-covered stairs led underground.

"I'm going first. Wait here a minute, then come down. You never saw me. I never saw you," the man said. "Forget what I look like. I'll do the same."

I nodded, more concerned with gulping down air than with responding. The man slid down the stairs. I put my hands on my hips and concentrated on breathing. When I felt like my lungs weren't going to explode, I shouldered my heavy purse and plodded down the grimy stairs to the subway platform.

It was close to one o'clock in the morning now. A couple of homeless guys slept over a steam vent, while a bored transit cop read a comic book inside his bulletproof booth. The Asian man had vanished like a puff of smoke blown away by the wind. I clutched my stun gun and tried not to look nervous.

A train rumbled into the station a minute later. I paid for a token and sank onto a hard plastic seat. I was the only passenger. The doors hissed shut, and the train slid away from the platform. I let out a breath. Safe. For now.

On the ride home, I thought about Striker. He'd recognized me. The question was what would he do now?

I chewed my lip. Striker would go back to the Fearless Five's supersecret headquarters and tell them Carmen Cole was up to her old tricks again. Given Tornado's suicide and my involvement in it, they'd try to figure out what I was up to, if I was trying to expose the rest of them.

They'd start investigating me, just like I was investigating them.

And they'd have a much easier time of it. If Hermit was the technological wizard he or she was rumored to be, the superhero had hacked into every part of my life by now. Hermit most likely had my bank records, credit history, library card number, grade school report cards, everything. He was probably reading the story about my doomed wedding and superhero ex-fiancé at this very moment. Other than the usual little prick of pain, the thought didn't bother me. I had nothing to hide. My humiliation was public record, and I was the one who had made it that way.

My thoughts turned back to Striker. The image of him spotlighted between the two cars flashed through my head. His pictures didn't do the man justice. I'd seen plenty of superheroes before. Hell, I'd even slept with one. But something about Striker captured my imagination like no one else ever had. Those piercing eyes, those perfect, chiseled lips, that hard, sculpted body that just begged to be touched.

And kissed. And caressed. And covered with whipped cream.

Striker had looked good. Very, very good. Mouthwatering good. Toe-curling good. On a scale of one to ten, Striker was definitely a thirteen and a half. I wondered if he looked as fantastic out of that costume as he did in it. Somehow, I knew he did. And by the looks of it, he hadn't been wearing a sculpted codpiece so many of the macho, male superheroes favored. Heat flooded my body. I shifted on the hard seat and fanned myself with my hand.

I shook my head. Why was I thinking about how well Striker filled out his leather costume? So what if he had the perfect body with lots of muscles in all the right places? Most superheroes did. It was practically a job requirement. Superheroes couldn't afford to let themselves go. Their adoring publics wouldn't let them. Nobody wanted to see overweight, out-of-shape superheroes. It just wasn't done. Fiera's pinup calendar was proof of that.

It had to be hormones. I hadn't had a decent date, much less sex, in forever. I'd gone without, and my hormones had kicked into overdrive at the sight of a sexy superhero. That's why I was lusting after Striker. That's why I was imagining the feel of his lips on mine. That's why I was fantasizing about peeling that leather suit off his body and seeing if he was as rock-solid as he looked.

That pair of searing gray eyes filled my memory. They burned into mine, as if they could see into the very depths of my soul. A shiver swept up my spine.

Hormones or not, it would be a very, very long time before I forgot about those amazing eyes.

The next morning, I flipped through The Exposé. The drug-bust story covered the front page, along with police photos of the dealers in various states of pain and agony. I scanned the story, written by one of the newspaper's many crime reporters. The police had confiscated over a hundred pounds of heroin. Chief Newman said the arrests had come about through an anonymous tip. He didn't confirm or deny that Striker and the Fearless Five had been involved. Perhaps he didn't know. The police always seemed to be the last to know anything in Bigtime.

I threw down the paper and paced around my apartment. Every time I made a lap, I stopped and stared out the living room windows into the street below. People bustled down the sidewalk, coffee and cigarettes in hand. Cars jockeyed for room, while horns blared out their harsh notes. Vendors hawked everything from magazines to giant pretzels to knock-off watches in loud, obnoxious voices. Another typical day in Bigtime. My eyes scanned the crush of people, peering into the alleys, squinting into every nook and cranny. Looking for someone. Looking for him.

Looking for Striker.

I knew he would seek me out. By now, the Fearless Five had figured out I was investigating them, trying to uncover their identities again. They wouldn't be pleased by the realization. I'd half expected Striker to be waiting in my apartment when I got home last night, hiding in the dark shadows, ready to spring out and order me to cease and desist with my investigations like any good superhero would. But everything had been as I'd left it, and there were no nasty surprises waiting inside.

No strange phone calls, no sudden knocks on the door, no windows breaking in the middle of the night. Nothing. Striker hadn't shown himself. Still, I knew he was coming, that he would be here soon. To my surprise, I was eager to see him again, although I couldn't quite figure out why.

My eyes scanned over the crush of people again, looking, searching, seeking.

There he was!

My heart stopped. A figure clad in black crouched on top of a city bus rumbling down the street toward my apartment building. That lithe form. That hard body. That elaborate snakelike headdress—

Wait a minute. The bus stopped in the street below, and I got a good look at the figure riding on top of it. The costume was black, but the figure squeezed inside it was definitely female. I sighed. It was Black Samba, another one of the city's resident superheroes. Along with some weird voodoo hoodoo powers, snakes were her thing, and they wrapped around her arms like multicolored bangle bracelets. She also liked to dance, hence her name.

The bus pulled back into traffic. I turned away from the windows and sighed. Malefica's deadline drew closer with every passing second. I didn't have time to waste worrying when Striker would appear on my doorstep. Not if I didn't want to end up looking like a radioactive snow bunny.

There were no society events scheduled for the evening, so I returned to the Bigtime Public Library. This time, I gathered information on the Terrible Triad. Every newspaper column, every glossy magazine spread, every journal article written about the ubervillains. I copied them all, stuffed them in a trash bag, and headed home.

It was late when I unlocked the door to my apartment and stepped over the threshold. I flipped on the lights, threw my keys down on a nearby table, and walked over to the alarm system. I punched in the code. I shivered and glanced at the thermostat. Sixty-five degrees. I frowned. The thermostat was set at seventy-two. It should be a lot warmer than that in here—

My fingers stilled for a second. Then, I leaned forward

and fiddled with the thermostat, pretending to punch in an elaborate command. My eyes scanned what I could see of the living room. One of the windows was open. A cool breeze invaded the room and fluttered the white curtains.

There was only one problem. I hadn't left the window open. I never did, not since the first time a kid had slipped inside and hidden two pounds of rotten fish under the sofa. Someone had broken into my apartment. Another, more disturbing thought popped into my frantic, confused brain.

He might still be in here.

For a moment, I wanted to scream and bolt through the door. Instead of running, I reached out into the hallway and picked up my garbage bag filled with papers. I knew who had come calling while I wasn't home. I was just surprised it had taken him this long.

I lugged the bag over to the coffee table and plopped it down. The table creaked under the weight.

"Whew!" I said for the benefit of whoever might be listening and wiped a bit of imaginary sweat from my forehead. "That one was even heavier than the last batch. Time to take a shower."

I walked down the hall like everything was perfectly normal, even though my heart pounded and blood roared in my ears. I went into the bathroom and closed the door not quite all the way. I stood at the crack, listening. Nothing. Was complete silence one of his superpowers? For once, my memory failed me. My jumbled brain couldn't recall.

I turned on the water in the sink. The steady hiss drowned out the rapid beating of my heart. I reached under the toilet and yanked off a piece of duct tape. A gun fell into my sweaty hand, along with an extra clip of ammo. It comforted me. I was pretty sure who my intruder was and that he wouldn't hurt me, but it was better to be safe than sorry. I racked back the slide and stuck the clip in my waistband. My hands trembled.

I took a deep breath to steady myself. Then, I tiptoed to the door and squeezed through the opening. I padded down the hall, as silent as any mouse. I stood in the pool of darkness that separated the hall from the living room and kitchen. I held the gun up, waiting, watching, listening.

Come out, come out, wherever you are . . .

A long, tall shadow detached itself from the refrigerator and headed for the open window. I raised the gun and aimed at the shadow's back. I pulled the trigger.

I wasn't fast enough. The shadow whirled around, sensing my presence. A dart hit the spot where he'd been standing a moment ago. So I fired again.

And again.

And again.

And again.

He kept moving. Dart after dart followed him through the kitchen. Glasses shattered and dishes broke as the tiny missiles hit them. Damn, he was fast, even for a superhero. A hollow click rang out, followed by another, then another. Out of ammo.

"Oh, bloody hell."

I popped out the clip and jammed in the fresh one. *Slow, slow, slow!* I was moving too slow, like I was underwater. I expected a body to slam into me at any second. Or a gloved hand to yank the gun from my shaky, sweaty grasp. But nothing happened.

I snapped up the gun. The shadow stilled. We stood there in a silent standoff. Then slowly, oh so slowly, he eased forward into the light that spilled in through the window.

Striker.

He looked just the same as he had last night. Black suit. Black mask. Black hair. Silver swords. Gray eyes. But the effect was far more devastating up close and personal. A dark, dangerous air buzzed around him like an electric current. He stood still, sizing up the situation. Striker was a predator. I was just his chosen prey for the evening.

I licked my lips. Hot, nervous sweat trickled down the back of my neck, plastering my hair to my skin. My hands shook. The gun bobbed up and down. I steadied my grip.

Striker pried a dart out of the kitchen wall and held it up by the feathered end. His movements were lithe and fluid and controlled like those of a jungle cat. He seemed unconcerned with me and my gun.

"Tranquilizers." I answered his silent question. "With enough juice in them to knock out an elephant. Striker, I presume?"

He nodded.

"I assume you know who I am."

He nodded again.

We stood there in silence. I kept my gun leveled at him. Striker leaned back against the wall like he owned it. His gray eyes slid over my body in a frank, assessing way that made me tremble from head to toe. I felt like a fattened calf on the auction block being inspected by would-be buyers. I wondered if Striker liked what he saw. The thought startled me. I looked down at my faded, ripped jeans, battered sneakers, and T-shirt that read *0 TO BITCH IN 7.7 SECONDS OR YOUR MONEY BACK*. Probably not. Ugh.

"How did you know I was in here?" His voice was deep and rough and rich, with an edge of cool sophistication. The sort of voice that made women melt. Including me.

"It was cold." I, on the other hand, squeaked like a mouse caught in a trap. "You forgot to shut the window."

"I see."

More silence.

"So, what do you want?"

Striker blinked. "Excuse me?"

"What do you want? I assume there was a reason you broke into my apartment. Or is it something you do for kicks?"

"You want *me* to tell *you* the reason I'm here?"

"Yes," I said. "Aren't superheroes supposed to be honest, forthright, and have outstanding morals? Isn't that part of the job description, along with helping little old ladies cross the street?"

Striker hesitated, as if he didn't know what to say. "Shut up," he growled.

"Excuse me?"

"Not you." He pointed to his ear. "One of my colleagues is listening in on our conversation. He's laughing at your last statement. Evidently, he doesn't think I'm very forthright."

"Oh." I wondered which one of the Fearless Five was tuning in to our tête-à-tête. Probably Hermit, given the fact that Striker had some sort of listening gizmo in his ear.

The silence gathered around us once more. Striker stared at me with his piercing gray eyes. The dark current snapped and hummed around him like a live wire. The man oozed danger and sensuality. Every part of my body tingled and tightened in response. And in anticipation of something I couldn't quite identify.

I dropped my eyes from his face. My gaze landed on his fantastic chest and slid down his rippling stomach to his . . . I snapped my head back up. My cheeks flamed.

"Look, I've had a really long day, and I'm tired. I would like nothing more than to take a shower and go to bed, plus my arm is starting to cramp from holding this gun. So, why don't you just tell me what you want? Who knows? I just might give it to you. You can be on your merry way, and I can get some sleep."

"Why don't you put the gun down first, and then we'll talk."

I chewed my lip. "Might as well. I imagine you could take it away from me before I could blink if you wanted to."

Suddenly, Striker moved. He sprang at me like a panther leaping upon a plump little bird. I blinked once before he pulled the gun out of my hand. I didn't even feel him do it. For a moment, he stood there in front of me, so close that his breath kissed my face, so close that I could see the flecks of electric blue in his hypnotic eyes. My heart slammed against my rib cage.

"I did just take your gun away. Quite easily. But hold on to it if it makes you feel better."

He stepped back and tossed the weapon to me. Somehow, I managed to catch it.

"Well, there's no reason to get all cocky about it," I muttered, trying to hide my intense reaction to him.

I stumbled forward on shaky feet and put the gun on the coffee table. I sank down into the groove on the sofa, kicked off my sneakers, and propped my feet up on the trash bag. I tried to look tougher and stronger and calmer than I felt.

Striker leaned against the entertainment center. "What's in the bag?"

"Papers."

"What sort of papers?"

My eyes flicked over the table. "The sort of papers you've been going through, judging by the mess you've made."

"More papers on me?" A hard edge crept into his voice. It cut me like a razor.

"Not exactly."

"Then what sort of papers, *exactly*?"

"Papers on the Terrible Triad. Malefica, Frost, Scorpion, their various escapades."

Striker cocked his head to one side, listening to whatever his comrade said. "My friend says you're telling the truth. That all you've been doing all night is making copies at the library. Why are you gathering information on the Triad? Given our . . . previous meeting, I thought I was the one you were after."

"Not exactly."

Striker jerked his head at the table. "Those papers tell me otherwise. You've gathered quite a bit of information on me, and I saw you on top of that roof last night. I assume you weren't there to buy some drugs. Are you trying to uncover my identity? Planning to expose me to the world?"

I hesitated. "Not exactly."

"Then what are you doing, *exactly*?"

"I don't have to tell you that."

Striker's hands curled into fists. His gray eyes bored into mine. They glowed with barely suppressed anger.

I shivered under the intense scrutiny. I didn't think Striker would hurt me. The superhero code of ethics wouldn't allow him to. Then again, I hadn't thought Tornado would commit suicide either. Or that Matt would cheat on me. I wasn't the best judge of character when it came to superheroes.

"You wouldn't believe me if I told you," I mumbled.

"Try me."

I weighed the pros and cons. Oh, what the hell? I'd probably never get another opportunity to talk face-to-face with Striker. I might as well lay my puzzle pieces on the table.

I rolled up my T-shirt. Two bruises colored my arms in angry purple and garish green. "Your good friend Malefica paid me a visit a few nights ago. Or rather she made me pay her one. Two goons kidnapped me and drugged me.

When I woke up, I was in some kind of factory. Malefica was there with Frost and Scorpion."

Striker's eyes bored into me like hot laser beams. My temperature shot up about ten degrees. "I'm listening."

"Frost had some animals that he'd done experiments on. They were . . . they were . . ." I took a deep breath to steady my shaky nerves. The memory of those poor creatures made me sick. I could still feel their pain and horror. "He had changed them. Into monsters. Malefica told me that unless I discovered your identity in a month's time and gave it to her, she would turn me over to Frost and let him do the same thing to me."

"I see."

Silence.

"But I have a plan," I continued.

"A plan?"

"Yes. I've been gathering information on you in hopes of uncovering your true identity."

"And what happens if you do? How does that help you, other than keep you out of Frost's grasp? Or perhaps get you back in the good graces of the editors at *The Exposé*?" Striker's voice could have frozen boiling lava.

"Simple." I picked up a wayward Rubik's Cube and fiddled with it. "I use you to lead me to Malefica. I uncover her real identity and give it to you. You and the rest of the Fearless Five go after her, while I slip off into the sunset. You apprehend your greatest enemy, I don't get turned into a yeti, and we all go home happy, except for Malefica and her boys, who will hopefully get twenty-to-life in a secure facility for insane ubervillains."

"I see. Why not just concentrate on Malefica? Why drag me into it?" His voice was quiet and calm, but I could hear the anger in it. Striker didn't approve of my master plan.

"Because I need you to lead me to Malefica. That's how it works. The superheroes always lead me to the ubervillains, not the other way around." I slid a row of colors into place. My hands trembled, and I hoped Striker didn't notice how much he affected me.

"What makes you think I have anything to do with Malefica?"

I looked up at him. "Karma."

"Karma?"

"Karma." I got up off the sofa and paced around. I couldn't sit still. Not when he stared at me like that. "Good and evil always balance each other out. Superheroes and ubervillains are always connected in some way. They're like magnets, always attracting and repelling each other. It's fascinating. Malefica is somewhere in your life. She might be a friend, a girlfriend, a business partner, maybe even your wife. You just don't know it or refuse to see it."

Striker paused. His eyes turned inward, mentally sorting through every person in his life, trying to figure out who might fit the mold.

"Come up with any suspects? Anybody sneak off in the middle of an important business meeting? Any girlfriends fail to show up for dates? Any so-called friends have odd, unexplainable injuries?"

"No," he growled.

"Too bad."

I finished my Rubik's Cube and put it on the bookshelf.

"So, I've told you my plans. How about taking off that mask?" I asked in a bright, cheery voice to hide my nervousness. "I'm sure you'd be much more comfortable without it. I've always wondered how you people breathe through those things. They look terribly thick. And I really don't see how you move around in those leather suits either. Or is yours some sort of special spandex?"

Striker crossed his arms over his chest and gave me a cold look that would have made Frost icy with envy.

I shrugged. "It never hurts to ask. And it would make my job a lot easier."

He didn't respond.

"Look, I don't want to expose you. I'm not going to reveal your identity to anyone. I promise. I'm through with that. For good."

Striker's eyes slammed into mine. "Why should I believe you?"

"Because of what happened to Tornado."

The words just popped out. A muscle in Striker's clenched jaw twitched. His eyes grew dark and stormy as a thundercloud. I shrank back against the bookcase. I didn't need my inner voice to tell me I'd just stepped way over the line.

Still, there was something I had wanted to say for a long time, something I needed to say, whether he believed me or not. I turned my back to the superhero, unable to meet his damning, angry gaze. "I'm sorry. I truly, truly am. I never meant for that to happen. If I'd had any idea Tornado would react that way, I never would have written the story. I hope you can accept my apology and sympathy for your loss."

The silence deafened me. I turned. The apartment was empty.

Striker had left the building.

★ 8 ★

I stared at the swirls in the ceiling above the bed.
Noon sunlight peeked through the closed curtains and
warmed my bedroom. I should have been up hours ago,
hard at work on my superhero jigsaw puzzle. Instead, I lay
in bed, replaying the events of the past night over and over
again in my head.

I couldn't get Striker out of my mind.

I had been face-to-face with one of the most powerful,
revered superheroes in the world. Striker munched on bur-
glars at breakfast, snacked on evildoers over lunch, and ate
ubervillains for dinner. Oh, the irony. A few months ago,
the encounter would have been a dream come true, a
chance to confront one of the mysterious, masked cru-
saders up close and personal. Now, the whole affair left a
sour, bitter taste in my mouth.

Superheroes and ubervillains had always been abstract
thoughts to me, puzzles to be solved. I'd never considered
them to be people too, with thoughts and feelings and

emotions. I had been too angry and hurt and self-righteous to do that. Matt and Karen had ignored my feelings, so I'd steamrolled over everyone else's.

Seeing Striker made that impossible. The hurt in his piercing gray eyes when I mentioned Tornado had hit me like a sledgehammer. His pain, his anguish at the loss of his friend. You could almost drown in the intensity of it. The feeling increased my own guilt tenfold.

And yet, despite his anger, there was something about Striker that had made me want to go to him, to brush his black hair off his face, and tell him everything was going to be okay. I wanted to comfort him in some small way. Yearned to. The depth of the feeling surprised me, shook me to the core. But acting on this strange feeling, of course, had been—and would always be—out of the question.

I sighed. Tornado was gone. There was nothing I could do about that, other than struggle to live with my own guilt and shame.

I could, however, do something to help Striker and the rest of the Fearless Five. I threw back the covers.

Time to go to work.

I padded into the living room and ripped open the trash bag on the coffee table. For the next few hours, I sorted through and organized all the information on the Terrible Triad, as well as the papers Striker had disturbed during his nocturnal visit. Every so often, I stopped and glanced at the windows. Striker's presence lingered in my apartment, an invisible ghost haunting me. Where was he? What he was doing? Would he ever come through my window again?

After mooning for the better part of five minutes, I focused my attention on the task at hand. As far as the Terrible

Triad was concerned, there wasn't much to go on. Little had been written about the group except for the usual articles about how evil they were, their epic battles with the Fearless Five, and so on and so forth. Those same professors with way too much time on their hands had written another set of journal articles about the ubervillains' costumes and what the colors said about each one's inner child.

Frost had penned several papers in some less-than-reputable scientific journals about his various experiments involving animals. I skimmed through one of the stories. Most of the information dealt with radioactive isotopes, the effects different chemical compounds and doses produced, and other things far beyond my understanding. I flipped to the next page, which contained before-and-after pictures of Frost's handiwork. More mutated animals. I gagged and threw the story aside.

The intellectual media paid little attention to Scorpion, but he regularly appeared in a variety of mainstream wrestling and other sporting magazines. Most of the stories dealt with his tendency to crash professional wrestling and other strongman fights. Scorpion had a habit of leaping into the ring and taking on all the competitors at the same time. He always won, leaving a trail of broken bones and mangled bodies in his wake.

I moved on to Malefica. The ubervillain never wrote anything herself, and she never did anything to get herself mentioned in the media, other than try to take over the city every few weeks. She was a ghost, just like Striker.

However, one fashion magazine had devoted an entire spread to Malefica's sense of style. Evidently, the editors found her bloodred leather ensemble to be terribly sophisticated and the height of haute couture among the superhero-ubervillain set. The photos showed how Malefica's ensemble had changed. Ten years ago, diamonds, rubies, and gold thread had adorned her costume, which the editors thought was rather cartoonish and over the top. Since then, Malefica had developed a classier, more understated style with her sleek, jewel-free cat suit, cape, and thigh-high boots. I wondered what the fashion editors would think of the Bulluci sandals she sported now. They would probably approve.

By the time I reviewed the material, I had a headache the size of Texas. I squinted at the small print just to get the words to focus. I rubbed my aching temples. Either I was concussed from all the falls I'd taken, or my eyesight was going the way everything did as you aged—south. Great, something else to worry about. Going blind at the ripe old age of twenty-eight. On the bright side, if my vision worsened, I wouldn't be able to see myself when Frost turned me into the Abominable Snowwoman.

The thought didn't cheer me up.

After reviewing papers for a couple of hours and getting nowhere, I took a break to go do another necessary evil.

Shopping.

I needed to replace the little black dress and shoes that Frost and his two goons had ruined the night they'd kidnapped me. I'd put it off as long as I could. Shopping wasn't my favorite activity. Not even close. Perhaps I'd enjoy it more if I actually had some money to spend on all the pretties I saw. Most journalists get rather pitiful salaries, and I'd decided long ago I'd rather eat on a regular basis than wear the latest designs by the likes of Fiona Fine and Bella Bulluci.

I slapped on some makeup, combed out my tangled hair, and headed to Oodles o' Stuff, the biggest department

store in all of Bigtime. You could find anything you
wanted in the massive building, from shoes to clothes to
makeup to consumer electronics. I headed for the subbasements, where all the sale items were kept.

On the way down the escalator, I spotted not one, not
two, but three superheroes. Gentleman George tried on
some silk ties and ascots on level three, the Toastmaster
showed off his new line of kitchen gizmos on level two,
and reformed ubervillain Shrieker signed copies of her tell-
all memoir, *Both Sides Now*, on level one.

Superheroes loved Oodles. The store gave them dis-
counts on everything, and in return, the superheroes tried
to keep their building-leveling battles away from the historic structure. Also, it didn't hurt to have the heroes mingle with the other customers. It made the muggers and
shoplifters think twice.

I reached the second subbasement and shoved my way
through the maddening crowd. Regular folks also loved
Oodles, especially the subbasements, which had the best
bargains around. It was the only place where you could get
a slightly imperfect Fiona Fine original for under a hundred bucks. If, of course, you wanted to look like an abstract painting. With feathers.

I grabbed the first black dress that fit and was seventy-
five percent off, picked up some high heels that weren't
too monstrous, and got the heck outta Dodge. With my
shopping complete for the next two months, I went home
to change.

That night, I suffered through another boring society
soiree, the annual fundraiser for the Bigtime Symphony
Orchestra, held at the spacious and lavish Bigtime Con-
vention Center and Orchestra Hall. Naturally, the fundrais-
ing committee had chosen a musical theme for the event.
Plastic music notes, paper pianos, and cardboard violins

dangled from the ceiling, while members of the orchestra played classics by the likes of Mozart and Bach.

All the usual suspects attended. Sam Sloane and his supermodel of the week. Fiona Fine wearing her latest sequin-covered monstrosity. Even Morgana Madison came out for the event.

I tapped my finger against my champagne glass. This was supposed to have been my night off, but Sandra had called in sick. Instead of working on uncovering Striker's identity, I'd been called in to cover another bit of society fluff. I'd done my interviews and taken notes in record time. All I needed was a quote from the orchestra's conductor, and I could go write my story. I wandered through the orchestra pit, where the bar had been set up, waiting for the conductor to finish schmoozing with his rich patrons before I pounced on him.

"I didn't realize they let just anyone into these things," Fiona sniffed. The tall blond elbowed me out of the way and ordered a double gin and tonic.

"Hello, Miss Fine," I said in a sweet, sugary tone that would rot teeth. "It's good to see you again too. Tell me, did you make your dress yourself, or did it come out of a paint-by-numbers catalog?"

Fiona's pink lips pressed together. Too bad her face didn't crack from the strain. I glared at the haughty fashion designer, daring her to make a scene. I wasn't afraid of these people, and I wouldn't be cowed by them. Not anymore. I didn't even care if I kept my lousy job on the society beat. Let the editors at *The Exposé* fire me for offending Fiona Fine. The threat of being dumped into a vat of radioactive goo made my other trials and tribulations pale in comparison.

"Carmen, what a pleasant surprise," Chief Newman's deep brogue cut in.

Fiona gave the police chief a heated look, grabbed her drink, and flounced away. The chief appeared at my elbow. He had traded in his usual subdued suit and tie for a brand-new tuxedo. He looked quite distinguished, and many of the wealthy widows eyed him like hungry vultures flying over a piece of fresh meat.

"Hello, Chief. Good to see you."

Newman lowered his voice. "Listen, I know it's a lousy time to talk business, but I want you to come down to the station tomorrow and take a look at a couple of bodies we found out by the marina."

"Bodies? Why?"

"They might be your two kidnappers. They match your description."

"How did they die?" I asked.

"They froze to death in one of the big fish freezers down by the docks."

For a moment, my vision fuzzed over. I shook my head, and the world returned to normal. Still, I couldn't stop the chill slithering up my spine.

"They probably got drunk and wandered into the freezer by accident. We found several beer cans at the scene. The coroner says their blood alcohol levels were off the charts."

I knew better. Frost's icy handprints covered this one. My inner voice chattered. He'd murdered his two henchmen. The question was, why? Had they stepped out of line? Or were Frost and the rest of the Triad trying to send me a message?

"Are you ready for me, Miss Cole?" The conductor, a thin man with a receding hairline, interrupted our conversation.

I felt stiff, frozen inside. Every movement was an effort. "Sure thing, Mr. Muzicale. I'll see you tomorrow, Chief."

"Just come by when you get a chance. I'll be in all day."

The chief strolled away. Matronly, marriage-minded society types trailed after him like sharks drawn to blood in the water. I focused my attention on the balding conductor and plastered a big, fake smile on my face.

"Tell me, Mr. Muzicale. What does the Bigtime Symphony Orchestra have on tap for patrons this season?"

Two hours later, I put the finishing touches on my story and sent it to the society editor. After getting the usual response, I walked over to Henry's desk. He wore his typical sweater vest, khakis, and bow tie. Henry had skipped right over his youth. He wasn't even thirty yet, but he already dressed like an old man.

His nose hovered next to the flickering computer monitor. His fingers danced over the keyboard in a rapid, staccato rhythm.

"Henry? Henry?"

No response. I put a hand on his shoulder. A static shock sparked and cracked between us.

"Yikes!" Henry jumped a foot out of his chair. "You scared me!"

"Sorry for the interruption." I shook my tingling hand. "I was wondering if you had compiled that list for me."

Henry blinked. "Sure. I've got it here somewhere. Let me check."

He dug through a tall stack of papers. Minutes ticked by. I frowned. Even though his desk was Chaos Central, Henry could usually find a pin in less than a second. What was up with him?

Ten minutes later, Henry yanked a thick binder out from under a pile of half-empty, take-out Chinese cartons on the back of his desk. I wrinkled my nose. The paper containers reeked of two-week-old General's Chicken.

"Here you go. All the info on the fifty wealthiest citizens of Bigtime."

"Thanks, Henry." I stuffed the binder into my purse. "By the way, did someone named Lulu call you?"

Henry pushed his glasses up his nose. "Yes, yes, she did."

"And what did you think of her?"

"She seemed like a very nice woman."

I arched an eyebrow. "A nice woman? A nice woman you might take to dinner if you could tear yourself away from your computer long enough?"

Henry fiddled with his glasses again. "Um, well, you see . . ."

"Never mind, Henry. I'll let you two work it out. I just wanted to make sure she'd called you and got the ball rolling."

Henry and Lulu had made contact. My inner voice whispered with satisfaction. The rest would take care of itself. Who knew? Maybe Lulu could introduce Henry to Bella Bulluci's men's collection and get rid of those horrid polka-dot bow ties. Or at least get him to stop wearing stripes with them.

I told Henry good night and made my way through the gauntlet to the elevator. I rode down to the ground floor, brushed past the doorman, and hurried out onto the sidewalk.

"Hey, baby. Where you off to? Why don't you come over here and sit on Daddy's lap?" my familiar harasser cooed from his stoop.

"Get a life, loser," I snapped and kept walking.

After two blocks, I stopped. A faint scuffle sounded behind me. I turned, but there was no one on the deserted street. I didn't even see any headlights coming in my direction. No people, no cars, nothing. A shiver slid up my spine. I eased a hand down into my purse and grabbed my pepper spray. I continued on, quickening my strides.

The uneasy feeling continued for several more blocks. My inner voice murmured, and I knew who was, well, stalking me.

"Oh come out," I snapped. "I really hate playing hide-and-seek, especially with superheroes. You're all so much better at it than I am. It's *so* not fair."

I scanned the long, dark shadows. I squinted hard, but saw nothing unusual, just walls and parked cars and expired meters. "Well, are you going to show yourself or not?"

A couple of college-age kids with backpacks slung over their shoulders plodded down the steps of the Bigtime Public Library. They heard the tail end of my conversation with my invisible friend, because they gave me a wide berth and giggled as they passed. They probably thought I was some drugged-out hooker talking to myself. They disappeared around the corner. More laughter floated on the air.

I tapped my shoe on the pavement. It had been a long day, and I was exhausted. I didn't want to play any games tonight. "Hello? Is anyone out there? Striker?"

He didn't appear. After a long, tense moment, I let out a breath. If Striker wanted to follow me home, so be it. I couldn't stop him. If he was even out there to start with. Maybe I was just imagining things due to my odd, intense desire to see the sexy superhero again.

I turned around to continue my trek home. Striker stood in front of me.

I shrieked and stumbled back. My heel caught in a crack in the sidewalk. My arms windmilled. My body tilted backward. I closed my eyes, bracing for the inevitable, painful impact.

It never came. I opened my eyes. Striker had caught me. The superhero loomed over me. His arms supported my back, and he held me like we were ballroom dancers frozen in an elegant dip. His hot breath brushed against my cheek as soft as a butterfly's kiss on my feverish skin. He smelled of musk and the cool night, and his leather costume felt smooth and supple under my grasping fingers. Striker's firm, hard thigh lodged between my legs. He shifted his weight, rubbing my thighs ever so slightly. My breasts tightened at the sensual contact, and a warm sensation flooded my veins. I couldn't breathe. Striker's eyes widened. Hot, electric blue sparks flared to life in their silvery depths. A current snapped and hummed between us. For a mad, mad moment, I thought Striker might lean in and kiss me, capture my lips with his. I parted my own. I wanted him to. Oh, how I wanted him to. Every molecule of my overheated body screamed at him to do it.

Striker pulled me upright. His hands slid down my back, scorching my skin through my jacket and the thin silk of my dress. He held on to me a moment longer than necessary, then dropped his hands. My head felt light and airy as a cloud. I didn't know if I was dizzy from the abrupt change in elevation or from the feel of Striker's strong arms around me. Maybe both.

"Don't do that," I snapped, trying to hide my hormonal flare-up. "Do you want to give me a heart attack?"

Striker shrugged. "Sorry. You said to come out. I was just waiting for the kids to go by. How did you know I was following you?"

"It was quiet. Too quiet," I said in a deep, serious voice.

Striker folded his arms over his chest.

"It was a dark and stormy night?" I tried again.

He looked up. The moon glittered like a giant opal in the sky.

"I just knew, okay?"

Curiosity filled Striker's eyes, but I didn't feel like explaining myself. He had his secrets, I would keep mine. Including the fact I was desperately, dangerously attracted to him.

"So are you going to walk me home or what?" I shoved my hands into my jacket pockets. "It's rather cold. I'd really hate to get frostbite and rob Malefica and Frost of their chance to turn me into a monster."

Striker gestured at the deserted street. I began to walk, and the superhero fell in step beside me, sliding from shadow to shadow like the creature of the night he was. A block went by, then another, then another. I wasn't sure what to say to him, given the way our last conversation had gone. It hadn't been a smashing success.

"So, how was your day?" I asked.

"Excuse me?"

"How was your day? Bust any more drug runners? Apprehend any thieves? Have any building-leveling fights with ubervillains?"

"Why do you ask?" Suspicion colored Striker's deep voice.

I closed my eyes a moment, letting his rich tone wash over me. Even his voice was sexy. "I'm just making conversation. That's what people do, you know. There's no ulterior motive. I promise."

"Well, I got up this morning, went to work—" He stopped.

"Went to work and what?"

"I can't tell you that."

"Well, what did you do after work?"

"I can't tell you that either."

"Well, what did you have for lunch?" I snapped. "Surely that's not top secret superhero information."

"Steak with mashed potatoes and a side salad," Striker replied. "And a piece of chocolate cheesecake for dessert."

I gave up on conversation after that. I was too jealous of the cheesecake to continue.

We strolled along. I looked at Striker. His silvery eyes glowed like a cat's in the twilight, and his hair glistened under the fluorescent streetlights. My gaze traced over his lean, muscled form. His black leather suit clung to his body like a second skin. The man certainly filled it out well. My eyes dipped lower. In all sorts of places. My cheeks flushed. Despite the chill in the air, I felt very warm.

Focus, Carmen, focus. I pulled my thoughts back to the matter at hand. Striker knew what I was up to. So why had he sought me out? He should have been busy burying all traces of his real identity from my prying eyes. Instead, he walked me home like we were a couple of teenagers out on a date. Maybe he'd mistaken me for a little old lady who needed help crossing the street. I bit back a laugh. Not likely.

Several minutes later, we arrived at my apartment building, and I still hadn't come up with any answers to my burning questions. Or a way to cool this sudden sexual fire inside me.

"Well, here we are," I said. "Home, sweet home. Thanks for the company."

"You know, you really shouldn't walk on the streets at night by yourself," Striker said. "It's not very safe, especially now that Malefica has targeted you."

"Yeah, well. It's cheaper than taking a cab all the time. Some of us have to live within our means."

"Why do you say that?"

I eyed Striker's supple leather suit and the two swords that peeked up over his shoulder. "Your getup there probably costs more than everything I own put together. It's obvious you're not a poor man, Striker. If I had to guess, I'd say you're just another bored billionaire who does this for kicks in his spare time. Right? Tell me, are you hooked on the adrenaline rush or just a slave to the noble idea of making the world a better place?"

Striker's eyes darkened to a stormy gray. He didn't reply. Ah, so I'd hit the nail on the head. Perhaps Henry's list would be more useful than I thought.

I fished my keys out of my battered purse. "Did you want something else? It's been a long day, and I'd like to go inside and get some sleep."

"The reason I followed you tonight was to offer you protection," Striker muttered.

My mouth dropped open. "Protection?"

"Yes. We can protect you from Malefica and the rest of the Triad until we figure a way out of this mess."

All I could do was just stare at him. Then, reality kicked in. "How could you protect me? Put me up in a safe house somewhere with round-the-clock guards?" I shook my head. "Sorry, I've read that story before. Everything would be fine for a while. But one day, your guard would be down, and Malefica would come for me. Besides, I can't go into hiding and keep my job. Like I said before, I'm not independently wealthy. Protection isn't really an option for me."

Still, the offer touched me. Despite everything I'd done to them, the Fearless Five was still willing to help me. Perhaps there was a reason they called them superheroes after all. I stared down at the sidewalk. "I appreciate the offer. I really do. And I want to thank you for it. I know it must have been a difficult decision, given my history with Tornado."

Silence greeted me. I looked up. I whirled round and round, but Striker had disappeared into the night. There was no sign of the sexy superhero.

How the hell did he do that?

★ 9 ★

I stood in front of my dresser, brushing my wet hair. A cold chill swept through my body, and a familiar current flooded the room. I glanced into the mirror. He was there behind me.

I put down my brush and faced him. Without a word, Striker pulled me into his arms. His lips captured mine. They were just as warm and firm as I'd imagined. I opened my mouth, and his tongue slipped inside. I loved the clean taste of him, the feel of his muscled arms around me, his musky scent. He filled up my senses until there was nothing else.

Striker laid me down on the bed. I pulled him on top of me, enjoying the feel of his weight on my feverish body. My clothes disappeared. So did his leather suit. Only the black mask that covered his face separated us. His gray eyes burned into mine. I kissed him, long and hard and deep. Our hands explored each other's bodies with hungry purpose. He trailed his fingers down my breastbone over my quivering stomach. I opened my legs, and he sank his fingers into me.

I cried out. Waves of pleasure rippled through my body. Striker stroked me until I was dizzy with desire. Then, he pulled back. I whimpered at the loss of contact, at the loss of his touch. Striker loomed over me. His eyes shimmered with the brilliance of a thousand stars. I knew what he wanted. It was the same thing I did. I opened my legs once more, and he plunged into me. He began to move—

I gasped and sat up. My eyes flew around the dark room. The door was shut, the windows locked. Everything was in its place. No sexy superheroes lurked in the shadows that pooled on the floor around the bed. Alone. I was alone. All alone. It had been a dream. Just a dream. I flopped back against the pillows.

Damn.

After a long night of heated dreams, I walked down to the police station the next morning. I met up with Chief Newman, and we headed for the morgue in the basement.

I'd been to the morgue many times before when I'd been working the investigative and police beats. It was a dark, depressing place that smelled of harsh chemicals and decay. Sometimes, I thought I saw the blood of all the murder victims puddling on the floor and dripping down the walls. Not a pleasant vision.

We entered the viewing area. A glass partition separated us from the autopsy room. The coroner, a tall, square man, stood on the other side of the glass in front of a large metal table. Blue toes peeked out from under two white sheets.

"I'll warn you, this isn't a pretty sight," Chief Newman said. "Are you ready?"

I nodded. The coroner pulled back the sheets.

I gagged and turned away.

"Easy, easy," the chief rumbled. He put a hand on my arm to steady me. "Is that them?"

"Yes."

I forced myself to turn back and look at the two bodies. I recognized my kidnappers, despite their condition. Their skin was pale as ice and looked twice as hard, while their hair had turned an unnatural white. Blue and purple veins popped out on their faces, reminding me of some kind of macabre spider's web. The men's eyes and mouths gaped open, frozen in sheer terror. Even their tongues had turned blue. Even though the men were dead, I could still feel their horrific fear as they realized what was about to befall them. A chill crawled up my spine. This was what Malefica and Frost had in store for me if I didn't uncover Striker's identity.

"We haven't identified them yet, but it's only a matter of time. Why don't you go back home and get some rest? If I find out anything, I'll give you a call," Chief Newman said in a comforting tone. "I don't think there's anything more you can do here."

Dazed, I made my way back up to the ground floor. My stride quickened with every step. I stumbled outside and started to run. But even as my sneakers smacked against the concrete, I knew I couldn't outrun Frost or my own inevitable, chilly fate.

My days fell into a pattern. I spent the better part of the morning and afternoon doing research, searching for the slightest clue that would tell me who Striker and Malefica really were. I went to the latest society bash at night, wrote my story, and left. More often than not, Striker popped up outside *The Exposé* and walked me home. He never said much, but he was always there, watching me.

I didn't know whether to be frightened or flattered. I strained to hear his silent footsteps, peered into the shadows hoping to get the smallest glimpse of him, breathed in the night air in hopes of catching a trace of his musky scent. It was pathetic, but I could no more stop myself from searching for Striker than I could quit breathing.

And I always knew when he was around. My inner voice slyly whispered his presence to me. An electric current surged through my body, and I felt all warm and tingly inside. And when I finally spotted him, well, my hormones kicked into overdrive. It was all I could do not to drag him into the shadows and kiss him senseless.

But I could never, ever do that. I could never have Striker. I could never even do anything as simple as just be his friend.

Every time I looked at Striker, I could see the pain of Tornado's loss in his silvery eyes. Striker's grief, his sorrow, radiated off him. It intensified my own guilt and shame.

Every day, I told myself there could never be anything between Striker and me.

Never.

But oh, how I wanted there to be.

One night about two weeks after our initial meeting, a cool breeze kissed my back while I worked in the kitchen. Electricity charged the air, and my stomach tightened.

"Hello, Striker."

I stirred the pasta salad I was whipping up for dinner. I'd left work early for a change and hadn't seen Striker on my way home. I'd been planning to drown my disappointment in a bowl full of food. A poor substitute, I know.

"How do you always know it's me? I could be a burglar."

I stared at the superhero, who leaned against the refrigerator. "Well, I don't have any other superheroes stalking me. At least, not yet. Besides, a burglar could never be as quiet as you are."

"And yet you always know when I'm here."

I wasn't about to tell Striker about my inner voice, my gut instincts. He'd just laugh. He had real superpowers, not strange, imaginary twinges like mine. As I stirred the pasta salad, Striker's gray eyes traced over my body. I gripped the spoon tighter to keep from shivering.

More than once, I wondered what Striker thought about me. Why he kept coming back to see me. Whether he felt anything at all toward me. Sometimes, I almost thought I saw a shimmer, a faint spark of desire in his eyes when I neared him. But that was just my wishful, sex-starved imagination.

It had to be. Striker could never want somebody like me. Somebody so out of his league. Somebody so unworthy.

I dumped the pasta in a bowl and turned around. Striker stood between me and the kitchen table. I hesitated. I didn't want to get within arm's reach of him. Didn't want to get close enough to see the blue flecks in his silvery eyes. Didn't want to smell him. Didn't want to feel his hot breath on my cheek. I would only be tormented that much more by my attraction to him—and the complete hopelessness of it.

But this was my apartment, not his. It was bad enough Striker waltzed in whenever he wanted, and I did nothing to discourage him. I wouldn't let him dictate where I walked too. I squared my shoulders and stepped forward.

"Excuse me," I said.

Striker moved back a fraction of an inch. I squeezed by, so close that I brushed up against his tall form. The brief contact made me hum and spark deep down inside, like a live wire ripped free from its power source. All my previous intentions to keep my distance burned away. I longed to reach out and touch Striker, to see if his chest was as hard and muscled as it looked, to see if he was really here, and not some figment of my feverish, overactive imagination.

I dropped the bowl onto the table and sank into my chair. I grabbed my glass of water and downed half of it in one gulp. My hand shook.

It took me a moment, but I composed myself. I pointed to the chair across from me. "Sit down. Have some food. I made plenty. Too much just for me."

Striker eyed the pasta with suspicion.

"Oh, it's not drugged or poisoned or whatever you think." I stabbed a bite of the creamy salad with my fork, chewed, and swallowed. "See? I haven't keeled over yet."

Striker hesitated, then dropped into the other chair. I dished us up some pasta. A roll of crusty French bread and sharp cheddar cheese completed the meal. We ate in silence. I kept my eyes fixed on my food so I wouldn't stare at Striker like a schoolgirl with a movie star crush.

"This is really good." Striker helped himself to some more food.

"You sound surprised."

Striker shrugged. "It's a nice surprise. You don't strike me as a woman who likes to cook."

I smiled. The backhanded compliment pleased me. But then, I scowled. Why did I care what Striker thought of me? Why did I listen for his footsteps? Why did his mere presence affect me so? It had to be the costume. I'd always been a sucker for guys in black leather jackets. A superhero suit wasn't much different. It was just bigger. And tighter. And filled out a lot better . . .

I chugged down the rest of my water. We finished our meal. I gathered up the dishes and dumped them in the sink. Striker leaned against the refrigerator as usual. I turned to face him.

"So, now that I've fed you, want to take off your mask for me?" I asked the question every time I saw him.

"No."

Unfortunately, the answer was always the same.

"I'm going to find out who you are eventually. You could save me a lot of trouble. Not to mention all the money I've been spending on highlighters and photocopies and sticky pads."

Striker stared at me, his gray eyes dark and hooded.

"Why do you do it, anyway?" I blurted out. It was the one question I'd never been able to puzzle out the answer to, despite all my superhero and ubervillain exposés.

"Do what?"

I gestured at him. "The whole superhero thing. Fighting evil, battling ubervillains, the whole shebang. It's not like you get paid to put yourself in danger."

Striker looked at me as though the answer was self-explanatory. "I have a gift, powers I can use to help others, powers I can use for good. It's a calling for me. It's something I have to do."

"But why hide your true identity if what you do is so noble? Why wear the mask and the costume?"

"A secret identity is the only way superheroes can exist, the only way we can lead any semblance of a normal life. I don't fight evil all the time, you know. I have other interests and hobbies and responsibilities. If we didn't wear masks and costumes, people would never leave us alone. They'd want us to help them with everything. We'd never get any work done. Not to mention the fact that ubervil-lains could pick us off one by one." Striker's voice was cold and hard.

"But what about your friends and family? Why hide what you do from them?"

His lips tightened. "Because if they were ever captured by an enemy, they could be forced to reveal my true iden-tity."

"But don't they have a right to know? You put them in danger just by doing what you do. Maybe if they knew, they could take better care of themselves—and you." I per-sisted with my questions, even though I was antagonizing the superhero. I couldn't stop myself. I wanted answers. Wanted satisfaction. That, and I wanted him.

Striker crossed his arms over his lean chest. "Really? Like the way you took care of the Machinator?"

I froze.

"Oh yes. I read your story about your would-be wed-ding. How you caught your fiancé cheating with your best friend, how you discovered their alter egos, how you ex-posed them. Tell me, Carmen. Why do *you* do what you do? Are you trying to punish every superhero for your fi-ancé's infidelity? Does his betrayal still hurt that much?"

My mouth dropped open. How dare he! How dare Striker question *my* motives. I wasn't the one who crept around in the shadows. I wasn't the one parading around in skin-tight black leather. I wasn't the one hiding myself from the world.

Rage and hurt bubbled up inside me. Needles pricked the pieces of my broken heart. My arm jerked forward, and I slapped Striker. The crack roared like thunder in the small kitchen. My hand left a red welt on his exposed cheek. In seconds, it faded away, as though I had never even hit him. The sight only fueled my anger.

"I forgot. You regenerate. Neat trick. I guess I'll just have to hit you harder."

I raised my hand to hit him again. Striker grabbed my arm and pulled me forward. His breath brushed my flushed face. My breasts flattened against his supple leather suit, and my body hummed at the touch. I stared up into his masked face. Striker's silver eyes glowed in the faint light. Hot, blue sparks glittered in the depths of his hypnotic eyes.

My inner voice shouted out a warning. For once in my life, I ignored it.

I pressed my lips to his.

Striker stilled, as shocked by my action as I was. He started to pull back. I wrapped my arms around his neck and drew him closer. He wasn't walking away from me. Striker wasn't disappearing into the shadows. I wasn't letting the superhero slip through my fingers.

Not tonight.

His lips opened as if to say something. My tongue plunged inside his hot, moist mouth. Teasing. Testing. Tempting.

Striker's hands wavered in the air like a drowning man debating on whether to reach for a life preserver. The sane thing, the safe thing, would have been to stop. To end the kiss. To step back. But I didn't want to be sane tonight. I wanted Striker to drown. In me. With me.

I continued my exploration of his mouth. My tongue slid across his teeth. I nibbled the corner of his lips and trailed soft kisses down his neck. Striker's hands settled on my back. He growled and yanked me to him.

Our lips melded together. Our tongues dipped and darted and dodged, finding each other time and time again. Striker's hands settled on my waist, pulling my hips toward his. Mine roamed over his slick leather suit. The material felt as smooth as silk under my frantic fingers.

Striker's erection burned against my thigh. He wanted me just as much as I wanted him. Good.

My anger and frustration and confusion melted into a tidal wave of hot, liquid desire. We spun around and around in the kitchen. Tasting, caressing, driving each other mad. Dishes shattered on the floor. Chairs flipped over. Food spilled everywhere.

The air sparked and snapped between us. Electricity hummed through my body, burning me from the inside out. I'd been jolted out of the half-alive state I'd been trapped in for so long. Everything felt more vivid, more intense, and far more pleasurable.

We stumbled into the living room and fell onto the sofa. Striker's gloved hands roamed over my body.

"Not enough," he muttered. "Not nearly enough."

He ripped off one glove with his teeth. The other followed. Striker lifted my T-shirt over my head. My bra unsnapped with a whisper. The shock of his bare hands on my body heightened my desire. I ached for him. Striker's warm, sure hands stroked my taut breasts, cupping them, circling my stiff nipples. I arched my back in pleasure. He dipped his head. Striker's wet tongue trailed down my breastbone, and he closed his mouth over my nipple. I gasped.

He ran his tongue round and round my nipple, while his hands moved down my body. My jeans popped open. With sure, hot strokes, Striker trailed his hand down into my underwear. I opened my legs, and he dipped his finger inside me. Wave after wave of pleasure cascaded through me. I was drowning in a waterfall of sensations. I shuddered and cried out.

"Better," Striker murmured in a hoarse, husky voice. "Much, much better."

I thrashed on the sofa. A whimper escaped my throat. I wanted to touch him like he was touching me. Pleasure him as he was pleasuring me. My fingers clawed at the slick leather, seeking some sort of entry. Somehow, I found a zipper, yanked it open, and shoved my hand inside. Striker's flesh was as warm and solid as I'd dreamed. More so. My fingers trailed down his sculpted abdomen, past his navel. I took him in my hand, stroking him. That, too, was just as hard and solid as I'd thought it would be. Striker's breath quickened.

"Carmen," he murmured in my ear. Raw need filled his rich, deep voice. "Carmen."

The pressure inside me reached a fevered peak. It needed to be released. Now. I lifted my hips off the sofa. Striker slid my jeans down. My panties followed. I yanked on the bottom half of his suit, exposing his erection. He pulled a condom out from somewhere inside his suit and covered himself with it. None too soon.

I crossed my legs around his waist. He slid inside me, filling me.

Our eyes locked.

"Striker," I whispered. "Striker."

Slowly, we moved together. We rocked back and forth. Every thrust went deeper. Every thrust pulled me under even more. I was caught in an undertow I couldn't escape. One I didn't want to escape.

Striker kissed my neck. I ran my hands up and down his back. Our strokes grew quicker, faster, surer. Desire had swallowed us both whole.

Oh. My. God.

That single thought kept running through my head the next morning. Somehow, after making frenzied love to Striker, I'd drifted off to sleep. I'd woken up on the sofa in the middle of the night, a blanket covering my naked body.

The only thing I'd still had on were my socks. Striker, of course, was long gone. He'd even shut the window on his way out. How considerate of him. I wondered if he treated all his late-night conquests with such respect.

Now, I sat on the sofa, the blanket still wrapped around me. Early morning sunlight peeked in through the windows, illuminating my apartment and the colossal mess I'd made of my life.

What had I done? What the hell had I been thinking?

I hadn't been thinking. I'd ignored my inner voice, and to my utter shame and mortification, I'd had sex with a superhero. And not just any superhero. Striker. The superhero whose identity I was trying to uncover. The superhero who had every reason to hate me.

I groaned.

I wasn't the sort of woman who slept around. I'd had only a few lovers—my college boyfriends, Matt, and Striker. I'd dated Matt for almost a year before we'd had sex. Yet somehow, I'd slept with Striker after knowing him only a few weeks. And I didn't even know the *real* him. He was just a guy in a leather costume and a mask who followed me around and broke into my apartment on a regular basis. How kinky was that? I had no idea who he was. He could be married for all I knew. I smacked my hand against my forehead. Adultery. I didn't need to add that to my list of sins. My karma was already black enough.

But the worst part was I couldn't get Striker out of my mind. I could still feel his lips on mine. Still feel his hands caressing my body. Still feel him moving deep inside me. It made me want him all over again. I felt warm and squishy inside just thinking about him. If Striker were to slide through my window right now, I'd welcome him with open arms. Hell, I'd probably pounce on the poor man and demand he pleasure me again and again and again. I buried my nose in the blanket. It smelled like him. Musky, manly, sexy. I sighed.

Sex with Matt had been good. Sex with Striker the superhero had been, well, super. All right. Better than super. Fantastic. Amazing. Earth-shattering. Everything I'd ever dreamed of and more.

But there was more to it than just sex. I'd felt safe in Striker's arms. Completely safe. And even cared for. That thought, the need for it to be true, rattled me. Striker had stirred up emotions I thought I'd buried for good after the brutal breakup with Matt.

Snap out of it, Carmen! So what if I'd had sex with Striker? It didn't mean anything. According to all the articles I'd read, superheroes sleeping with people they'd saved wasn't uncommon. Some of them even got off on having anonymous sex with strangers. And on the flip side, there was a whole cult of people called *Slaves for Superhero Sex* who put themselves in danger just so they could get rescued and make time with a superhero.

At least I wasn't that far gone.

Yet.

Besides, it wasn't like Striker and I could ever have a *real* relationship. There was too much bad karma between us. He was a superhero, and I was a nosy reporter. The two just didn't mix, no matter how much chemistry we might have.

And did we have chemistry. I'd been so hot for Striker I thought I might spontaneously combust. Judging by the way he'd called out my name, Striker had had just as good a time as me. At least, I hoped so.

I shook my head to clear away my charged thoughts. I'd chalk up last night to a temporary bout of insanity and the fact that I hadn't had sex in over three years. Maybe the drug Frost had knocked me out with had some sort of weird pheromones in it. Maybe that's why I was so attracted to Striker. Or maybe the superhero sprayed his costume with some woman-attracting musk that made him irresistible to the opposite sex. My weak excuses did little to comfort me, but they were all that I had.

At least we'd used protection, and I'd started taking the pill again recently in hopes of dating and having sex sometime in the near future. So I didn't have to worry about getting knocked up by the superhero. How embarrassing would *that* be? Unless, of course, Striker had some sort of weird, superstrong sperm that could thwart any attempts to counteract it. Were supercharged sex organs part of being a superhero? I'd seen some sort of journal article on superhero-and-ubervillain reproduction during my research, but I couldn't remember the details.

My inner voice chattered, and another alarming thought popped into my mind.

What if Striker had been wearing an earpiece, as he did so many nights when he dropped in? The other members of the Fearless Five could have heard every word, every sound, every moan and cry of pleasure. They could even be dissecting our night of passion at this very moment.

My cheeks flamed. I buried my face in my hands.

Oh. My. God.

★ 10 ★

Somehow, I pulled my thoughts away from Striker. I took a long, hot shower, cleaned up the mess we'd made in the kitchen during our fit of passion, and got dressed.

That night, I attended the annual Fall Ball, hosted by the Bigtime Debutante Society. It was the night when all the proud, marriage-minded mothers introduced their daughters to Bigtime society and made them go trolling for suitably rich husbands.

My eyes roamed over the crowd. I studied all the men, comparing them to Striker. I wondered if one of them sported a black leather suit underneath his tuxedo. Wondered if one of them had a mask hidden in his jacket pocket. Wondered if one of them was thinking about what had happened between us last night. Wondered—

High-pitched laughter caught my ear. A cluster of twenty-something debutantes gathered around Sam Sloane, giggling at his every word. For once, the billionaire appeared to be a little flustered by the hungry, female attention. He seemed distracted and kept glancing around, scanning the crowd. Who could he possibly be searching for? People flocked to Sloane. He didn't have to seek out company of any kind—female or otherwise. And where was his latest supermodel? The billionaire looked rather exposed without a towering blond clutching his arm.

I stared at Sloane. Wondering. Comparing. Contrasting.

Maybe.

Maybe not.

Oh, he had black hair like Striker, but so did lots of rich businessmen. It was practically a job requirement on the society scene. If you weren't a thirtyish playboy with dark good looks, then you were fifty-plus, with a mane of silver hair, and searching for trophy wife number three. Besides, Sloane just didn't seem to have Striker's intensity. Sloane was as handsome as the next playboy, but he couldn't turn me into a puddle of mush with a single glance. Still, for some reason, my eyes strayed back to him again and again. Perhaps I should use Henry's list to dig a little deeper into Sam Sloane, just to be sure he wasn't Striker.

Sam Sloane, Nate Norris, Devlin Dash. Each of them and a dozen others fit Striker's general description. I paid special attention to Dash, who always sported a pair of silver-rimmed glasses, usually a dead giveaway. But Dash seemed too quiet and introverted to be the leader of a team of superheroes like the Fearless Five. All he did was wander around, sip champagne, and look at the paintings that adorned the walls.

After an hour of sizing up every man on the premises, I gave up. If Striker was hidden among the high-society crowd, I wasn't going to discover his identity tonight. There were just too many suspects.

I was finishing up my last interview when excited whispers cut through the air. A group of people clustered around an older man. A fancy cell phone flickered in his hand, and I spotted an SNN logo on the tiny screen.

"What's going on?" I asked, shoving my way through the crowd.

"The Terrible Triad's on a rampage," a matronly mother piped up. "They've ransacked the Complete Computer Company already, and they're at the Super Duper Sweeper Upper Vacuum Cleaner Plant right now. Everybody's wondering where the Fearless Five are. Why they haven't stopped them yet."

My breath caught in my throat. Where the Terrible Triad were, the Fearless Five would soon follow. Including Striker. I dashed out of the ball, flagged down a taxi, and leapt into the backseat.

"The Super Duper Sweeper Upper Vacuum Cleaner Plant. And step on it."

"What's the address?"

"How the hell should I know? Just follow the police cars and the sound of the explosions."

"What are you?" the driver asked. "One of those weird superhero chasers?"

"Something like that," I muttered. Superhero-obsessed slut was more like it.

The cabbie double-timed it, and ten minutes later, we stopped a block away from the plant. I shoved the fare at him, scrambled out of the taxi, and started running. Now, running toward the scene of an ubervillain crime spree wasn't the smartest thing in the world to do, especially when Malefica wanted to turn me into a monster. But I couldn't stay away. Not if there was even the smallest chance he would be there. *Striker . . . Striker . . . Striker.* My footsteps pounded out his name as I sprinted toward the plant.

The cops were already on the scene. Police cars, SWAT vehicles, and a couple of tanks crouched in front of the plant, a square, squat building in one of Bigtime's blue-collar neighborhoods. Lights swirled on top of the vehicles, bathing everything in a harsh, red glow. I dashed past the old ladies in their curlers and housecoats, and the kids in their baggy sweats. A beefy cop held up his hand, but I flashed my press pass at him and zoomed by before he could protest. Sirens screeched, and walkie-talkies cracked and squawked. I made my way as close to the front of the barricade as I could, grabbed an official-looking guy in a dark suit, and shoved a tape recorder into his face.

"Carmen Cole with *The Exposé*. What's the situation?"

"In case you haven't noticed, we've got three ubervillains on the roof who don't want to come down. That's the situation," he growled. The guy pulled his arm free and turned back to his fellow policemen.

I craned my neck up. Sure enough, the Terrible Triad stood on top of the two-story building. Malefica put her hands on her hips. Frost cradled his infamous freezoray gun in his arms, while a large metal briefcase dangled from Scorpion's meaty hand. I eyed the briefcase. What could there possibly be of value at a vacuum cleaner plant?

The three of them stared down at the crowd, unconcerned by the cops' considerable show of strength.

"Put your weapons down and your hands up!" a cop roared through a bullhorn.

Malefica just laughed. The pealing cackles sent chills up my spine. She turned to Frost and gestured at the policemen. The thin ubervillain stepped forward. His icy eyes swept over the crowd.

"Damn that's cold!" a cop close to me muttered.

Something hit the ground next to my feet. It had been a gun at one time, but now a solid lump of ice covered the weapon. One by one, the cops dropped their frozen guns. Even the ones on the tanks iced over. Frost sneered.

"Your puny weapons are no match for me!" the ubervillain shouted. "And your lack of intellect is too small to calculate!"

Scorpion cracked his knuckles. He looked like he wanted to drop the briefcase and dive off the roof onto the cops below. Malefica waved and blew kisses to the crowd. Some of the men cheered her name and let out low whistles and catcalls. At least, until their wives glared at them.

The policemen exchanged nervous glances. A couple checked their watches. They were outmatched, and they knew it. I looked for Chief Newman, but I couldn't spot him in the crowd. And where were the Fearless Five . . . ?

Suddenly, a fireball slammed into the building where the Terrible Triad stood. Three more figures popped up on the far side of the roof. The Fearless Five had arrived. Fiera flashed by in all her flaming glory and hurled a fireball at Scorpion, who ducked out of the way. Mr. Sage focused his gaze on Frost's gun, trying to rip it out of his hand with his telekinesis, while the ubervillain tried to put the deep freeze on him.

But I only had eyes for Striker. He ran at Malefica as if to tackle her, but she used her telekinetic powers to pick up a couple of cement blocks and throw them at the superhero. The blocks slammed into his chest, and Striker fell to his knees. I gasped. My knuckles whitened around my tape recorder. But the superhero got right back up and went after Malefica again.

For the next ten minutes, the two groups tried to kill each other and level the surrounding neighborhood. Fireballs, rubble, and more flew through the air. Explosion after explosion roared out. Grunts, shouts, and curses floated down from the rooftop.

The spectators oohed and aahed at the pyrotechnic show.

Girls played with Fiera action figures. Boys crossed mock Striker swords. Teenagers punched each other with foam Scorpion fists. Just another typical superhero-ubervillain battle in Bigtime.

With a loud groan, part of the roof collapsed. All sorts of things smashed and cracked and shattered. A cloud of smoke puffed up, obscuring the roof. Everyone screamed and leapt back except me. I couldn't move. Not until I was sure that Striker was okay. It was suddenly very important to me that he was all right.

"Let's go!" Malefica shouted above the roar of the crowd.

A horrible screech rang out. It was like a thousand ice picks stabbing into my brain at the same time. Agony, pure agony. I stuck my fingers in my ears to try to block the noise, but it didn't work. The sound intensified. Just when I thought I couldn't stand another second of it, the terrible noise stopped. I shook my head, trying to clear away the painful fog. All the cops around me wore similar, dazed expressions.

"What the hell was that?"

"I don't know."

"Are the Fearless Five okay?"

"Did the Triad escape?"

"Is anyone hurt?"

Murmurs and whispers filled the air. My eyes went back to the collapsed roof. Seconds ticked by. Minutes passed. Still no sign of the Fearless Five. Come *on*. The superheroes had to be okay. Striker had to be okay.

Finally, just when I was about to leapfrog over the police barricade and run to the demolished building, three figures climbed back up onto the part of the roof that hadn't collapsed. The crowd cheered. Mr. Sage gave a halfhearted wave. Fiera shot a few sparks off her fingertips. Striker just stood there, looking at the mess and the cheering crowd.

"Striker! Striker!" I shouted.

I knew he'd never hear me, one voice in a thousand. But for some reason, his gaze turned in my direction. Our eyes locked. All the emotions, all the hot touches and whispered caresses of last night, flashed through my mind. I'd come to the battle site because I wanted to see Striker again. Because I wondered if he'd felt all the things that I had. If he wanted me as much as I still wanted him.

Evidently, the answer was a resounding no. Striker stared at me for a moment, then turned and disappeared into the dark night.

Once all the excitement died down, I took a taxi to The Exposé, wrote my society story, and left. I walked as slowly as I could back to my apartment.

Striker didn't show up during my walk home, and he wasn't waiting for me inside. He'd seen me at the vacuum cleaner plant. I knew he had. Did he think I just went down there for my health? But he didn't come to me. Disappointment filled my heart, along with anger. What had I expected? Roses? Chocolates? A mushy card? A repeat of last night's performance?

Still, though, I unlocked one of the living room windows, just in case.

Striker didn't come to me that night. Or the next. Or the next. He didn't follow me home from work. He didn't pop into my apartment. The superhero quit stalking me. He melted into the shadows from which he'd come.

Typical. Sleep with a guy, and he disappears. In a way, it

was comforting to know some things were predictable. Even if my hormones and emotions weren't.

The days flew by all too quickly, despite Striker's absence. Time passed, until I had only three days left before Malefica's deadline.

I threw down my highlighter. I'd been working nonstop for the last three weeks, and I was no closer to uncovering Striker's identity than when I started. I'd slept with him, for crying out loud, and I still couldn't figure out who he was. How pathetic was that? I fumed for a moment, then picked up my blue highlighter. I didn't have time to be discouraged or angry. Every second counted.

I flipped through the list of the fifty richest men and women in Bigtime that Henry had provided me. Notes and scribbles and highlighted passages dotted the pages. I'd crossed off some of the names right away. After all, ninety-year-old widows with rheumatoid arthritis weren't the stuff superheroes were made of. Ubervillains, perhaps, but not superheroes.

I'd been depressed to find out exactly how rich the rich and famous of Bigtime were. Morgana Madison topped the list with assets in excess of fifty billion, not counting the stacks of cash and ropes of diamonds she probably had secreted away in foreign banks. When I'd first come to Bigtime, I'd dug into my boss, wondering if she could be one of the villains I was after. You had to be extremely lucky or do some extremely illegal things to accumulate that much wealth, and ubervillains loved money. The only thing they coveted more than wealth was power. Morgana had plenty of both. But she always seemed to be at a society function or on some overseas teleconference call when the Triad or other ubervillains tore through town.

So, I moved on. Berkley Brighton, Joanne James, Nate Norris, Bella Bulluci. All the usual suspects were also on the list. Or were they?

I frowned. I'd been over the list a dozen times, but I had a nagging feeling I was missing something. The list seemed . . . short. I flipped through the pages and counted the names. I came up with forty-eight. I counted again. Forty-eight. And again. Forty-eight. Odd. Henry was usually so thorough in his work. I'd never known him to make a mistake before. Who had Henry left off? I closed my eyes and went through a mental list of Bigtime's richest, but I couldn't put my finger on the missing billionaires. I had the forty-eight richest men and women. Two more probably weren't going to make a difference, but I didn't want to overlook anything at this stage of the game. It was fourth and long, the clock was running down, and I was miles away from the end zone.

I picked up the phone and dialed Henry.

"Hi, this is Henry Harris . . ." His answering machine clicked on after five rings.

"Henry, it's Carmen. There's some missing information on this list you gave me. I really, really, *really* need the missing info. I'm on a tight deadline. Call me back as soon as you get this, either at home or on my cell. Thanks." I rattled off my numbers and hung up.

Henry was probably lost somewhere in the land of gigabytes. I drummed my fingers on my thigh. Who knew when he'd get around to calling me back? I'd get the information myself. I grabbed my purse and coat and headed for the Bigtime Public Library.

For the next few hours, I surfed through stock holdings and perused tax reports. Finally, I gave up. It was almost midnight and closing time, and I still couldn't pinpoint the two missing billionaires. I went to the office, but for once, Henry wasn't there. Curiouser and curiouser. Perhaps he'd finally asked Lulu out to dinner. Either way, I'd have to get Henry to give me the missing information tomorrow.

I left *The Exposé* offices and began my trek home, right past my nightly harasser's stoop.

"Hey there, sweet stuff," the familiar, obnoxious voice called out.

"Get over yourself, loser." I was in no mood to be hit on. Men. They were all the same, superheroes or not. They all wanted one thing. Sex. Once they got it, it was *hasta la vista*, baby.

"Bitch," he muttered.

I kept walking. Sneakers squeaked on the pavement, and I glanced over my shoulder. A large man emerged from the shadowy doorway. Even though it was chilly, he wore a sleeveless white shirt. Tattoos covered his muscled arms, and a large, gold cross dangled from a thick chain around his neck. My inner voice whispered in warning. I picked up my pace.

He dialed a series of numbers on his cell phone. "The corner of Seventh and Thirteenth. Now. See you, bro."

I glanced up at a nearby street sign. That was the block the two of us were on. Not good. I pulled my pepper spray out of my purse and crossed the street. The man jogged over as well. I glanced around, praying for a taxi to miraculously drive by. None came. There was no one on the street besides the two of us.

Suddenly, as if in answer to my prayers, two men stepped into view about a block ahead. A wave of relief hit me. The two men stood there, watching me walk. I slowed. It was almost as if they were waiting for me. I stopped. The man behind me kept coming.

"You ready to have a little fun now, bitch?" he called

out in a mocking tone. "Me and my boys are hot to trot to-night, if you know what I mean."

My inner voice screamed. I ran. The men laughed. I dashed across the street and into an alley. Footsteps pounded on the pavement behind me. I ran faster than I'd ever run before. My heart slammed against my ribs. My lungs burned. My legs ached. Still, I ran. My life depended on it.

I rounded a corner and skidded to a halt. Dead end. I whirled around, ready to run again, but the men blocked the alley. My eyes darted around. Desperate. No way out. I flipped the nozzle on my pepper spray and tried to re-member self-defense moves from my various classes. My fingers trembled. Sweat dripped down the back of my neck.

The men circled me. I turned first one way then an-other, trying to keep an eye on all of them at the same time. Suddenly, they lunged at me. One of them knocked the pepper spray from my hand, while another slapped me across the face. Pain flooded my body, and I tumbled to the ground. Two of the men grabbed my arms and yanked me to my feet. I kicked out. They easily avoided my awk-ward, flailing blows.

In a moment, it was over. Two of the men pinned me against the wall. The rough brick dug into my back, cut-ting through my jacket and T-shirt. I kept struggling, twisting and turning and trying to break free, but it was no use. They both had about a hundred pounds of muscle on me. Still, I fought. I had to. I had to get away, or I was in for something more horrible than anything the Terrible Triad could ever dream up.

"Now, sweet stuff, we're going to have a little fun." The tattooed leader grinned. Gold-capped teeth glistened in his mouth.

Bile and fear and terror rose up in my throat. My inner

voice screamed and wailed. I was going to be raped. Perhaps worse, if there was such a thing.

The leader pushed my jacket aside and ran a finger down my chest. "Now, let's get to the sweet stuff."

He eyed me in a cold, casual way, like I was a piece of meat he was about to sink his teeth into. The callous disregard enraged me, breaking through my fear. I wasn't going down without a fight. Carmen Cole never gave in, not even when things seemed hopeless. So, I did the only thing I could—I spat at him. "Go to hell and die, you bastard."

The man wiped the spit off his face. Blackness filled his empty eyes. He stared at me a moment, then backhanded me. I cried out in pain. Blood pooled in my mouth. The men chuckled, and the leader reached for me.

His hand never touched me.

A force yanked him back with a furious vengeance. He hit the wall on the other side of the alley and slumped down.

Striker leapt out of the shadows. My heart swelled. I had never been so grateful to see anyone in my entire life.

"Let her go." His voice was harsh, demanding, furious.

"No need to get all heroic, bro," one of the men said. "There's plenty here to share."

Striker didn't respond. His gloved hands tightened into fists.

"If that's the way you want to play it, bro, we're game."

The two men jumped at Striker. My knees buckled with relief, and I slid to the ground.

Seconds after that, so did the men.

Fists pummeled flesh. A tooth clinked away into the darkness. Bones snapped like dry twigs. The men whimpered for mercy.

I struggled to my feet. My vision clouded over, and I

squinted through the fog. Striker towered over the three men, who curled into fetal positions. The leather-clad superhero stepped over them and came to me.

"Are you okay, Carmen?" His voice sounded gentle, concerned.

"I'm fine, Striker." For some reason, I felt unnaturally calm. Disjointed even, as though I was standing outside my own body.

"I—"

"I said I'm fine. I'm going to go home now. Good night."

I grabbed my purse and pepper spray, and hobbled down the alley and onto the main street. I didn't turn around to see if Striker was following me. He was. I could feel his eyes on me. A taxi cruised by. Where the hell had the cabbie been five minutes ago? I lurched into the street, waved my hands, and flagged down the car.

"Are you all right, lady?" The driver stared at me in the rearview mirror.

"Fine. Just drive." I gave him my address.

I stared at the back of his bald head, thinking of nothing in particular. Lights and streets whizzed by, but I couldn't quite focus on them. Ten minutes later, the taxi pulled up to my building. I paid him and got out. Every movement hurt, stabbing through some of the strange, calm cocoon that wrapped around my mind. I brushed by the doorman, who gave me a bored look, and got into the elevator. I concentrated on the buttons. Five more floors. Three. Two. One. The elevator pinged open. I cringed at the sound and dashed to my apartment. My hands shook as I put the key in the lock.

I went through the apartment, double-checking to make sure every window was locked. I bolted the door and dragged a chair in front of it. Then, I stripped off my clothes and threw them away. I wanted nothing to remind me of this night and what had almost happened. Nothing.

I got into the shower. The white tile cooled my burning feet. I turned the water on full blast as hot as it would go and scrubbed everything hard—three times. I leaned against the shower wall. The water cascaded over me. The steady hiss blocked everything out. Everything except my memories of the last hour. Blood mixed with the water around my feet.

I got out of the shower, dried off, and put on a pair of plaid, fleece pajamas. I peered at my face in the bathroom mirror. The would-be rapists had split my lip open with their slaps, and a nasty-looking, purple bruise had formed under my right eye. I ran my tongue around the inside of my mouth. No loose teeth, though. I dabbed some ointment on my swollen face, took a couple of aspirin, and turned out the light.

After triple-checking the door and windows, I padded into the bedroom and put my stun gun and pepper spray underneath my pillow. They hadn't done me much good before, but I wanted them near. I drew back the comforter, snuggled underneath the soft sheets, and curled into a tight ball.

As I lay there, the rest of my odd calm cracked and flaked and peeled away, like old paint chipping off a house. The alley. The men. Their hands on me. The images invaded my mind, whirling round and round like a kaleidoscope. Then, the tears came, slowly at first, trickling out of the corner of my eyes like a leaky faucet. I did nothing to hold them back. I couldn't have, even if I'd wanted to. Soon, my whole body shook with intense sobs and muffled cries. The enormity of what had almost happened hit me like a tidal wave.

Even though I'd escaped being raped, I would never be

the same. Before, I'd roamed around the city at all hours of the day and night, never really worrying about the danger. Getting mugged, getting raped, getting murdered, those things happened to other people. Never to me or anyone I knew. I'd always felt relatively safe. Or at least before Frost and his goons had kidnapped me. Even that had been a fluke, a freakish, once-in-a-lifetime event. What had happened tonight could happen to me again.

At any time.

In any city.

Now, I would always look over my shoulder and wonder who was walking behind me, what they might want to do to me. Malefica and Frost's tubs of radioactive goo had frightened me. But now, their threats seemed petty, almost cartoonish, in comparison to the attack tonight.

Suddenly, a quiet stillness filled the room. He was there watching me have a nervous breakdown. And probably enjoying it immensely.

"Go away," I said through my sobs, embarrassed and ashamed of my cosmic meltdown.

"I just wanted to make sure you were all right."

"I'm fine. Now please, go away. I don't want you to see me like this."

"Like what?" Striker asked in a gentle tone.

"Frightened, weak, crying my eyes out. It must seem so pathetic to you." I closed my eyes and squeezed back the tears. I wouldn't cry again until he left. *I would not.*

Striker sat down on the edge of the bed. It dipped with his solid weight. "Superheroes aren't perfect, you know. Just because some of us have superstrength doesn't mean we never get scared. We have fears and insecurities and worries too."

I rolled over to look at him. "Fear? What fear? I didn't see any fear in you tonight. You took out those guys like it was nothing, just like you took out the drug runners a few weeks ago." *Just like you made love to me.*

"I *was* afraid tonight. Afraid for you. I saw the men chase you into the alley. I was afraid I wouldn't be quick enough to save you, fast enough to stop them."

"That's not the same thing."

"Yes, it is."

I let out a snort. "You almost sound like you care."

His eyes locked with mine. Some emotion I couldn't quite identify shimmered in the silvery depths. "I do."

"Then why haven't I seen you since . . . that night?" It was a question I'd asked myself a hundred times. A thousand times.

He dropped his eyes. "I've been around. I just—I didn't know—I couldn't—"

Striker reached out. He hesitated, then put his hand on my head. He stroked my damp hair. The image of my would-be rapists flashed through my head. Instead of Striker's gentle touch, I felt their cruel hands marching all over me.

My stomach churned, and I rolled away from the superhero. "Please just leave."

Striker didn't listen. Instead, he lay down on the bed next to me and drew me into his arms. I let him. I was weak and scared and terrified, so I let him hold me.

The tears came back. For the second time that night, I did nothing to stop them.

★11★

I woke up early the next morning. I opened my eyes, and the room slowly came into focus. The last thing I remembered was crying my eyes out while Striker held me. Was he still here? I heard nothing over the sound of my own quick breathing. I rolled over.

Striker was gone. Only a slight indentation in the bed revealed he had ever been there to start with. Relief washed over me. Mornings after were always tricky. I'd never really known what to say to Matt or any other man in my bed first thing in the morning. They had been few and far between. What could I say to the superhero whose secret identity I was trying to uncover after he just saved my life? What could I say to someone who could give me incredible pleasure one night, then hold me so gently the next?

What the hell could I say to a man I'd come to care about?

Nothing.

Carmen Cole, reporter extraordinaire, superhero-ubervillain exposer, could never say anything to Striker.

Never.

I got out of bed. My vision blurred, and the room zipped around. I sat back down. After a moment, my head cleared. I was really going to have to stop falling down and getting the stuffing beat out of me. I padded into the bathroom to assess the damage.

I stared into the mirror in horror. Malefica wouldn't have to work too hard to turn me into a monster. My lip had doubled to twice its normal size. A few cuts and scrapes slashed across my face, and a lovely purple bruise had taken up residence high on my right cheek. The bruise went along nicely with my puffy, bloodshot eyes. The faces of my attackers popped into my head. Imaginary hands brushed my body.

The phone rang, chasing away the horrid memories. For now.

"Hello?"

"Carmen, it's Henry. Are you okay? You don't sound too good."

I didn't feel too good either. Every muscle ached, my head throbbed, and my stomach still churned with fear. "I'm fine, Henry. What's up?"

"I got your message. I don't know what happened. It must have been a glitch in my computer program, but I left off the last two names. I didn't save a copy of the information, though. If you still want it, I would have to go back through and recompile it."

My brows knit together. Henry saved everything, even old gum wrappers, by the looks of his overcrowded desk. What was going on with the computer guru?

I walked into the kitchen and looked at the calendar on

my refrigerator. Two days to go until Malefica's deadline. The two missing billionaires weren't going to save me. Nothing could. "No, that's okay. Never mind. It's not that important."

"Well, okay. I guess I'll see you at the benefit tonight then."

"Benefit? What benefit?"

"The benefit for Yee-haw!, the therapeutic riding program."

I groaned. That couldn't be tonight. I glanced back at my calendar. Sure enough, there it was spelled out in big blue letters.

"What's wrong?"

"Nothing, nothing at all." One of the biggest social events of the year, and I looked like death warmed over.

"Lulu invited me to go with her," Henry said in a shy tone. "We had dinner last night. We really hit it off. I'm glad you gave her my number."

"That's nice, Henry. Really it is."

"Are you sure you're okay? You sound kind of tired."

"Yeah, that's it. I'm tired. I had a rough night last night. Couldn't sleep a wink." It was partly true.

"Okay, well, I'll let you go. See you tonight."

"Bye, Henry."

He hung up. I wanted nothing more than to crawl back into bed, pull the covers up, and never come out again. I couldn't do that, though. I owed Lulu, and I'd promised her I would cover the benefit and write a wonderful story. I wanted to pay off my debts before my meeting with the Triad. This would be the last opportunity I had to write an article about the riding program. Hell, it would probably be the last story I wrote for the society page. No more flat champagne, no more moldy cheese, no more dealing with the likes of Fiona Fine.

That was a little something to look forward to before Frost turned me into a female version of Bigfoot.

Several hours and a couple of pounds of makeup later, I arrived at the Bigtime Museum of Modern Art. The museum, located across the street from the library, was the crowning jewel of art and culture in Bigtime. Wide marble steps led up to the entrance, which was framed by massive columns. The building itself towered several stories into the air. An enormous banner draped over the entrance read: YEE-HAW COPPERS! BENEFIT FOR BIGTIME'S FINEST TONIGHT.

After I gave my engraved invitation to the doorman and showed him my wrinkled press pass, I entered the museum and made my way to the main gallery. I paused at the entrance. The museum always took my breath away. White lights ran up the shining marble columns and lent a soft glow to the enormous room. Cherub angels played and danced in the frescoes on the ceiling, while paintings splashed the walls with vibrant colors. Classical music whispered in the background. Everything gleamed and glistened as if it had been personally spit-shined.

People dressed in designer tuxedoes and glittering gowns clustered around long tables set up in the middle of the gallery. Pricey watches, diamond rings, concert tickets, movie roles. All were being auctioned off for charity. Waiters distributed champagne and fancy finger food to the crowd.

A motor whined, and Lulu zoomed up with Henry in tow.

"Sister Carmen, good to see you," Lulu said. "Nice dress."

"Thanks." I'd forgone my basic black for a lovely lavender ball gown with a poofy skirt. It was the only thing that looked halfway decent with the outrageous purple eye shadow and thick makeup I'd slathered on to hide my bruised, battered face. "You look nice too."

Lulu had chosen a vivid blue dress with silver trim that was one of Fiona Fine's more restrained designs. The color brought out her flawless pale skin and accented her dark eyes. And the neon blue streaks in her hair.

"Why, Henry, I don't think I've ever seen you in a tuxedo before."

"It's only for special occasions." The black man tugged at his bow tie, probably wishing it had polka dots on it. His silver glasses gleamed in the soft light.

"Well, it looks wonderful. The two of you make quite the dashing couple."

They both blushed and exchanged shy smiles. Henry took Lulu's hand. I grinned. So far, my inner voice had been right on target. At least I'd done something good these last few weeks.

"If you'll excuse me, Sister Carmen, I have to mix and mingle with all these society types and remind them to open their checkbooks before they leave."

Lulu and Henry moved off into the crowd. I dug my notepad and tape recorder out of my purse. Time to go to work.

This night, I went well beyond my usual spiel. I talked not only to the major power players but to every single person I could corner. This was more than likely going to be my final story. I wanted to make it one of the best I'd ever written, even if it was going to end up buried on the back page of the society section.

I finished my last interview and grabbed a glass of champagne. I wandered out of the gallery and looked at the various pieces of art housed in the adjoining areas. Paintings by the likes of van Gogh and Renoir adorned the slick marble walls, while bronze sculptures pondered what they meant from the middle of the floor. I roamed into a room devoted to medieval weapons and suits of armor. I strolled past the displays. Silver swords glittered on the walls, reminding me of Striker.

Why had he been so kind to me last night? Had he really been concerned about me? Did he actually care about me? Or was comforting weeping and wailing women just part of being a superhero? Did I mean anything at all to him?

"Fascinating, aren't they?" a deep voice said.

I turned. Sam Sloane stood a few feet away from me. Reclusive billionaire, eligible bachelor, and all-around, It-on-a-stick Sam Sloane.

"Don't you think?" he asked.

I glanced around. There was no one else within earshot, no one else in the entire room. He must be talking to me.

Sam Sloane talking to me?

"Um, yes. Fascinating."

"The craftsmanship is incredible." He pointed to one of the swords and explained the process by which blind Tibetan monks handcrafted the instrument.

I paid little attention to what he was saying. I couldn't get over the fact I was actually standing next to Sam Sloane and that he was talking. To me of all people.

My inner voice chirped. Why would Sam Sloane deign to talk to me? He hated reporters, especially ones from *The Exposé*. I frowned. And where was his supermodel of the evening? Usually, nothing could tear Sam Sloane's dates off his arm, not even buckets of free champagne. The idea of becoming Mrs. Sam Sloane was far more intoxicating.

"Is something wrong? You're frowning."

I snapped out of my reverie. "Oh no. Everything's fine. I was just thinking how hard it must be to make a sword if you were blind. I imagine you'd cut yourself quite a bit."

His lips twitched with amusement. "Yes, I imagine you would."

High heels clicked on the floor, and a tall blond sashayed into the gallery. I stifled a groan. Not *her* again.

Fiona Fine flounced up to us. The fashion designer wore a gown of shimmering silver beads that brought out every curve of her perfectly perfect body. Her eyes flicked over me, and she put her hand on Sloane's arm. I immediately got the message.

"Sam, what are you doing in here?"

"Just looking at the swords."

The two of them exchanged a long, tense look. I could have cut the air between them with a dull spoon.

"We really must get back to the benefit. *Chief Newman* was looking for you," Fiona emphasized.

A shadow fell over Sloane's face, and he turned to me. "Please excuse me."

"Thank you for telling me about the swords," I said.

Fiona shot me another nasty look and led Sloane away as fast as she could in her towering high heels. I frowned. What was that all about?

Although I'd gathered more than enough information for my story, I stayed at the benefit and kept an eagle eye on Sam Sloane. He shook hands, greased palms, and worked the room like the business tycoon he was. He seemed equally comfortable talking to ancient widows as he did flirting with their twenty-something granddaughters. Sloane charmed everyone. Well, almost everyone.

Joanne James didn't seem very impressed with the businessman. At one point, Sam tried to engage her in conversation, but Joanne ignored him, downing another glass of champagne. Then again, Joanne was hard to impress. She was one of Bigtime's wealthiest women—and the black widow of the society circuit. The forty-something, multiple divorcée was always on the lookout for her next husband.

From the way she went from man to man, I'd always thought that Joanne had to have some sort of seductive superpower. And that she was really an ubervillain in disguise—maybe even Malefica herself. Joanne had the same sort of fantastic body as the ubervillain, and she was about the right age. I stared at Joanne, wondering if she was the one threatening to drown me in radioactive goo unless I did her bidding. She could do it. Joanne was someone you didn't mess with. She hadn't gotten to where she was today by being the shy, retiring, wallflower type.

Joanne's eyes settled on Berkley Brighton, the whiskey billionaire, and she strolled away from Sloane without a backward glance. Maybe he just wasn't rich enough for her.

Morgana Madison also wasn't a fan of Sloane's. The two ignored each other all night long, even when they were talking to the same people. According to business reports, they wanted to buy the same computer company and were currently locked in their latest business battle.

However, one person had a very keen interest in Sloane—Fiona Fine. She kept a grip on his arm the rest of the night. It was a wonder the poor man didn't have claw marks. Evidently, Fiona didn't want me anywhere near him. I wondered when the fashion designer had become so protective of Sloane. The two were friends but had never been an item. The couple made their way to Chief Newman, who stood next to Lulu and Henry. Lulu said something, and they all laughed. Suddenly, Sam Sloane turned, as if he could sense me staring at him. Our eyes locked. My inner voice whispered.

And I knew.

I knew.

I knew who I'd had incredible sex with. Who had made me feel so passionate, so alive, so vibrant. Who had saved me from my would-be rapists. Who had held me so tenderly while I'd cried.

I couldn't believe it. I couldn't wrap my mind around the fact.

Just like that. Out of the blue. The puzzle pieces snapped into place. The picture came into focus. All my research, my encounters with Striker, the folks on the society circuit, the list of the richest men and women in Bigtime—it all finally fit together.

I knew who Striker was. And Fiera, and Mr. Sage, and I had a sneaking suspicion about Hermit too. I could have smacked myself for not seeing it sooner. They had been there right under my nose the whole time, just as I suspected. The irony of it all made me take a long swig of my champagne. The golden bubbles rose to the top of the glass and fizzed out.

So what the hell was I going to do now?

★12★

I sat in my apartment and brooded.

Roamed around the library and brooded.

Wandered through the park and brooded.

I spent the better part of the next day brooding in and around the greater downtown area of Bigtime.

To tell or not to tell, that was the question.

After writing a glowing story about the benefit, I stayed up all night filtering through facts, following the money trail, and checking dates and times. There was nothing conclusive, but I could see a pattern, tiny little threads that would lead me to Striker's real identity and a bona fide Page One exposé of epic proportions. He'd been careful, but not quite careful enough. They never were, in the end.

On my way home from the park, I passed a newsstand. I elbowed my way through the crowd, bought a copy of the day's edition of *The Exposé*, and flipped to the society pages. The headline on the front of the section screamed:

YEE-HAW INDEED! BENEFIT RAISES OVER $3 MILLION FOR

RIDING PROGRAM, POLICE DEPARTMENT. Story by Carmen Cole. I couldn't remember the last time a story of mine had made the cover of, well, anything. At least I was going to go out on top, or at least on top of the society section. Plus, Lulu and the chief had a nice chunk of change to put toward their various do-good programs.

I tucked the newspaper under my arm and walked on. An hour later, without meaning to, I found myself at the corner of Seventh and Thirteenth streets. There it was, right over there, an alley that ran between two of the high-rise buildings. I slowed, took a deep breath, and crossed the street.

The alley seemed far less sinister than it had that night. It was just an alley, three brick walls strung together, stone piled on stone. My eyes swept over the scene. They had pinned me to the wall *there*, and they had all fallen over *there* when Striker had pulled them off me. My body still ached from the brutal assault, and my battered face had turned several interesting shades of green and purple. But no physical trace of the attack remained in the alley, other than the raw memories and jagged echoes in my mind. My fist tightened around the bottle stuck in my jacket pocket. I always kept one hand on my pepper spray now, even during daylight hours.

I took a long, last look at the alley. Then, I stepped back out onto the main street. I squared my shoulders. There was only one thing I could do. I flipped open my cell phone and punched in a number.

"Talk to me."

"It's Carmen. I need to meet."

"Are you sure about this? Really, really sure?" Lulu asked.

"Positive."

The two of us were back in Paradise Park, next to the fountain where the nymphs danced in their never-ending circle. I chewed on a big cone of strawberry cotton candy I'd snagged while walking past one of the carnival vendors. Lulu sat silent, although her laptop hummed like a drowsy bee. Five minutes had passed since I told Lulu what I wanted. The information queen had spent the last four trying to talk me out of it.

But I'd made my decision, for better or worse. I wasn't going to give up Striker to Malefica, not after he'd saved me. I owed him that much, no matter what else had happened between us. My original plan had been to use Striker's real identity to lead me to Malefica's. But with just twenty-four hours left until the ubervillain's deadline, I didn't have enough time to uncover her real identity, unless she ripped off her mask herself for the whole world to see. But I wasn't just going to roll over for Malefica either. I had a plan. A stupid, probably fatal plan, but a plan nonetheless.

"Can he get me the stuff?" I asked. "I need it by tomorrow. And I need to know how to use it."

"He can, but it will be expensive on such short notice, especially the lesson."

Lulu rattled off a prospective price. I winced. It would pretty much deplete my nest egg and ensure a steady diet of macaroni and cheese for the next few years. Then again, if things went wrong, I wouldn't have much use for money anyway. "I can pay it. Do it."

Lulu began to type.

An hour later, I knocked on the door of one of the nicer brownstones in one of the nicer neighborhoods in Bigtime. An intercom cracked to life, and a security camera swiveled around to focus on Lulu and me.

"What's the word?" a gruff male voice asked.

"The word is *boom-boom*," Lulu replied.

The door buzzed open. A tall, thin man waited inside. A diamond twinkled in his ear, while glasses perched on the end of his hawklike nose.

"Jasper, what's going on?" Lulu asked.

The two engaged in a complicated handshake.

"Not much, L. This your friend?"

"Yeah. I told her you could help her out."

Jasper peered at me. "You got the money?"

"I've got it," I said. "You got what I want?"

"Always. Follow me, ladies."

Jasper walked farther back into the house. To my surprise, the inside of the brownstone was just as nice and normal as the outside. Overstuffed, slightly chintzy furniture crouched in the spacious rooms, along with cabinets full of crystal knickknacks and several bookcases.

Jasper came to a metal door and stopped. He punched in a series of codes, and we went down through several more doors before reaching a small, cramped workroom. Twisted bits of metal and wire littered a long table, along with tools of every shape and size. I didn't even know the names for most of the devices. Jasper pulled a heavy lead box out from a safe underneath the table. He opened it, revealing some small metal balls and even more wires.

"You sure you want to do this?" Jasper asked. "This stuff is pretty potent."

"Teach me everything you know. By the way, will you take a check?"

Lulu waved her hand. "Forget it, Sister Carmen. Your money's no good here. I've got this one."

"But——"

"But nothing. That story you did was terrific. Calls have been pouring in, and we've raised more money than ever before. I owe you this and the next three favors. Deal?"

"Deal," I said, not being one to look a gift horse in the mouth.

I just hoped I'd be around long enough to collect on our bargain.

I did absolutely nothing that night. I played hooky from work, took a catnap, and whiled away the hours in whatever manner I saw fit.

I finished the thriller I'd been reading. I solved all of my Rubik's Cubes and snapped the final piece of my latest jigsaw puzzle into place. I ate deep-fried, fatty foods and didn't even think about exercising. I didn't bother with makeup and wore the most comfortable pair of sweats I owned. I was a condemned woman, and I thoroughly enjoyed my last free hours on earth.

Mostly, though, I thought about Striker and his alter ego. About our passionate night together. About how he'd held me so gently when I needed it the most. I thought about what this strange thing was between us and tried to puzzle out my attraction to him. I wanted to know if I'd meant more to him than just a one-night stand. Striker had come to mean a lot more than that to me, whether he realized it or not. Despite my best intentions. Despite everything.

Finally, the day arrived.

The day.

I went for a walk early the next morning to check out the scene of my impending demise. Laurel Park perched on the outskirts of Bigtime. It was a small area that catered to families and senior citizens who liked to explore the many trails or feed the pigeons that populated the grassy lawns.

I strolled through the winding paths until I found the

bench Malefica had mentioned. Children shrieked and played on a wooden swing set nearby, while their parents kept a watchful eye on them from under the shelter of a picnic awning. I stretched and did jumping jacks until they left, then did a little more exploratory work and put my plan into action using Lulu's generous gift. I power walked through the rest of the park and headed back downtown. There was one more thing I needed to do.

I bought a dozen red roses from a street vendor and made my way to Bigtime Cemetery. A row of pines separated the cemetery from Paradise Park and muted the wild, calliope music of the carousel. A wrought-iron gate surrounded the lush, green expanse, and tombstones and angel statues dotted the manicured lawn. Old women wearing towering hats and gardening gloves planted purple pansies in a bed of dirt. Nearby, a man clutched a tattered picture and stared at a fresh grave twenty feet away. Tears ran down his wrinkled face.

I headed for my destination. My stomach twisted. It always did when I came here. Row 17. Plot 325. An ordinary grave, topped with a simple, white marble tombstone that read *TRAVIS TEMPLETON TEAGUE. BELOVED BY ALL.* Tornado action figures marched across the top of the stone, while flowers, teddy bears, and cards clustered around the bottom. Six months had passed since he'd died, and people still left mementoes on his grave. I laid my roses next to the others.

I stared at the tombstone, my heart aching. After Travis's suicide, I'd dug deeper into his past, frantic to figure out why he'd killed himself. I learned Travis was an only child. His parents died when he was a teenager, and he'd been raised by an uncle. Travis worked three jobs to put himself through Bigtime University. Eventually, he founded a company specializing in wind power and other alternative sources of energy. The company's innovative technology made him rich, but Travis didn't forget his struggles. He gave gobs of money to charity and started college scholarships for inner-city kids. Travis always paid his taxes on time, and he'd never gotten so much as a parking ticket. Everyone described him as kind, caring, and considerate.

Travis aka Tornado Teague had been a good man. And I'd killed him.

Even now, I wondered why. Why had he done it? Had Travis snapped because of the exposure? Been unable to handle the rabid media attention? Worried about the anonymity of his fellow superheroes? Whatever Travis's reason, my exposé had been the catalyst. Guilt tightened my chest, making it hard to breathe. Tears streaked down my face.

After a moment, I wiped them away. I couldn't change the tragedy I'd caused, but I could prevent another one from happening.

Or die trying.

I went back to my apartment and took a long shower, as if the water could cleanse my soul and wash away my guilt. I put on my makeup with care and slipped into my favorite pair of faded jeans and a T-shirt that read I'M SMARTER THAN I LOOK. I hoped the logo would be true tonight. I wanted to look my best, even if I was going to my own funeral.

I took a last look around my apartment at all my books and puzzles and knickknacks. It had been my home ever since I'd come to Bigtime. It was a cozy space, and I was going to miss it. I ran my fingers over the finished jigsaw puzzle on the kitchen table. The peaceful scene of floating water lilies did little to soothe my taut nerves.

I took the notes I'd written to the landlord and Chief

Newman and propped them up on the kitchen table. The letter to the landlord instructed him to donate my clothes and books to local charities, while the missive to the chief explained what had happened to me.

I picked up the final note I'd written. To Striker. The superhero had been conspicuously absent the last few days. I had neither seen him nor felt him watching me. I wasn't sure whether I was grateful or annoyed over the lack of attention. I left the note for him on the coffee table among all the papers and articles I'd collected on the Fearless Five.

Don't worry. Your secret's safe with me. Thanks again for the rescue the other night. Carmen.

It was terribly short, but for once, I hadn't known exactly what to write. What could you say to a superhero you'd slept with? Thank you? Atta-boy? Keep up the good work? Striker had been unbelievably kind to me, despite the fact I was trying to uncover his identity, despite the fact I'd driven his friend to commit suicide. Despite everything. Words couldn't express how grateful I was for my rescue. Perhaps what I was about to do would. It might even help my karma a little bit. Maybe I'd come back as a bird or a butterfly, instead of a cockroach.

I grabbed my supplies and stuffed them in my jacket pockets. I let out a long breath.

Time to go to work.

I took a taxi to the park, got out, paid the fare, and checked my silver watch. Eleven forty-five. Right on time. I walked slowly through the park and scanned the shadows. But my friendly neighborhood ubervillains were nowhere to be found. I kept my hands in my pockets, made my way to the appropriate bench, and sat down.

"Come out, come out wherever you are," I whispered.

The birds didn't sing, the bugs didn't chirp. All was quiet and still and hushed, but they were out there in the shadows watching me. I could feel their eyes on me.

At exactly midnight, they appeared. Scorpion lumbered out of the shadows to my left. His bald head gleamed under the faint moonlight. He cracked his knuckles together and grinned. Frost appeared from the right and crossed his arms over his skinny chest. Malefica came at me straight on, her enormous, thigh-high red boots crushing the dewy grass with every step like she was Bigfoot lumbering through the forest.

"Well, well, if it isn't our good friend, Carmen Cole," Malefica purred. "Right on time. I do so like punctual people."

I shrugged. "It's a habit of mine."

She turned to Frost. "You owe me a hundred thousand dollars. He didn't think you'd come. Didn't think you were smart enough to realize it was your only option. Or that you had the spine to show up."

"Really?" I said. "And here I thought he didn't have a brain."

"I have more of a brain than you've ever dreamed of," Frost snapped back. "I've been educated in the finest schools on the East Coast. Where did you graduate from? Hillbilly High?"

"Enough," Malefica interrupted. "We all know why we're here. Let's get down to business. Your month is up, Miss Cole. What I want to know is this—did you find out the answer to my question?"

"Yes. Yes, I did."

"So you know who Striker is?" Breathy excitement colored Malefica's voice. "His true identity?"

"Yep. I know his name, age, marital status, and shoe size. It's eleven and a half, if you're curious. I know just about everything about him except whether he prefers boxers or briefs. Is that enough information for you?" Striker liked to go commando under his black leather suit, but I wasn't about to share that little tidbit with Malefica.

She licked her ruby red lips in anticipation. "Who? Who is he?"

"I'm afraid I'm not going to tell you."

Malefica laughed. The gleeful chuckle grated on my nerves. "Oh please. You're going to tell us. Either now, when you can still pass for a *moderately* attractive woman, or later, after Frost has dipped you in his freezeterium like an overgrown Easter egg."

The three of them started toward me.

"Ah, ah, ah. I wouldn't do that if I were you." I took my right hand out of my pocket, exposing a small metal tube. A blue light glowed on top of the device.

Malefica's eyes narrowed. "What is that?"

"It's a remote-trigger device," I said. "A bomb switch, in layman's terms. You see, I've rigged myself, this bench, and the entire area where you're standing with enough explodium to kill us all."

The three ubervillains looked at the ground beneath their booted feet.

"You're bluffing," Frost sneered.

I turned my gaze to him. "No, actually I'm not. I'm not much of a scientist like you, but I've learned quite a bit about explodium in the last few days. It's a radioactive isotope. Makes dynamite look like a firecracker. Packs enough punch to take down entire city blocks with just a few ounces. Just imagine what it would do to those icy good looks of yours. Shatter them in an instant, I imagine."

Frost gave me a, well, frosty look. Scorpion clenched and unclenched his hands into giant fists, as though he wanted to pound me into oblivion.

"Did I mention that any move on your part, one way or the other, and the bomb goes off? The whole area is wired. If I let go of this trigger, the bomb goes off. If I so much as sneeze, the bomb goes off."

"So much for your brilliant plan," Frost hissed at Malefica. "Your little pet project is going to blow us to hell and back!"

"Shut up!" Malefica plastered a bright smile on her face. "Miss Cole, I'm sure we can come to some sort of arrangement. There's no need to get violent."

I arched an eyebrow. "Really? What sort of arrangement? Let me guess. You're going to offer me money and power and all the usual perks, right? Perhaps even offer to make me some sort of partner in your evil empire. Then, of course, when my guard is down and you no longer have any use for me, you'll shove me into one of those vats or come up with some equally clever and painful way of killing me. Sorry. I've read that story before. I don't like the ending."

Malefica's green eyes grew as hard as marbles. "Pity. I would have so enjoyed double-crossing you. I guess I'll just have to settle for killing you now."

Her eyes began to glow. She rose into the air, using her telekinesis to move out of range of the bomb. She sailed through the air and set herself down forty feet away. Malefica raised her hands, picked up Scorpion and Frost with her mind, and put them down near her next to the wooden swing set. It happened in seconds.

Something tugged on me, and a giant, invisible fist tried to pull the bomb trigger out of my hand. I yanked my hand back, but the invisible fist was stronger. It pried my fingers open and closed itself around the trigger. I swiped at it, but the device dodged my grasp. The trigger floated through the air until it was in Frost's line of sight.

Frost stared at it, and ice formed on the device. A mo-

ment later, it looked like a very large ice cube. Malefica let
go of it, and the trigger clattered to the ground. Useless.

"It seems that your little plan has hit a snag. No trigger, no bomb, no explosion. Pity." Malefica laughed and
blew me a kiss.

Frost pulled out his freezoray gun and leveled it at me.
"Shall I put her on ice?"

"I say we just tear her apart with our bare hands," Scorpion chimed in. His poison-tipped talons gleamed in the
moonlight.

"No, I think we need to come up with something a little more special for Miss Cole for refusing to go quietly."
Malefica tapped her booted foot on the grass. "How about
Frost hits her with his freezoray gun, then you shatter her
icy limbs one at a time?"

"Works for me," Scorpion replied.

"I hate to interrupt," I called out. "After all, it is terribly fascinating to watch you three plot my demise, but
there's something you should know."

"Oh really?" Frost sneered. "What are you going to do
now? Plead for your life?"

"No. I just thought you should know I've got another
trigger." I took my left hand out of my pocket and held up
the metal device so they could see it.

I hadn't rigged the ground in front of me or the bench
or even myself. I just said that to keep the ubervillains
away. Without superpowers, I could never go toe-to-toe
with any of them, even if I had a bottle of pepper spray the
size of a jumbo jet. Instead, I'd rigged the swing set. According to Jasper, explodium produced a concentrated
blast with no shrapnel and no debris. It sucked everything
in toward itself. His bombs had a blast radius of no more
than twenty-five feet, meaning I should be safe at this distance.

By moving away from me and my supposed bomb, the Terrible Triad had floated right into my trap. I might have been crazy trying to take on the Triad by myself, but I didn't have a death wish.

Malefica's eyes began to glow again. I knew I only had seconds before she yanked the second trigger out of my hand.

I loosened my grip—

A silver sword sailed through the air. It embedded itself in a nearby tree, which burst into flame.

"No, no, no!" Malefica shrieked.

Striker leapt out from the shadows and landed on Scorpion. The two went down in a pile of flailing arms and legs. A line of flames cut the two off from Malefica and Frost.

"Hit her, Frost!" Malefica screamed. "Hit her now!"

Frost pulled the trigger on his freezoray gun.

I threw my hands up, still clutching the trigger. Instead of an icy blast, something stung my shoulder. I looked at my jacket, where a tiny dart stuck out. What the hell—

Another tree erupted into flames. Frost threw switches and raked back the slide on his fancy-looking gun. Scorpion and Striker struggled on the ground. They rolled over and over each other, hitting, punching, kicking, clawing. They sounded like a marching band clanging and crashing together. A trashcan zipped up into the air and zoomed toward Malefica. She held out her hand, stopping it.

Still holding the bomb trigger, I ran around the bench. While grateful for Striker's intervention, I couldn't help but be annoyed. Another three seconds, and Malefica and Co. would have been snoring through dirt. Permanently. My problem, Striker's problem, would have been solved. Now, I couldn't blow the bomb without catching the Fearless Five in the blast. Plus, I had no desire to be in the middle of a superhero-ubervillain battle. They'd destroy the whole park before they were done. This time, I didn't have a police barricade to keep me a safe distance away.

A figure with flaming hair and fists emerged from the shadows to my left. I put my hands up to ward off the intense heat and light.

"Stay out of the way!" Fiera hissed.

The superhero ran past me. Sparks landed on my jacket and roared to life. With one hand, I ripped off the smoldering cloth and stomped on it. My inner voice cried out. Something came up fast behind me. I hit the ground. A metal trashcan sailed over my head and off into the darkness.

I scrambled to my feet. Malefica stared at me. The ubervillain's eyes glowed neon green with hate and rage. Another trashcan came at me. I ducked back behind the bench. The can hit it and rattled off.

Out of the corner of my eye, I spotted a green-and-white figure. Malefica saw him too. She picked up another bench with her mind and tossed it at Mr. Sage. One of the discarded trashcans zoomed through the air to meet it. The bench and the can seesawed back and forth, creaking and cracking and groaning. Another wall of fire roared up between Malefica and Mr. Sage.

"Let's go!" Malefica screamed. "Now!"

Frost hit another button on his gun and pulled the trigger. A shrieking sound ripped through the air, just like it had at the vacuum cleaner plant. I clapped my hands over my ears, but it wasn't enough to block out the excruciating wail. My brain felt like it was on fire. Mr. Sage, Striker, and Fiera clutched their heads in agony, but the noise didn't affect the Triad. They scampered away and vanished into the dark woods on the far side of the park.

After a few seconds, the sound faded away. The fires

snuffed out. I stood. The superheroes clustered together, checking to make sure no one was seriously injured. They turned toward me.

"Thank you—"

My vision fuzzed over. I shook my head. The world spun around, and a searing pain roared to life in the back of my skull.

"Carmen? Carmen!"

Striker's voice sounded long and slow, like he was underwater. I staggered back and forth. I squinted as hard as I could, but I couldn't focus. What the hell had Frost injected me with? My throat closed up. I couldn't talk. Couldn't breathe. My foot snagged on something, and I tumbled to the ground. I tried to hold on to the bomb trigger so I wouldn't blow us all to bits, but my fingers felt numb, lifeless. The metal device slid from my grasp.

The light on top of the trigger flashed once.

An enormous roar ripped through the air.

Heat washed over me.

Then, everything went black.

PART TWO

Superhero Central

★ 13 ★

The machine was the first thing I was aware of. It beeped and buzzed and made it impossible for me to sleep. I frowned. I didn't have any sort of machine in my bedroom, other than my old clock radio. Had it suddenly gone haywire?

My eyes fluttered open. A blurry haze covered my vision. Slowly, the tile ceiling came into focus. The harsh fluorescent lights made me squint. I frowned again. My bedroom ceiling wasn't tiled, and I didn't have fluorescent lights. A muscle in my arm twitched. Pain shot up my shoulder.

The pain brought back memories of the battle between the Fearless Five and the Terrible Triad. Frost had shot me with some sort of dart before his gun had produced that horrid noise. I recalled lots of fire and trashcans flying through the air. Everything else was a bit foggy. Had the Fearless Five defeated the Terrible Triad? Or had it been the other way around? Did the bomb go off? I couldn't remember.

I sat up on my elbows and realized I was in a hospital bed. An IV dripped some sort of clear fluid into my arm. Another machine sounded out my heart rate and blood pressure every few seconds. Still more machines burped out information.

Several microscopes and other medical paraphernalia perched on a nearby table. Latex gloves peeked up out of a box. A large metal sink ran along one wall, and a long window with thick glass looked out onto an empty hall-way. A set of hydraulic double doors sat at the far end, leading out to . . . where?

I wasn't in a hospital or doctor's office. Although the room had the antiseptic feel of an infirmary, it was too large to be your average hospital room, and the equipment seemed far too advanced. I couldn't see anything beyond the doors, and I couldn't hear anything except the whines and chirps of the various machines. No nurses, no doctors, no other whimpering patients. A ball of fear formed in my stomach.

Where the hell was I?

I threw back the bedsheets. A pair of white pajama pants, socks, and a loose T-shirt covered my body. Not your typical backless hospital gown. Who had put the clothes on me? And why? I looked like a rat ready to be dissected in a lab. Perhaps this was Frost's lair, the place where he readied his test subjects before he experimented on them. My alarm grew.

I tumbled out of bed and started toward the door, but the wires from the various machines yanked me back. I ripped the IV out of my arm. Blood trickled out of the small wound. I tore off the heart monitor and other patches at-tached to my body, silencing the annoying machines. I staggered over to the double doors.

"Hello? Hello!" I beat my hand on the door. "Can anyone hear me?"

No one answered.

I looked for a button or switch or trigger for the door, but the only things that greeted me were the smooth, blank walls. I cupped my hands together and peered out the long, narrow windows. A hallway branched off in both directions, and I spotted a ten-digit keypad outside. A red light blinked on the device, indicating the door was armed or locked or whatever. Somebody didn't want me to leave this room.

I was a prisoner.

Well, not for long.

I scoured the room, opened the metal cabinets, and looked for anything useful, anything that could help me escape, anything I could use as a weapon. I didn't know who exactly was waiting outside the doors or what they might have in store for me, but I wanted to be prepared no matter what.

The cabinets contained medical supplies—gloves, syringes, bandages. I also discovered a box full of packets of brown pills with the initials *RID* on them. I squinted at the tiny print. *Radioactive Isotope Diminisher*. Interesting, but not helpful. I threw the pills back in the box and kept searching, but the cabinets held no other secrets.

I turned my attention to the odd machines in the room. Most of them were squat, square, metal contraptions with all sorts of knobs and controls and wires. I had no idea what they did, and after I determined that they were of no use to me, I didn't care.

I searched the rest of the room but found nothing that would help me escape. I plopped back on the bed. Frustrated, I kicked the IV stand with my foot.

Not smart.

My toes hit the unyielding metal with a loud crack. A strangled cry of pain escaped my lips. I leapt up off the bed and hopped around on one foot.

Once the throbbing subsided, I hobbled over to the IV stand, a tall metal pole with four legs. I took the bag of fluid off the hook at the top and unplugged the various wires that anchored the stand to the bed. I hefted it in my arms. It would make an excellent battering ram. I took a long hard look at the locked double doors, held the stand out like a lance, and ran toward the doors as fast as my socked feet would let me.

The stand skidded off the door.

I bounced back. My feet slipped sideways. I barely caught myself before I busted my ass on the hard, slick floor. Once I regained my balance, I picked up the stand and tried again.

And again . . .

And again . . .

And again . . .

After ten minutes, all I had succeeded in doing was putting a few scratches on the metal doors. I wasn't going to get out that way.

I turned my attention to the window and chewed my lip. I'd avoided the window until now for a number of reasons. First of all, I didn't want to get a face full of glass trying to get out, not to mention the noise it would make when I shattered it. Still, it was my only way out. I didn't want to be in the room when my captors came back for me, whoever they might be.

I yanked the sheets off the bed, ripped them into long thin strips, and wrapped them around my hands. I wound more strips around my head and face until I looked like a mummy come to life. I took hold of the stand and went over to the window. I closed my eyes a moment, gathering my thoughts. Then, I picked up the IV stand, raised it high, and turned my head away from the window. I shoved the metal stand through the glass with all my might.

It didn't shatter.

I frowned and rammed the stand through the window again.

It still didn't shatter.

I tapped on the window. It was made of some sort of thick substance more like plastic than glass. I peered at the surface. Tiny cracks ran out from the spot where I'd hit it.

Well, it was a start.

I stabbed the window with the stand over and over and over again. Ten minutes later, small cracks and fissures dotted the surface like the delicate threads of a spider's web. I wiped the sweat off my face. Escaping was hard work. I studied the lines and cracks. A couple more good, strategically placed whacks should do it.

I picked up the metal pole again. On the fifth whack, the stand punched through the window, which exploded outward. It sounded louder than a sonic boom in the enclosed space. The flying glass shredded my makeshift gloves. A few pieces stung my arms like small, angry bees.

An alarm blared to life.

Uh-oh.

I threw down the stand, stepped over the broken glass, climbed out the window, and started running.

Ten minutes later, I slumped against the wall, gasping and panting for breath. I felt like I'd been running for hours and hours. My lungs ached and burned with the effort, and a throbbing stitch pulsed in my side. I pushed away from the wall. I didn't have time for such weakness. I had to escape.

Somehow.

It was proving to be more difficult than I'd imagined. The first hallway I'd run down had branched off into another hallway. That hallway had branched out into another hallway. The place was huge. It reminded me of some medieval castle, complete with a labyrinth in the dungeon that poor prisoners like me never escaped from. And the blaring alarm was giving me a killer headache.

I walked as fast as I could. No more running blind. I had to think, get some direction. I came to another branch in the hallway. I went left and kept going left at every new intersection.

Finally, I reached a large set of doors, yanked one open, and slipped into a massive kitchen. I squinted in the semi-darkness. Pots and pans and big spatulas hung from metal racks. Gleaming knives and other cutlery sat in thick wooden blocks. Rows of refrigerators and freezers flanked the walls. Another dead end.

A door snicked open at the other end of the room. I grabbed a frying pan from an overhead rack and ducked behind one of the refrigerators, which was roughly the size of a humpback whale. Soft footsteps whispered. A black shadow pooled on the floor, growing larger and larger. I tensed, ready to strike. My heart hammered against my ribs. Blood roared in my buzzing ears. My breaths came in shallow gasps.

A figure strolled into view. I leapt out and swung the frying pan at its head. Too slow. The figure turned and grabbed my wrist, bending it downward. I dropped the pan, and it skittered off into the darkness. I lashed out with my free fist. The figure caught that hand too. A body pinned me against the refrigerator and pressed into mine. Visions of the almost-rape flooded my mind. I shrieked and struggled, trying to get away from my assailant.

"Carmen! Carmen! Calm down! It's me."

Striker's deep voice cut through my panic. I quit fighting. My senses flared to life, and I realized what a cozy position we were in. His leg rested between mine, spreading them apart. I could feel the sleek leather fabric of his suit through my thin pajama bottoms. He shifted his stance, and a heavy wetness gathered between my thighs at the intimate contact. Striker's gloved hands held my wrists against the refrigerator. His arms brushed the sides of my breasts, which swelled in response. My nipples hardened, and I panted for breath once more.

Electric blue flecks sparked to life deep in Striker's silver eyes. For a moment, I thought he might lean forward and kiss me, capture my lips with his. I wanted him to. Oh, how I wanted him to. I burned for him to do that and much, much more.

Striker hissed. He let out a long breath, pulled back, and dropped his arms. I bit my lip.

"I've been looking everywhere for you," he said. "Why did you break out of the infirmary?"

"I didn't know where I was or who had me. I figured I didn't want to stick around to find out."

"Don't you remember what happened at the park? That we defeated the Triad?"

"Not really. It's all kind of a blur."

The alarm stopped. The silence seemed strange after the constant blaring.

"How are you feeling?" Striker asked, concern evident in his voice.

"Not too bad, I suppose. Got my morning walk in today anyway." A sudden chill swept over me. My head throbbed. The veins in my eyeballs twitched. "Actually, I'm kind of cold. Do you think you could—"

I pitched forward headfirst.

In addition to his other superpowers, Striker had excellent reflexes. He caught me before I hit the floor.

My eyes fluttered open. For the second time that day, I found myself staring at a tiled ceiling.

I sat up, back in the same room I'd woken up in. The same machines beeped and chirped and hummed, and an IV dripped into my arm. A piece of cardboard covered the shattered window. However, there was a new addition to the room.

Striker.

He sat in a chair in the corner, staring at me. "How are you feeling?" Striker asked, his silver eyes bright.

"Okay, I suppose." My throat felt like it had sand in it. "Can I have some water, please?"

Striker walked over to the sink, his stride fluid and graceful, and turned on some sort of fancy-looking filter. I eyed his backside while he filled a glass. Even his ass was perfect. He handed the water to me, and our fingers brushed. A tingle shot up my arm, and I gulped down the cool liquid. Some of the sand cleared out of my throat, but my body still burned.

"How long have I been unconscious?" I asked.

"This time, only a few hours. Before that, almost three days."

"Three days? What the hell did Frost shoot me with?"

"We're not sure, but we think it was some kind of tranquilizer. Evidently, it had some residual effect as well, which your journey through the manor didn't help. That's why you passed out again."

"Oh."

I tilted my head. Striker looked rather silly wearing black leather in the all-white hospital room, especially with the two swords peeping up over his back. Sexy, but silly too. What was going to attack him in here? A nasty microbe? I felt a sudden urge to giggle.

"What's so funny?" he asked.

I smoothed my face over. This was no laughing matter, and I knew it.

"You know, you can take off that costume. I know who you are," I said in a quiet voice. "I've known for a while now."

Striker froze.

I gathered up what was left of my courage. "So why don't you take off the mask, Sam? Or should I call you Mr. Sloane?"

★ 14 ★

Striker let out a deep breath. He reached up, and his fingers touched his black mask. They lingered there a moment, and Striker closed his eyes. Then, he yanked the leather over his head.

Sam Sloane stared back at me.

I studied him. Black hair flopped over his forehead, and a long, thin scar slashed a white line down his right cheek. His nose was slightly crooked, as though it had been broken once upon a time. He was a handsome man, but his eyes were what set him apart. They were the brightest, most brilliant silver eyes I had ever seen. The sort of eyes a woman could lose herself in forever.

I compared the man before me to the masked superhero. Now that I knew exactly what to look for, the mask really was a thin disguise and did very little to hide his features, especially his intense eyes. How had no one uncovered Striker's true identity before? Why hadn't I seen it before?

"How did you figure it out?" he asked.

"You made a mistake at the charity benefit. You spoke to me. Why would billionaire Sam Sloane talk to me? He hates reporters, especially the ones from *The Exposé*. But you talked to me, made polite chitchat. And I wondered—why? The answer was *he* wouldn't. Sam Sloane would never talk to *me*. I'm a reporter, I'm the enemy. But Striker would. He would want to talk to me and see how I was doing after the attack and . . . everything else. So I watched you the rest of the evening, trying to figure it out. And it just came to me. I just knew. I went back and looked through all the files I collected and found some facts to support my theory."

"In a way, I'm glad you know." Sam poked his fingers through the eyeholes in his mask. "I wasn't looking forward to running around in my costume the whole time you were here."

I glanced at the white walls. "Where might *here* be?"

"Sublime, my manor on the outskirts of Bigtime. We're in a sublevel in the left wing."

"Ah."

I'd heard about the luxurious estate while covering the society beat. It was the crème de la crème of houses in Bigtime. Sublime featured several hundred spacious rooms full of all sorts of pricey antiques, art collections, and more. The manor could house an army of people and had been the scene of many a society benefit. The grounds were just as impressive, if not more so, than the house. They featured an extensive network of gardens full of exotic, fragrant flowers in addition to fish-filled ponds, marble fountains, and even a bird sanctuary or five.

"So where are the others?" I asked.

"Others?"

"Fiona Fine, Henry Harris, Chief Sean Newman."

"Why would those people be in my house?"

Sam's voice was calm, cool, controlled, but I detected

the faintest bit of shock in it. I was getting better at reading him.

"Because they're the other members of the Fearless Five."

Sam's eyes drifted to a light on the ceiling. My inner voice chattered.

"Is there a hidden camera up there? Are they watching us right now from some superduper secret control room deep in the bowels of this place?"

"Yes, yes, they are."

I looked up and waved. "Hi, guys. What's up?"

"Are you sure you feel okay?" Sam asked ten minutes later. "Maybe you should spend the day in here resting."

"I'm fine," I said for the twentieth time. "Now, can we please get out of here? I'd like to take a shower and clean up." I glanced down at my white pajama ensemble. "And put on some real clothes, if you have any."

"Actually, we brought all your things here."

I blinked. "You did?"

"Yes. I let myself into your apartment after we fought off the Triad. The chief and I packed up your stuff and brought it here."

"But how did you know I was going to the park? I made it a point not to tell you."

"I went to your apartment to check on you, just like always, but you weren't there."

"Just like always?"

Sam dropped his eyes. "I've been swinging by your building at night to make sure you were safe."

"How long have you been doing that? Since the night I was attacked?"

"No. Not since that night. The other night. The night we were . . . together."

"Oh."

I didn't know what to say. All this time I had thought he didn't care. That I hadn't mattered to him. That that night had been nothing more than satisfying sex between two willing partners. But he had been watching me, looking out for me. The knowledge thrilled me. My heart lifted.

Sam continued with his story. "Since you weren't in your apartment, I nosed around. You had the meeting written down on the calendar on your refrigerator in big letters. I knew the month was probably up. I saw the notes you left on the table and figured out the rest. You should have told me that it was time, Carmen."

I stared at the floor. "I didn't want anyone else to get hurt. It was my mess. I wanted to get out of it myself."

"Really? Is that why you had a couple of pounds of ex-plodium taped to that swing set?"

"I was hoping I could eliminate the Triad by myself. Or at least go out trying."

Sam raised a black eyebrow. "You wanted to commit suicide by blowing yourself to kingdom come?"

"It would have been better than what Frost had in store for me."

He didn't argue.

Suddenly, a horrible thought flashed through my mind. "What about the others? Are they okay? They didn't get caught in the blast, did they?"

Sam shook his head. "No. Everyone's fine. Fiera was closest to the swing set, but obviously, the fire didn't hurt her. The rest of us were out of range."

I closed my eyes. Thank heavens. I couldn't have lived with myself if I'd hurt another superhero, especially a member of the Fearless Five.

Sam slipped the IV needle out of my arm and put a small bandage over the wound. His skin felt warm and smooth on my own. More tingles spread through my body. I closed my eyes, enjoying the sensation, remembering how good, how solid the rest of him had felt against me. In me. Sam's ragged breath brushed my hair, and I knew he felt it too, this strange magnetism, this odd chemistry between us.

"Come on," Sam said, breaking contact and stepping away from me. "Since you're bound and determined not to rest, I'll show you to your room."

Sam led me through a series of long hallways. "We're a couple of hundred feet underground here, in case you're curious."

"Three hundred thirty-seven feet to be precise. I saw the construction invoice when I was investigating you," I said. "Underground construction is a giant red flag. It practically screams *supersecret underground lair*, both for superheroes and ubervillains. It's like drawing a great big bull's-eye on yourself. I can't tell you how many people I busted on underground construction bills alone. The Kilted Scotsman, the Blue Berserker, Shrooma."

Sam's face tightened at the mention of the other superheroes and ubervillains I'd exposed. I shut up. I was blathering anyway, trying to fill the silence. It was an annoying habit I developed whenever I was nervous or guilty or both. Being in the Fearless Five's headquarters was more than enough to make me feel guilty, given Tornado's suicide. And queasy. As for Sam, well, just thinking about him was enough to get me worked up in a completely different, totally unacceptable way.

We arrived at an elevator. Sam punched in a series of numbers on a keypad next to the doors. They slid open. He punched in another code on a pad inside the elevator. The doors pinged closed, and the elevator rose.

I studied Sam. He stared straight ahead at the smooth door. I couldn't decide who was sexier—Sam Sloane or Striker. He looked damn good either way. My eyes trailed down Sam's lean, firm body. I imagined him stopping the elevator, turning to me, taking me into his arms, peeling the white pajamas from my body, and then—

I shook my head. I really needed to get some new fantasies. Ones that didn't star Sam aka Striker Sloane. I'd almost died a couple days ago, and now I was thinking about jumping him in an elevator. What the hell was wrong with me?

Several floors later, the elevator stopped. Sam punched in yet another code. The doors slid open, revealing a small black space.

"Where are we?"

"This leads out to the wine cellar." He hit some more keys, and another door opened.

We emerged in the far corner of a massive wine cellar. Rack after wooden rack of bottles stood like quiet sentinels in the damp, cool space. Sam flipped open a panel in the wall and punched in one final code. The secret door slid shut, and he closed the panel.

I eyed the labels as we walked by. From the stories I'd done on the society beat, I knew the bottles in Sam's cellar went for thousands and thousands of dollars apiece. He probably even had some Brighton's Best whiskey stashed away somewhere, just like Malefica had in her secret lair. A vague thought stirred in my mind. Brighton's Best—

Sam opened another door, and the thought fled. We climbed up a flight of stairs and emerged into a wide hallway. Gilded mirrors lined the walls. A crystal chandelier dangled hundreds of feet overhead. Ivory and jade statues peeked out from wall recesses. Wide marble stairs led up to the top floors of the manor.

I tried hard not to gawk. I'd been to high-society affairs before at some of the finest homes in Bigtime, but Sublime blew me away. Everything whispered of money and elegance and power. It was enough to make a middle-class country gal from Tennessee feel, well, just a little inadequate. All right, downright inferior. Especially when I was wearing a lab rat getup and smelled like I hadn't had a shower in days. All the opulence reminded me once again of the painful fact that I was way out of my league when it came to Sam Sloane. Hell, I wasn't even in the same time zone.

Sam wound his way up the stairs and past yet more lavishly filled rooms. He came to a set of doors at the very end of one hallway, and we entered an enormous room.

"This is your suite. There's a bedroom, bathroom, walk-in closet, and living room complete with a TV, CD player, DVD player, and all the other usual bells and whistles."

It was all that and a bag of chips too. A couple of bags. *Big* bags. I worked very hard to keep my jaw from dropping open. The suite was three times the size of my apartment and just as richly furnished as the rest of the manor. One of the silver-embroidered throw pillows on the sofa probably cost as much as all the furniture in my apartment. Put together. And tripled. The electronics also blew my mind. The entertainment system Sam showed me was state-of-the-art with the latest and greatest technology and remote controls. I even spotted a laptop on the writing desk that was almost as big as the TV. It looked like it could run a couple of countries all by itself. I pinched my arm. Just to make sure I wasn't dreaming. Or dead.

"Your stuff is over there." Sam pointed to a pile of boxes next to the wall near the king-size bed. "And here's the intercom. I've had it connected to my room. Just push the button if you need something. If I'm not in my room, the call gets routed throughout the manor. It might take a few minutes, but Henry or someone else will answer you."

"You mean you don't have a trusty butler with a stuffy British accent to do your bidding and help you slip into your superhero getup? I thought that was a requirement for all you rich, superhero types," I quipped. "How terribly disappointing."

"Sorry. I tried the whole servants thing, but it just didn't work. Servants are too nosy for their own good. I have some crews come in a couple of times a week to cook, clean, and take care of the grounds, but that's it. If you know where I can find a trusty butler with a stuffy British accent to do my bidding, please, let me know."

Sam grinned. His white teeth contrasted with his dark, tanned face. His pale eyes sparkled, and little laugh lines appeared at the corners. The effect devastated me. My heart skipped about twenty beats. No wonder every eligible debutante in Bigtime wanted to hook Sam Sloane. The man was gorgeous from head to toe. I knew. I'd seen most of him.

"Dinner is at six sharp. Everyone will be there. We need to talk about what our next move should be. I'll come back up and get you then. In the meantime, make yourself comfortable. Try to relax."

My eyes drifted to the bed. I'd like to relax in that, all right, with Sam next to me. Or on top of me. Or under me. I wasn't picky. I pushed the wicked thought out of my mind.

"Thanks."

Sam winked at me, walked across the room, and closed the door.

I sank down onto the plush bed. A silly little grin turned up the corners of my mouth. He'd winked at me! Sam Sloane had winked at me! Then, reality intruded, as it so often did. My grin faded away. What was wrong with me?

Mooning over Sam would get me nothing but trouble, and I didn't need my karma to get any worse.

And, of course, there was the fact that I'd made the superhero-dating mistake before with Matt, although technically I hadn't known he was a superhero. Still, all the long hours, mysterious disappearances, and strange injuries had been difficult to put up with, to say the least. And then there was the betrayal of Matt cheating on me with Karen, my best friend and the local ubervillain. I had no desire to repeat that. No desire whatsoever.

Well . . .

Maybe just a little . . .

A teeny, tiny bit of desire . . .

I growled. Maybe Frost had given me some kind of bizarre love potion in addition to the tranquilizer. Maybe that explained my odd attraction to Sam and my fascination with his brilliant eyes. I snorted. *Yeah right*.

More than likely I was feeling the so-called *superhero swoon* effect. It was a well-known fact that after someone was saved by a superhero, she usually developed a mad, mad crush on her savior. The victim bought the hero chocolates, flowers, and other trinkets and made a pest of herself until the superhero oh-so-gently told her they could never be together. It was a well-documented phenomenon. Countless journal articles had been written about it, often by bitter female researchers who had been under the effects of the *superhero swoon* once upon a time.

Except, in my case, I'd actually slept with said superhero before he'd saved me. And no matter how I tried to deny it, I wanted to again. And again. And again. I groaned and flopped back on the bed. There was no way things could ever work out between Sam and me, no matter how super the sex had been.

There were just too many things between us, namely

the ghost of a dead man and a malicious ubervillain who wanted our heads on a silver platter. Malefica was out there somewhere plotting her revenge, trying to get me back in her sights. I couldn't bear it if something happened to Sam because of me. But what could I do to stop it?

I mulled over the predicament, pushing possible options around in my mind like the pieces of a jigsaw puzzle. I sat up and squared my shoulders. I would go to dinner tonight and be nice and polite to everyone, even Fiona Fine. Then, I would pack up my things and leave Sam Sloane and the rest of the Fearless Five alone.

Forever.

It was the only chance I had to keep Sam and the others safe from Malefica's wrath.

And the only way I could keep my shattered heart from taking another pummeling at the hands of a superhero.

★15★

After spending fifteen minutes chastising myself and vowing never to look at Sam Sloane ever again, I stripped off my hospital clothes and took the longest bath in the history of mankind. Well, one of the longest.

Like the rest of the suite, the bathroom had everything a girl could want. Bath beads, exotic body oils, even scented soap-on-a-rope. I threw a couple of different scents into the swimming-pool-sized tub and filled it to the brim with the hottest water I could stand. I plunged into the bubbles and scrubbed myself down.

When I finished, I wrapped myself in a fluffy white bath towel and unstopped the tub. I watched the soapy water swirl down the drain. If only my troubles could disappear so easily.

Sam knocked on the door at exactly six. The super-hero had shed his skin-tight leather suit for a perfectly fitted tuxedo. The black coat and white shirt only enhanced his dark good looks. My heart fluttered.

Sam's silver eyes flicked over my body. I looked down at my ensemble, a less-than-glamorous combo of faded jeans, worn-out sneakers, and a T-shirt that read *LOVE JUST WEIGHS A WOMAN DOWN*. A pink anvil covered with hearts crushed a woman to death on the front of the shirt. I cringed, aware once again of the enormous socioeconomic gap between us. I looked like a bag lady next to Sam.

"I didn't realize we were dressing up for dinner. If you give me a few minutes, I can change—"

"No, no. You look fine. It doesn't matter. I should have told you. It's something we do around here. There's no reason to change."

Superheroes who dressed up for dinner? Odd. I wouldn't think they would have time to do something so fancy, what with all the crime in Bigtime. I wondered what other strange, superhero behavior I was going to witness tonight.

"Are you ready?" Sam asked.

Ready to face the friends of a superhero I'd driven to commit suicide? Sure, no problem. I did that every day and twice on Sundays.

Or not.

A ball of nerves knotted up in my stomach, and I let out a long breath. "As ready as I'll ever be."

"Don't worry. Nobody blames you for Travis's death," he said in a gentle voice. "Everything will be fine."

I didn't believe him for an instant. They all blamed me, and I knew it.

I could feel it in my very soul.

Sam led me down various hallways and flights of stairs until we reached the dining room. I stepped over the threshold and stopped. A chandelier the size of a compact car hung over the table and bathed the room in a pure, white light. A table filled with delicate china, antique crystal, and lit candles crouched below. Impressionist paintings in silver frames adorned the walls, while gleaming suits of armor stood guard next to them. I felt small and insignificant and shabby in the enormous room, which could easily hold a couple hundred people. The others clustered around one end of the long, square table. They rose, and I realized they were just as dressed up as Sam was. Henry and the chief wore dark tuxedos, while Fiona sported a bright blue gown.

"Carmen, good to see you," Chief Sean Newman rumbled.

"Hi, Carmen." Henry gave me a shy wave.

Fiona remained silent. The other's woman anger and loathing for me radiated from her with the heat of a thousand suns. Beads of sweat popped out on my face. If Fiona got any hotter, my hair would light up like a Christmas tree.

"Chief, Henry, Fiona."

I stared at the unmasked superheroes. They stared back. The knot in my stomach ballooned up to the size of a basketball. Tension blanketed the air like a heavy fog.

"I think we all know each other," Sam said. "Why don't we sit down and have dinner?"

He walked over to the table and pulled out a chair next to Henry. My knees shook, and I sank into it. Fiona and Chief Newman faced me across the table, and Sam took his place at the head. Silver trays of cheeses, fruits, and vegetables filled the table, along with tureens of steaming soup, bowls of salads, and a turkey large enough to feed a third world country. A luscious-looking chocolate cheesecake perched at the far end.

"Dig in, dig in, don't be shy," Sam said. "There's plenty to go around."

The others picked up their silverware and passed around the various platters and bowls. Once everyone had been served, we dug into our food. Silverware and cutlery clinked together, creating a pleasant-sounding symphony to accompany the meal.

I picked at my food. I had no appetite for the fantastic spread, even though I hadn't eaten in several days. The ball in my stomach spread up into my throat. I could barely breathe.

Fiona had no such problem. The fashion designer took three portions of everything and wolfed them down in record time. She was on her fourth helping of mashed potatoes and gravy before the others finished their first. It was fascinating, in a gluttonous sort of way. The gusto and speed with which the other woman ate transfixed me. Watching food disappear from Fiona's plate would make for excellent time-lapse photography.

"What are you staring at?" Fiona snapped.

"Nothing," I said. "It's just . . . how can you eat so much and stay so thin? What's your secret?"

"I have a high metabolism. I can eat whatever I want and never gain an ounce. I burn all the calories away. Literally." Her blue eyes flicked over me. "Unlike some people."

I sucked in my less-than-flat stomach. I wasn't fat, but I didn't have a supermodel's perfect, stick-thin figure. I never would without liposuction and some sort of serious eating disorder. Still, I put my fork down.

Once everyone had finished, Chief Newman picked up the chocolate cheesecake. "Would you like some, Carmen?"

I started to say no when a smirk flitted across Fiona's face. "Yes, please. I'd love a piece."

Chief Newman passed me the dessert. I helped myself to a piece of cheesecake and took a big bite. The chocolate melted in my mouth, and I polished off the rest of it.

Fiona Fine and her perfect figure be damned. Life was too short to count calories. Especially when I had a malevolent ubervillain to worry about.

The others dawdled over their cheesecake, and my curiosity crept up over my nervousness. The reporter in me yearned to ask questions. Just like always.

"So, do you all live here at Sublime?" I asked.

"Not exactly," Sam replied. "We all have separate apartments and homes. However, everybody does have their own suite of rooms downstairs that they can crash in whenever we come back from a mission."

"Downstairs? I thought we were on the bottom floor."

Sam made a gesture with his hand. "You know, *downstairs*."

"Oh."

"I have a question for you, Carmen. How did you figure out our identities?" Henry asked, his glasses gleaming in that dim light. "We're all dying to know."

"Well, like I told Sam, he made a mistake. He talked to me at the benefit, and I wondered why. Sam Sloane would never talk to me. Then, Fiona came in and dragged him away from me because Chief Newman wanted to see him. I just had a feeling about the four of you. I saw you standing together, and everything just fit. Sam talking to me, the chief wanting to see him, Fiona pulling him away. Later that night, I went back home and started digging into your backgrounds. I found some more information that confirmed my hunch."

Fiona let out a snort. "You had a feeling? What are you, psychic now?"

"No," I said in a defensive tone. "I'm not psychic. I just get these feelings sometimes, little flashes in my head. I just know things. It's a gut instinct, I guess, an inner voice that whispers to me."

"Interesting," Chief Newman murmured. His blue eyes darkened. "Very interesting."

"And what about me?" Henry asked. "How did you figure me out? Nobody knows what Hermit looks like or what powers he has."

I smiled. "You made a mistake too, with the list I asked you to compile of the fifty richest men and women in Bigtime. The Henry Harris I know would never leave two names off a list like that, and it certainly wouldn't be because there was a flaw in his computer program. When I realized the two names you had left off were Sam and Fiona, I knew you were Hermit."

Henry looked at Fiona. "I told you she'd figure that out."

Fiona sniffed. "Yes, well, I suppose anyone can count."

I glared at the other woman.

Sam cleared his throat before things got any more heated. "We all know why we're here. The question is what do we do now?"

"Actually, before we talk about that, I have something I want to say to all of you. Something I've wanted to say for a long time." I took a deep breath. This was the reason my stomach had been overtaken by a basketball. Still, it was something I had to do, something I needed to do, no matter how difficult it was. I swallowed. The ball blew up to gigantic proportions.

"I just wanted you all to know how sorry I am about Tornado, er, Travis's death. If I'd known how my article would have affected him, I never would have written it. Never. I hope you can accept my apology and my sympathy. I truly am very, very sorry for your loss."

Sam's eyes glittered. Henry stared at his fork. Chief Newman interlaced his fingers.

Fiona stood. Her blue eyes burned into me, and my own temperature rose in response. Sweat gathered and trickled down the small of my back. Fiona threw her napkin down. Sparks flew from her fingertips and smoked on the white tablecloth. She stalked away, her shoes leaving black scorch marks on the floor. She wrenched open the door, walked through, and slammed it shut.

The door had other ideas. Pulled on by Fiona's incredible strength, it kept going. The door exploded through the wall and zipped through the air. It skidded to a halt two rooms over.

Fiona never looked back.

Well, that certainly had not gone well. I was lucky Fiona hadn't reduced me to a pile of ash on the spot. Or squeezed me until I popped like a piece of bubble wrap. I turned a wary eye to the others, wondering what other superhero powers I was about to witness.

"You'll have to forgive my daughter," Chief Newman said. "Travis was special to her. His death has hit her very hard."

My mouth dropped open. "Your daughter?" My research had never revealed any familial connections between any members of the Fearless Five. How could I have missed that? More importantly, how could such a kind, calm man like the chief have such a hot-tempered, obnoxious daughter like Fiona?

"Yes, Fiona's my daughter. It's something we keep to ourselves for our safety. She has her mother's temper."

Chief Newman reading my mind and answering my silent questions unnerved me. Had he sensed my nervousness and fear the whole evening? Was he peering into my thoughts even now? Did he know about Sam and me . . . ?

I immediately cut that thought off.

A ghost of a smile drifted across the chief's face. "Yes, I did sense your nervousness, and yes, I am reading your mind, Carmen."

"Stop that!"

Henry gave me a small grin. "Unfortunately, having your mind read comes with the territory around here."

I eyed one of the empty soup tureens. I wondered if putting it on my head would block my thoughts from Chief Newman. Or maybe I could make myself a hat out of aluminum foil. That was good for keeping the aliens away. At least, that's what all the crazy homeless people at Paradise Park claimed.

Chief Newman chuckled. "I imagine that would look rather funny, Carmen."

I gave him a sour look. He chuckled again.

"Even though Fiona has decided to leave, we still need to discuss our next move," Sam reminded us.

The mood darkened.

"First things first." Sam turned to me. "You've got to stay here at Sublime, where you'll be safe."

"Until when?"

"Until we figure out a way to stop Malefica for good."

"How long might that be?"

"I have no idea."

"I can't stay here forever. What about my job? My apartment? My overdue library books? I have a life, you know." I clapped a hand to my head and groaned. "I bet they've already fired me. I haven't been to work in almost a week."

"Actually, I took care of that," Chief Newman said. "You've been given a brief sabbatical from the newspaper, and your rent's been paid up through the end of the year."

"How did you manage that? I've already used up all my vacation days for the entire year." I'd blown through them after Travis Teague's suicide. There was something about driving a man to take his own life that made you want to never be seen again.

The chief laced his fingers together. "I merely called up some of the editors and told them what a valuable employee you were, what a hard worker. They were more than happy to give you the time off."

"What he means is that he hypnotized them into doing what he wanted," Henry added. "It's one of his more useful powers."

"You hypnotized my bosses?"

"I prefer the term *suggestive encouragement*." The chief's blue eyes twinkled.

"Oh. That doesn't matter. I still can't stay here." Panic strained my voice. "I just can't."

I didn't belong here among all the glitz and glamour, and I didn't belong within twenty feet of any superheroes. I certainly didn't need to be in such close proximity to Sam Sloane for any length of time. Given my intense attraction to him, eventually I'd do something stupid, like lock him in my room and beg him to make love to me again. My heart had already been broken once. I couldn't risk it a second time, especially not with my bad karma with men and superheroes. And everything else for that matter.

"You can stay here, and you will," Sam snapped.

His authoritative tone grated on my nerves. If there was one thing I hated, it was when another person tried to tell me what to do. No matter how sexy the person might be. "It's my life, and I want to get back to it as soon as I can. I'll do what I want to."

"And if you want to keep it, you'll stay right here where it's safe, where we can protect you."

My blue eyes narrowed. Sam glared at me, his silver gaze shimmering with emotion.

"Why don't we just take it one day at a time and see what develops?" Chief Newman suggested. "There's no need to make a hasty decision now we might regret later."

I drummed my fingers on the table. Besides my un-wanted, relentless attraction to Sam, my other major prob-lem was Malefica. If I left the safety of Sublime and went back to Bigtime, she'd track me down faster than a South-ern bloodhound treeing raccoons. I'd felt Malefica's rage, her absolute hatred of me, at the park. I had dared to stand up to the ubervillain, and Malefica hadn't liked it. Not one little bit.

I shuddered to think what would happen if she got her inch-long nails into me. How could I deal with this threat? Despite my reprieve from work, I couldn't spend the rest of my life hiding from the Terrible Triad. There had to be a way out of this mess. I turned the problem round and round in my mind.

Besides her superpowers, Malefica's only real advantage was her anonymity. That, however, was something I could change. And it would drastically level the playing field.

"Did you guys bring *all* my stuff from my apartment?"

"Yes. We shoved everything into those cardboard boxes in your suite," Sam replied.

"All of it? Even the papers I had on the coffee table?"

"Yes, why do you ask?"

"Because if my notes are here, I can get back to work."

"On what?"

"Uncovering Malefica's real identity."

The three superheroes exchanged worried glances. I stood and paced back and forth beside the table.

"Don't worry. I'm not going to expose you or dig up your deepest, darkest secrets, but we need to uncover Malefica's identity. If I do that, I can serve her up to you, just the way she wanted to give me to Frost. You guys can ambush her, and she'll never know what hit her. Once she's safely locked away for the remainder of her natural life, I can get back to mine, and you guys can go back to saving Bigtime on a weekly basis. Everyone wins. It's the same game plan I had in the beginning, the same one I told Striker about. Except now, I have *all* your identities. That should make Malefica much easier to unmask."

"Do you think you can really do that?" Henry said. "Uncover her identity? I've been trying for years."

I shrugged. "I've done it before. It's really not difficult. You superheroes and ubervillains aren't nearly as clever as you think you are."

The three men stared at me.

"Well, you're not," I said in a defensive tone. "Anyone with half a brain and a little bit of time can figure out who most of you are. C'mon. What sort of lame-ass disguise is a pair of glasses and skin-tight spandex anyway?"

★ 16 ★

I started Operation Unmask the next morning. By nine o'clock, I'd dressed, put on my usual war paint, and was ready to face the day and my superhero hosts. I opened the door to my room and stuck my head outside. An empty hallway greeted me.

"Hello? Is anyone out here? Hello?"

Silence echoed back.

I pushed the intercom button. It squawked.

"Um, Sam? Are you there?"

No one answered. So much for my call being routed through the manor. Perhaps I was the only one up. Maybe superheroes slept late because they fought crime into the wee hours of the morning. Matt had certainly never been able to get up early. *Matt.* For once, it didn't hurt to think about him. No needles of pain pierced my heart. Maybe I was finally getting over his betrayal. Or maybe I just had bigger things to worry about at the moment, like keeping my head attached to my body and free of frostbite.

I pushed the intercom button three more times, but no one responded. I'd just have to navigate the twisting hallways alone. I saw no one, and nothing moved or stirred. The gigantic house soaked up sound, hushing the plop of my sneakers on the thick carpet and the rustle of my jeans. The only other people I spotted were the figures in the various paintings that lined the walls, along with the marble statues and suits of armor. Their empty eyes followed me wherever I went. Creepy.

Finally, I stumbled across the kitchen. It, too, was deserted. I settled myself on a stool next to a long skinny island in the middle of the open space. Surely, the others would come down—or up—for breakfast, given the fancy dinner they'd had last night. Meals seemed to be a group affair around here.

But ten minutes later, I was still alone. I hadn't heard a whisper of movement. My stomach rumbled, reminding me how long it had been since I'd had a substantial meal. I chewed my lip and stared at the stainless steel refrigerators. Sam had told me not to be shy. Of course, I wasn't shy by nature, not by a long shot, but it didn't hurt to have permission from the man of the manor.

I scooted off my stool and opened the refrigerators. Cheeses, meats, vegetables, fruits, breads, juices, milk, and more. It was better than a grocery store. My mouth watered. I helped myself to some fresh fruit, orange juice, bagels, and cream cheese. I rustled through the various drawers and cabinets until I found some dishes and silverware, carried my plates to the island, and chowed down. Ah, the breakfast of superheroes. Or nosy reporters.

Twenty minutes later, I popped the last bite of bagel into my mouth and polished off the rest of my juice. No one had appeared. I put my dirty dishes in one of the sinks that lined the walls. Well, if no one was going to find me, I was just going to have to find them. Like usual.

I went back upstairs, paying careful attention to the layout of the hallways and various rooms. This time, I made it back to my suite in only five minutes. I tried the intercom again. No response.

I picked up my two boxes of notes on the Terrible Triad and the Fearless Five and lugged them down to the kitchen. I left them on the island and scouted out the rest of the first floor. I wandered through all sorts of theme rooms. There was a room filled with portraits, a room of statues, a room of crystal figurines, and even a game room with multiple pool tables and a big-screen TV. Finally, I found what I was look-ing for—the wine cellar. I trooped back to the kitchen, re-trieved my boxes of notes, and hauled them down to the cellar. I pushed open the door with my foot and walked past the rows and rows of wine bottles. I wrinkled my nose at the sour, musty smell.

I went to the far corner. Empty walls stared back at me, and I felt along them. The stone felt cool and smooth and slightly damp under my probing fingers. I ran my hands up and down and sideways. My fingertips snagged on a jagged spot. A-ha! There it was. I took a step back. If you knew where it was, the secret panel looked just as fake as the plastic rocks people hid extra house keys in and put in their yards. I pried the panel open with my fingernails.

I squinted at the keypad. I hadn't caught all of the numbers yesterday when Sam had punched in the three-digit code, but he'd started with a 5. I tried various com-binations for the next ten minutes. The keypad beeped each time I entered the wrong combination. Frustrated, I smacked it with my hand. It beeped again. Stupid com-puter.

I leaned in and stared at the numbers. It was your typical ten-digit keypad, with an enter key and a few other sundry buttons to one side. I scanned the device, looking for fingerprints or telltale grooves or smudges—anything that would tell me which numbers were used. If I only knew the other two numbers, I could try all those combinations until one of them worked. I saw nothing out of the ordinary, except for the fact that a piece of paint had been chipped off the number 5. I leaned closer. In fact, the number 5 looked as if it was the only number ever touched. Hmmm. My inner voice whispered.

I punched in 555.

The door slid open. 555 for the Fearless Five. How . . . predictable. Why hadn't I tried that combination first? It was so obvious. You would think superheroes desperate to keep their identities secret would be a little more creative. It was worse than using your birthday as your bank account PIN.

I gathered up my boxes, blew out a long breath, and stepped into the elevator.

The elevator descended into the underground depths of Sublime and floated to a stop. I punched in 555 again. So far, the code on every one of the doors had been the same. The doors pinged open. I shook my head. Some security system. A child could break in here. What would the Fearless Five do if Malefica and her friends came to call one day?

I stepped into the hallway. "Hello? Is anyone down here? Anyone at all?"

No answer.

I felt sneaky, tiptoeing and creeping around the manor, stealing breakfast for myself, and now breaking into the

supersecret superhero lair. I squared my shoulders. I'd
tried to call Sam, and I'd called out to anyone who might
be lurking nearby. He was the one who hadn't answered.
I'd done nothing wrong. For a change.

I hauled my boxes through the labyrinth of hallways,
past the sick room where I'd woken up yesterday. Someone
had already replaced the glass window I'd broken. Well,
they were certainly efficient. I wondered which one of the
superheroes moonlighted as a glazier. Or perhaps Sam had
a contractor on call to come out and repair anything around
the manor that mysteriously broke. I wondered how he explained all the accidents. I imagined Fiona melted her
share of furniture, doors, and walls. *Oops, it just broke* would
only work so many times before a normal person got suspicious. Perhaps the contractor was paid to look the other
way. Or maybe Chief Newman hypnotized him into forgetting.

I passed more sick rooms, five in all. A long glass window on my right revealed a gym full of treadmills, elliptical
trainers, stationary bikes, and other complicated-looking
equipment. A hot tub bubbled on one side of the room, and
I spied a wooden door that probably led to a pool or sauna.
Interesting. I'd never thought superheroes would have to
work out to stay in shape. Of course, it would be terribly
embarrassing for a superhero to let himself or herself go,
what with all the skin-tight spandex and leather they wore.
After all, there was only so much flesh you could shove into
a size 0 catsuit.

The brotherhood of superheroes and ubervillains probably frowned upon beer bellies, love handles, and stretch
marks. There was probably even a superhero-ubervillain re-
quired attributes job application. Some long-winded form
you had to sign before you could officially join up with the
latest and greatest superhero or ubervillain team. *Only tall,*

svelte women with big breasts and small waists, and muscle-bound men with chiseled biceps and rock-hard abs need apply.

I sucked in my own squishy stomach. Good thing I wasn't a superhero. I'd definitely flunk that portion of the standard requirements. Sam wouldn't, though. I thought back to that night in my apartment and the feel of his sculpted stomach under my searching fingers. Rock-hard didn't do them justice. His abs were probably carved out of slick, sleek marble. Other things had also been rock-hard . . .

After a minute, I realized I was smiling and staring at nothing. I pushed away my lustful memories and walked on. Farther down the hallway was an even bigger version of the game room I'd seen upstairs. Clusters of chairs and couches crouched around entertainment centers filled with TV sets and stereo systems. A couple of pool balls sat on a table next to some abandoned cues. Someone's game had been interrupted. A foosball table jutted out from one wall, along with a variety of pinball machines. I spotted shelves upon shelves full of CDs, DVDs, books, and even some board games. What did superheroes play to get themselves pumped up for battle? Carly Simon always worked for me. What did they listen to after they returned home? Jimmy Buffett was my choice for that.

Next, I passed the kitchen I'd explored during my escape attempt. It, too, was even larger than the one upstairs. Two refrigerators bore the name *Fiera.* The fiery superhero could eat two whole refrigerators' worth of food by herself? I wondered if that was on a daily or weekly basis. Fascinating . . . and a little disgusting. What would the fanboys say if they learned that detail? It probably wouldn't distract them from admiring Fiera's other ample assets.

I continued on, past five doors with the names *Striker, Mr. Sage, Fiera, Tornado,* and *Hermit* embossed on them.

Everyone had his or her own personal suite underground, just like Sam had said. How cozy. I paused in front of the door marked *Tornado*. My inner voice whispered, and I reached for the doorknob. No. I wouldn't look in there. I dropped my hand. I had no right to snoop through the things of a dead man. No right at all. Especially this dead man. One I had driven to commit suicide.

I walked on, shadowed by my guilt and sadness. Finally, I reached a set of double doors. There was no window cut into the wall, so I couldn't peek inside. Curious, I pushed one of the doors open and found myself in the biggest private library I'd ever seen. It almost rivaled the Bigtime Public Library for space and grandeur. Books and magazines and encyclopedias fought for space on the floor-to-ceiling shelves. A large film screen hung halfway down one wall, while a massive table dominated the middle of the plush room. The hardwood floor gleamed underfoot in the places where it wasn't covered by thick, colorful Persian rugs. It was the closest thing to a control room or Superhero Central that I had seen. Surely, somebody would come in here sometime soon to check up on something. Either way, I was tired of lugging my heavy boxes down the never-ending hallways, so I sat them down on a small table in the far corner. I roamed through the room, peering into the bookshelves, pulling down maps, spinning the glossy globes round and round.

Finally, I moved over to the table, which boasted five chairs. Computers and wires and high-tech gadgets surrounded one chair. I smiled. Henry's seat. A series of burn marks and scorches marked Fiona's place. Two other chairs revealed nothing about their occupants. A layer of dust covered the fifth and final chair, as if it hadn't been used in a while. I knew whose chair that used to be. A hard lump of guilt formed in my throat. I stared at the enormous *F5* insignia carved into the heavy wood and traced my fingers over it. My vision blurred for a moment, then cleared. I shivered, suddenly cold.

The door banged open. I yelped and turned to face it. Fiona stood in the threshold, her mouth open in surprise. Surprise that melted into anger. "What the hell are you doing in here?" Fiona's blond hair burst into flames.

Uh-oh.

★ 17 ★

Of the four superheroes I could have run into while snooping, Fiona aka Fiera Fine was last on my list. Sparks shot out of her clenched fists, fists that looked like they wanted to pummel me into oblivion.

"Um, well, I was just—"

"How did you get past the security doors? And the codes?" Fiona's eyes narrowed. They glowed with a red-hot intensity.

"Well, you see—"

"Are you spying on us?" Flames licked at her fingertips. "Secretly working for Malefica?"

"Of course not!"

My eyes darted around, looking for some means of escape. I took another step back and bumped into the table. I scooted around it, putting it between myself and the fiery superhero. Not that it would do any good, since it was made of solid wood.

Fiona stepped forward. "I'll get to the truth—one way or another."

"Carmen! There you are!" Henry said, entering the library. "I've been looking everywhere for you."

I had never been so grateful to see him and his polka-dot bow tie.

"I found her roaming around in here like she owned the place." Fiona crossed her arms over her chest. Smoke rose from her body. "Evidently, she managed to get past the security doors and codes upstairs."

Henry blinked. "You did? How?"

I shrugged. "I figured it out. You know, 555 isn't the safest thing to use."

"I've been telling Sam that for years," Henry replied. "But no. The code has sentimental value, he says. It's the only thing we can all remember, he says—"

Fiona shot him a heated look.

"So, er, what are you doing in here?" Henry asked, changing the subject.

I pointed to my boxes. "I brought my things down. I was going to start working on Malefica's identity. I thought you guys might have some high-powered gizmos or information that might help me."

"So you thought you'd sneak down here and snoop around while no one was watching?" Fiona said, her eyes suspicious slits in her face.

I put my hands on my hips. "I tried using the intercom. Nobody answered. I called out. Nobody answered. I ate breakfast, and nobody showed up. I did everything but dial 911 to try to get somebody to answer me."

Fiona glared at me. I returned her hot stare, even though sweat dripped down the back of my neck. I wasn't going to give the other woman the satisfaction of looking away first. Not unless my eyeballs started to melt.

Henry looked back and forth between the two of us. "We might have some things that you can use, Carmen. I'm not sure exactly how you go about doing what, er, you do."

"It's really pretty simple."

"Well, you two have fun," Fiona said. "Some of us have to go to work today."

She flounced out of the room and slammed the door shut behind her. The wood shuddered but remained in its frame. I winced at the big bang.

"I bet you guys go through a lot of doors around here."

"You have no idea," Henry replied. "Don't mind Fiona. She's just had a rough time of it since—"

"Since Tornado committed suicide." I finished his sentence.

"They were engaged. They were really crazy about each other. She took his death a bit harder than the rest of us."

No wonder Fiona hated me. Even though I didn't think it was humanly possible, I felt even guiltier than before. Driving somebody's fiancé to commit suicide was definitely not good for one's karma. My own turned a little darker. Soon, it would be as black as Malefica's surely was.

"So, where are Sam and Mr. Sage? I mean Striker and Chief Newman?" I shook my head. "What do I even call you guys? Henry or Hermit? I'm not familiar with superhero etiquette." I'd never had to worry about such niceties before. No superhero in his or her right mind had ever wanted to talk to me.

"Generally, when we're out on a mission or when we have our uniforms on, we call each other by our superhero names. The rest of the time, we use our real names."

"Okay, got it. So where are the others?"

"The chief is at work. He said he'd try to drop by after his shift. Sam had some big business deal to tend to. He'll be holed up in his office upstairs the rest of the day."

"Oh." A wave of disappointment washed over me. I'd been looking forward to seeing him, to just being near him. I bit my lip. His absence was for the best, though. Hadn't I made a solemn vow last night to keep my distance from Sam Sloane? Here I was longing for his presence, for a mere glimpse of him. Geez. I was a mess.

"Well, we should get started. I have some files to go through. I'm trying to track down the Triad through their Internet accounts." Henry booted up one computer after another. "So far, I'm not having much luck."

I walked to the table where I'd put my boxes. I tugged the top off one and pulled out a stack of papers.

"You could work over here at the table with me," Henry suggested. "There's plenty of room."

I stared at the empty, dust-covered chair. My stomach twisted. "No, I'm fine where I am."

A few minutes later, I was ready to throttle Sam and Chief Newman. They had made a complete mess of my carefully compiled and filed papers. Evidently, the two men had just shoved everything into the boxes without trying to keep it organized. As a result, all the papers were mixed together and out of place. I finally just dumped the contents of the two boxes on the floor, sat down in the middle of the snowy pile, and began sorting through it all. Again. Henry's staccato, gunshot-loud typing accompanied my work.

After about an hour, silence intruded on my thoughts. No more *rat-a-tats* sounded. Henry had quit typing. I looked up. He stared blankly at the screen. His fingers rested on top of the keyboard. He seemed totally absorbed in whatever he was looking at.

Curious, I walked across the room and peeked over Henry's shoulder. Rows and rows of numbers and letters flashed on the screen. In an instant, they were gone, replaced by even more numbers and letters. A strange, bluish-white glow connected his hands to the keyboard. Even though the light crackled and sparked like electricity, it didn't seem to bother Henry. He didn't move a muscle, not even to blink. I stared at his chest to make sure he was still breathing. How strange. I reached out my hand—

"Don't touch me," Henry said. "Or you'll get the shock of your life."

I froze.

Henry's hands lost their glow. His dark eyes cleared. He blinked several times.

"What were you doing?" I asked.

"Mind-melding with the computer. It's my power."

"Your power? I thought Hermit didn't have a power, that you just—" I bit off my words.

Henry pushed his glasses up his nose. "That I just provided technical support to the group? That I'm just some computer geek who spends his time hiding in a black van while the others go out and fight? A lot of people think that. But I do, in fact, have a power. I can open my mind up to computers and other electronic devices and use them. It's called mind-melding. It's actually a pretty useful skill. The human brain is far more complex than any computer and operates several times faster. I can view hundreds of characters in mere seconds. I also have a photographic memory, which comes in handy when you're sorting through billions of bytes of information."

"I see." I fell silent for a moment. "How did you get it? Your power? Were you born with it? Or did something happen to you to cause it?"

"No." Henry stared at his flickering computer screen. The light made the white dots on his bow tie gleam. "When I was a kid, I spent most of my time in my room, playing fantasy games on my computer, trying to hack into the FBI directory, your usual crazy kids' stuff."

I blinked. I'd done my share of stupid stuff as a kid, but I couldn't ever remember trying to hack into the FBI mainframe. Drink a few wine coolers, sure. Break into a secure government network, not so much.

Henry continued with his story. "I didn't have many friends, except for a few people I'd met online, and those didn't really count. Anyway, one night when I was sixteen, there was this huge electrical storm. The rain was coming down so hard you couldn't see two feet in front of your face. It was one of the worst storms we'd ever had, before or since. It flooded most of the city and knocked out the power for days. Despite all this, I was on my computer in the middle of the storm, since we still had electricity. My mom told me to turn it off, but I wanted to finish this game.

"Lightning hit the power line outside. Thousands and thousands of volts of electricity surged inside the house right into my computer. But it didn't stop there. The body is a wonderful conductor of electricity, you know. The current ran up my fingers and throughout the rest of my body."

"Did it hurt?" I could see it in my head. Henry typing away, when suddenly . . . *BAM!*

"Not really. I blacked out after the first few seconds. When I came to, it was almost like something had snapped open inside my head, like a light had been turned on. I could see things I hadn't been able to before. I could reach out to the computer and make it do anything I wanted."

"How did you get involved with the Fearless Five?"

"Mr. Sage sensed me. He's always on the lookout for spikes in psychic energy. He felt my . . . transformation. At first, I didn't understand what had happened, and I got terrible headaches. Mr. Sage found me. He taught me how to control my power, how to use it to benefit others. Mr. Sage and the rest of the group needed somebody who understood computers and could do what I could. So, I joined the group, and the rest is history."

"Do you ever regret it? Having powers, I mean? Not being . . . ordinary?"

"Sometimes. I like helping people, I really do, but being a superhero is a full-time job. And it's an awesome responsibility. There's always somebody who needs help or wants to rule the world. Sometimes, I wish I could be just like everybody else. Plus, mind-melding can give you one killer headache, particularly if you run into a virus or some nasty security firewall on the Internet." Henry took off his glasses and pinched the bridge of his nose.

His story awed and humbled me. I couldn't imagine being a teenager who suddenly developed this fantastical power. I wouldn't have been able to handle it. Yet Henry had become a good, kind man despite having this power thrust upon him. He truly was amazing.

"Well, from everything I've seen and read, you do a great job, Hermit," I said. "I'm sure everyone is grateful that you do what you do. I know I am."

Henry smiled.

I grinned back. "Now, if you feel up to it, why don't we use that power of yours to track down an ubervillain?"

"I'm always up for that." Henry slid his glasses back on his face. "Let's go get her."

We spent the next two hours going through files and reviewing all the information we'd gathered on Malefica and the rest of the Terrible Triad. The answer to Malefica's real identity was hidden somewhere among my papers. I could feel it. I just didn't know where to look. Yet.

Henry left to go to work at *The Exposé*, but I stayed in

the library. By the time I finished reorganizing my papers, it was close to six. I stretched my arms up over my head. My bones snapped and popped in a pleasant way. My stomach rumbled. Time for dinner. Malefica would have to wait until tomorrow.

I turned off the light and left the library. I walked back down the hallways, rode the elevator up to the wine cellar, and made my way to the kitchen. It was deserted, just like this morning. This time, I didn't hesitate. After all my hard work, I was in the mood for a little comfort—Southern style. I gathered up the necessary ingredients for a bona fide Southern feast. Soon, chicken sizzled in a hot skillet, while biscuits baked in the oven. Peach tea chilled in the refrigerator.

"Something smells good."

I shrieked at the sound of Sam's deep voice. A spatula slipped from my fingers.

"How many times do I have to tell you not to do that?" I clutched a hand over my racing heart.

"It's one of my many talents," he replied.

I glared at him. Or at least I tried to. He leaned against the side of the refrigerator. A navy blue business suit hugged his body to perfection and brought out his brilliant eyes. He looked good. Too good. I turned back to the stove so he wouldn't notice the flush in my cheeks. It was a good thing he couldn't read minds, because mine was once more full of lustful thoughts.

Sam walked over and snitched a piece of chicken from the pan.

"Stop that. It's not ready." I swiped at him, but he easily ducked out of the way. Stupid superhuman reflexes.

"Mmmm. Tastes ready to me. Where did you learn to cook like that?"

I sniffed. "I, sir, am a Southerner. And every Southerner,

no matter the gender, learns at a very young age to make three essential things—fried chicken, buttermilk biscuits, and iced tea. All of which I have prepared tonight and will soon be dining on."

"Care if I join you?"

I looked into his eyes. They were the most unusual color, and varied with his mood, from dark, gunmetal gray when he was angry or upset to light silver when he was calm and relaxed, like now. I realized I was alone with Sam aka Striker Sloane, the one person I should be avoiding at all costs, other than Malefica. I thought back to that night in my apartment and how it had all started in my kitchen.

I dropped my gaze to the crispy chicken. "Um, well, I'm not sure I made enough for two people."

"Don't worry. I don't eat nearly as much as Fiona does."

I laughed. Despite my earlier vow, I wanted to have dinner with Sam. Wanted to know the man behind the mask. So, I did something I shouldn't have.

"I'd love to have some company," I said.

We settled ourselves at the island in the middle of the kitchen. Sam loosened his silk tie, while I filled our plates.

"Mmm-mmm. I think I'm in heaven." Sam rolled his eyes for emphasis and took another bite of his buttered biscuit.

I laughed again. "I wouldn't go that far, but it certainly beats flat champagne and moldy cheese."

"Ah, the gourmet cuisine of the Bigtime society crowd."

For the next half hour, we regaled each other with tales from the society scene. Sam talked about how hard it was to avoid all the money-hungry debutantes and their marriage-minded mothers, while I spun horror stories about the drunken businessmen who hit on me, even though their stone-cold-sober wives stood all of two feet away.

The conversation moved on to other topics. I told Sam about my childhood and what it was like to grow up in the Tennessee hills. He told me about taking his father's small construction business and turning it into a multibillion-dollar empire that included everything from newspapers to computer companies to farming interests. Sam liked football, hockey, and other contact sports. I told him about my fascination with puzzles. We talked about favorite movies and books and music and more. If it hadn't been for the fact that I was in hiding, Sam was pretty much stuck with me, and we'd already had sex, I would have sworn I was having the best first date of my life.

I'd never found someone who was so easy to talk to. Sam and I chatted about everything—except that night in my apartment. That was the one topic I didn't know how to bring up or even what to say. *Was it good for you too? What was that thing you did with your hands that drove me crazy? Want to do it again?* I didn't have the courage to ask Sam any of those questions, especially the last one.

Suddenly, Sam cocked his head to one side. "Nine o'clock already."

"How do you know that?" I didn't see any clocks in the kitchen.

"There's an antique grandfather clock in the main hallway. It chimes the hours."

I could just barely hear the faint murmur. "You must have amazing hearing."

"Supersenses, remember?" Sam stood. "I'd love to stay, but I have to go downstairs. I'm on call tonight."

"You go ahead. I'll clean up." I rose from my stool as well.

"No, you cooked. I'll clean up."

We both reached for the same plate, and our hands collided. A jolt of electricity zipped up my arm at his touch. I stared into Sam's eyes. They really were the most brilliant eyes I'd ever seen. Eyes that could look right into your soul. I wondered what he saw in mine. Wondered if he could see how attracted I was to him. Wondered if he could see how much I desired him.

"Carmen, what's happening between us?" Sam asked, his silver eyes burning into mine.

I tugged the plate out of his hand, turned away, and dumped it in the sink. "I don't know what you're talking about." I made my voice light and cheery, even though I trembled inside.

"I'm talking about the night in your apartment. The night we made love."

"Oh. That." I closed my eyes to try to block out the memory. But I couldn't.

"Oh, that? Is that all you have to say?"

I faced him. Sam's eyes were dark and guarded, his body tense like a coiled spring.

"Honestly, I don't know what to say, other than it happened, and we can't change it."

"I don't want to change it."

"Then what do you want?" My heart smashed against my ribs with every breath like waves continuously crashing on a sandy beach. The wrong word, the wrong look from Sam, and my heart would break once more.

"I want to know how it happened. Why. If you enjoyed it. How you felt . . . afterwards. If you thought about me." Sam ran his hand through his thick, dark hair. "I don't know about you, but I don't do that sort of thing."

"What sort of thing?"

"Sleep with people I barely know."

"Never?"

Sam shook his head. "Never. I don't sleep around, especially not with the women I save. I'm not that kind of superhero."

"Why not? I'm sure you get lots of offers." He had to, given how scrumptious he looked in his tight, leather suit.

"It's not fair. They don't owe me anything, especially not their bodies. I save people because I want to, not because I expect some reward."

"And what about your personal life? When you're Sam Sloane?" All the tall, beautiful supermodels I'd seen him squiring around Bigtime danced through my head.

He sighed. "Not then either. I have a hard time trusting women, letting them get close to me, what with the secret identity and all."

"So why did you sleep with me? I would think after what happened with Tornado you would hate me. That you would want nothing to do with me. Ever." The words popped out before I could stop them.

"After Travis died, I did blame you, Carmen. I did hate you."

Sam's words pierced my heart. I closed my eyes.

"But I came to realize that Travis's death wasn't your fault."

"Of course it was," I snapped. "How could it not be?"

Sam shook his head. "You might have exposed him, but he's the one who decided to take his own life. Travis made that decision, not you, Carmen."

"But I drove him to it," I whispered. My stomach turned over.

"No. I don't think that and neither should you. Being exposed is a fear every superhero lives with. It's one of the job hazards. Travis knew that, he accepted the risk. We could have gotten through it, if only he'd given us a chance to."

Sam's words did little to comfort me. He might not

blame me for Travis's death, but I knew the truth—it was my fault. It would always be my fault.

I'd learned the answer to one of my burning questions. I had to know the other one. "But why sleep with me?"

He stared at me as if the answer was obvious. "You're a desirable woman, Carmen."

I snorted. "Oh get real."

"Excuse me?"

"Sam, you're an incredibly handsome man. You look better in a business suit than any guy I've ever seen. Not to mention the fact you're smart, charming, and incredibly rich. You're every woman's fantasy. And when you put your superhero suit on, well, let's just say it doesn't hurt matters." I gestured at my ratty jeans and T-shirt. "I, on the other hand, am not the stuff men's dreams are made of."

Sam titled my chin up until my eyes met his. "You're a beautiful, strong, intelligent woman, Carmen Cole. A man would have to be a fool not to want you."

The sincerity in his eyes startled me. Could billionaire Sam Sloane really be attracted to me? Could he want me like I wanted him? Could our time together actually have meant something to him?

The image of Matt and Karen doing the deed flashed through my head. "Tell that to my ex-fiancé."

"He was an enormous idiot to let you get away." Sam grinned. "Besides, have you seen Crusher lately? She's almost as ripped as Scorpion. That can be a little intimidating, even for a superhero."

His catty comment brought a smile to my face. I stood on my tiptoes and kissed his cheek. "Thanks for that. And for lying."

Sam stared at me. Then, he backed me up against the sink and put his hands on either side. I caught a whiff of his musky, manly scent. His silver eyes locked with mine.

"What—what are you doing?" I asked, breathless.

"Proving to you I'm not lying."

Sam lowered his lips to mine. For a moment, I couldn't think. Couldn't breathe. Couldn't believe this was happening again. I'd never thought it would. Never thought I would be this lucky.

Sam nibbled at my lips. I opened my mouth, and he slipped his tongue inside. Desire exploded deep within me. Every part of my body hummed and throbbed at Sam's firm touch. At the feel of his lips on mine.

"I can't think straight whenever I'm near you. All I want to do is touch you, Carmen. Taste you. All of you," Sam whispered. He pressed hot kisses against my throat.

I buried my hands in his thick, silky hair and pulled him closer. I wanted him to touch me. All of me.

Sam picked me up and set me on the edge of the sink. His hands trailed up my leg to the junction of my thighs, stroking my wet heat. I hissed. The touch scorched me, even through the thick denim of my blue jeans. I ran my hands up and down his back, marveling at his taut muscles. Why did the man always have to have a shirt on? He'd look so much better without one. He'd feel so much better without one.

We kissed again, long and hard and deep. Sam's hands ran up my body and dipped under the bottom of my T-shirt. His hands cupped my swelled breasts, while his fingers traced over my hard nipples. Waves of pleasure cascaded through me. Thank heavens I'd decided not to wear a bra today.

Sam pushed my shirt up, and I shivered as the cool air hit my flushed skin. I wrapped my legs around his waist and leaned back, knowing what he wanted. It was the same thing I did. Sam dipped his head to my stomach. He kissed his way up my chest and took my exposed nipple in his mouth. He ran his tongue round and round and round until I felt dizzy from the pleasure of it.

I moaned, on fire, burning alive from the inside out. There was only one thing that could quench the heat in me, the raging need. Sam.

Suddenly, Sam froze, his tongue hot and wet on my breast. A second later, someone called out.

"Sam? Are you up here?" Fiona's lilting voice echoed through the manor.

My eyes widened. Fiona was the very last person I wanted to find out about Sam and me. She'd fry me alive.

"She's coming this way," Sam said.

I dropped my arms from Sam's neck and pushed him away. I pulled my T-shirt down, darted around him, ran to the island, and lunged onto my stool.

"Carmen, wait—" Sam put his hand on my arm.

Sweat popped out on the nape of my neck. My temperature shot up at least five degrees.

"Well, isn't this a cozy little scene?" Fiona Fine called out from the doorway.

I froze. And tried not to think about what had just happened between us. It was a good thing Fiona wasn't a psychic like her father.

"Mind if I join you?" she asked.

Fiona pulled out a third stool at the head of the island and wormed her way in between Sam and me. She sat down and flipped her long, blond hair over her shoulder. Every strand landed perfectly back into place. I eyed Fiona's outfit. The fashion designer had on a neon pink dress dotted with black-and-white spots. She looked like a cross between a flamingo and a Dalmatian. Somehow though, Fiona still looked fabulous. I stared down at my T-shirt that read

ADDICTED TO SHOPPING, CHOCOLATE, AND MEN. NOT NEC-
ESSARILY IN THAT ORDER. Truer words had never been
printed. I was addicted all right. To Sam Sloane.

"We were just finishing up dinner," Sam explained. His
voice was cool and calm, even though we'd been engaged
in some hot 'n' heavy action a minute before. How had he
regained his composure so quickly? My heart was still beating so fast I thought it might explode.

"Really? I'm famished." Fiona reached for a piece of
chicken.

"Actually, Carmen cooked tonight. You should try her
fried chicken. It's excellent."

Fiona's hand hovered over the plate. I watched as the
other woman debated with herself, weighing her burning
hunger against her intense dislike of me. Fiona dropped
her hand.

"Actually, I had chicken for lunch. And fried chicken
isn't terribly good for one's figure. Too much fat, too many
calories."

"I thought you weren't concerned about calories, what
with your fiery metabolism and all," I said in a snide tone.

Sam coughed, although it sounded more like a laugh.
Fiona glared at both of us.

"Your loss," I continued on in a cheerful voice, trying to
take my mind off my latest encounter with Sam. "I make
excellent fried chicken. The best there is, or so I've been
told."

Fiona gave me a sour look.

"So how was your day, Fiona?" Sam asked, changing the
subject.

"The usual. Made some sketches for the new collection.
Screamed at my suppliers. Sewed my fingers off. By the way,
Sam, I have some more models I'd love to introduce you to.
Really *beautiful* women." Fiona shot me a pointed look.

I gripped the counter so hard my knuckles turned white. "So that's where Sam gets all his dates from. I didn't know you ran an escort service, Fiona."

I was being bitchy, but I didn't care. Images of beautiful, buxom, blond models drooling all over Sam floated through my mind. I felt fat and inadequate and depressed. My ego deflated like a popped balloon. Who was I kidding thinking someone like Sam could be interested in me? I hadn't even been able to keep my ex-fiancé away from my ex–best friend. How could I hang on to superrich, supercool, supersexy Sam for any length of time? Sure, we had great chemistry, but it took a lot more than that to make a relationship work.

"I take the models out as favors to Fiona, that's all." Sam responded almost as if he knew my dark, depressing thoughts. "Being seen with me helps them get other jobs. It ups their credibility or something like that. I'm not sure how it works."

"What it means is that the model is attractive to wealthy men. Wealthy men have wealthy wives or well-off ex-wives. Those wives want to look good for their husbands or potential husbands. They see a wealthy man with a model, and they want to look like her. Specifically, they want to wear what she's wearing in hopes of pleasing their men. So I let Sam take out my models, wearing my latest designs. The models get some exposure, Sam has some fun, and my business goes through the roof. Everybody wins."

Fiona's logic made sense in a weird sort of way. I hadn't thought she had anything more than a pretty face and hot disposition going for her. Maybe there actually was a brain beneath that golden hair. Still, I didn't like the *Sam having fun* part. Not one bit.

Fiona tore into a biscuit and slathered it with butter.

"Speaking of well-off ex-wives, I did have a problem today with Joanne James."

Sam raised an eyebrow. "Oh really? And how is Joanne?"

Although Joanne James was one of Bigtime's wealthiest women, she was also a notorious miser. The divorcee never met a penny she couldn't pinch a few more cents out of. I'd come to dread any society event she was involved in. Joanne James's champagne was not only flat, but watered down as well. Her cheapskate tendencies were another reason I'd always thought she might be an ubervillain. Evil types didn't like to part with their money, not a nickel of it, unless they absolutely had to.

"She tried to tell me that I had charged her too much for the couture gown I designed for her. I had a written contract right in front of her with the exact price and her signature on it, and she still insisted I was overcharging her. I wanted to scorch her with my eyeballs. I almost set her dress on fire with her in it. Who does she think she is? I'm Fiera, for crying out loud. Protector of the innocent. Defender of democracy. I don't cheat people."

Fiona's hair hissed and sizzled. I scooted away from the sudden flare-up. Maybe I should cut down on the bitchy remarks. Making Fiona, er, Fiera mad could be hazardous to my health.

Fiona raged on for another ten minutes about Joanne James and her cheapskate tendencies. I made mental notes. The hot-tempered fashion designer had quite a way with words. She spat out several four-letters ones I'd never heard before.

While Sam tried to calm Fiona down, I gathered up the rest of the dirty dishes, dumped them in one of the stainless steel sinks, and rinsed them off. A chill swept over me, and my vision blurred. The room spun around, and I put my hands on the countertop to keep myself from falling.

"Are you okay?" Sam asked, putting a hand on my back. The warmth drove away the cold and ignited a fire of a different sort deep inside me. What was it about him that affected me so?

I shook my head. The world returned to normal, but I felt tired. My head throbbed. "I'm fine. It's just been a long day. I'm going to take a shower and go to bed. Good night."

I left the kitchen, trying hard not to collapse. I didn't want to get dragged back down to the sick bay. Sam started to follow me, but Fiona called out to him. Sam hesitated.

"I'll be fine." I waved him away. I needed some time to myself right now. Time to think.

"Call me if you need anything. Anything at all."

Our eyes locked. I shivered at the heat in his gaze. I needed something, all right. Him. That was the problem.

Sam headed back into the kitchen. I crept through the manor with one hand on the wall. After about five agonizing minutes, I reached my room, shut the door, and collapsed on the bed.

I stared up at the ceiling, and my thoughts turned to Sam. I closed my eyes, remembering every detail of the evening. His quick wit, his smile, his laugh, his voice. The way he kissed me. The way he touched me. The way he melted my defenses. If Fiona hadn't walked in, we would have made love in the kitchen.

Damn.

I sighed. It was for the best, though. I didn't need to get any more involved with Sam Sloane. We could never have a future together. There was too much bad karma between us.

My inner voice chided me. I was already in too deep. I'd learned so much about the billionaire-turned-superhero tonight, and I wanted to know even more. What his hopes and dreams were, how and why he'd become a superhero, whether he thought about me as much as I did about him.

Sam.

His brilliant silver eyes were the last thing I thought of before my strange symptoms overcame me.

★18★

For the next two days, I worked feverishly on Malefica's identity, stopping only to eat and collapse into bed at night. There were no more intimate moments with Sam. No more long talks. No more make-out sessions in the kitchen. I kept my distance from him, and he did the same. I didn't know whether to be hurt or relieved the superhero didn't press the issue. It was for the best, but I still wanted him desperately. Dreamed about him even.

After dinner, the others put on their superhero suits and went out to apprehend the criminals that prowled the streets of Bigtime. There were no run-ins with the Triad, but it was only a matter of time. Malefica, Frost, and Scorpion were out there somewhere, plotting their next move. They were up to something. My inner voice constantly grumbled about it. I just didn't know what it could possibly be.

While the Fearless Five made the streets safe, I was left alone to pace through the halls of Sublime. I never went with the Fearless Five on any of their forays into the real world. They kept that part of themselves separate from me, and I respected their privacy.

But that didn't keep me from watching them on TV. Every night I went down to the underground library and tuned the monitors to SNN, the Superhero News Network. The round-the-clock TV station was dedicated to, you guessed it, all things superhero. From in-depth profiles to the latest action-figure and video-game releases, the station covered everything that had anything to do with superheroes. But the station got its biggest ratings from its live coverage. At least once a day, the anchor went out to some reporter on the scene of an ongoing superhero-ubervillain battle. Or one of the reporters interviewed Swifte or some other hero about his latest, greatest rescue of a grandma wandering out into traffic or a kitten from a towering tree. Sometimes, they even read the latest diatribes and demands from ubervillains like Mad Maria or Noxious or Captain Sushi.

I sat down, put my feet up on my table, and flipped on SNN. When I'd first come to Bigtime, I hadn't watched SNN. I hadn't wanted the station's stories to influence my own reporting or color my investigations into the Fearless Five. I hadn't wanted to hear something on SNN and spend weeks investigating it only to discover that some newbie had gotten her facts wrong.

But now, I watched the channel every night. It was the only way I could keep track of the Fearless Five on their missions. The only way I had of knowing whether or not Sam was coming back safe and sound. That had suddenly become very important to me.

I sat through a program about how the Invisible Ingénues were, well, invisible to men and had a hard time finding dates. Suddenly, the anchor touched his earpiece. His words grew sharp and clipped.

"We interrupt our regularly scheduled programming to

take you out live to the streets of Bigtime." The anchor turned to two chairs that looked empty. "Sorry, girls."

"Don't worry. We're used to it." A soft, feminine voice floated through the monitor.

"We now take you to our woman on the street, Kelly Caleb. Kelly, what's the situation?"

The camera cut to a young, thin, pretty blond woman with a wide smile and unnaturally white teeth. "Well, James, it seems that Bigtime's favorite superheroes, the Fearless Five, have cornered a gang of armed robbers in an alley across the street. The superheroes picked up the robbers' trail after they tripped the silent alarm at Jewel's Jewel Emporium in downtown Bigtime. Let's see how the Five are faring."

The camera zoomed over to the alley, and I perched on the edge of my seat. I had an urge for popcorn.

A body flew out of the dark hole and landed with an audible crack on the sidewalk. The robber, who was wearing black clothes and a tattered ski mask, let out a low groan. Five more bodies followed in quick succession.

Striker strode out of the shadows, followed by Fiera and Mr. Sage. My mouth went dry. Good grief, the man knew how to wear leather well. Especially on TV. I wasn't the only one who thought so. The camera panned across the street, where a large group of twenty- and thirty-something women stood behind a police barricade.

"Striker! Striker! He's our man! If he can't spank us, no one can!" the women cheered in unison.

They shook their booties and waved and clapped. A couple of them even sported cheerleader uniforms and sparkling silver pom-poms. Tramps.

Kelly Caleb trotted over to the superheroes as fast as her stilettos would let her. She ignored Fiera and Mr. Sage and stuck her microphone in Striker's face.

"Striker, Kelly Caleb with SNN. What's the situation?"

Striker seemed baffled by her obvious question. He gestured at the moaning, groaning robbers. A couple of cops came over and started slapping handcuffs on them. "The robbers have been apprehended, as you can see. The police are taking them into custody."

Kelly opened her mouth to ask him something else, when a woman shoved past her.

"Striker! I love you! Be mine!"

The woman, one of the pom-pom carriers, wrapped something that looked like a bra around Striker's neck, pulled his head down, and kissed him on the mouth.

I gasped. The brazen hussy!

The kiss went on . . . and on . . . and on . . . I threw my Rubik's Cube at one of the monitors. It bounced off and dropped to the floor.

"Get your hands off him, you slut!" I shouted.

Fiera came to Striker's rescue and yanked the woman back. "That's enough of that," she snapped. "Have a little respect for yourself, lady."

For once, I was grateful to the hotheaded superhero. Any other time, I would have thought Striker looked like a clown with a white bra draped over his black suit. But I wasn't in a humorous mood now.

"Time to go," Mr. Sage said. "Kelly, thank you for your interest and stellar reporting, as usual. Until next time."

Mr. Sage kissed her hand. Kelly blushed and stuttered something incoherent. Smooth. Very smooth. Mr. Sage was another hero who knew how to work the media.

The Fearless Five jogged away. The women screamed for Striker to stop. Bras, panties, and other articles of clothing sailed after the sexy superhero. My hands curled into fists. A large black van skidded to a halt at the end of the street. The door slid back, and the superheroes dived inside. The van sped away, trailed by sex-starved women shouting phone numbers and lewd suggestions.

I snapped off the monitor and glared into space. Striker wasn't their man. He was mine. I sighed. No, he wasn't mine either. No matter how much I wanted him to be.

Another day passed, and I was still no closer to uncovering Malefica's identity. I threw down my pen in disgust. I'd been over and over all the information that I had. Nothing. Nada. Zip. Zilch. Zero. Malefica might as well have not even existed as far as I was getting.

I picked up a Rubik's Cube from my makeshift desk in the library, slid the rows of colors round and round, and muttered obscenities about Malefica's parentage.

"Carmen, that's not very nice," Henry chided, staring at me over the top of his computer monitor.

"Well, Malefica's not a very nice person," I snapped.

I finished the Rubik's Cube, put it down, and scooted over to the far side of my desk, where I had started a jigsaw puzzle. I'd completed the border yesterday. Now, I was trying to fill in the center of the puzzle, a picture of purple pansies. However, the cheery colors did little to ease my frustrations.

After a few minutes, the puzzle pieces blurred. My head started to throb. I groaned and closed my eyes.

"Another headache?"

"Unfortunately." I rubbed my aching temples.

According to Chief Newman, I was still feeling the aftereffects from the dart Frost had shot me with. The chief hadn't been able to identify the exact drug the ubervillain used. I reached for the giant bottle of aspirin perched on my desk, poured out two pills, and swallowed them.

"Maybe you need a break," Henry suggested. "We're

going to do some training this afternoon. Would you like to watch?"

"Training?"

"It's something we do once a month. We go through battle simulations, plot strategies, test our powers, things like that. War games. It's Sam's way of making sure we stay fresh and sharp."

I eyed the piles of papers on my desk. Anything sounded better than sorting through more boring articles detailing Malefica's impeccable sense of style and expensive tastes. Plus, I was more than a little curious to see the Fearless Five in action again.

"Let the games begin," I said.

Henry led me down a hallway I hadn't explored. This one twisted and turned like a snake writhing along the floor. It went deeper and deeper underground until it seemed as though we were in the middle of the earth itself.

We reached a thick metal door, and Henry punched in the 555 code. The door slid open, revealing a long hallway with various rooms branching off it. Sam, Fiona, and Chief Newman stood in the center of the hallway, already in costume.

"There you are, Henry. We've been waiting for you," Mr. Sage said.

I drank in the sight of Striker. His black leather suit hugged every part of his firm body. Our eyes met. The superhero shot me a quick smile, which I shyly returned.

"What's she doing here?" Fiera hissed. Her hair sparked and cracked with fire. "Don't we have any secrets left?"

"She wanted to watch," Henry said.

The tall black man went to a door marked EQUIPMENT and punched in the code. He gestured at me, and I walked inside. The others followed.

My mouth dropped open. Rows and rows of superhero suits hung behind glass doors along one side of the room. The colorful costumes provided a bright, almost gaudy, contrast to the gray, metal walls. Another glass case contained boots and gloves and masks galore, all lined up from largest to smallest and sorted by color. Stacks of swords identical to the two Striker carried glistened from their place on steel racks anchored to another wall. Whips, utility belts, and various other odds and ends sat on stands in the middle of the room just waiting to be grabbed and used. The area contained enough suits and gizmos to equip an entire army of superheroes. I truly was in Superhero Central.

"This is incredible. How much money do you spend on all this stuff?" I whispered.

"Too much. Why do you think I'm such a ruthless businessman? Somebody's got to pay for all of this," Striker quipped. "Being a superhero isn't cheap."

Fiera put her hands on her hips. "My fashion designs accounted for a good portion of our budget last year. Certainly more than Henry and my father's meager contributions."

"Yes, well, some of us aren't independently wealthy," Henry replied. "Ask Carmen. She knows how badly journalists are paid, especially those at *The Exposé*. Morgana Madison has Striker beat in the ruthless category."

"She's something, all right," Striker said in a wry tone.

A vague thought swirled around in my mind. Something connected to karma—

"Can we get started already?" Fiera asked. "I have clients I need to see later."

The thought went down the drain of my brain.

Henry walked to a door marked TRAINING. He entered the code, and it slid open. We trooped inside. The room reminded me of a recording studio. A control panel with thousands of buttons and switches and lights lined one wall. A window situated over the panel overlooked a sunken, metal room the size of a football field. I eyed the scorch marks on the walls and floor below. Interesting.

Striker, Fiera, and Mr. Sage clustered around a locker. Each one grabbed a silver helmet and put it on. The helmets had black visors that covered the superheroes' eyes, along with microphones attached to one side. Henry punched buttons and threw switches on the control panel.

"Everybody turn his or her helmet on," he said.

The visors darkened, and flickering lights reflected down onto the superheroes' faces. The visor seemed to be some sort of interactive screen. Curiouser and curiouser.

"Now the chinstrap," Henry said.

The three superheroes ran the straps underneath their chins and snapped them to the opposite side of the helmet.

"Whenever you're ready, guys," Henry said.

"Enjoy the show." Fiera gave us a mock salute.

The three superheroes opened a metal door and pounded down a flight of stairs to the room below. The door clanged shut behind them.

"Aren't you going downstairs too?" I asked Henry.

"No, I don't need to. This is my job—to stay in the van and provide technical support. Today, I'm running the simulation instead."

Henry waited until the superheroes had made their way to the middle of the gigantic area. Then, he hit more buttons. "We're going to replay the incident in the park when the Triad attacked you. Watch the room."

I peered out of the window and scanned the walls and floor. The big metal room was a big metal room. Not much else to see . . .

Wait a minute. I squinted. Something was coming up out of the metal floor. It looked like . . . grass.

Grass?

I leaned forward until my nose pressed up against the window. I squinted. My eyes weren't playing tricks on me this time. It *was* grass.

A green, velvety carpet sprouted up out of the floor, while the roof took on the appearance of the night sky, complete with a crescent moon and a sprinkling of stars. Trashcans popped up out of nowhere, along with picnic tables. Walking trails zigged and zagged over the grass. In less than a minute, the room went from an empty metal box to a perfect replica of Laurel Park.

"It looks so real," I whispered.

"Doesn't it?" Henry aka Hermit said. His bow tie perked up with pride. "Computer chips and monitors embedded in the walls and floors project the 3-D images. Some other adjustments I've made pump in sounds, smells, wind, everything. The grass even *feels* real."

A woman walked on one of the paths and sat down on a bench near the swing set. I blinked.

"Is that *me*?"

"You bet. I recorded the whole incident. All of our costumes have cameras imbedded in the *F5* insignia, so I was able to record the battle from different perspectives. I took the images of you, digitized them, and inserted a composite into this simulation. We try to make things as authentic as possible."

I didn't know whether to be flattered or creeped out that I was starring in a Fearless Five training simulation. I stared at the image of myself. One thing was for sure—I needed to do something different with my hair. It looked like a rat's nest of auburn tangles.

A series of beeps caught my attention. "What's that?"

Hermit pointed to five monitors, three of which had rows of pulsing lines. "There are a variety of sensors embedded in the chinstraps that tell me everybody's heart rate, blood pressure, other vitals signs, and the intensity of any pain they feel."

"Pain?"

"Not only do things look and feel real, so do any injuries that occur, even though it's just a mixture of holograms and computer images. Nobody actually gets hurt. Sort of like a Jedi mind trick."

"That's incredible," I said. "Did you think of all this by yourself?"

Hermit shrugged in a modest sort of way. "Most of it. Striker came up with some of the concepts and told me what he wanted. I designed all of the electronics. Mr. Sage helped with some of the illusions and sensations."

"Speaking of Striker, where did he and the others go?"

The superheroes had disappeared.

"They've gone to wait in the spots where they started the attack from."

I watched myself sit on the bench. Moments later, an image of Scorpion appeared, followed by ones of Frost and Malefica. It was a bit disconcerting and disorienting to see myself clutching a bomb trigger and threatening ubervillains with annihilation. What the hell had I been thinking? I felt as though I'd stepped outside my body. In a way, I had.

Striker launched himself out from behind a tree. He crashed into the image of Scorpion, and the two of them fell to the ground. Fiera lit up another tree, and the battle was on. Things progressed just as they had in real life, with the Fearless Five defeating the Terrible Triad.

I frowned. Something wasn't right. It almost looked as if the Triad had retreated on purpose, instead of being beaten back. Something about the smile on Malefica's face bothered me. The ubervillain was cocky, but her ear-to-ear grin seemed out of place when she was under attack from three of the world's greatest superheroes. Something was wrong with the whole scenario. My inner voice murmured.

The battle ended. I watched myself pass out. Striker picked up my body. Too bad I wasn't really in the room. I wouldn't have minded being close to the superhero again, even if I was drugged and unconscious.

"That was the first run. We always do the first one just the way events transpired in real life," Hermit explained. "Now, we'll do other configurations and methods of attack and see how things might have played out differently.

"Okay, guys. Mix it up this time." Hermit spoke into one of the microphones that jutted up from the control panel. His voice echoed in the enormous metal room.

The scene reset itself. Once again, I watched myself walk through the park, sit down on the bench, and threaten Malefica with my bomb. The Fearless Five appeared, and the fight commenced.

Fiera threw a fireball at Malefica, who used her telekinesis to send it flying through the air. The red-hot ball of energy smacked into the window in front of me. I screamed and threw my hands up, expecting to be burned alive.

"Don't worry," Hermit said. "The glass is bulletproof, shatterproof, and Fiera-proof."

I lowered my hands. My face turned tomato red. Of course the glass was fireproof. It would have to be to withstand Fiera's fury. Despite the computer guru's reassurance, I took a small step back. Just in case.

The rest of the battle didn't go as well as it had before. Malefica knocked out Mr. Sage with a trashcan to the head, Frost hit Fiera with his freezoray gun and gave her frostbite, and Scorpion body-slammed Striker to the ground and raked his poisoned talons across the superhero's face. Even though it wasn't real, I had to stop myself from screaming at the sight of Striker being injured.

"Everybody catch their breath, and let's go again," Hermit said.

The superheroes got to their feet. The scene rewound.

They fought battle after battle after battle. Sometimes, the Fearless Five won, but more often than not, the Terrible Triad triumphed. The groups were fairly evenly matched, but the Fearless Five seemed out of sync during the fights. They bumped into each other, made mistakes, and targeted the wrong members of the Triad with their powers. Striker against Scorpion was a fair matchup, as was Fiera against Frost. Regeneration versus poison, fire versus ice. Their powers balanced out. But Mr. Sage versus Scorpion ended in disaster every time, as did Fiera against Malefica. In short, the Fearless Five needed another superhero, someone to round out their attacks and powers.

A wave of guilt swallowed me. They used to have someone else, someone to watch their backs and turn the tide in their favor. The Fearless Five used to have Tornado.

Hermit ran a final simulation, which the Fearless Five won, and the superheroes quit for the day.

"So what did you think?" Striker asked when we were back in the equipment room. He peeled off his mask, grabbed a towel from a nearby locker, and wiped the sweat from his face.

All I could do was just stare at Sam. The man was gorgeous, even when covered in shimmering sweat. My eyes traced over his costume. I wanted to strip the smooth fabric away from his body and . . .

"Carmen?" Sam asked.

I pushed away my lustful thoughts and opened my mouth to respond when Fiona cut in.

"We kicked ass like we usually do. We're superheroes, for crying out loud. Enough said," Fiona crowed.

Evidently, Fiona had already forgotten the simulation in which Frost had turned her into a giant, flame-shaped ice sculpture.

"Ah, you must be one of those," I said.

"One of *those*?" Fiona's red-and-orange catsuit glowed. "What do you mean by that?"

Sweat popped out on my forehead. I wanted to kick myself as soon as the words left my mouth. Why did I say things like that out loud where other people could hear them? The others looked at me with questions in their eyes. In for a penny.

"It has been my experience that a great many superheroes and ubervillains think their powers make them special, make them better than everybody else. And that because of this, they have the right to do whatever they want, whenever they want."

Fiona sniffed. "Of course our powers make us special. That's why they call us *superheroes*."

I shook my head. "No, actually they don't. Your powers just make you different, not special. It's a common misconception, particularly among ubervillains. It's where a lot of your *I'm-all-powerful-and-destined-to-rule-the-world* psychotic dreams and schemes come from."

"Really? Can you melt metal with your eyeballs? Make fireballs shoot out of your fingertips? Defeat ubervillains with one hand tied behind your back?"

"No, I can't," I replied in an even tone.

"Then you don't know what you're talking about. You wouldn't last two seconds against Malefica."

Fiona took a seat on a nearby bench and unzipped her

chunky boots. The superhero ignored me like I was a bug crawling on the wall. My temper flared up, and my foot tapped out an angry, staccato rhythm.

"Can you play the piano like Beethoven? Or sing like Carly Simon? Can you take five pages' worth of quotes and turn them into a usable story ten minutes before deadline? I don't think so, unless you have more hidden talents I don't know about. We all have our special skills. They don't make us better or worse than each other. Just different."

"You're just jealous," Fiona snapped. "Most people are."

"No, I'm not. I don't want superpowers. I have enough problems, in case you haven't noticed, which is why I'm here with you."

"Hopefully, not for long," she growled.

I glared at Fiona. My hands curled into fists. She was getting on my last nerve. If the superhero didn't have the ability to reduce me to a pile of ash, I would have punched her. Fiona should be grateful for her superpowers—they were all that was saving her from a knuckle sandwich.

Sensing my dark, violent thoughts, Chief Newman stepped between us. "That's an interesting theory, Carmen. Why don't you meet me in the library? We can discuss it further."

"Fine."

I continued to glare at Fiona. Suddenly, the superhero's face blurred, and a massive headache roared to life inside my skull. My veins quivered and pulsed with every breath. A chill ran down my spine, and I put my hands on my head.

"What's wrong?" Sam asked. His silver eyes darkened with concern.

"Nothing," I muttered. "Just another superhero-induced headache."

★19★

I stumbled back to the library, grabbed my bottle of aspirin, and downed two of them. Only a few more rattled around inside the plastic container. Almost empty. I might as well buy stock in the pills as fast as I was popping them. I plopped down in my chair in the corner, leaned back, closed my eyes, and massaged my aching temples. Frost's mystery drug combined with Fiona's cattiness made for one hell of a headache.

"Feeling better?" Chief Newman asked, entering the library a few minutes later.

"I will once the aspirin kicks in. The headaches never seem to last long. A few more painful minutes, and I should be fine."

"I'm still trying to identify the drug Frost injected you with. I can't quite nail it down. Once I do, I should be able to stop the headaches and the blurry vision."

"I hope so."

"I know Fiona doesn't help matters."

I snorted. "You could say that again. I know she's your daughter and your comrade in arms, and she has every right to be angry with me because of Travis. I try to be nice to her, I really do, but something about her just makes me—"

"Burn with anger?"

I nodded. "It's a cliché, but true."

"But what you said about having powers is right. Sometimes, Fiona forgets that. Sometimes, we all do."

"How did the two of you even—"

"Get our powers?" Chief Newman finished my question.

I nodded.

"We were born with them."

I blinked. I hadn't encountered many natural superheroes or ubervillains during my investigations. Most got their powers as a result of exposure to radioactive waste, animal bites, or magical objects. Not to mention the occasional superintelligent, talking animal with plans of human enslavement and world domination.

"As a child I knew I was different," Chief Newman explained. "I could see things others couldn't, glimpses of the future. I could feel others' emotions, almost see the thoughts that danced through their heads. Sometimes, if I concentrated, I could even move objects with my mind. Eventually, I learned to develop and control my power."

"What about Fiona?" I leaned forward, my headache forgotten.

Chief Newman's blue eyes grew distant with memories. "I met her mother, Finola Fine, when I was in my twenties. Finola was a fiery Irish lass with quite a temper. She didn't have any powers, but she was very understanding of my desire to use mine to help others. A few years later, Fiona was born. I watched her closely, of course, trying to determine if I'd passed my gift on to her. To my surprise, her mother's temper had combined with my powers and created something quite unique."

"Fire-based powers."

Mr. Sage nodded his head.

"But how did you guys even—"

"Become superheroes in the first place?"

I sighed. "I really wish you would quit doing that. It's rather disconcerting. Some of us like to finish our own sentences."

"Sorry. It's a bad habit of mine. Finola died of cancer when Fiona was in high school. That was a dark time for us." A shadow passed over Chief Newman's face. "Fiona knew what I did in my spare time. With her mother gone, she demanded I take her along. Said she wanted to look after me. I said no at first, but Fiona can be quite stubborn, a trait she gets from her mother."

Fiona? Stubborn? I never would have guessed.

"One night, I gave in. Fiona had been making my costumes for years and had already designed one for herself. She even had a superhero name already picked out—Fiera. To my surprise, we worked well together. It was nice to have someone to watch my back after all those years alone. At first, it was just Fiera and me. We would go out and catch criminals or fight other minor ubervillains like the Hunter or the Prankster or Johnny Angel. One night, we ran into Striker. He was after the same thieves we were. Of course, being a billionaire, Striker was much better equipped to be a superhero than we were. He had a leather costume, twin swords, and lots of fancy computer equipment. We were in store-bought masks and the homemade costumes Fiona had sewn."

"Striker helped us apprehend the thieves. Over the next few months, we ran into him again and again. We seemed to be on the same wavelength, so we joined forces. Striker brought Tornado on board, and I found Hermit a few months later. The five of us just gelled. The rest is history."

The scenes flashed through my mind. Mr. Sage and Fiera stalking criminals on the streets, running into Striker, Tornado and Hermit joining the group, the five of them forming one of the greatest superhero teams in the world. A few months ago, I would have taken this knowledge and splashed it all over the front page of *The Exposé*. Now, I felt as though I'd been trusted with a precious secret. I almost felt like one of the gang. Or at least a sidekick. Almost. I certainly had the sidekick habit of needing to be rescued every few minutes down pat.

But the Fearless Five's backstory, no matter how intriguing, still didn't help me figure out how to deal with Fiona. Or help me find a cure for these killer headaches. I rubbed my temples.

"Has Fiona always been so . . . combustible?"

"Oh yes. You should have seen her as a child whenever she didn't get her way. We went through a lot of furniture, tables, lamps, chairs." Chief Newman grinned. "It was a good thing we lived next door to the fire department. Although the firefighters thought Fiona was quite the little arsonist."

I smiled at the chief's joke, but my thoughts turned to a more serious matter. "Can I ask you something?"

The chief looked at me. His blue eyes glowed. "You want to know why Henry and I were still your friends after Travis died."

I nodded. "I don't understand it. The two of you should have hated me, should still hate me for what I did. But you never showed the slightest bit of anger towards me. Not once."

"That's because it wasn't your fault, Carmen."

"Of course it was," I snapped.

"Suicide is a person's choice. You might have exposed Travis, but he was the one who decided to end his life. He made that decision himself. If anyone is to blame, it's me."

"What? Why?"

"I should have sensed Travis's pain, his intentions." Raw pain filled the chief's eyes. Lines of grief etched his face.

The sight only fueled my own guilt. Despite the chief's kind words, I was to blame for Travis's suicide. Nobody else.

Chief Newman let out a long breath. "Unfortunately, Fiona hasn't accepted Travis's decision yet. She still misses him terribly. We all do, and we all loved him, but Fiona more so than any of us."

"So how should I handle her?" I asked. "I don't want to fight with her anymore."

"You could try explaining the reasons you started exposing superheroes. Fiona might be hot-tempered, but she's not unreasonable."

It was worth a shot. What was the worst Fiona could do to me? Fry me like a slab of bacon? Melt my eyeballs out of my head? My veins throbbed and pulsed in my skull. Melted eyeballs didn't sound so bad. They would be much more preferable than the ten-trombone parade marching through my mind.

I popped another aspirin into my mouth. On the bright side, if Fiona reduced me to a pile of ash, I wouldn't have any more headaches.

I didn't get a chance to corner Fiona until that afternoon. The superhero strode through the halls of Sublime, her impossibly high heels pounding on the marble floors. How on earth did she walk in those things?

Fiona entered the wine cellar, and I followed the hollow echo of her footsteps. I hurried over to the secret door and jabbed the keypad. After several long seconds, the elevator arrived. I dashed in and punched the appropriate buttons. It descended. The elevator slowed, and the doors opened. I dashed down the hall, wanting to catch up to Fiona before she got to the library. I didn't want to try to explain myself and my actions in front of everyone. I rounded a corner. Up ahead, Fiona opened a door and went inside. I skidded to a halt in front of Tornado's room.

Uh-oh.

I stood outside. How was I supposed to handle this? I didn't want to disturb Fiona in what was a moment of private, personal grief. I chewed my lip. And yet . . . I had to go into the room. I wanted to explain to Fiona why I'd done the things I'd done. I needed to. We would never be friends, but I wanted her to understand, wanted her forgiveness.

Do it . . .
Do it . . .
Do it . . .

The inner voice whispered in my head, the voice I never doubted.

I reached for the door handle.

When I eased open the heavy door, I found myself in the middle of a suite remarkably similar to mine upstairs. Bedroom, living room, bathroom. Glossy magazines about meteorology leaned on a coffee table next to a half-eaten piece of moldy toast. The bedsheets had been thrown to one side as if someone had just gotten up. A man's clothes lay scattered on the floor, and a thick layer of dust covered everything. The room smelled like old mothballs. I knew nothing had been touched in six months. This was exactly the way Travis Teague had left his room the day he committed suicide. Guilt sparked to life in my stomach. For a moment, I couldn't breathe.

Fiona sat on a low, long sofa in the middle of the living room. She clutched a silver picture frame in her hands. Tears slid down her pink cheeks and evaporated off her flushed face.

"Um, Fiona? Can I talk to you a minute?"

"Get out," Fiona snarled. "I don't want you in here."

I felt physically sick from the hurt and anger in her voice. I took a step back. I should go.

No . . .

Not yet . . .

Must explain . . .

My inner voice whispered, and I squared my shoulders. I walked over to the couch, sat down on the far end, and squinted at the picture in Fiona's hands. Travis Teague beamed at her from beneath the glass.

"He seems like he was a nice man."

Fiona stroked the picture with her fingertips. "He was a nice man, the best man there was, until you came along and ruined everything."

I took a deep breath. "I don't mean to intrude on your grief, but I want to explain to you why I did what I did. I'm not asking for your forgiveness. That's too much to ask. But maybe if I tell you the reasons why, you might be able to at least understand."

"Never. I'll never understand you and your twisted obsession with us. You ruined our lives. And for what? To sell a few more thousand copies of that rag of a newspaper you work for?"

Fiona's eyes burned into me. My temperature shot up about five degrees. Sweat trickled down my neck.

"Not exactly," I replied.

Fiona's hands gripped the picture frame so hard I thought it would crack. A diamond ring glowed like a white-hot star on her left hand. A diamond ring . . . An idea popped into my mind.

"You know, I was engaged at one time," I said in a cautious voice.

"Good for you. What was he, blind? Or just deaf and dumb?"

I bit my tongue. Although I wanted to snap back at Fiona, I would say my piece and go. The rest was up to her.

"No, he wasn't blind or deaf or dumb. His name was Matt. He was a very nice man. Loving, kind, considerate. He always remembered my birthday and never left the toilet seat up. We dated for a long time. The day he proposed to me was one of the happiest days of my life. I thought we would be together forever. Build a house with a white-picket fence, have a couple of kids, get a dog. But things didn't quite turn out that way."

Fiona said nothing, but I could feel the other woman struggling to contain her curiosity. That was the thing about stories. You always wanted to know how they turned out, even if they ended badly. They hooked you like a fish, and you couldn't wriggle away until you'd heard the whole thing.

"So what happened?" Fiona asked. "Where is this Matt character?"

"He's back in Beginnings, my hometown, doing what he used to do."

More silence.

"So why didn't you marry him?"

I smiled. I'd hooked the superhero. "I was going to. It was our wedding day. I was in my dress, and the wedding was less than thirty minutes away. But I was having second thoughts. I felt as though Matt was keeping something from me. Something big. He'd been acting strangely, coming home at odd hours and whatnot."

"What did you do?"

"I went to Matt's room to ask him what was bothering him. I found him rolling around on the bed with Karen, my best friend and maid of honor." The scene flashed through my mind. This time, though, it didn't stir as much anger and hurt as it used to. I could look back on it calmly, rationally, and not turn into a hulking, green monster.

Fiona sniffed. "Must have sucked to have been you."

"That wasn't the worst part."

"There's something worse than catching your fiancé and your best friend together on your wedding day?"

"There's always something worse. In my case, it was the discovery my beloved fiancé was actually the Machinator, the superhero. During all the rolling around, their clothes had come undone and his costume peeked out from under his shirt."

Fiona arched a blond eyebrow. "You were engaged to the Machinator? The guy who can control machines with his mind?"

"Yep. And my best friend was Crusher. You can imagine my shock, not just at finding the two of them together, but also at the fact they were a superhero and ubervillain. They were going at it like bunny rabbits. And do you know what they blamed their transgression on? The reason they told me they *had* to sleep together? Radioactive waste. Can you believe that?"

Fiona gave me a look that was almost pitying. Almost.

"After that, I snapped," I continued. "I took pictures of the two of them in their costumes right there on the bed. They ran in the newspaper the next day. But exposing the two of them wasn't enough for me. It didn't take the hurt away. It didn't ease my pain. So I made a vow to myself, to the whole world. Nobody was going to be fooled like I was ever again. Nobody. I went from town to town, newspaper to newspaper, exposing superheroes and ubervillains. Finally, I wound up in Bigtime. You know the rest."

Fiona stared at the picture in her hands.

"Funny, isn't it?" I let out a bitter laugh. "How one event can affect the lives of so many. But that's karma for you."

"Karma?"

"Destiny. Fate. Kismet. What goes around comes around. Karma."

Fiona didn't reply.

I stood. My time with the superhero was up. I'd said what I needed to. "I wanted you to hear my side of the story, and now you have. You can hate me if you want to. Avoid me, berate me, whatever. I deserve all that and more. No matter what the others say, it's my fault that Travis is dead. If I could take it back, I would. But I can't. That's the really bad thing about karma. You don't get any second chances. At least, not in this lifetime."

★20★

After that, my relationship with Fiona changed. She no longer disparaged or mocked every single thing I did. Just every *other* thing. It was a truce. Of sorts.

Another day passed. I stared at my papers and graphs and flowcharts. I was still no closer to uncovering Malefica's identity. I snatched the paper in front of me, wadded it up into a tight ball, and tossed it at the trashcan. It bounced off the top of the massive pile and landed on the floor. I glared at it, wishing I had Fiona's ability to make it burst into flames.

I'd spent the last three hours poring over a variety of documents relating to the Terrible Triad and had gotten absolutely nowhere. I rolled my neck around to relieve some of the tension and looked at one of the clocks on the walls. Nine-thirty. Quitting time.

I pulled open the door to the library and ambled down the hall. A loud scuffle up ahead caught my attention.

Who could that be? The others were all taking a rare night off so they could catch up on their other lives. Sam was plotting his next business takeover, Henry was at work writing about the latest, greatest computer advancements, Chief Newman was hot on the trail of a group of thieves who'd hit three banks in the last two days, and Fiona was busy coming up with new color combinations that would make a flamingo neon pink with envy. Or just give the poor creature a massive headache.

I reached one of the training rooms. Inside, Striker jousted with invisible enemies. His swords zipped through the air, and he moved with the easy grace of a dancer. My eyes traced over him, especially since he was clothed in his black leather costume. My heart fluttered, and my hormones kicked into high gear. Oh, the things that man did for a leather suit. It was practically criminal.

I hadn't seen much of Sam. We had both been avoiding each other ever since that night in the kitchen when we'd almost made love. It was for the best, but still . . . There was something about him that made me weak in the knees. And it didn't have anything to do with radioactive waste. At least, I didn't think it did.

I knocked on the window, and Striker waved me in. I pushed open the door.

"Hey, I thought you had a business meeting tonight."

"It got moved to next week."

"Oh." I shifted from one foot to the other. "Care if I watch you? I need to unwind before I go to bed."

"Help yourself."

I settled on the padded floor in a corner of the room. Striker resumed his stance. He dodged and darted like a panther on the prowl, and his swords sliced through the air as he cut down enemy after enemy. Suddenly, he turned and threw one of the swords behind him. It landed in the middle of a target. He made a strange motion with his wrist. The sword flew back out of the target and landed in his hand. Striker went through another series of attacks before landing in a low crouch.

I clapped. Striker straightened and bowed to me.

"Very impressive. I think you killed everything in your way."

"Thanks. That's the plan." He wiped the glistening sweat from his forehead.

I glanced at the two swords dangling from his hands. "How do they work? I've always wondered."

"Get up, and I'll show you."

Striker put one of the swords on a nearby rack, then offered his hand to me. I took it, and he pulled me up. My body brushed against his, and his musky scent filled my nose. A warm sensation flooded my veins, and my whole body tingled. I stepped back.

Striker held out a sword, and I took it. Although it was made out of some silver metal, the weapon was surprisingly lightweight. It curved a bit at the end, like a scimitar, and the simple, unadorned pommel fit nicely into my hand. I swung the sword back and forth a few times. It felt as light as a pencil.

Striker reached for the sword, and I gave it back to him. Our fingers touched for a brief moment. A jolt of electricity zinged through me. The air between us hummed and sparked and snapped. Striker cleared his throat and pointed to the pommel. He slid open a small compartment.

"The swords each contain a microchip in the hilt, along with a propulsion motor," he explained. "These microchips are linked to the one in the insignia on my costume." He pointed to the *F5* shape stitched across his leather-bound chest. "I control the swords with nerve impulses. In other words, I move my hand a certain way, and the swords automatically come back to me. It's something Henry and I dreamed up."

"Amazing," I said. "I always thought they were magical or something."

Striker put the sword away and laughed. The warm, husky sound made tingles shoot through my body. "Not quite."

I stared at him, curious to know more about the sexy superhero. "So, how did you get your powers? If you don't mind my asking."

"I don't mind. My father's construction company was erecting a building near the Bigtime Nuclear Power Plant. Travis and I decided to go down to the site one night and goof off, ride our skateboards and bikes around, things like that. We were thirteen." Striker's eyes grew dark and gray with memories.

"My father warned us not to get too close to the edge of the site that bordered the power plant. There were all kinds of pools of radioactive waste and other nasty things there. Of course, we did get too close. I rode my bike down a hill, lost control, and fell into one of the pools. It looked like green sludge, only it glowed. I couldn't swim very well then. The sludge was thick and heavy, and I thought I was going to drown. Travis didn't hesitate. He dove in and pulled me out. We crawled back up the hill."

"I don't remember much after that, just lying there and feeling things happen in my body. I passed out. When I came to, my senses were heightened. Even though it was after midnight, I could see in the dark. I could smell things better, hear better. Everything seemed amped up, magnified. I stumbled around in the dark for a few minutes, trying to get my bearings. I fell and cut my hand. I looked at it, and the skin began to . . . move. The wound

sewed itself shut. Later, I realized I had the ability to regenerate or heal quickly."

"What about Travis?"

"He'd been affected by whatever was in that pool too.
He eventually woke up. When he did, the wind picked up.
It howled around us like a tornado. I was scared to death,
but Travis never moved a muscle. He seemed . . . comforted by the wind somehow."

"You know the rest of the story. He became Tornado, and
I became Striker. Eventually, we hooked up with Fiera and
Mr. Sage. Hermit joined the group later. The Fearless Five
were born. But no more. Now, Tornado's gone. My best
friend is gone. Forever." His voice ended with a whisper.

And it's all my fault. I put a hand on his arm, wanting to
comfort the superhero. "I'm sorry. I'm so, so sorry."

Striker stared into my face. His eyes burned as bright as
two silver stars. I moved closer to him, drawn by his hypnotic gaze.

"Carmen," he whispered.

Striker leaned down and kissed me. A thousand things
sprang to life inside me. Guilt, desire, heat, longing, more
desire. I wrapped my arms around his neck and drew him
closer. Striker growled in response. This felt good—right
somehow. For once, the voice inside my head didn't chatter
at me to stop or keep my distance from the hunky superhero. Maybe I just couldn't hear it over the rapid thump
ing of my heart. Maybe I didn't want to hear it.

The kiss deepened. Our tongues dueled back and forth.
Teasing. Tasting. Tempting. Striker picked me up as though
I weighed nothing and pulled me closer. I wrapped my legs
around his waist, feeling his hard body flex beneath my
own. Striker's hands moved to cup my bottom, and a low
growl escaped his throat.

"I want you, Carmen. Heaven help me, but tonight, I need you."

I pulled back and stared into his eyes. Guilt, desire, longing. All those emotions and more swirled in the silvery depths. The same emotions reflected in my own eyes. The safe thing to do, the sane thing to do, would have been to stop. To walk away. To pretend like this never happened. To pretend like there was nothing between us.

But I'd never been one to play it safe. I didn't care about the past or the future or my own bad karma with men. All that mattered was the two of us and this moment, these feelings between us.

"Then take me to your room," I whispered. "Take me there. Now."

Striker didn't have to be told twice. We were outside the door to his suite before I knew exactly how we'd gotten there. I twisted the knob open. Striker carried me inside and kicked the door shut with his heavy boot. He set me down in front of him, and I moved back into his arms. I drew his head down to mine, delving into the hot, moist depths of his welcoming mouth. Striker's hands roamed up and down my back, kneading, caressing, sculpting. His erection pressed into my thigh, letting me know he wanted me as much as I wanted him. It was nice to be wanted. Very, very nice.

He walked me backward until my legs hit the edge of the bed. Striker leaned over me, and I let gravity do the rest. I sank onto the bed and pulled Striker down on top of me. The weight of his hard body on mine only fueled my desire.

Striker rained hungry kisses down my neck. Cold chills swept through my hot, aching body. I tangled my fingers in his thick, black hair. It felt smoother than satin. Striker moved back up to my mouth, and we exchanged another long, heated kiss that left me panting for breath. We broke apart for a moment. Striker's eyes glowed like white-hot coals, contrasting with the black mask that covered his chiseled face.

I tugged off his mask and threw it aside. "I want Sam Sloane to make love to me tonight. Not Striker."

"You've got us both, Carmen. You've got us both," he whispered before capturing my mouth with his again.

We lay there on the bed kissing for a long time. Slow kisses, deep kisses, lingering kisses.

Sam sat up and pulled me onto his lap. "I want to taste you, Carmen. All of you."

He drew my T-shirt up over my head. I shivered as the cool air hit my bare skin. We kissed once more, and then he reached around my back and undid the clasp on my bra. My breasts spilled into his smooth, waiting hands. I gasped at his firm touch.

"You're so beautiful," Sam whispered.

He leaned down and took my nipple into his hot, wet mouth. I arched my back, letting out little moans of pleasure. His other hand moved down to the clasp of my jeans and farther on into my panties. I rose up on my knees and parted my legs. He plunged his fingers inside me. Sam stroked me, slow at first, drawing lazy circles and figure eights with his nimble fingers. I whimpered. It was so pleasurable it was almost painful. I felt like a champagne cork about to pop from all the built-up pressure. Finally, I did.

"Sam!" I screamed and shuddered my release.

As I lay there, spent and euphoric, Sam continued on with his explorations. The rest of my clothes followed my T-shirt and bra and sailed to the floor. I gave myself over to Sam's masterful touch. Kissing. Licking. Caressing. From head to toe, he explored my body as if I were some unknown continent he'd just discovered and was eager to conquer.

I happily surrendered.

But I burned for him, yearned to touch him the way he was touching me, longed to feel him inside me. My fingers probed and prodded and plucked, but I couldn't quite find a way to get through the thick leather that covered his body.

"Damn superhero suit," I muttered.

Sam laughed. "Let me."

He stood up. Sam grabbed some sort of zipper or toggle and yanked off the top part of the suit, exposing his perfect chest. He shucked off his boots, peeled off his pants, and stood there, naked before me.

I eyed his sculpted chest, his rippling six-pack abs, his long, hard erection. My mouth went as dry as a cotton field in the summertime. The man was beautiful, perfect, gorgeous. A true Adonis come to life. And he wanted *me*. I still couldn't believe it.

Sam came back to bed and reached for me. I pushed him onto his back, avoiding his seeking hands.

"Oh no," I said in a wicked voice. "It's my turn to play."

So I did. Teasing. Tasting. Tempting. Tormenting him just the way he had done to me. I ran my tongue down his chest, following the trail of dark hair that led southward. Sam smelled of musk and tasted of salty sweat. The combination was more intoxicating than any drug I'd ever had. I closed my hand around him, stroking his hard, swollen shaft.

"Carmen!" His fingers twisted the silken sheets beneath us.

"What?" I asked in a taunting tone. "Am I doing something wrong? Maybe you'd like it better if I did something like this." I ran my tongue up and down him.

He moaned in response. I continued my ministrations.

I loved the feel of him, the smell, the taste. He filled up my senses until there was nothing else.

"That's enough of that," he finally growled.

Sam reached over, yanked open the nightstand drawer, and drew out a condom. Superspeed must have been another one of his powers, because he had it on before I could blink or mention that I was on the pill.

Sam grabbed my hands. He pulled me up on top of him, flipped me over, and slid inside me all in one smooth motion. I gasped at the full length of him filling me. I wrapped my legs around his waist, and Sam began to move over me. I met him kiss for kiss, thrust for thrust, moan for moan.

We moved faster, harder together. The bed rocked back and forth in time. We called out each other's names and rode that final wave of passion to its ultimate destination.

Afterward, we lay there in silence, nestled in each other's arms.

"Wow," I said when I got my breath back. "That was certainly something."

"Yes, it was." Sam leaned up on his elbow. His silver eyes glowed in the semidarkness. "I don't know what it is about you, Carmen, but I just can't seem to control myself whenever you're around."

I laughed. "Ditto."

I turned over to stare at him and felt him harden against my thigh. I arched an eyebrow. "No way. You can't be ready to do that again."

Sam grinned. His fingers trailed down my body and slid inside me, making slow and steady circles. "Don't you know endurance is one of my superpowers?"

I shook my head, unable to breathe, unable to concentrate on anything else except the heat roaring through my body.

So Sam showed me exactly what he meant.

Five more fabulous times.

* * *

The next morning, I rolled over and bumped into something warm and hard. My eyes popped open. Sam snuggled next to me, his face calm and smooth in sleep.

For a moment, I just looked at him. His face, his chest, his glorious body. My inner voice sang with happiness. Somehow, in the course of the past few weeks, Sam Sloane had come to mean a great deal to me. Somehow, he'd become my friend and my lover.

And what a lover he was. The sex had been fantastic. Everything I'd ever dreamed of and then some. But there was more to it than that. I cared about Sam. A lot. More than I wanted to admit to myself. More than was wise, given my track record with men, especially superheroes.

I was falling in love with him.

And I didn't know what to do about it.

I thought about the puzzle, trying to make the pieces fit together in some sort of order. But the edges were too rough, too raw, too new. I couldn't make sense out of my feelings.

Since I didn't know the answer to my silent questions, I rolled over and eyed the clock on the nightstand. After ten. I groaned. I hadn't meant to sleep so late. Then again, I hadn't planned on staying up most of the night making love to a superhero either. Funny how things never turned out the way you expected. That was karma for you. I just wondered how I was going to end up paying for my glorious night with Sam. What cruel thing would fate throw my way?

I shoved that thought aside and focused on the present. I leaned over and kissed his cheek. Sam's silver eyes opened. They brightened at the sight of me.

"Hey, sleepyhead."

"Hey there yourself." Sam pushed a lock of hair back

over my shoulder. Heat flared to life inside me at his gentle touch.

I kissed him lightly on the mouth and scooted back. I slipped out of his grasp and moved around the room, picking up and putting on my discarded clothes.

"You know, you could stay here with me." Sam patted the mattress. "There's plenty of room."

I eyed the thin sheet that just barely covered his fantastic body. It took all of my willpower not to shuck my clothes and throw myself on top of him. "As much as I'd love to stay and let you show me some more of your *superpowers*, duty calls. You have to go to work, and I still have an ubervillain to track down." Plus, I needed some space, some time to think about what had happened.

I sat back down on the bed and pulled on my socks and shoes. Sam watched me run my fingers through my auburn hair in an effort to get some of the tangles out of it.

"Carmen, about last night—"

I put my fingers to his lips. "Don't say anything. Last night was wonderful. One of the best nights of my life. Let's just leave it at that, okay?"

After a moment, he nodded. I kissed him once more, got to my feet, and opened the door.

Fiona stood outside, her hand poised in midair as if to knock.

I froze. Uh-oh.

Sam came up behind me, a sheet wrapped around his lean waist. "Carmen, what's the matter—"

Fiona's eyes widened. Her mouth dropped open. Her hair flamed to life. "Are the two of you—are you—are you *sleeping* together?"

I grimaced at the high-pitched screech. My karmic retribution had come around already to bite me on the ass. I should have known better.

"How could you do this, Sam? Are you *insane*?"

"Fiona—"

"No." Her hair sparked and hissed. "Don't you dare try to explain this. She's the one who exposed Tornado, who wanted to expose us all for no other reason than the fact that she wanted to. She killed him, Sam, just as surely as if she'd pushed him out that window. Or did you conveniently forget that when she was screwing your brains out?"

Sam's face paled. Guilt flashed in his eyes.

"I hope she was worth betraying us, Sam."

Fiona stared at me so hard I thought my hair would catch fire. "You bloody bitch," she snarled. "Wasn't it enough for you to find out who we all really are? Wasn't it enough for us to rescue you from Malefica? Wasn't it enough for us to bring you here? When will you be satisfied? When you've completely destroyed us?"

"Fiona—"

"And do you know what the worst part is? I almost felt sorry for you the other day when you told me your sob story about your fiancé and best friend. What a fool I was. You expose Tornado, get us to rescue you and keep you safe, and now you've even seduced Sam. You're nothing but a manipulator. You've done nothing but use us all from day one."

"It's not like that—"

Her balled fists burst into flames. "Don't you ever speak to me again, Carmen Cole. Don't even look at me. You're lucky I don't drop-kick your ass all the way back to Bigtime. We should have let Malefica and Frost have your miserable, worthless, rotten hide. Saving you is a mistake I'll regret to my dying day."

Sam stepped forward and held out his hand. "Fiona, stop. That's enough. Quit attacking Carmen. We're both adults and what happened between us was perfectly mutual—"

"Shut up, Sam. It's obvious what part of your body you're thinking with at the moment. And it's definitely *not* your brain. I don't want to hear your sorry excuses."

Fiona stomped away. The carpet smoldered with every hot step she took. Smoke poured off her body and blackened the walls.

"I'm sorry about that," Sam said in a quiet voice. "She's wrong, you know."

"No," I whispered. "She's right. She's absolutely right. I did it. I exposed Travis because I was angry and hurt, and he killed himself because of it. Because of my need for revenge. Everyone knows it. You're all just too kind to say it to my face."

Sam gripped my shoulders and made me face him. "Carmen, you're not responsible for Travis's death. If anybody is, I am. He was my best friend. I should have known how troubled he was. I should have sensed something, anything. I'm the one who's to blame, not you."

Guilt and pain and grief darkened Sam's silver eyes. The sight burned me more than Fiona's hot words ever could. My heart cracked. I'd caused him so much pain. I'd caused them all so much pain.

I was such a sad cliché. A woman scorned who had to take everyone else down with her. Sam, Striker, had asked me once why I did what I did, why I'd exposed all those superheroes and ubervillains.

Spite. Jealousy. Anger. Revenge.

Those were the real reasons. Not because superheroes lied or ubervillains stole or even because of my own warped view of karma. No, I'd wanted revenge on Matt and Karen, and I'd used everyone else as my scapegoats. A man was dead as a result of my haughty, selfish actions, and his friends were grieving his loss. I'd hurt the wrong people. I'd hurt *Sam*, the one person I would never, ever want to bring harm to.

"Carmen, it's not your fault. It never was," Sam said.

His words only increased my self-loathing. I'd made such a mess of everything. How could he stand to look at me? To touch me? I couldn't bear my own self. Sam might not blame me for Travis's death now, but one day he would. The newness would wear off our relationship, and he'd realize that he was so much better than me. That I didn't deserve him. He'd find someone else. Someone more suitable. Another superrich superhero to share his life with. I couldn't bear that. I couldn't bear being tossed aside for someone else. Not again. Not from *Sam*.

I closed my eyes to try to shut out the image of Sam. But I couldn't. It was seared into my mind. My heart.

"This was a mistake, Sam. A huge mistake."

"Carmen—"

I backed up. "No, don't touch me. I just—I can't. I'm sorry."

I turned and ran down the hall.

⋆ 21 ⋆

I took the elevator and ran back upstairs to my room. But I couldn't outrun the pain in Sam's eyes. The pain I'd caused.

Tears trickled down my flushed face. I sank onto the bed and buried my head in my hands. What had happened to my steely resolve, my complete determination to stay away from Sam Sloane? Some determination. With one kiss, it melted faster than a bag of chocolate in Fiona's hot hands.

A long sigh escaped my lips. I'd just slept with a man who had been mourning his best friend. And the dead man's fiancée had caught us not quite in the act. Guilt rose up in me like a tidal wave. No good could come of this. My karma darkened, blackened with every second.

But I was halfway in love with Sam aka Striker Sloane. I loved his dry wit, his sense of duty, his kindness toward others. And oh, the way he kissed me. I got all tingly inside just thinking about it.

My guilt, my shame warred with my feelings for Sam. I couldn't leave Sublime, not without risking another run-in with Malefica. Despite everything, I didn't want to die or be turned into a monster. Deep down, I was a coward.

I paced the length of my suite, trying to figure out some solution to my latest catastrophe, some way to right all the wrongs. I decided to avoid the others like the plague. Especially Sam. It was the only thing I could do. If Sam walked past me, I would stare at the floor until he passed. If he spoke to me, I would not reply. There would be no more longing glances. No more heated kisses. No more nights of hot superhero sex.

I would uncover Malefica's real identity, give it to the Fearless Five, and get the heck outta Dodge. I didn't belong here at Sublime among all the finery any more than a piece of coal belonged in a jewelry store. I didn't belong underground with the superheroes. And I certainly didn't belong with Sam Sloane. Damaged, hazardous goods. That's what I was. A giant pool of radioactive waste that infected everyone who came into contact with me. I wanted, no I *needed* to go back to my safe, boring life. The one where nobody touched me, where nobody had the power to hurt me, and where the damage I did was limited to the society pages of *The Exposé*.

So, I would avoid Sam. I *would*. The safety of my heart—of everyone's hearts—depended on it.

Two more nights passed. I held firm to my decision to avoid the superheroes. I only came out of my suite when they were busy with their day jobs or out chasing crimi-nals. Whenever I did bump into the others, I averted my eyes, mumbled some excuse, and ran away. Fiona glared at me whenever our paths crossed, wanting to boil me with her hot gaze. Chief Newman and Henry didn't say anything, but Fiona had told them about Sam and me. The knowledge glittered in their eyes.

Avoiding everyone wasn't my only problem. I still hadn't been able to uncover Malefica's identity. I was missing something, something obvious among my papers and flowcharts and notes. I could feel it. Too bad I had no idea what it was. Still, I worked feverishly at it, determined to leave Sublime before I brought another disaster down on Sam and the rest of the Fearless Five. Plus, my headaches had gotten even worse, to the point where they were almost debilitating. My vision blurred at least once an hour, and I was popping aspirin like a crack addict constantly in need of a fix.

After spending the morning fruitlessly searching through my papers, I went outside to the expansive gardens, hoping a little sunshine and fresh air would clear my mind and ease my throbbing head. Or at least cheer me up.

The gardens were exquisite. Flowers of all shapes and sizes lined the dirt beds and filled the air with their fragrant scents. Roses, orchids, tulips, pansies, and more brightened the ground with their rainbow of colors. Hummingbirds darted in and out of the blossoms, along with bees and other nectar-seeking insects. More birds sang from the trees that towered over the gardens. It was a virtual paradise.

I ambled along the crushed-shell paths, stooped over, and plucked a rose off a massive bush. I twirled the bright flower in my hand and plucked the petals off one by one. *He loves me, he loves me not, he loves me . . .*

"Enjoying the gardens?"

I shrieked. Sam stood behind me. He looked oh-so-elegant in a dark blue suit and polished wingtips. My heart warmed, despite my best intentions.

"How many times do I have to tell you? Don't do that!"

Sam shrugged. "Sorry. Sneaking up on people is a habit of mine."

"I thought you had a meeting." My eyes darted around, looking for some means of escape. What excuse could I use to get away? Allergies? A bee sting? A sudden aversion to beautiful flowers?

"It got canceled. I thought I'd come out and get some fresh air. The chief thought it would be good for me. He thinks I've been working too hard."

My inner voice whispered, and my eyes narrowed. "The chief? That's the same thing he told me." He'd shouted out the words this morning as I ran down the hall away from him.

We stared at each other.

"I guess he wanted us to run into each other," I said.

"I guess so."

I shifted from one foot to the other. "Well, I was just going back to the house."

"Can I walk with you?"

I couldn't see a polite enough way to tell him no, so I gave in. "Sure." The truth was I missed him terribly. I wanted to be close to him, even if it was only for a little while.

We left the gardens and strolled across the massive lawn. The house stood like a sleeping giant about a half mile away. I kept three feet of space in between us. I wasn't about to tempt fate—or myself—again.

"So do you want to talk about it?" Sam asked.

"About what?"

"Our night together."

I stopped. My face flushed. "Oh. That."

"Yes, that." Sam cleared his throat. "I wanted to say I'm sorry."

"Oh." Disappointment swept over me. Evidently, he hadn't felt the things I'd felt during our time together. Even now, my fingers itched to touch him, to pull him toward me and lose myself in his hot embrace.

"I'm sorry because I was hurting, and I took advantage of you."

"That's okay. I don't mind. You can take advantage of me anytime."

Sam raised an eyebrow.

"Er, what I mean is . . . um, if you feel the need . . . I mean, if you want to . . ." My voice trailed off under his intense scrutiny. "Never mind."

"Anyway, I wanted to apologize. I've been avoiding you because of that . . . and other things. I thought you should know why."

"I've been avoiding you too." I sighed, suddenly tired of dancing around Sam Sloane. "Look, I like you, Sam. I really do. You're a great guy. Intelligent, funny, charming, a good kisser, and more gorgeous than any man has a right to be. The other night was absolutely fantastic. One of the best nights of my life. Certainly the best sex of my life."

"But . . ."

I took in a deep breath. "But it would never work out between us. We live in two completely different worlds. You're a billionaire playboy. I'm a lowly society reporter. You're a superhero. I exposed superheroes for a living. And with Tornado's suicide and Malefica lurking around, there's just too much bad karma in the mix." Every single thing I said was true, but the words still hurt. My inner voice whimpered.

"And I'm pretty sure Fiona would fry me alive if she found out I was sticking around a second longer than necessary," I said in an effort to lighten the mood. That was me. Plucky to the bitter, bitter end.

A ghost of a smile crossed Sam's face. "Fiona probably would fry me too."

We stood there on the lawn, still and silent. My eyes locked onto Sam's handsome face, memorizing every curve, every line. Soon, memories would be all that I had left. A dull ache formed in my heart.

I stuck out my hand before I did something stupid, like beg him to kiss me. "So, just friends then?"

He stared at my outstretched hand for a long, long moment. "Just friends then."

Sam took my hand. All the feelings and sensations of the other night flashed through my head. Tangled sheets. Hot kisses. Slow caresses. I gritted my teeth to keep from pulling him toward me and picking up where we'd left off.

Suddenly, Sam cocked his head to one side, listening. He dropped my hand.

"What is it?" I heard nothing other than the tweet of the birds and the occasional drone of a bumblebee.

Sam frowned. "It sounds like a helicopter."

"A helicopter? Is that something to worry about?"

"No, but it's odd because Sublime extends out in all directions for several miles. And no one can fly over the estate without my permission." He shrugged. "It's probably somebody who's just gotten off course. It happens."

I opened my mouth to reply when an icy wave of pain shot through my body. I doubled over. I felt numb, frozen inside. My teeth chattered. My dull headache exploded into a raging migraine. My vision went black. My inner voice screamed.

"Carmen? Carmen!"

"I don't . . . feel so good," I mumbled.

I pitched forward. Sam caught me and lowered me to the ground.

"Cold . . . so . . . cold." My teeth bounced together like a child's rattle.

Sam took off his suit jacket and draped it over my body. "Lie still. I'm going to get help."

"No! Stay with me," I said, clutching at him.

"I have to, Carmen. I'll be back soon. I promise."

Sam cupped my cheek in his warm hand. Blue waves seemed to surround his body. And there was something behind him. I squinted. A black helicopter hovered overhead. Fear crawled up my spine.

"Go! Leave me!" I shouted to Sam.

The roar of the helicopter's motors drowned me out. Flower petals and dead leaves fluttered up into the air and whipped around like shrapnel. Trees bowed under the sudden gust of wind. The helicopter landed on the green lawn. The door slid open, and three figures emerged. My heart sank.

Uh-oh.

Malefica, Scorpion, and Frost sprinted toward us. Sam crouched over me.

"Run! Go!" I screamed.

"I'm not leaving you!"

The three ubervillains came closer . . . and closer . . . and closer. I looked toward the house. Where the hell were the others? Hadn't they heard the chopper land on the lawn? Didn't the house have some sort of alarm system? Shouldn't the ground open up to let rockets come flying out or something?

The ubervillains stopped a few feet away. Sam stood. His hands clenched into fists. Somehow, I managed to sit up.

"Well, well, if it isn't Sam Sloane," Malefica drawled. "Or should I call you Striker?"

Sam didn't reply.

"Nothing to say? No witty remarks? No pithy come-back? What a pity. Take him out."

Sam launched himself at Scorpion. The ubervillain threw Sam over his shoulder with ease. Sam hit the ground rolling and bounced right back up. A blue streak zapped through the air and hit the superhero in the chest. He rocked back on his heels and wobbled like a seesaw. Sam's eyes opened wide and grew glassy. Then, he fell to the ground.

"Noooo!" I screamed. "No! No! Noooo!"

I tried to crawl toward Sam, but the pain pulsing through my body was too great. Every part of me ached with cold. I slumped to the ground, panting for air. Every breath was an enormous effort.

A pair of strappy red sandals strolled into view. Even though every muscle in my body screamed at me to stop moving, I looked up past them.

Malefica loomed over me. A smile stretched across the ubervillain's ruby red lips. "Well, well, if it isn't my good friend Carmen Cole. Feeling a little ill? Pity."

"What have you done to Sam?" I mumbled through my frozen lips. "How did you find us?"

"Oh, don't worry about Striker. He's not dead. Yet."

Fear blanketed my heart like an icy shroud.

"As for you, remember that dart Frost shot you with? It contained a radioactive isotope, which lives in the human body a very long time. After a few days have passed, the isotope mutates and gives off a particular amount of radiation that's very unique. And very easy to track if you have the proper equipment. Think of it as a sort of homing beacon. You led us right to Striker."

I closed my eyes. So this had been Malefica's real plan all along. To use me to track down Striker. That was why the Triad had retreated from the park that night. That was why the Fearless Five had driven them away so easily. I'd played right into the ubervillains' evil hands.

Frost stared at me like a doctor examining a patient. "Hmmm. Interesting side effects. See how blue her lips are? I bet her body temperature has dropped at least two degrees in the last few minutes. Are you cold, Miss Cole? Feel like your insides are made out of ice cubes? Hmmm? Have you had any migraines or problems with your vision lately?"

I didn't reply.

"Well, if you're not going to be a cooperative test subject and tell me how you're feeling, I have no further use for you. Shall I take care of her once and for all?" Frost asked.

I stared into the black eyehole of Frost's freezoray gun. My eyes widened. I was about to get dead.

Malefica tapped her long nails on her lips. "Leave her. The rest of the Fearless Five will take care of her when they find out we have Striker. After all, someone has to be the bearer of good news. Get him back to the helicopter."

Scorpion picked up Sam's limp form, slung him over his massive shoulder, and lumbered away. Frost followed.

Malefica leaned down until her green eyes were level with mine. "I just wanted to thank you, Carmen. You played your part perfectly."

"You'll pay for this," I spat out.

"I doubt it. Without Striker, the Fearless Five are nothing but a bunch of second-string superheroes. With him out of the way, we can pick the others off one by one by one until there's no one left. Once the Fearless Five are gone, Bigtime will be mine. After that . . . who knows? And you made it all possible."

Malefica straightened. "Please remember to give my regards to Fiera and the others. And my sympathy on their untimely loss." She laughed, her voice filled with malicious glee and triumph.

I glared at the other woman. If looks could kill, Malefica would have been stone-cold dead. Too bad I didn't have that particular superpower.

Malefica blew me a kiss and sidled away, her curvy form swinging with every step. She boarded the helicopter and shut the door. The motor roared to life. In seconds, the helicopter was airborne. It roared across the sky and disappeared from sight, taking Sam and the Terrible Triad with it.

Then, the pain came again, stronger this time, and I knew no more.

PART THREE

Bigtime

★ 22 ★

"I'm fine," I snapped. "Will you quit shining that light in my eyes?"

"You most certainly are not fine, Carmen," Chief Newman retorted. "We found you lying on the lawn, as cold and unconscious as a rock. If what Malefica said is true, you've been under the effects of a powerful drug for days now. You don't just recover from that. Now, hold still."

I waved his hand and the light away. "I'm fine. You gave me those *RIP* pills. I feel much better."

"Those are *RID* pills, *Radioactive Isotope Diminishers*. They will absorb the radioactivity in your system and cleanse your body of the drug. But they're not a cure-all, especially for something as nasty as what Frost slipped you."

"Whatever. The point is I feel much better."

I slid off the hospital bed and stood. The world swam back and forth. I wobbled.

"Fine, huh?" the chief asked.

He eased me onto the bed. I was back in the sick bay in

another pair of clinical, white, lab-rat pajamas. I'd woken up an hour ago to find Henry, Chief Newman, and even Fiona clustered around me with concerned looks on their faces. Their alarm had grown by leaps and bounds as I described how Malefica, Scorpion, and Frost had kidnapped Sam. Fiona and Henry had dashed out of the room in hopes of trying to track down the Terrible Triad, while Chief Newman had stayed to tend to me.

Luckily, I'd only been passed out for about ten minutes before Henry had found me. The three of them had been running through some battle simulations underground. By the time they came back to the library, heard the alarm, and raced outside, it'd been too late to save Sam and almost too late for me. Fiona had carried me inside, where the chief poured just about every drug known to superheroes down my throat, as well as poking and prodding me with all sorts of cold, metal devices. In addition to being the chief of police, Sean was also a first-rate doctor.

I stared straight ahead as the chief shined his small penlight into my eyes. I swung my feet back and forth, and tapped my fingers against the metal rail on the bed. I didn't need to be here. I needed to be in the library with Henry and Fiona trying to locate Sam. I needed to be doing something, anything but sitting still.

"It's not your fault, Carmen," the chief said in a gentle tone.

"Yes, it is. Malefica used me like a puppet, and I didn't even know it." A bitter taste filled my mouth. "And now Sam's going to pay the price. If only I'd seen what she was up to. I knew there was something wrong about the attack in the park. I could feel it. You guys didn't beat the Triad back. They left because they'd done what they'd needed to do—infect me with their radioactive tracking drug. Too bad I didn't realize what it was."

"None of us did. Not even me, and I'm the one who's psychic. Don't beat yourself up. It's happened to all of us at one time or another. The important thing now is that you rest and get your strength back. We'll find him, Carmen. We will."

I looked at the chief. "What do you see now? What do your visions tell you? What's going to happen to Sam?"

The chief shook his head. "I only see pieces, fragments of futures that could be. Some of them are quite unpleasant and better left unsaid."

Panic swelled up in my chest. "But some of them are pleasant, aren't they? *Aren't* they?"

"Yes, some of them are. The future's a funny thing. You can never tell exactly how it's going to turn out until you're in it. It's constantly changing as people act and react to each other. That's the trouble with relying on visions or premonitions to guide you. They're terribly unpredictable. Like Malefica's plan. It depended on several things going exactly her way. Frost hitting you with the drug, us taking you in, you agreeing to stay here, and so on and so forth."

"Well, I'm going to derail her plan this time, whatever it is." I stood again. "I'm going to find her, find out who she is and what dark hole she's hiding in, and then I'm going to find Sam."

The chief blinked at the vehemence in my voice. "I'm not going to be able to stop you, am I?"

"Not unless you chain me to the bed."

"Very well. But I want you to stay seated and take frequent breaks. Agreed?"

"Sure," I replied, even though I had no intention of resting a single second until I'd uncovered Malefica's true identity and, more importantly, where the ubervillain was holding Sam.

I retrieved my jeans and T-shirt from the plastic bag

the chief had put them in. I dressed as fast as I could and hurried off to the library.

I threw open the door. Fiona and Henry were already inside. Henry had all of his computers fired up, and his mind plugged into them. A bluish-white glow emanated from his fingertips, and his eyes were far away and distant behind his thick glasses. Document after document flashed on the flat screens.

Fiona stalked around behind Henry. Her cat suit fit her perfect body like a second skin, and sparks flew from her hair. Fiera was all suited up and ready to go.

"Will you go pace somewhere else?" Henry snapped. "I'm trying to work."

"No." Fiona spotted me in the doorway. "What the hell are you doing here? Get out. We have work to do."

"So do I."

I ignored Fiona, walked over to my desk, and sat down. I stared at the mounds of papers and notes and charts that littered the area. Time to go to work. This time, I had to find the answer. This time, I had to uncover Malefica's real identity.

This time, Sam's life depended on it.

An hour later, I rubbed my aching head, opened my aspirin bottle, and downed three of the hard, white pills.

"Anything, Henry?"

"Nothing. Absolutely nothing. I checked all the airports and helipads, although I knew they probably wouldn't go anywhere near those. Nothing. I hacked into the local FAA system, but I couldn't find any mention of a black helicopter taking off or landing anywhere within fifty miles of Bigtime. I expanded my search out to a hundred miles. Nothing. It's like they disappeared off the face of the earth."

"There has to be some way to track them down," Fiona said. "They can't disappear. They're not the Invisible Ingénues, you know."

The superhero stalked around the room. Her shoes *click-click-clack*ed on the hardwood floor. Fiona had been pacing nonstop for the last hour. Every step slammed another ice pick of pain into my brain. I massaged my throbbing temples.

"Will you please stop pacing back and forth? The noise is driving me insane." I stared at her high-heeled boots. "I don't even see how you can walk in those shoes—"

Shoes . . .

Sandals . . .

Strappy, red sandals . . .

My inner voice whispered. I flashed back to my first meeting with Malefica. The ubervillain's long, red shoes *tap-tap-tapped* in front of my face.

"*Nice sandals,*" I croaked. "*Bulluci's fall collection?*"

"*Good eye,*" Malefica said. "*Now get up. We have things to discuss.*"

"Carmen? Carmen, are you okay?" Henry asked. "You have a strange look on your face."

"Bulluci's fall collection," I whispered. "Bulluci's fall collection!"

"Why are you babbling on about fashion designers at a time like this?" Fiona growled.

I ignored her, grabbed my Rubik's Cube, and twisted it round and round in my hand. There was something else, something important swimming around in the back of my mind. I thought back, concentrating on that meeting, trying to remember every detail, every single snippet of conversation . . .

"*Would you like something to drink?*" Malefica asked.

"*No,*" I said.

"Are you sure? It's Brighton's Best."

And I remembered . . .

Malefica reclined in the leather chair behind the desk. She took a long pull on her drink then set it aside. Unless I missed my guess, the glass was a Hilustar tumbler.

"Brighton's Best. Hilustar tumblers. Bulluci's fall collection. That's it! That's it! That's it!" I shouted.

The pieces clicked together in my mind like a jigsaw puzzle. I grabbed Fiona's hot hands and jumped up and down with glee.

"What are you going on about? Have you finally lost what little bit of sanity that you have?" Fiona yanked her hands away.

"No," I said. "But I've just figured out a way to find out who Malefica really is."

★23★

"What are you talking about?" Fiona asked. "You've been trying to uncover Malefica's real identity for days now with no success."

"That's because I was overlooking something. Henry, I need you to start hacking and see who's ordered red sandals from Bulluci's fall collection, Brighton's Best Scotch whiskey, and Hilustar crystal tumblers in the last six months. And I need to know where everything was shipped."

"But I—"

"Just do it, Henry. Trust me."

Henry and Fiona exchanged *oh the-poor-girl-she's-finally-snapped* looks. I paid them no attention. Instead, I dug around on my desk until I found the list of the fifty richest men and women Henry had compiled for me so many weeks ago.

Ten minutes later, Henry handed me a stack of papers. "There you go."

I whipped out my blue highlighter and cross-referenced the names on the lists with the wealthiest women in Bigtime. Many of the names appeared on one or two of the lists. The upper crust of Bigtime certainly liked their whiskey, and in large quantities. The amount of hard liquor some of the more genteel widows packed away in a month shocked me. Several of them needed a ride to Alcoholics Anonymous. Pronto.

But there was only one woman who had special-ordered red sandals, whiskey, and crystal glasses in the last six months who was among the richest women in Bigtime.

Morgana Madison.

The name stunned me. Could it be? Could my boss, the owner of *The Exposé*, really be one of the most feared ubervillains in the world? She always seemed to be somewhere else when the Triad struck. I shook my head. *Seemed to be.* That was the problem. Appearing at society functions and taking phone calls weren't iron-clad alibis. Phone logs could be altered, meetings could be rescheduled. During any event, Morgana could have gone off to powder her nose, slipped out of the bathroom, committed an hour's worth of crime, mischief, and mayhem, and slipped back in before anyone noticed she was missing. It would be difficult, but not impossible, to pull off. Not with Malefica's psychic powers. She could probably give someone a subtle mental command and make him think he'd seen her when he really hadn't. Or any number of other things to protect her secret identity. Just like Chief Newman had done when he got me time off from work.

Fingers trembling, I went back through the lists and double-checked all the names. Morgana Madison. I triple-checked. Morgana.

I closed my eyes and pictured Morgana Madison and Malefica, putting the two of them side by side in my mind.

They were the same age, height, and weight. They had the same facial features and curvy figures. I thought back to the day in the newsroom when I'd exposed Tornado and the silent toast Morgana had given me. My inner voice whispered. All of a sudden I knew, I just *knew* Morgana was really Malefica.

"Morgana Madison is Malefica," I whispered. "Incredible."

Henry looked up from his computer. "What? What did you say?"

"Morgana Madison is Malefica. It's her. It is."

Fiona arched an eyebrow. "And you know this how?"

I held up the papers. "From these. Listen. When Malefica kidnapped me, she was wearing a new pair of Bulluci sandals."

"So what? She has good taste. Bella Bulluci is a great designer. Even I'll admit that," Fiona said.

"But that's not all. She took me to her office and drank Brighton's Best whiskey from a Hilustar crystal tumbler. I didn't think anything of it at the time."

"Those are pretty expensive items," Henry said, picking up on my train of thought. "Not a lot of people could afford one of them, let alone all three."

"Exactly," I beamed. "Everyone knows how much ubervillains love to flaunt their wealth. I cross-referenced the names on the list Henry compiled for me of the richest men and women in Bigtime with people who had purchased these items in the last six months. Morgana Madison is the only name that's on all of the lists."

Henry's fingers slid over the keyboard like he was playing a piano. "Let me pull up some photos of the two of them."

Seconds later, the three of us stared at pictures of Malefica that Henry had recorded at the park and a photo of Morgana Madison that had appeared in the society section of *The Exposé*. Side by side, the resemblance was obvious.

I could have smacked myself for not seeing it earlier. For making a rookie mistake and not digging deeper into Morgana from the very beginning. I'd told Sam it was all about karma, that Malefica was in his life somewhere. It made perfect sense. Sam and Morgana hated each other in real life just as much as their alter egos did. Their business battles were just as brutal as the superhero-ubervillain duels they staged on a weekly basis.

"Bloody hell," Fiona said. "She's been right under our noses the whole time. I even made a dress for her earlier this year. She was rather bitchy about the price too."

"I never even suspected it might be her," Henry said. "And I've worked at *The Exposé* for years."

"But it *is* her." I pumped my fist. "Gotcha!"

Henry and I pored over the records, trying to determine exactly where the goods had been shipped to in hopes of locating Sam. Fiona ran off to tell Chief Newman we'd uncovered Malefica's true identity. This time, the slap of her shoes on the floor didn't bother me in the slightest. My headache had vanished as well.

"She's got shell company after shell company." I flipped through a stack of papers. "Look at all these corporations. She's got more branches than McDonald's."

Henry sat at the computer. His fingers glowed. "You've only got the parts I've printed out. The woman has her fingers into everything. Oil, natural gas, communications, construction. The list is endless."

"Wait a minute, wait a minute," I muttered. "I've got

the shoes. She had them shipped to her apartment in the city to start with. From there, a courier service picked them up. They went to her office at *The Exposé* and then out to her country home. Eventually, they arrived at the Snowdom Ice Cream Factory on the outskirts of Bigtime. You know what? She put the courier service on her credit card."

Stupid move. Ubervillains thought they were so smart. But all it took was one little receipt to blow their cover wide open.

"The ice cream factory? That place has been closed for over a year now," Henry said. "The company couldn't compete with the other big chains, all the workers were laid off, and the plant was shut down. Tracy, the business reporter at *The Exposé*, did a story on it. The building's been empty ever since."

I remembered the story. I closed my eyes and thought back to my first meeting with Malefica. I tried to recall every single detail of the building I'd been taken to. Concrete floors and walls, enormous steel vats, lots of catwalks, bitter cold. I frowned. Had there been any words on the giant metal vats? Any markings or letters on the doors or floors or walls? I couldn't remember. At the time, I'd been more concerned with being dropped into the radioactive goo than my surroundings. But it could have been an ice cream factory. It had all the necessary equipment. Plus, that might explain how Frost had been able to turn it into his own personal playground.

"I think that's it," I said. "It makes sense."

"Let me pull up the deed and blueprints," Henry said.

The glow from his fingertips brightened. I peered over his shoulder at the computer screen. A series of images flashed across it.

"Okay, these are the blueprints. It's a pretty big place and covers a couple of acres. Lots of entrances and exits. There don't seem to be any buildings near it. It would be the perfect place for the Triad to hide. Now, on to the deed and other paperwork."

A document popped up on the monitor. I ran my finger down the screen. "Bill of sale, estimated worth, acreage, utility hookups, blah, blah, blah. Wait. Here it is. The current owner of record of the Snowdom Ice Cream Factory is one Morgana Madison. That's it, Henry. That's where she's got him. I can feel it."

"I want to go with you," I protested. "You can't just leave me behind."

"We can and we will," Chief Newman said. "You're in no condition to go anywhere."

"I'm fine now. Do you want me to run a marathon to prove it? I will."

Chief Newman gave me a disbelieving look.

"Okay, so I couldn't run a marathon on my best day. But I do feel much better now." I really did. My headache was gone, and my vision hadn't gotten fuzzy since the chief had dumped those *RID* pills down my throat.

Chief Newman ignored me. The four of us stood in the equipment room. Fiona was ablaze in reddish-orange, while the chief was clad in Irish green with white accents. Now, they were Fiera and Mr. Sage, and they were ready to do battle with the Terrible Triad. Henry emerged from behind a row of lockers. A checkered, black-and-white costume covered his tall frame, and a mask complete with prescription eye goggles wrapped around his head.

"Nice costume," I said. "I didn't think that you actually wore one."

Henry shrugged. "I do. But nobody ever sees it since I'm in the van most of the time. Tonight, though, I'm going in with Fiera and Mr. Sage."

I itched to get in on the act. I grabbed one of Striker's swords from a nearby rack.

"I could really be of use to you guys—"

I didn't get a very good grip on the sword, and it plummeted downward. The metal weapon clanged off the floor, narrowly missing Fiera's booted foot.

Fiera grabbed the sword. "Give me that before you cut yourself." She put the weapon back in its proper place on the rack.

"You have to let me do something. I'll go crazy just sitting here waiting for you guys to come back," I whined.

"That's why I set up the big screen in the library so you can see, hear, and talk to us," Hermit said. "That way you'll know the moment we rescue Striker. The other computers have background information on Malefica, photos, stuff like that in case you wanted to investigate her more once we've gotten Striker back."

Sometimes, Hermit's efficiency was so annoying. I opened my mouth to protest, but Mr. Sage cut me off.

"We need to focus on finding Striker. We don't need any distractions. You want us to bring him back safely, don't you? We don't need to worry about the Triad capturing you, Carmen."

He had me, and he knew it. There was nothing more in the entire world I wanted than to see Sam safe and sound again.

"Fine. I'll stay here like a good little girl and play nice. Just bring him back. Please." My heart squeezed tight. I couldn't handle having another superhero's death on my hands. Especially Striker's.

"We will, Carmen." Mr. Sage put a comforting hand on my shoulder. "Don't worry. We will."

Mr. Sage and Hermit went to the library to grab a few more pieces of equipment, leaving me alone with Fiera.

"Well, good luck," I said.

"Thanks." Fiera turned toward the door. She stopped and looked over her shoulder.

"I've never liked you, Carmen. You know that, and you know why. I thought this was all part of some plan of Malefica's, some scheme the two of you had cooked up to trick us. And when I found you with Sam, I wasn't happy about that either. But you came through for us when it really counted. You found Striker. We couldn't have done it without you. I'm sorry I thought that you were working with Malefica."

"Apology accepted." I grinned. "Now, get out there and go get the man back."

The group roared out of the underground garage a few minutes later. I settled myself in the library to wait. I wasn't happy they'd left me behind, but I understood their reasons. They didn't need to worry about someone else, especially someone without superpowers. Their sole focus should be on rescuing Striker before it was too late.

The minutes dragged by. It was after seven now. Malefica had kidnapped Striker a little over six hours ago. I tried not to think of what she might be doing to Striker at this very moment, the vicious ways she might be torturing him. But the images played over and over and over again in my mind like a CD stuck on one really bad song.

I buried my head in my hands. If anything happened to

Sam, I'd never forgive myself. Never. He'd been kind to me when no one else had, when I didn't deserve it. He'd saved me from those would-be rapists. Held me when I cried. Taken me in when I had no place else to go. Those were just a few of the reasons I'd come to care for Sam. Just a few of the reasons I'd come to love him.

Oh, how I loved him.

"Carmen, can you hear me?" Mr. Sage's voice cracked and echoed through the library.

I leaned forward and spoke into the microphone Hermit had rigged up next to one of his computers for me. "Loud and clear."

"We're here," Mr. Sage said. "We've hidden the van in the woods outside the ice cream factory. We're going in now."

"Be careful. There's no telling what Malefica might have in store for you." I swallowed. "Or what she's done to Striker." With the superhero's ability to regenerate, Malefica could torture him for hours on end.

"We will, don't worry. I'm turning on the camera in my suit. Over and out."

A moment later, a large bush came into view on the screen. A green, gloved hand pushed the thick limbs aside. A tall building lay about three hundred yards ahead. I perched on the edge of my seat. I was seeing exactly what Mr. Sage and the others were.

The superheroes crept toward the building. Nothing stirred. As they drew closer to the factory, I could tell that it had seen better days. Debris, mostly rocks and broken bits of rubble, littered the cracked, uneven parking lot. Graffiti and gang signs crawled over the walls, and all the windows on the bottom floors had been busted out. The setting sun caught on the delicate spider webs that spanned the empty windows and made them glisten like silver. The superheroes reached a metal door tucked away in one corner of the building. An exit sign swung in the breeze, creaking over their heads.

Through the microphone, I heard Hermit tap a few buttons on his handheld supercomputer.

"I'm not detecting any outer alarms or electrical devices," he whispered. "I've got no thermal images. Nothing within two hundred feet. The walls are too thick for my sensors to penetrate any deeper."

"Then, let's go in. But keep your eyes open," Mr. Sage replied.

"Always," Fiera chimed in. "Always."

Mr. Sage opened the door. Nothing but darkness lay inside.

"Here we go," Mr. Sage whispered.

"Good luck," I whispered back.

The superheroes stepped inside, and the door snickered shut. The camera on Mr. Sage's suit automatically adjusted to the faint light, allowing me to see just as clearly as if I had Striker's supersenses. Hermit took point, and the three superheroes eased into the factory.

They worked their way through a series of long hallways that turned and twisted back on each other. Finally, the superheroes reached a large open space. On the far side of the room, a few thousand feet away, an assembly line led deeper into the factory. A metal catwalk ringed the entire area.

"This is it," I said into the microphone. "This is definitely the place Malefica took me the night her goons kidnapped me. Everything looks just the way I remember it."

"Good," Mr. Sage whispered. "Let's find Striker and get out of here."

The three superheroes moved deeper into the abandoned factory.

My inner voice muttered. It all seemed too easy. If I were an ubervillain who had just kidnapped one of the world's greatest superheroes, I'd know his friends would come after him. I would have more security and guards around my supersecret lair than Fort Knox. At the very least, I would have set up alarms on all the outer doors to let me know if somebody was trying to break in. But there were no alarms; no loud, squealing sirens; no red, flashing danger signs. Nothing but eerie silence and the labored breathing of Fiera, Hermit, and Mr. Sage.

"That's funny," Hermit said. "There's a wall in front of us. That wasn't on the blueprints I found online."

"The Triad's probably done some remodeling," Fiera said. "You know how Scorpion likes to exercise—by smashing through walls."

They continued on. My uneasy feeling ballooned with every step the group took. They met no resistance, not even a couple of token, throwaway goons like the two who'd kidnapped me. The factory seemed to be deserted. There weren't even any rats or bugs crawling around in the rubble and broken pipes. Of course, Frost had probably used them all in his experiments. Still, something wasn't right.

I could feel it.

The group kept going. They reached the assembly line and crouched under it. I turned my attention to another computer, the one with all of the information on Malefica. I pulled up files and photos of the ubervillain. Document after document, photo after photo, zipped by.

I stopped when I came to an article that analyzed Malefica's fashion sense. It was the same story I'd read so many weeks ago in the comfort of my apartment. My eyes traced over the pictures that chronicled the changing looks of Malefica. There was something odd about the pictures, something I was missing. What was it?

I got closer to the screen, so close my nose almost touched the monitor, and looked at the sequence of photos. Over the years, Malefica had changed the color of her suit from bright crimson to a darker blood-red. She'd ditched the glittering rhinestones and sparkling rubies on her cat suit for a simpler, classier design. On the flip side, there was one constant. Her shoes were exactly the same in every picture . . .

It hit me. I knew what was wrong. In every single one of the pictures, Malefica was wearing boots. Red, thigh-high boots.

Boots—not sandals.

I chewed my lip and picked up one of my Rubik's Cubes. I turned the puzzle round and round in my hands. It was probably nothing. Perhaps the ubervillain had grown tired of her boots, as women were so wont to do with their footwear and other accessories. Perhaps she was now into sandals. Perhaps she had just wanted to show off her pedicure.

Still . . .

But maybe . . .

What if . . .

My inner voice nagged me. I thought back to the night in the park when I'd gone to meet the Terrible Triad. Malefica had been wearing boots then, because I remembered the way the enormous soles had flattened the grass. My frown deepened. But Malefica had sported sandals when she'd kidnapped Striker earlier in the day. Why would she switch from sandals to boots and then back to sandals? Superheroes and ubervillains rarely changed anything about their costumes once they got used to them. They might tweak them a little bit, as Malefica had done by removing the gaudy rhinestones from her cat suit, but they wouldn't change anything major. It made it too hard for the public to recognize and identify them, not to mention all the subsequent marketing headaches it created. So why would Malefica change her look now? Why now when she was hot on the trail of the Fearless Five?

I slid a row of colors into place on the Rubik's Cube. The answer was that Malefica wouldn't. Not unless she had specifically *wanted* me to notice her sandals. But why? Why would Malefica want that? What would that get her? What could she possibly gain from that?

I paced around the room and clutched the Rubik's Cube in my icy hands. The only reason I'd even recognized Malefica's shoes was because of my time on the society beat. A month before Malefica had kidnapped me, I had done a lengthy feature story on Bella Bulluci and her fall shoe collection. Bella had shown me a pair of sandals exactly like the ones Malefica had been wearing. The photo had run a good four columns wide across the top of one of the society pages.

I put the cube down, sat in front of Henry's computer, and went to *The Exposé's* Web site. I entered my password and searched through the archives until I found the story on the Bulluci sandals. It was your usual fluffy, society piece, but my eyes snagged on a sentence near the bottom. *The sandals are only available in sizes 6 through 9* . . . I riffled through the papers until I found the order form Malefica, er, Morgana had used to purchase the sandals. Her shoe size was 10½. Bigfoot, indeed. She'd had to pay another five thousand dollars to special-order them, and she'd added another three grand to the total to have them delivered by September 1—two weeks before the Triad had kidnapped me.

I grabbed my cube and started pacing again. Other

pieces of the puzzle snapped into place inside my head. The week before the Bulluci cover, I'd done a piece on fine liquor, including Brighton's Best whiskey. I remembered whistling when the salesman had told me how expensive it was. A week earlier, I'd written a glowing story about crystal, specifically Hilustar tumblers.

What if . . .

Could it be . . .

Was it possible . . .

The society page editor had assigned me all of those stories. The society editor, like all the others, had to get her story ideas approved through the managing editor, who reported to Morgana Madison, aka Malefica. It would have been easy for Morgana to whisper into the managing editor's ear and get me assigned to certain stories. Everyone in the newsroom knew what a good memory I had. I could still recall names, dates, and places from stories I'd written in college. Like all journalists, I was a compendium of useless facts I'd picked up during my years on the job. A cold, iron fist wrapped itself around my heart and squeezed tight.

What if Malefica had been planning something far more sinister than kidnapping Striker all along? What if she wasn't through with her plan yet? What if this was just the beginning?

I stalked around the room, twisting and turning the cubed puzzle in my hands. I flashed back to the night in the factory and the tour that Malefica had taken me on. I hadn't thought too much of the ubervillain's secret lair. It was a run-down factory. The only thing that had looked remotely sinister besides the vats of goo and mutated animals had been the bank of computers plugged into those four glass tubes. But what could Malefica do with those?

I clicked the last row of colors into place on the Rubik's

Cube. There had been four glass tubes next to the computers. Not one, not two, not three, but four. Four, man-sized, glass tubes. Suddenly, I knew.

I just *knew*.

The Fearless Five were walking straight into a trap.

And it was all my fault.

★ 24 ★

I dropped the Rubik's Cube, lunged forward, and grabbed the microphone on the table. "Hermit! Mr. Sage! Fiera! Can you hear me? Come in! Come in now!"

"Ouch!" Hermit's tinny voice echoed back to me. "There's no need to shout, Carmen. I can hear you just fine. What's the matter?"

"It's a trap. Malefica set up this whole thing. She wants to capture all of you, not just Striker. Get out! Get out now!"

"What? What is she babbling about this time?" Fiera said.

"Are you sure, Carmen?" Mr. Sage asked. "Everything seems to be quiet. Hermit's just gotten a possible location for Striker."

"Yes, I'm sure. Leave! Right now! Before it's too late!"

"Okay. You heard her. Let's go."

"But what about Striker?" Fiera asked.

"We'll have to come back later. We can't risk it if Malefica's expecting us."

Mr. Sage turned. Suddenly, a brilliant blue light flashed in front of the camera. Mr. Sage stumbled back.

"Run," he said in a weak voice. "While you still can—"

The superhero went down on his knees and flopped over on his back. The camera on his suit pointed straight up. I had a lovely view of the iced-over, thick, metal pipes that hung down from the ceiling, but nothing else. Scuffles, loud crashes, and bangs cracked and shrieked through the microphone. Fiera let out a string of curses. Hermit shouted something unintelligible. The blue light flashed over Mr. Sage two more times. And then . . .

Silence.

Complete, utter, chilling silence.

"Mr. Sage? Mr. Sage?! Fiera?! Hermit?!" I shouted into the microphone. "Answer me!"

No one responded. I opened my mouth to yell at the superheroes again when I heard something. I listened.

Click-click-clack.

The sound grew louder and louder and louder. My heart sank. That sound had echoed through my nightmares many times.

A long, dark shadow fell over Mr. Sage. A flash of red blocked my view for a moment. The figure pulled back, and Malefica stared into the camera. Her green eyes bored into the lens.

"I can't see you, Miss Cole, but I know you're watching. Pity you couldn't be here in person to witness the end of the Fearless Five. It's going to make for a hell of a good story." Malefica laughed in triumph.

A bitter taste filled my mouth. A tight, hard knot formed in my stomach. My inner voice wailed.

"Then again, I have you to thank for my victory, don't I? Have you figured it out yet? Probably not. Few people can rarely see the big picture. Let me fill you in. I owe you that much." Malefica leaned closer to the camera, like she was sharing an important secret with her best friend. Me. "I've been after the Fearless Five for years. But all my plans to eliminate them always backfired. Until now. I knew your reputation for unmasking superheroes. It's the reason I hired you to work at *The Exposé*. You did your job beautifully, until Tornado's oh-so-tragic suicide. I, of course, wanted you to unmask the rest of the Fearless Five, but you had a change of heart. Pity what guilt does to a person. Of course, I've never had a problem with it.

"I had to find some way to get you back on track, some way to motivate you. That's why I kidnapped you and let Frost threaten to turn you into his latest science project. It worked like the proverbial charm, and you went back to your old Nancy Drew ways. I knew your snooping around would attract the attention of the Fearless Five and that they'd take you in to protect you from me. With Frost's tracking drug, you led me right to Striker. Then, came the tricky part of my plan. How to get you to lead the rest of the Fearless Five into my trap?"

I closed my eyes. I felt physically ill.

"The answer was obvious. I had to let you unmask me. I couldn't make it too easy, of course, or you might suspect something. So how to do it? Again, the answer was obvious. Any beat reporter worth her salt comes to know a great deal about the people she covers. How they think, what's important to them. What do rich people care about? What would a society beat reporter write stories about? Money, expensive baubles, pricey trinkets. I tossed a few breadcrumbs your way, namely the Bulluci sandals, and left a paper trail you could easily follow. I knew you'd figure it out sooner or later. You didn't disappoint me, which is why I'm going to spare your pathetic life."

Malefica smiled. "Aren't you going to say something?

Tell me how I'm going to pay for this? Threaten me with bodily harm? Vow to get your revenge come hell or high water?"

Tears trickled down my cheeks. I'd thought I was so clever, figuring out Malefica's real identity. I was nothing but a colossal fool.

"Guess not. Pity. One more thing, Miss Cole. Don't bother trying to expose my real identity to the world now. No one will believe you."

"Why not?" I whispered.

"Because as of this morning, you were officially fired from *The Exposé*. Something to do with your mentally fragile state—and the fact that you'd broken into my office, threatened me, and stole some petty cash. Lies, of course, but very believable ones, with police reports and other documentation to back them up. Well, I guess this concludes our business. Enjoy the rest of your evening. I know I will."

Malefica blew me a kiss and reached toward the camera. Her hand covered the lens. Something ripped and snapped.

Then, the screen went black.

I sat there, stunned. Malefica had been using me the entire time. All this time, I'd thought I was the one in control, but Malefica had been pulling my strings like I was a child's puppet. Now, the Fearless Five were going to pay the ultimate price for my stupidity and arrogance. If they hadn't already. Sam and the others were going to die.

I buried my head in my hands and sobbed.

Hot tears dripped down my face into my hands and then slid down my arms. A few of the salty drops splattered onto the computer keyboard.

"Ouch!"

I lurched back from the keyboard and rubbed the spot

on my elbow where the computer had zapped me. Water and electricity do not mix. I should have remembered that from my story on the Electric Eelinator.

"Stupid computer. I'm trying to have a breakdown here," I muttered.

But the shock jolted me out of my sobbing fit. I took deep breaths and wiped away the rest of my tears. Now was not the time to cry. The Fearless Five were in danger because of me. I had to do something to help them. And not just because they were righteous superheroes. I'd come to think of them as my friends these last few weeks. Even Fiera. And Striker . . . well, he was something more entirely. Much, much more.

But what? What could I possibly do? I could call the police, but they wouldn't believe me, not without Chief Newman around to vouch for me. Morgana Madison had made sure of that. Anyway, Bigtime's finest would be no match for the Triad. They'd be slaughtered like newborn lambs. I couldn't handle any more blood on my hands.

I picked up my discarded Rubik's Cube. The only people capable of rescuing the Fearless Five were other superheroes. But I didn't know any superhero who would help me after what I'd done to the brotherhood. And I couldn't exactly go through the yellow pages and call them up. Where was the Serious Samurai when you needed him?

I let out a long breath. It was up to me now. There was no one else.

Oh, I had no illusions about myself. Not anymore. I was definitely not a superhero. I didn't have superstrength. I couldn't form fireballs with my hands. I couldn't read other people's minds. I didn't have anything to rely on, except myself. A ball of fear knotted in my throat. I didn't think that I was strong enough, that I would *be* enough.

Malefica's cackle of triumph echoed through my head.

The ubervillain had threatened me, manipulated me, used me like a tissue, and then tossed me aside. I wasn't anybody's patsy. Not anymore. I slammed the cube down onto the table.

I wasn't a superhero, but I was seriously pissed off. Malefica was going to pay for what she'd done to me and the Fearless Five. She'd made one major mistake and miscalculation. Everybody knew you didn't piss off a Southern woman. We might look all sweet and nice and innocent, but every single one of us had a memory an elephant would envy and a mean streak to match. I was no exception. I never forgot, and I very rarely forgave.

"I am woman, hear me roar, Malefica," I said. "I'm coming to get you, bitch."

★25★

The first thing I did was try to get the camera back online. I fiddled with switches and turned dials and pushed buttons. Nothing. No sound, no video, no feedback. I couldn't see anything happening inside the factory, not even the evil tortures Malefica was subjecting my friends to. Perhaps it was better that way.

Since the camera was dead, I would have to do things on my own. I'd have to go in blind. I sat and thought for a minute. Then, I walked over to my desk, picked up a phone, and punched in a number I knew by heart.

"Talk to me."

"You want blueprints of the Snowdom Ice Cream Factory so you can bust in and save the Fearless Five from the vile clutches of the Terrible Triad?" Lulu asked.

I could hear the disbelief in the other woman's voice. "I

know I sound a little nuts right now, but it's the truth, I swear."

"Have you been drinking? Or were there pills involved?"

"No, I have not been drinking. Or popping pills." That wasn't entirely true, but I was in no mood to confess to my growing dependence on aspirin. "Listen up. I'm only going to tell this story to you once."

I told Lulu everything. How I'd been kidnapped by Malefica, why I'd started digging into the Fearless Five's real identities again, the battle at the park, my time with the superheroes, Malefica's dastardly plan. Of course, I left out a few pertinent details like the real identities of the Fearless Five. However, I had no such qualms about unmasking Malefica, despite her threats that no one would believe me.

"Morgana Madison?! You've got to be kidding me, Sister Carmen. She's one of the most respected businesswomen in Bigtime—not to mention the richest. Why would she masquerade as an ubervillain?"

"Who knows? Maybe she's a thrill-seeker. Maybe her parents didn't love her enough as a child. Maybe she was dropped on her head when she was a baby. I don't really care what drove her to her life of crime. I just want to stop her and rescue the Fearless Five. Do me a favor. Pull up a photo of Malefica off the Internet and compare it to one of Morgana. That's all I ask. If you don't believe me then, you can hang up."

Through the phone, I could hear Lulu pounding away on her computer. The typing stopped, and Lulu let out a low whistle.

"Well, well, well, as I live and breathe. Hello, Malefica. Or should I call her Morgana Madison?"

"I don't know," I said. "There's some weird superhero-ubervillain etiquette about that I don't really understand. I'm sticking with Malefica. Or *the bitch that must die*. Whichever you prefer."

"Meow!" Lulu purred. "So Sister Carmen, what exactly do you need?"

"First of all, I need the blueprints for the ice cream factory. Get the originals from city hall if you can. I think Malefica tampered with the ones that Hermit found online."

"Got it. What else?"

"I need you to see if you can find someone who used to work at the factory. Someone who remembers the layout, what kind of chemicals the workers used, what's the best way in and out of the building, that sort of thing."

"Why?" Lulu asked.

"It never hurts to have too much information. I want to know as much as I can about the building before I go in."

"Anything else?"

"Remember your friend Jasper? I need some more supplies from him. As soon as possible."

"Are you sure that's a good idea? From what you've told me, you almost blew yourself up the last time Jasper gave you some supplies."

The memory of the fiasco in the park gave me another headache. I reached across my desk for my bottle of aspirin. I shook it. Empty. I'd grab some from the sick bay on my way out.

"I don't have a choice, Lulu. Not unless you've got a superhero or five up your sleeve."

"Sadly, that's the one commodity I can't quite seem to get my hands on. I'm working on it, though."

"Meet me at the Wolf's Den as soon as you've got everything. It's an all-night diner that's about five miles away from the factory."

"I know the place, but it will take me some time to get this stuff together. I'm not Swifte, you know."

"How long?" I ground my teeth together.

Every minute, every second counted. I didn't know how long Malefica would keep the Fearless Five alive. My guess was not very long. Malefica would gloat for a while, then get bored with her prisoners. After that—I didn't want to think about what would happen.

Lulu's fingers snapped against the keyboard. "I can get what you need and be there in an hour."

I glanced at the clock. It was almost ten now. "Fine. See you there."

"Be there or be square, Sister Carmen."

I hung up the phone and went over to the round table in the center of the library. I stared at the five empty chairs and the *F5* insignia. I brushed my fingers over the carved wood. I would save the Fearless Five. I would.

Or die trying.

I put aside my raging emotions and ransacked the library, searching for anything that might help me in my upcoming battle. I found nothing I could use, unless I wanted to brain Scorpion with a very thick encyclopedia. I didn't think that would slow down the ubervillain for a second, although a book without pictures might confuse him.

Next, I jogged down the hall to the equipment room. I jabbed in the code, and the door slid open. I walked toward the colorful leather costumes hanging behind the glass door and reached for the handle. My hand dropped to my side. No. I wasn't a superhero. I wasn't going to play dress-up and pretend to be one at this stage of the game. I was Carmen Cole, the woman who lived in jeans and a T-shirt.

The woman who was probably going to die in jeans and a T-shirt.

No use thinking about that right now. When Malefica got her hands on me or Frost dumped me in a vat of radioactive goo. That would be a good time to have a proper panic.

I turned and surveyed the rest of the room. Striker's gleaming silver swords caught my eye. I went over and picked one up. I twirled the sword in my hand. It weighed less than a feather. A weapon I didn't know how to use was better than no weapon at all. I grabbed another sword off the rack. And two weapons were definitely better than one. I found a scabbard for the swords and strapped them to my back. I spent a few minutes practicing pulling the swords out and putting them back in the leather slots.

Once I'd familiarized myself with the swords, I tore through the rest of the room. I found nothing else remotely helpful. No guns, no knives, no quarterstaffs, no throwing stars. Nothing. You'd think Sam would have invested a little more money in weapons given how much he spent on the rest of the group's equipment. But that was a superhero for you. Always confident his power would be enough to see him through any battle. That was the problem with having superpowers—you came to rely on them too much. When they went away, as they so often did, you were left defenseless, helpless. It had happened to the Colorful Crusader and countless others.

Still, reliable or not, I would have given anything to have a superpower right now.

My next stop was the sick bay. Again, I found nothing helpful. The room was filled with odd machines and other devices much too complicated for me to understand, let alone find any use for. Odd drugs with bizarre, never-ending names and too many vowels sat inside most of the cabinets and drawers. I had a rule about medicine—I never took anything I couldn't pronounce.

A box on one of the counters caught my eye. More *RID* pills. Evidently, it was Mr. Sage's drug of choice. I turned the box over and read the label. *Caution: Take one pill per day as needed to absorb and diminish radioactive isotopes. More than one pill per day may result in serious side effects, such as nausea, dizziness, headaches, and fatigue. Extreme overdoses could result in death. Consult your doctor for more information.*

Big metal vats of radioactive goo flashed through my mind. My inner voice whispered. I had a funny feeling I'd be taking a cold, cold bath before the night was over. What the hell? I wasn't likely to live through this little adventure anyway. Maybe they'd help my headache.

I downed ten of the pills.

Once I was done scouring the underground lair for weapons, I took the elevator upstairs and paced through the silent halls. My sneakers squeaked on the slick marble floors. The eyes of the statues and paintings followed my every step.

The manor seemed so empty without the others in it. I kept expecting to turn a corner and run into Sam carrying a briefcase full of papers from his latest business meeting. Or see Fiona snacking on a couple dozen pizzas in the kitchen. Or find Henry and Chief Newman playing pool in the game room.

I made my way to my room and plopped down on the thick bed. I glanced at the alarm clock. A little after ten. I closed my eyes, then opened them. I sat up. I got off the bed and paced around the room. I stared at the clock. Exactly two minutes had passed.

I couldn't sit still until it was time to meet Lulu—I'd go crazy. So, I took a quick shower to kill some time. I turned the water up as hot as I could stand it and let it soak into my body, as if it would linger there and drive away the cold of the factory. Once I'd dried off, I put on my favorite pair of faded jeans, sneakers, and a T-shirt with POW! and BIF! and BAM! and other cartoon words on it.

I took extra care with my makeup. I was going to war, so I put on all my paint. Foundation, powder, eye shadow, mascara, lipstick. After all, a girl should look her best when she was about to meet her inevitable doom and death. A leather jacket completed the look. It wasn't Bulluci's fall collection, but it would have to do.

I grabbed a couple of CDs out of the cardboard boxes that littered the floor and tossed them into a bag with the swords and scabbard. I needed to psych myself up a little bit for the mission at hand. Okay, a lot. A *whole* hell of a lot.

I took a long, last look at myself in the mirror. Fear, panic, worry. All those emotions and more swirled in my troubled blue eyes. Tension tightened my face underneath all the makeup. I blew out a long, long breath. My emotions, my fears, my concerns didn't matter anymore. All that was important now was saving Striker and the rest of the Fearless Five.

It was time to go to work.

★26★

I walked to the garage attached to the far side of the manor and flipped on a switch. Row after row of cars, motorcycles, and vans gleamed under the bright lights. I randomly picked a set of keys off a pegboard near the door and hit the alarm button. The lights on a silver Aston Martin lit up. Not a bad ride. Not a bad ride at all.

I opened the driver's side door, slid inside, and put my bag of swords in the passenger seat. I adjusted the mirrors, fastened my seat belt, and popped in a CD. Carly Simon's deep, husky, angry voice blared out, singing about people being vain, among other things.

My spirits lifted just a bit. "Ready or not, here I come. Carmen Cole, reporter extraordinaire, to the rescue."

I stomped down on the gas.

Thirty minutes later, I tapped my fingers on the side of my parfait glass. The dark dregs of a triple-chocolate milk shake clung to the bottom of the container. I glanced at my watch. Eleven-fifteen. Lulu was late. My inner voice chattered. I couldn't wait any longer. I had to go. Now. I put a ten-dollar bill on the table and stood.

The door chimed open. A motor sounded, and Lulu zoomed into the diner. The Asian woman zipped over to me. The cobalt streaks in her black hair gleamed under the bright lights. I sank back down into my cherry-colored vinyl booth.

"Sorry. Traffic was terrible," Lulu said. "Yeti Girl was throwing cars around the freeway. Swifte showed up and helped the cops tranq her, but it took them forever to get the debris off the road."

"I was about to give up on you."

"Now, you should know better than that, Sister Carmen. I always deliver. I'm better than the post office. If you'll step outside with me, I have the items you requested."

I followed Lulu out to the parking lot. A black van not unlike the one the Fearless Five used sat in the shadows. Lulu knocked once on the door. It slid open, revealing Jasper. He smiled at me.

"Step into my parlor," Lulu said.

A hydraulic lift hissed to life. Lulu strapped her chair to the device, which picked her up and deposited her inside the van. Once Lulu was settled, I climbed inside and shut the door behind me.

"You remember Jasper."

I nodded at the bomb expert.

"He has the items you wanted."

Jasper opened a black duffel bag at his feet. He pulled out a device shaped like a cherry with the stem attached. "These contain a very concentrated form of explodium. Think of them as minigrenades that pack a hell of a punch. I've made ten of them for you."

"How big a punch?" I asked.

"Let's just say you wouldn't want to be anywhere within fifty feet of them when they go off. You can throw them, and they'll explode on impact, or you can set them on a timer to detonate when you choose. I would suggest the latter method, unless you're the Baseballer. I've included a remote trigger for you, or you can set the time on the bomb itself and watch it count down, just like in the movies."

Jasper demonstrated how to arm the bomb and made me do the same. When he was convinced I sort of knew what I was doing, he pulled another device out of the bag. This one was shaped like a pineapple.

"And this is the big bang. The boom-boom if you will. This bomb has enough explodium in it to level a building—something Lulu said you might be interested in."

"You've got that right." I'd like nothing better than to destroy the Triad's lair, after I'd saved Striker and the others.

"Again, it has a remote trigger or you can set the timer." Jasper showed me how to operate the device and made me repeat the steps back to him.

"And that concludes my business here. Enjoy." He winked at me. "Don't blow yourself up, Carmen. You're becoming one of my best clients."

I wasn't sure what to say. I'd never thought I'd be on a bomber's preferred client list. Although, if he gave me a discount, it might be worth it.

Lulu handed Jasper a thick brown envelope. "Thank you for your speedy assistance, Brother Jasper. Have a good evening."

Jasper pocketed the envelope. "You girls have fun. Try not to destroy too much of the city."

He opened the van door, got out, and shut it behind him.

"How much money did you give him?" I asked.

"Two hundred fifty thousand dollars. He wanted an even half million, but I talked him down."

"Lulu!" I closed my eyes. My nest egg looked like a single chicken feather compared to that dollar amount. A moldy, moth-eaten feather. "I don't have that kind of money. I'll never be able to pay you back. Not in a million years."

Lulu waved my hand. "I told you. The next three favors are on me, remember? Besides it's time somebody taught Malefica and her crew a lesson."

The hard tone in her voice caught my attention. "What do you mean by that?"

Lulu stared at her legs. And I just *knew*.

"Malefica's the reason you're in that chair," I whispered.

Lulu nodded. Her black hair bobbed back and forth. "Five years ago, the Triad broke into the Complete Computer Company. They wanted the company's new microchip. I was there doing an internship. The Fearless Five showed up, and a big battle ensued. In the confusion, Malefica grabbed me. She used me as a human shield so she and the Triad could get away. We went up to the roof, and Malefica forced me into a helicopter. We took off and hovered over the building. The Fearless Five came out on the roof. And—"

"And Malefica dropped you out of the helicopter," I finished.

"Striker tried to catch me, but he missed. I didn't fall that far, maybe twenty feet, but I broke my back and messed up my spinal cord. Hence the wheelchair."

I put my hand on Lulu's arm. "I'm so sorry. Why didn't you tell me before?"

Lulu shrugged. "It didn't matter. You can't change what happened. Nobody can." Her dark eyes drilled into mine. "But Malefica needs to pay for what she's done. Not only to me, but to you, to the Fearless Five, to every person she's ever hurt or used or manipulated. If you're going to go after her, I'll help you any way I can."

Lulu handed me a folder filled with papers. "I got the original blueprints from city hall just like you wanted. You were right. Malefica had tampered with a set I found online. I also found an old-timer who worked at the ice cream factory for over thirty years. He said the best way in and out of the plant is through this loading dock here. From your description, he figures Malefica's office is there, and the computers and the Fearless Five are probably here." She pointed to the locations on the map. "See these Xs? If you place your bombs there, you should be able to bring down the whole building. Jasper was kind enough to mark the structural hot spots for me."

"Thanks, Lulu." I stuffed the papers into the bag with the bombs. "Now, I want you to promise me something."

"What?"

"If I don't make it back—"

"You will. You'll be fine," Lulu protested.

"Be real. I'm going up against three of the world's most vicious ubervillains. I have a very, very slim chance of survival. I have a better chance of winning the lottery, and I don't even play. The most I can hope for is to free a member of the Fearless Five and hope he or she can get the others out."

"I have faith in you, Sister Carmen. You've made it this far. You'll find a way to survive."

"Thanks for the vote of confidence. But if I don't make it out, I want you to expose Morgana Madison. Tell the whole world she's really Malefica, but do it anonymously. She's already discredited me, and I don't want her to come after you too." I pulled a CD out of my jacket and handed it to Lulu. "All the information you need is on here. Photos, documents, the money trail. Leak it to *The Chronicle* and SNN first. They'll eat it up. It'll go national in five seconds. We can have our revenge, one way or the other."

"It'll be my pleasure." Lulu palmed the disc. "Take care, Sister Carmen. Good luck."

"Thanks," I said. "I'll need it."

I got out of the van and shut the door behind me. Lulu cranked the motor and drove away. I watched the taillights fade into the dark night, carefully picked up the bag of bombs, and walked to the borrowed Aston Martin. The bag went in the back, while I slid into the front seat.

Ten minutes later, I steered the car off the side of the road. The ice cream factory towered in the distance about a quarter mile away. I drove the car into the woods where it couldn't be seen, parked, killed the headlights, and got out. The ground felt moist and springy underfoot, and the scent of pine trees and sap tickled my nose. A crescent moon hung like a silver lantern in the sky. It might be the last moon I'd ever see. I shoved that unpleasant thought aside.

I grabbed the swords and scabbard, took off my leather jacket, and tossed it in the car. The night air chilled my skin, but I had no doubt that I'd soon be much, much colder. I strapped on the scabbard and put the two swords into their slots. The weapons felt odd on my back. I picked up the black duffel bag and eased it over my shoulder.

I walked through the woods toward the ice cream factory. A few bugs chirped in the deep shadows. Bullfrogs bellowed, and owls hooted in the treetops. Dry leaves crackled under my sneakers, their earthy aroma mingling with the sticky sap of the pine trees. The sounds and smells of the woods comforted me. I was a country girl at heart, no matter how long I'd been in the big city.

I reached the edge of the woods, crouched down, and peered through the trees. The ice cream factory towered above me. With its shattered windows and graffiti-covered walls, the building looked like it belonged in the middle of a war zone. I stopped where I was, looking, listening. Nothing moved outside the building, and I couldn't detect any noise or movement inside.

I checked the swords on my back and the bag slung over my shoulder one more time. Everything was in place. It was now or never.

I crept forward.

Using the trees for cover, I skirted around the building until I came to the loading dock entrance. I pulled out Lulu's blueprints and double-checked the location. Right on track. I stuffed the papers into my back pocket, got a firm grip on the duffel bag, and darted across the parking lot as fast as I could. I eased myself up against the building, then stopped and waited, looking, listening. Nothing, except my ragged breaths and the frantic beating of my heart.

I crept over to the door and tried the knob. It turned, and I inched open the door. No alarms sounded, no sirens blared. I snuck inside and closed the door behind me. I stood at the entrance a moment, letting my eyes adjust to the dim light. I was in a large, square room. Empty buckets and barrels littered the floor, and I tiptoed through the debris. Goose bumps covered my bare arms. It couldn't be more than thirty degrees inside the factory. Evidently, Frost was up to his usual tricks.

I peeked around the corner. The room opened up into

the main factory floor. A catwalk crisscrossed over my head. No one in sight. I turned right and headed for a metal support beam in the center of the wall. According to Jasper's directions, I should plant the first bomb here. I took one of the cherry-shaped devices out of my bag, flicked a switch to arm it, and nestled it next to the beam. I paused every few seconds to look and listen. Nothing. I grabbed some loose pieces of brick and piled them over the bomb to hide it. It wasn't much of a disguise, but hopefully it would pass a casual inspection. I let out a breath. One down. Lots more to go.

I repeated this process over and over, making a circle around the inside of the factory, until I'd planted all of my bombs. Luckily, the points Jasper had marked on the map were away from the very center of the factory, where Malefica was holding the Fearless Five.

Once the final bomb was in place, I pulled out the remote trigger and programmed it to detonate the bombs in one hour. If we weren't out in an hour, we weren't getting out at all. I stuffed the duffel bag and remote trigger down a metal grate about twenty feet away from the last bomb. I also ripped up the blueprints and threw the pieces down the grate as well, and piled bricks on top of it so it couldn't be seen. The Terrible Triad might find some of the bombs and disarm them, but it was unlikely they could get to them all without the trigger.

My hands shook. Now came the hard part. I reached over my back and drew the two swords out of the leather scabbard. I twirled them in my hands to get a feel for them. I took a long breath and blew it out to steady my ragged nerves. I could do this. I'd planted the bombs without being detected. All I had to do now was free the Fearless Five. If they were still alive.

I closed my eyes and thought of Sam. His eyes, his smile, the way his lips felt on mine. My heart tightened. He had to be alive. He just had to be. They all had to be alive.

I tiptoed through the factory. I moved slowly, cautiously, and kept to the shadows. I passed the room where I'd been held on my last visit. I went by and ducked under a set of metal stairs. Icicles hung like jagged daggers from the underside. I peeked around a tall canister. Through the maze of pipes, I spotted the cages that contained Frost's pet projects. The animals must be sleeping because I didn't hear any moans or growls or howls. I gulped. The cages stood right next to the giant vats of radioactive goo.

Suddenly, a large shadow fell over me. Knuckles cracked together.

Uh-oh.

I turned. Scorpion stood right behind me.

He swatted the swords out of my hand. They hit the icy floor and slid away. I tried to run, but he grabbed me by the back of my shirt. He picked me up like I was a naughty puppy and dangled me in front of him.

"Little girls shouldn't play with toothpicks," he said.

Scorpion slung me over his shoulder and scooped up the swords.

"Put me down, you big bully!"

I struggled and tried to slide free, but my strength was no match for the ubervillain's. A tractor trailer going over a hundred would have had a hard time slowing him down. All I could do was pound my fists against his back like an indignant child.

Scorpion climbed up a set of stairs. Laughter floated down. Scorpion reached the top. I swayed from side to side, catching sight of the vats below. Fog rose up from them. I shivered.

"Malefica, Frost, look what I found creeping around the factory—a little mouse," Scorpion said.

He dumped me on the floor, and a pair of red boots came into view.

"Well, well, well, what do we have here?" Malefica said, her green eyes lighting up.

Uh-oh.

★ 27 ★

"Carmen!" Sam shouted.

My heart lit up like a firecracker at the sound of Sam's voice. I looked past Malefica and spotted him standing in one of the glass tubes. I drank in the sight of him. Lines of fatigue etched his handsome face, which was tight with worry. Other than that, Sam looked no worse for wear. My eyes flicked to the others in the tubes next to him. They all looked a little beat-up but not seriously injured. Fiona, Henry, and Chief Newman stared back at me. My heart plummeted. None of them were wearing their masks. Malefica had unmasked them, all of them. She knew who they were.

The ubervillain paced around me. I got to my feet.

"She had these with her." Scorpion held out the swords.

Malefica waved her hands, and the swords floated toward her. "Running with sharp objects? Tisk, tisk, Miss Cole."

The swords sailed over and landed in front of Sam's tube. He eyed them like a starving man staring at a thick, juicy steak.

"What did you think you would accomplish by breaking in here?" Malefica asked.

I didn't reply.

"Surely you didn't think you could defeat us," Frost sneered. "That would go against all the laws of science, logic, and chance."

I shrugged. "It was a thought. Everybody gets lucky every now and then. I thought tonight might be my night."

"Well, it was a bad thought. In fact, it's the last one you'll ever have," Malefica said. "You know, I was going to let you live out the rest of your pathetic life, wracked by guilt over your part in the demise of the Fearless Five. I was going to enjoy tormenting you from afar. It would have been a pleasant diversion. Not anymore. You've caused far too much trouble, popping up like this just as we were about to get on with things. I hate delays of any sort."

"I'm sorry, am I keeping you from an important dinner date?"

Malefica backhanded me. Pain exploded in my cheek. I rocked back, but I didn't fall to the ground. I refused to give her that satisfaction. Sam hissed.

"You pathetic woman. You still haven't figured it out, have you? Do you even know what this is all about?"

"Of course I know what it's about," I mumbled through my split lip. Blood pooled in my mouth, and a few drops spattered onto the icy floor. "It's what superhero-ubervillain battles are always about. You've captured the Fearless Five. You've unmasked them, and soon you're going to kill them."

Malefica shook her head. "Your vision is so shortsighted. I want more than to merely unmask the Fearless Five. I want their powers as well."

I froze. My eyes flew to the tubes and the computer.

"Let me explain it to you, Miss Cole," Frost said in a

patronizing voice. "I, being the brilliant scientist I am, have designed a complicated superhero suction system. My glass, power vacuumers will suck the superstrength right out of the Fearless Five, along with the rest of their powers." He preened like a proud father over his monstrous device. "The powers will be transferred through the computer and reconfigured so we can absorb them through this tube."

I followed Frost's gloved finger. Another glass tube, one I hadn't noticed before, sat on the far side of the computers. Glass, power vacuumers? So that's why the Triad had robbed the vacuum cleaner plant. Frost had needed parts for his gruesome project.

Malefica smiled. "Of course, when we have their powers, we'll be invincible. No one will be able to stop us . . ."

I tuned out the rest of the ubervillain's chatter and threats. I glanced at my watch. Forty minutes until the bombs went off. Hopefully, Malefica would keep talking right up until the last second. My eyes flicked up. Frost stared at me. Uh-oh.

"She looked at her watch," Frost said, interrupting Malefica's rant. "You might want to make sure the area is secure before you do away with her."

"What are you scheming now, Miss Cole?" Malefica's eyes glowed.

I could almost feel the other woman peering into my mind. I had to think of something, anything, but the bombs. Something completely unrelated to bombs and explosives and . . . Coconut! That was fairly inane and harmless, although I hated the taste of it. *Coconut, coconut, coconut . . .* I repeated over and over in my mind.

"She's planted several bombs in the building." Malefica rattled off a list of locations. "Go disarm them, now."

Scorpion lumbered down the icy stairs. My heart sank.

So much for my backup plan. What was wrong with me? Was my mind that simple? Was I an open book any psychic could read?

"Should we abort?" Frost asked. "He might not find them all in time."

"No." Malefica turned her head to look at the other ubervillain. "As long as he gets most of them, we'll be all right. Keep going."

I was out of options. It was time to do something drastic. I eyed Malefica, shifted my feet, and prepared to spring.

Suddenly, a giant invisible hand picked me up. I yelped. The hand closed around me, pinning my arms to my side. I felt like the damsel-in-distress in one of those old black-and-white *King Kong* movies.

"As for you, Miss Cole, I'm afraid you have outlived your usefulness. You really should have listened to me. I don't make idle threats."

Malefica waved her hand. Slowly, I moved. I floated about twenty feet up into the air, up over the metal railing, until I dangled right over one of the vats.

The radioactive liquid bubbled and gurgled below. White fog drifted up from the vat, and the bottoms of my sneakers iced over. My stomach morphed into a giant ball of fear. Terrified, I looked up and locked eyes with Sam. I saw the panic and fear in his eyes and knew it was reflected in my own.

"Sam," I whispered.

Malefica twitched her hand, and I plunged into the vat.

Cold.
No, *icy*.
No, *frigid*.

No . . .

Words couldn't describe the sensation, although it was rather funny I was trying to find a way to explain what it felt like to freeze to death.

The liquid closed over me like a shroud. It poured into my ears and mouth and forced its way down my throat. It tasted like old, crystallized, vanilla ice cream. Blech. And it was cold, colder than death. Colder than anything I'd ever felt before. It made the harshest winter, the bitterest wind feel balmy by comparison. I froze on the inside and outside. I immediately lost feeling in my fingers and toes. Ice formed on my clothes and in my hair. I couldn't move. Couldn't see. Couldn't breathe . . .

Suddenly, the invisible hand yanked me up out of the liquid. I coughed and gasped for air. My teeth rattled together like dominos.

"How's the water?" Malefica asked. "Let's go for another dip."

I plunged back into the vat. The cold was worse this time, if that was possible. The frigid sensation worked its way up my arms and legs. My internal organs iced over one by one . . .

I flew up out of the liquid again. Malefica danced me around like a puppet. Bits and pieces of ice broke off my clothes and disappeared into the fog below. I couldn't feel anything. Not my fingers, not my toes, not even my own eyes as they struggled to blink.

"Not quite done yet," Malefica cackled and blew me a kiss.

I went into the vat for a third time. The cold engulfed my body. Something cracked open in my head and trickled down into the back of my eyes. I floated away on a cold cloud . . .

Just when I thought this was the end, the invisible

hand lifted me up out of the goo. I stood frozen and stiff in midair, a human icicle come to life.

"I think that's enough." Malefica waved her hand.

I sailed through the air and landed on the metal platform in between Malefica and the caged superheroes. I couldn't move or speak or even whimper. I could barely make myself breathe. Fiona's horrified face swam in front of my eyes. Sam shouted, but his voice seemed far away.

"Well, I have to say, Frost, I'm most impressed. That stuff really packs a punch. Is she still alive?"

Frost peered at me. "For the moment. She won't last much longer."

Malefica leaned down. "There's one more secret I want to share with you before you depart this earth, Miss Cole. Something I've been keeping to myself for six delicious months now."

I struggled to focus on the ubervillain. My vision had gone haywire, along with everything else. Malefica looked like a jumbled mass of black waves all bouncing off each other.

"You see, I know how guilty you've been feeling over Tornado's death. But I just want to tell you this—your guilt was for nothing. He didn't commit suicide. I killed him."

"What? What are you saying?" Fiona demanded, pounding her fist against the inside of her tube.

Malefica turned to the superhero. "Haven't you figured it out yet? You superheroes . . . so gullible. Never thinking about the big picture. Pity."

"I got an advance copy of Carmen's story identifying Travis Teague as Tornado. I was thrilled when I got the news. As Morgana Madison, it was so easy to arrange a meeting with dear Travis to talk about investing in his wind power company. Once I was in his office, I hit him with Frost's freezoray gun, then dumped him out the window. Don't worry. I'm sure he didn't feel a thing."

"You bitch!"

Fiona exploded into a roaring mass of red and orange and yellow waves. I could almost feel the heat from the other woman, even though the glass tube separated us. A small spark of anger sizzled up in me. Malefica had used me from the very beginning, used me to murder Tornado, to capture the Fearless Five. Now, she was going to kill them all, kill my friends, kill Sam, the man I so desperately loved. The cold returned, stronger this time. The little spark flickered and dimmed and faded away . . .

No!

I focused my energy on that spark. Anger was good. Anger meant I was still alive and not sliding into cold, cold oblivion. I stared at the dazzling waves dancing around Fiona. If only I could reach out and touch that warmth *somehow* . . . wrap it around myself . . . I might have a chance . . . I had to fight . . . I strained toward the fiery waves . . .

"Now, now," Malefica said to Fiona. "There's no need to get all upset. I could have let the poor girl die thinking she was responsible for Tornado's death. Instead, I've chosen to do the noble thing, the honorable thing, and confess my wicked, wicked sins. You should applaud me."

"You're despicable," Sam spat out. "Rot in hell."

"You first, darling." Malefica puckered her lips and blew a kiss to the trapped superhero.

Water dripped off my frozen, ice-covered fingers. It puddled in the floor underneath me. Still, I stared at Fiona. The flames around her flickered and dimmed. Her face paled. Somehow, though, I didn't feel quite as cold as before.

Frost circled me. "Interesting. She should be frozen solid by now. She must be made of sturdier stuff than I thought. Or perhaps the ambient temperature is slowly thawing her out. It will be too little, too late, though." He drew his freez-oray gun out from the holster on his utility belt. "Are you going to finish her off, Malefica? Or shall I?"

"You get back to work on the computers. I'll take care of Miss Cole."

Frost put his weapon away. He took up his previous post in front of the computer and began flipping switches and pushing buttons.

Malefica used her boot to roll me over onto my back. I made no sound, although I stared at Malefica. The ubervillain paid no attention to the hate burning in my eyes—or to the fact my skin was no longer quite as blue as Frost's costume. Malefica made a grand sweep with her hand, and Sam's two swords rose up into the air.

"I think I'll let Striker's weapons of choice be the means of your demise, Miss Cole. Watching someone die from hypothermia brought on by radioactive goo isn't terribly exciting. There's no blood, no spatter, no real artistry to it."

"Don't do this, Malefica. Please. She's an innocent. She doesn't even have any powers," Sam pleaded.

Malefica smiled. "What's this? Are you begging me to spare her life? She won't last more than a few more minutes either way, you know." Her eyes glowed. "Do you actually . . . care about her?"

Sam stared at my still form. He lowered his head.

"You do!" Malefica laughed. "How ironic. Striker has feelings for the woman who exposed him to me. How deliciously ironic."

The swords floated over my body.

"And now, Miss Cole, it's time for you to die." Malefica snapped her hands downward.

"No!" Sam shouted.

The swords zoomed straight at my chest.

★28★

"How ironic. Striker has feelings for the woman who exposed him to me."

Striker has feelings for . . .

Feelings for . . .

Feelings . . .

The words echoed in my mind. My lips twitched upward. He cared about me? Sam aka Striker Sloane actually cared about me?

The little spark of anger that I'd been holding on to blossomed into something much, much greater. I moved my head an inch. He stood in his glass tube, a look of utter despair and hopelessness on his handsome face. Sam. The strange, warm feeling grew inside me. The cold receded from my bones.

I moved my head back. The swords hovered above me. Behind them, I could see Malefica, and the waves that surrounded the ubervillain. They looked just like the waves

I'd seen around Fiona, except they were black, just like Malefica's twisted soul.

Malefica moved her hand. The swords plunged downward, about to make me the world's largest pin cushion. If I could have put my hands up, I would have. If I could have screamed, I might have done that too.

But I couldn't. I couldn't do any of those things.

All I could do was stare at the black waves and concentrate.

It was enough.

The swords stopped an inch from my chest. They hovered there like long, slender helicopters. Malefica frowned. She waved her hand. The swords backed off, then plunged at me again.

Again, they stopped.

I stared at the ubervillain. Malefica repeated the process a third time.

Again, the swords stopped short of plunging into my cold body.

"What are you doing?" Frost demanded, putting his hands on his thin hips. "Quit fooling around. Kill her already. We have superpowers to suck, you know."

"I'm trying," Malefica muttered. "I'm trying."

I wasn't quite sure why I wasn't dead yet. It had something to do with the black waves boiling around Malefica. They pulsated just a few feet away. They weren't hot like the waves around Fiona. These waves had a different sort of power. They felt like . . . the ocean. Perpetual motion. Like all you had to do was just think about something and it would move for you.

The waves around Malefica surged forward, and the swords came at me once more. I stared at the waves and pictured myself using their power to shove the swords back at the ubervillain.

The weapons stopped.

"What—what are you doing? Stop that!" Malefica shrieked.

"Malefica, what's going on?" Frost asked.

"It's . . . her! She's interfering with my telekinesis!"

"Impossible!" Frost scoffed. "You just aren't concentrating. Focus on the task at hand." He turned back to the computers.

"Fine," she muttered. "I'll do it myself. It's always more fun that way."

Malefica waved her hand. One of the swords flew through the room and embedded itself in the wall. The ubervillain took hold of the other one and towered over me. Malefica lifted the sword up high above her head. The black waves around her intensified.

My fingers fluttered.

The sword ripped out of Malefica's hand, hit the floor, and slid to a stop in front of Sam's tube. Malefica's mouth dropped open. She stared at me. For the first time, the ubervillain realized I wasn't frozen anymore. All of the ice had melted off my body. My skin was no longer pale and blue, my hair no longer white with frost.

"Your eyes," she whispered. "They're glowing!"

Malefica took an uncertain step back.

I stared at the black waves around the ubervillain and imagined using their power to pull myself into a sitting position. Beads of sweat popped out on my face. It took so much effort to concentrate, to focus, to try to move. And yet, slowly, oh-so-slowly, my body propped itself up.

"Carmen?" Sam said. "Carmen!"

I stared at the caged superhero. Soothing sapphire waves rippled out from his body. I could feel their healing powers, their ability to continually restore. If only I could use them to heal myself . . . I reached out with my mind toward the pulsating waves . . .

"Bloody hell," Fiona said. "Look at her eyes!"

"Everyone be quiet. Stop talking to her, Sam. Carmen needs to concentrate," Chief Newman said in a low voice.

"What's happening to her?" Henry asked.

"What happened to all of us," the chief replied in a cryptic tone. "Now be quiet and watch."

I barely comprehended the superheroes' conversation. All I was aware of were the soothing, soothing waves. I reached for them, and their power trickled into my body. A warm glow enveloped me, jump-starting my heart, restoring my circulation. My breathing grew easier. Pricks and needles of pain ran up and down my arms and legs. I wiggled my toes. I could feel them again.

Inside the tube, Sam fell to his knees. Sweat streamed down his anguish-filled face. I frowned. I was hurting him. I let go. Sam fell back against the side of the tube. Malefica's eyes flicked back and forth between us.

I rolled over onto my knees. Water dripped down my face and plopped onto the metal floor. I pushed myself up. My knees wobbled. I lurched over to the metal railing and hung on to it for support.

Malefica took another step back. "Frost, Frost! Quit messing with that stupid computer."

"What do you want? I'm trying to work here in case you haven't noticed. Just kill her already . . ." The ubervillain caught sight of my glowing eyes. His voice trailed off.

"What's in that vat I dropped her in?" Malefica asked.

"Nothing special. Just a mixture of radioactive isotopes and chemical compounds. Your usual goo." Frost studied me. "Although it seems as if it has quite a different effect on humans than on animals. How fascinating."

"Fascinating my ass! Look at her!"

Frost waved his hand. "So her eyes are glowing. No big deal. It's probably just a temporary effect."

Malefica shook her head. "You're wrong. I can feel the power pouring off her. Quick! Hit her with the freezoray gun!"

Frost sighed. "Always so demanding."

Snow-white waves rippled out from the ubervillain. Cold waves. I stared at the gun on Frost's side and reached for the power.

Frost went for his weapon. Too little, too late. A large block of ice encased his freezoray gun, rendering it useless.

I took a step forward.

Malefica and Frost looked at each other. Meanwhile, Scorpion appeared at the top of the stairs.

"I found several bombs. They've been shut down—"

"That doesn't matter right now. Scorpion, get her!" Malefica shrieked.

The giant, hulking ubervillain shrugged. "Okay."

He lumbered over to me, put his hand on my throat, and picked me up. "Now what?"

Malefica pointed. "Throw her back into the vat! Now!"

Scorpion raised me high into the air. I looked at Fiona and the red-hot waves that enveloped her. I put my hand on Scorpion's chest.

He dropped me like a hot potato.

At that moment, I *was* one. I used Fiona's power to superheat my hand. Scorpion now had a giant smoking hole on his chest. Blisters popped out on his massive form, although they began to heal within seconds due to his regenerative abilities.

"What's the matter, Scorpion? Am I a little too hot to handle?" I said, getting to my feet.

The ubervillain growled in pain. Malefica and Frost stared at me. Fear and confusion shimmered in their eyes.

"What's wrong? Can't take a little taste of your own medicine?" I said.

The three ubervillains didn't reply.

"Or perhaps you're frightened of me. Imagine that. The Terrible Triad quaking in their boots because of Carmen Cole. What a strange day this is turning out to be. Wouldn't you say?" I sounded crazy and I knew it. I felt crazy. All jumbled up inside.

Scorpion charged at me. I stared at Malefica and used the ubervillain's telekinetic power waves to pick up Scorpion and fling him across the room. He crashed into the computers, shattering them with his massive form. The blinking lights snuffed out like a candle. Scorpion groaned once and lay still.

Frost wasn't nearly so bold and daring. He ran. He clattered down the steps as fast as he could, toward the cages that held his pet projects. I grabbed Malefica's powers again. The locks on the metal cages popped off. I waved my hand, and the doors creaked open. Frost stopped. He turned to look at me.

"What are you doing?! My work!"

"Is about to come back and bite you in the ass. Just like karma."

I used Malefica's power to rattle the cages. Low snarls erupted from within. A white, furry head appeared. Then another, then another. Frost's mouth dropped open in horror. He backed up against the wall. The mutated creatures caught sight of him. They growled with one voice and advanced on him.

"No! Stop! I created you! I am your master! You have to listen to me—"

Frost went down in a heap of teeth and claws and fur.

"Behind you!" Sam shouted.

I ducked. A sword zipped by my head. Malefica stared at me, her green eyes glittering with hate and rage.

"Do you want to play too?" I asked. "There's plenty of me to go around."

"You get a little taste of power and you think you're something special," Malefica hissed. "You're nothing compared to me."

"You're the one who's nothing," I spat back.

The ubervillain threw her arms wide. Bricks, loose wires, small pieces of metal, everything that wasn't tied down rose into the air. Malefica shoved her arms forward and threw the mass of stuff at me at warp speed.

I hit the ground, and the debris sailed over my head. Most of it clattered off the railing and disappeared into the bubbling liquid below. Pieces cut my arms and hands and shredded the back of my T-shirt.

I scrambled to my feet and threw myself at her. We went down in a pile on the slick, cold floor. We rolled around, each trying to get the upper hand. Malefica slapped me across the face. I sank my teeth into her forearm. Blood filled my mouth, and Malefica howled in pain. She hit me in the head. We kicked and clawed and bit and scratched like two she-cats.

"Get her, Carmen!"

"Kick her bloody ass!"

"Atta girl!"

"Go Carmen!"

Cheered on by the superheroes' shouts, I positioned myself on top of Malefica, reared back my hand, and punched the ubervillain with all my might. I had never punched anyone in my entire life.

It felt good.

Really good.

Incredibly good.

So I did it again. And again. And again.

"Carmen! Carmen, stop! She's out of it!"

Sam's voice penetrated my rage. Malefica lay slack and silent underneath me. The ubervillain's beautiful face was a pulpy, bloody mess. I quit punching her and staggered to my feet. The world spun around. I lurched forward and grabbed the railing for support. My friends shouted something to me, but I couldn't quite make it out over the ringing in my head.

My inner voice screamed. I turned. Somehow, Malefica had gotten up. She ran at me, but I sidestepped out of the way. Malefica hit the railing. Her momentum carried her forward, and she flipped up and over the side. She shrieked once and splashed into the cold liquid below. And then—

Silence.

I stared into the white fog. The liquid gurgled and bubbled once.

"Carmen? Carmen! Are you okay?"

I lumbered around at the sound of Sam's voice. The four superheroes stared at me, worry in their eyes.

"I . . . think so."

I felt drained and utterly exhausted. But I couldn't stop. Not yet. Not until I'd freed my friends. I staggered over to the smashed computers. Scorpion was gone. A pool of black blood glistened on the floor where he'd been. I squinted at the buttons and switches and wires. My hands hovered over the twisted metal.

"Hit the switch on the far side of the computer. The one that isn't broken off like the others," Henry said.

I threw the switch, and the doors on the glass tubes hissed open. The superheroes tumbled out of their cages. They exchanged wary glances and slowly approached me. I looked at them. The waves of power still billowed out from them. I shook my head, and my vision cleared. The waves disappeared, and my friends came into focus.

Sam put his arms around me. I smiled at him. He had never looked more handsome.

"It's good to see you," he said.

"You too," I replied.

Sam's face swam before my eyes. I smiled again. Then, the darkness came, and I fell into its sweet embrace.

★29★

My eyes fluttered open, and I stared at the ceiling overhead. I recognized it immediately. Back in the sick bay again. A heart monitor beeped next to me, along with all the other usual medical devices. An IV pumped fluid into my arm.

I could feel someone else in the room. I turned my head. Sam sat in a chair next to the bed.

"Hey there, handsome," I croaked. My throat had about a gallon of sand in it.

His silver eyes lit up. "Hey there, yourself. How are you feeling?"

"Better. Still kind of tired and sleepy."

He reached out and took my hand. "You gave us all quite a scare, you know."

"Did I? I'm sorry."

Sam stroked his thumb over my hand. Tingles of pleasure ran up and down my hand at his warm touch. I twitched my fingers in response.

"Why are you doing that?"

"Just making sure I can still feel them," I joked.

Sam smiled. I'd never thought I would see him smile again. The effect was even more devastating than I remembered. My eyes traced over him. No cuts, no bruises, no nicks or scrapes could be seen on his face and arms. He looked completely healthy. Then again, he would be. He could regenerate, after all. My heart swelled with love and tenderness. Sam was safe. I'd never been happier.

"What day is it?" I asked, trying to take my mind off Sam's incredible smile.

"Friday."

"Friday the thirteenth?" Surely, I'd been asleep longer than just a day.

"No, Friday, the twentieth."

Sam filled me in on what had happened after I collapsed. Henry and Chief Newman had made sure the glass tubes and computers had been destroyed. Then, Fiona picked me up, and the superheroes had raced out of the ice cream factory. Moments later, the building exploded. Scorpion hadn't gotten to all of the bombs after all. The factory collapsed in on itself. While the superheroes had fully recovered from the effects of Frost's freezeray gun, there had been no sign of Malefica, Frost, or Scorpion since the explosion.

"Do you think they're dead?" I asked.

"I think Scorpion made it out. He crawled away while you and Malefica were fighting. I don't know about Frost. By the time we got down the stairs, the animals had all escaped. We're trying to track them down now. There was a lot of blood on the floor, along with some pieces torn from his costume. As for Malefica, it's possible she survived being in the vat. You did."

I flashed back to the factory. Malefica laughing, dropping

me into the vat. The cold liquid closing over me. Freezing me, squeezing the warmth, the life from my body. I trembled and pulled the covers up to my neck. I wondered if I would ever forget that awful, awful cold, if I'd ever be truly warm again.

"Don't think about that," Sam said. "You're safe now, Carmen. The Triad will never hurt you again. I promise."

A shiver slithered up my spine. My inner voice whispered. "I'm not so sure about that."

"Well, I am. Rest now. We'll have time to talk once you're completely well."

Sam kissed my cheek and smoothed my hair back. His gentle touch brought hot tears to my eyes. I cupped his head in my hands and pressed my lips to his. Desire flared to life deep inside me. I wrapped my arms around Sam's neck, drawing him closer, even as my tongue sought out his.

"If you keep kissing me like that, I'm going to have a hard time leaving," Sam murmured in a low, husky voice.

"Then don't," I whispered.

Sam disentangled himself from my greedy grasp. He pressed a kiss to the palm of my hand. "Unfortunately, I have to. The chief's orders. He told me in no uncertain terms not to do anything to upset you."

I arched an eyebrow. "You don't upset me. Quite the opposite in fact."

"I think the chief was speaking in code."

"Oh."

Sam smiled. "Sleep now. I'll be back soon."

"Promise?"

He crossed his heart. "Promise."

He kissed me lightly and left. The door hissed shut behind him. I touched my fingers to my lips. They still felt warm and tingly from his kiss. A goofy grin spread across my face. I sat up, wanting to go after him, to make sure this was real, that he was real, and not some figment of my frozen imagination. A rustle of fabric caught my attention.

Oh no. Not again.

I peeked under the covers. A brand-new pair of lab-rat, white pajamas covered my pale body. I sighed. In a way, it was comforting to know some things would never change.

The next day and several naps later, I felt well enough to get out of bed. My first order of business was to have Sam help me upstairs to my suite, where I took a long, hot bath and pulled on some clean, non-pajama-like clothes.

I felt more like myself in my usual uniform of jeans and a T-shirt. My stomach rumbled. I was starving. I turned sideways and looked at myself in the bathroom mirror. On the upside, being unconscious was certainly good for the diet.

Someone knocked on the door. I opened it. Sam was there, wearing an impeccable business suit just like always.

"Ready for dinner?"

My stomach rumbled again. I blushed.

Sam grinned. "I'll take that as a yes."

"You can take it any way you want to, as long as you feed me."

Sam held out his arm. I took it, and we walked downstairs. Sam opened the door to the dining room. Fiona, Henry, and Chief Newman waited inside. The three superheroes stood. When I entered the room, they clapped. Sam joined in as well. Fiona put her fingers to her lips and let out an ear-splitting whistle. The chief wiggled his hand, and an enormous banner attached to one wall unfurled. It read TO CARMEN.

My eyes widened. I ran to the table and hugged all the superheroes, even Fiona.

"Sit, sit," Henry said. "You're our guest of honor to-night." He pulled out the seat at the head of the table.

I sank into the chair and wiped away the tears that threatened to trickle down my face. Sam disappeared into the kitchen and returned carrying an enormous chocolate cake. Fiona waved her hand, and candles lit up on the smooth, frosted surface. It also said TO CARMEN. Henry rushed forward and put a glass of champagne in my hands.

"You guys, I don't deserve this."

"You most certainly do," Sam said. "All this and much more."

"No, it's too much," I protested.

"Nonsense." Sam lifted his glass. "I propose a toast. To Carmen!"

"To Carmen!" the superheroes shouted.

We raised our glasses high and clinked them together.

"We just wanted to show our appreciation," the chief said, his blue eyes twinkling. "If it wasn't for you, none of us would be here now."

"I don't know about that. You guys are the Fearless Five. You would have found some way to escape Malefica's evil clutches. You're superheroes. It's what you do."

"Let's not talk about that now," Sam said. A dark shadow passed over his face. "Tonight, we're celebrating our rescuer, Carmen Cole. So let's eat. Our girl's hungry."

They brought out dish after dish of food. My mouth watered. Fried chicken, mashed potatoes, biscuits, vegetables. All my favorites. I took big helpings of everything, wolfed them down, and went back for seconds.

"Slow down there, tiger," Fiona said. "You're giving me a run for my money tonight."

My fork froze over my mashed potatoes. I stared at Fiona, but I didn't detect any hostility in the other woman's tone

or gaze. I didn't even feel any warmer than usual. No sweat.
No flare-ups. Nothing.

"I'm just kidding," Fiona laughed. "I'll fight you for
the last piece of fried chicken."

I smiled. "You're on."

In the end, Fiona got the last piece of chicken. I retali-
ated by eating not one, not two, but three pieces of the
scrumptious chocolate cake. We ate and laughed and talked
and ate some more. It was one of the best nights of my life.

Once we'd finished dessert, the conversation wound
down. Even though I was grateful for the party and festive
atmosphere, there were still questions I needed answers to.

"So what exactly happened to me?"

The four superheroes exchanged glances.

"That's something we've talked about a great deal. We've
concluded it was a combination of many things all working together." Chief Newman shoved back his empty plate
and pulled a pack of *RID* pills out of his pocket. "Exactly
how many of these did you take before you stormed the ice
cream factory?"

"About ten or so."

Henry whistled. "You're only supposed to take one a
day. Didn't you read the warning label?"

I shrugged. "I figured warning labels didn't matter when
you were going up against the Triad and their vats of radioactive goo. I didn't really expect to make it out of the
factory alive."

"Just as I suspected," Chief Newman said. "It's a good
thing you took the pills. They absorbed most of the radiation you were exposed to. They saved your life."

"So what about . . . the other stuff?" I asked.

"Other stuff?" the chief asked.

"You mean when you burned Scorpion and threw him

around like a rag doll?" Fiona asked. "Or do you mean when you iced Frost's freezoray gun? Or perhaps you're talking about when your eyes went all neon blue and glowy, and you wailed on Malefica?"

I swallowed. "Um, all of the above, I suppose."

"Well, it's quite simple," the chief said. "For that brief time in the factory, you, my dear, had superpowers."

My mouth fell open. Superpowers? Me? "No way!"

"Believe it," Sam said. "We all saw what you did. Somehow, you found a way to use the Triad's power against them."

Deep down, I'd known that's what had happened to me. Hell, I'd been drunk with the power. A ball of worry took root in my stomach. Ever since I'd woken up, I had been hoping it was just a figment of my imagination.

The chief continued. "What we need to determine now is if it was just a fluke."

"A fluke?"

"A onetime occurrence," Henry said. "Sometimes, people gain or even lose superpowers after exposure to radioactive isotopes and other materials. Most of the time, the powers fade away after a few days."

"Oh." The tight ball loosened a bit. "How are we going to do that?"

"First of all, how did you feel after you came out of the vat? What did you see?" the chief asked.

"It was cold, colder than anything you could possibly imagine. My vision went haywire, and I could see these waves around you guys. The waves seemed to have different feels to them. I just . . . sort of . . . reached out for them and stuff happened."

Chief Newman and Sam exchanged a quick glance.

"Why don't you see if you can do that again?" the chief asked in a gentle voice. "If you feel like you're up to it."

I took a deep breath and let it out. I pushed my chair away from the table and backed up until I could see all four of them. My eyes zipped from Fiona to Henry to Chief Newman to Sam, and back again.

Nothing.

Not even a flicker of a wave or a splash of color.

Relief surged through me. I didn't see anything. Not one thing—

Wait a minute.

Sam shifted in his chair, and I spotted something out of the corner of my eye. I turned my head and squinted at him. Sam crossed his arms over his chest, and the faintest bit of color sparked around his arms. The air around him shimmered sapphire blue, just like before.

"Well?" Fiona asked. "Do you see anything?"

"Quiet, Fiona," Chief Newman said. "She's trying to concentrate."

I titled my head. Fiona's blond hair seemed to be glowing a rather red color. Fiona shot her father a sour look, and the color intensified. My eyes flew to Henry, who drummed his fingers on the table. Every time his fingers hit the smooth wood, they sent out small, bluish-white waves. I turned to the chief. Lazy green waves swirled about his head. I looked down at my hands and wiggled my fingers. Silver waves radiated out from me.

Uh-oh.

My shoulders sagged.

"You don't see anything," Sam said.

I shook my head.

"No," I said. "Unfortunately, I see everything."

★ 30 ★

I sank down into my chair. "I can't believe this is happening to me. To me, of all people." I laughed. "How ironic. How pathetically ironic. But I suppose that's karma for you."

"So what exactly do you see?" Fiona asked.

I told the others about the waves of energy around them.

"I'm red? Hmmm. I always thought I'd be more of a cool, silver color," Fiona said. "Or maybe blue to match my eyes."

I shot Chief Newman a look. He shrugged.

"So do you think you can do something?" Fiona asked.

"Like what?"

Fiona threw her arms out. "I don't know. Something, anything. You can still see the waves. See if you can still use them."

I stared at Fiona and reached for the waves of red-hot energy. A fiery power poured into my body, and I fluttered my fingers. The candles on the cake flared back to life even though I'd blown them out long ago.

"Bloody hell," Fiona said. "That's just like what you did at the factory."

"Unfortunately," I muttered. "Why couldn't it just go away? Do you think it might in a few more days?"

The chief shook his head. "Probably not. If it's lasted this long, then it's more than likely permanent."

I groaned and buried my head in my hands.

"Being an empath is nothing to be worried about or scared of, my dear." The chief put a comforting hand on my shoulder.

I frowned. "An empath? What are you talking about?"

"Your power. You're an empath. When you first came here, I thought you might have some latent ability. You kept mentioning how you knew certain things would happen right before they did. You called it instinct. It's really empathy, the ability to tune into the emotions and feelings of others and sense their thoughts and future actions. It's a rare gift. In your case, you seem to be able not only to sense other people's feelings but to actually see the psychic energy that surrounds them. In the Triad's case, you tapped into their powers and used them to your advantage."

"But I don't want to be an empath," I wailed.

The chief chuckled. "I'm afraid you don't have a choice."

I put my head down into my arms. "Fantastic," I muttered. "Just fantastic."

Soon after, I claimed I had a headache and wanted to go to bed. I left the others, including Sam, in the dining room and made my way up to my suite. I shut the door, flopped down onto the bed, and stared at the plush carpet.

I couldn't quite wrap my head around everything that had happened in the past week or so. I'd gone from getting

Sam kidnapped, to finding out Malefica's real identity, to getting the rest of the Fearless Five captured, to being dumped in a vat of radioactive waste, to somehow saving everyone. Oh yes, and now I had powers.

Superpowers.

I rubbed my aching temples. I didn't want powers of any kind, much less superpowers. But it seemed as though I was stuck with them. Whether I liked it or not.

The question now was what the hell was I going to do with them?

The next morning, I went out into the garden. I wandered among the flowers and tried not to think about the green energy rippling out of them. Flowers, plants, trees. Even the grass underfoot radiated waves of energy. All the untapped power pulsed and flowed around me, just begging me to reach out and latch on to it. I refused to give in to the temptation. I did my best to pretend like everything was normal, that my vision wasn't awash in shimmering, colorful waves. If I didn't specifically look for them, I could almost ignore the energy waves. Almost.

I frowned. My inner voice chirped. Someone was watching me. I stared at a bush up ahead—a bush with sapphire blue waves radiating out of it.

"I know you're there. Come out, Sam."

He pushed some branches aside and stepped forward. "How did you know—"

I pointed to my eyes. "I've got super-vision now, remember?"

"Yes, well, that's something I wanted to talk to you about." He peered at me, his eyes full of concern. "How are you doing?"

I shrugged. "As well as can be expected, I suppose. After

all, it's not every day you learn you've developed superpowers. So far, I've only hyperventilated once."

Sam smiled. "That's good. Superheroes really shouldn't hyperventilate. Especially those in the Fearless Five."

I froze. "What?"

Sam took a breath. "We want you to become the newest member of the Fearless Five."

My mouth dropped open. "You want me to *what*?"

"Join the Fearless Five," Sam repeated.

I shook my head. I felt like I had water in my ears. "I'm sorry. Could you repeat that one more time?"

Sam took my hands. "Join us. Be part of the team. Like you were when you went up against the Triad."

I flashed back to the factory. Something Malefica said echoed in my mind, and I stared up into his silvery eyes. "Was Malefica right? When she said you cared about me?"

Sam stared deep into my eyes. "Yes, she was. I've come to care a great deal about you, Carmen, despite my best intentions to stay away, to let you go back to your old life once the Triad was defeated. The question is, how do you feel about me?"

"I care about you too."

Suddenly, we were kissing. Sam plundered my mouth with his demanding tongue. I pulled him tighter to me and ran my hands up and down his muscled back. Everything felt just as good as it had before. Better, actually. But my inner voice chattered, and I couldn't stop the nagging thought running through my head. I pulled back and broke off the passionate kiss.

"What do you really want, Sam? Me or my new powers?"

He frowned. "What are you talking about?"

"I have to know. You want me to join the Fearless Five in one breath, and in the next, you're telling me how much you care about me. What do you really want?"

"I—I want both," he admitted. "I care about you, Carmen. I do. But I also think you'd make a great addition to the team. We would be the Fearless Five again."

My heart sank down to my ankles and bled out my shoes. Sam didn't want *me*. He didn't want Carmen Cole—he just wanted the superhero he thought I could be. "I see."

"So what do you say?" Sam asked. His hands settled on my waist, and his silver eyes glowed with hope and excitement.

It broke my heart.

I closed my eyes, drinking in his musky scent, savoring the feel of his warm hands on my body. For the last time. I stared at him, memorizing every line, every curve of his handsome face. Then, I stepped back.

"I'm sorry, Sam. I just—I can't," I said.

I turned and ran away.

★31★

One month later

I swirled the champagne around in my glass. Bubbles rose up in the golden liquid, then fizzed out.

Just like my life.

After leaving Sam in the garden, I'd spent a few more days at Sublime, recovering my strength and learning to control my newfound, unwanted power. The chief asked me to stay longer, but I'd packed up my things and moved back into my apartment. I couldn't face Sam, and I didn't want to learn about my power. I just wanted it to go away. I just wanted things to return to normal. I wanted to go back to the good ole days when people hated me for killing Tornado, and I was toiling away on the society beat.

I took a swig from the glass. In a way, things had returned to normal. I'd put everything back into place in my apartment, and the chief had hypnotized his officers and the editors at *The Exposé* into forgetting about Morgana's frame-up of me. I'd even resumed my duties on the society beat, although I was keeping a low profile. The newspaper was in quite an uproar. Lulu had more than kept her word. A few hours after I went into the ice cream factory, the computer whiz had leaked Malefica's real identity to the press, much to the chagrin of the editors at *The Exposé*. Given the fact Morgana Madison hadn't been seen or heard from in over a month, the editors had been forced to run the story and admit their conquering hero was an ubervillain. One who was missing in action. I bought every copy of the newspaper I could get my hands on and pasted them up all over my apartment. I didn't know if Malefica was alive or not, but her cover as Morgana Madison had been completely blown. To my complete and utter delight.

Tonight, I was at the annual holiday ball hosted by the performing arts center. Another night, another society benefit, another glass of flat champagne. My eyes roamed the crowd. All the usual suspects were in attendance.

Except Sam Sloane.

The broken pieces of my heart twisted in my chest. Sam had been noticeably absent from the society scene lately. I hadn't seen him since I left Sublime, although he starred in my feverish dreams every night. There, he would come to me, kiss me, make passionate love to me. All the while, Sam would whisper that he loved me for me—not for my new powers. Every morning, I woke up smooching my pillow and murmuring how much I loved him in return. My heart shattered all over again when I realized that it wasn't real. That Sam wasn't there beside me.

That he didn't love me.

I was torn between wanting to see Sam and glad I didn't have to face him. I certainly didn't want to see him with some skinny, perfect supermodel hanging on to his arm. And I didn't want to do something foolish, like throw myself at him and beg him to love me for me.

I stared into the crowd once more. This time, though, I concentrated. Waves of power shimmered to life, and the room erupted with color. Every person radiated his or her own unique shade. More often than not, the color, the feel of the waves corresponded to someone's personality. Blues often indicated a strong, take-charge soul, while greens were usually caring, compassionate people. Whites tended to be shy, retiring types, while reds, yellows, and oranges almost always surrounded loud, boisterous extroverts. In a way, it was almost like looking at someone's karma.

I quit concentrating. The waves vanished, and the colors faded. I sighed. Every so often I tested out my power, hoping it had deserted me. Hoping it had gone away. It hadn't, and it never would.

I gave my empty glass to a passing waiter. I'd already gotten quotes for my story. Time to leave. I turned and smacked into someone.

"Oh! Excuse me. I'm sorry."

"No need to apologize, Carmen," Fiona purred.

Fiona had been trying to corner me at every society benefit this week. So far I'd been able to avoid her. I could spot her heat signature a hundred feet away, but I'd been too depressed and distracted to watch out for her tonight.

"So, how are things?" Fiona asked, her blue eyes wide and curious. She was trying to look all sweet and innocent. She didn't fool me for a second.

"Fine. And you?"

"Well, I'm not so fine. Do you know why?"

I stared at Fiona's flamboyant dress. "Because you're wearing something that would make a peacock blush?"

Fiona sniffed and smoothed down the sequined ruffles on her colorful gown. "I'm going to chalk that comment up to your lack of fashion expertise. No, I'm not fine because Sam is not fine. All he does is mope around the house. He's been a real sourpuss lately. It's getting on my last nerve. I'm the one with the bad attitude, not him."

"Why are you telling me this?" I asked in a guarded tone. I didn't know what Fiona was up to.

"Because I think you should give Sam a call. He misses you."

Sam missed me. For a moment, happiness flooded my body. Then, all my doubts and fears roared back to the surface. "I've got nothing to say to him."

Fiona arched one of her perfect blond eyebrows. "I'd say the two of you have lots to talk about. Didn't you see him when Malefica dropped you into that tub of radioactive goo? He was frantic. Sam really does care about you, Carmen, whether you believe it or not."

I glanced around to make sure no one was eavesdropping on us and lowered my voice. "Listen to me. I'm only going to say this once. I'm not a superhero. I never will be. And that's what Sam really wants. He doesn't want *me*. He doesn't care about *me*. He just wants to add another member to the team."

"Oh come on," Fiona snapped. Her blond hair shimmered. "Wake up and smell the champagne, Carmen. Sam wants *you*. He doesn't care about your powers at all. For some reason I can't fathom, he actually cares about you."

"Even if he did, and that's a very big if, we could never be together." A sour, bitter taste filled my mouth.

"Why the hell not? You've *been* together plenty of times already."

"I'm not talking about sex," I snapped. "I mean we couldn't ever have a real, lasting relationship. There's too much bad karma between us."

"Like what?"

I threw up my hands. I'd only been talking to Fiona two minutes, and she had already exasperated me. "I'm talking about the fact I used to expose superheroes for a living. I'm talking about the fact my relationships with men, especially superheroes, never work out. I'm talking about the fact I almost got you all killed." I drew in a deep breath. "And then there's the biggie—Travis's death."

Sadness filled Fiona's eyes.

"Despite what Malefica said, I'm the reason he's dead. I led her straight to him."

"I miss Travis. I always will. But Malefica's the one responsible. She killed him, Carmen, not you. Even I see that now. I don't blame you anymore."

I arched an eyebrow.

"Well, maybe just a little bit," Fiona admitted. "We'll never be best friends, but I can tolerate your presence now—for Sam's sake."

"Gee, thanks for the ringing endorsement."

Fiona glared at me. This time, though, my temperature didn't shoot up. I used the energy waves in the room to buffer myself from Fiona's heated gaze. There were some advantages to having superpowers.

Finally, I looked away. I was tired. So tired of everything. "Why are you telling me this? You don't even like me."

Fiona shrugged. "I want Sam to be happy, and you seem to make him happy. Give him a chance, Carmen, that's all I'm asking." She turned on her high heel and flounced away. The ruffles on her dress floated around her like butterflies.

All I could do was watch her leave and try to squash the sudden hope that flared up in my shattered heart.

I went back to the newspaper and wrote my story. I waited for the usual e-mail response, packed up my things, and left. I passed Henry's empty desk on the way out. He'd been spending less and less of his spare time at the office and more and more of it with Lulu. I was glad the computer whiz wasn't in his chair. I didn't need another superhero telling me how to run my life.

I pulled on my jacket and stepped outside. After the attack, I'd tried to avoid walking home alone late at night. I wasn't afraid of being raped or mugged now. Funny what being dropped into a vat of radioactive waste did for your courage.

I ambled down the streets and brooded. I thought about Sam and the Fearless Five and Sam and Sam some more. I'd been so hurt by Matt. Did I want to take a chance on having my heart broken by another superhero? One who seemed to want my powers just as much as he wanted me? Suddenly, my inner voice screeched.

"Help! Somebody please help me!" a woman's voice rang out.

Somebody was in trouble. I picked up my pace. I turned a corner and found a young woman with her back pressed against the wall. Three men stood in front of the woman, who clutched her purse over her chest.

"Hey! What do you think you're doing?" I shouted.

One of the men glanced over his shoulder. I froze. It was the same man who had tried to rape me all those weeks ago. The same man Striker had reduced to a pile of mush. Why the hell was he walking around free as a bird? Maybe he'd taken up the bad ubervillain habit of not staying in prison more than a few days before busting out.

"Well, well, sweet stuff. How are tricks?" the man crooned. He grinned, and I noticed he was missing some of his gold-capped teeth. "Look's like we're going to get two for the price of one tonight, boys."

The men laughed. I took a breath to calm my nerves.

Striker wasn't going to swoop in and save me this time. I'd have to do it myself. The leader walked toward me, and I concentrated on him just the way Chief Newman had taught me. Slowly but surely, I spotted wavy lines of psychic energy emanating from his body. Black waves. Just like his soul.

The man drew closer, and I reached for the waves. He put his hand on my chest and drew me toward him. I ducked under the man's body and used his own power to flip him over my shoulder. He hit the sidewalk with a satisfying thud.

Another one of the men came at me. I tapped into his psychic energy and threw him back against the wall. The men shook off their injuries and came at me again. Once more, I used their own power to propel them back into the wall. They slammed against it so hard that bits of crumbled brick broke off. Dust thickened the air. The men staggered to their feet and lunged at me. For the third time, I sent them flying through the air. This time, they didn't get up.

The other man, seeing what I had done to his two companions, ran away.

I stepped over the groaning men toward the woman. "Are you okay?"

"I—I—I think so. How did you do that? It was amazing!" The woman's eyes were as big and round as marbles.

"Um, well, I take, um, karate lessons. Karate is all about using your opponent's strength against him."

"You saved me. You're my hero." The woman pumped my hand like she was meeting a rock star. "How can I ever thank you?"

"Call the police and report the men. I bet you're not the first woman they've attacked. And don't walk down the street by yourself at night. This neighborhood is dangerous.

You're just asking for trouble when you do that." Said the voice of experience. Me.

"I will, and I won't. Thanks again." The woman whipped out her cell phone.

She dialed 911. I ducked around the corner and hid in the shadows until I saw the flashing lights of a police car. Once the officer approached the woman, I eased down the street. I had no desire to be identified as the Good Samaritan and explain how I took out two men with my bare hands and scared another one away. My karate story wouldn't cut it with the cops.

"Nicely done, although I would have stuck around for the TV cameras. It's always good to remind people just how noble and heroic you are," a low, male voice murmured behind me.

I shrieked and whirled around, ready to do battle once more. To my surprise, Swifte stood behind me. I hadn't even heard the speedy superhero approach.

"What are you doing here?" I asked, wary.

"Nothing much. Just doing my usual patrols. I heard the woman scream and zipped over." Swifte eyed me. "And you were on the scene."

I froze. Had Swifte seen me take out those goons? Had he seen me use powers? Oh God, was he going to expose me as I'd exposed so many superheroes? For a moment, I couldn't breathe. That'd be some karmic retribution all right.

"Yeah. I got lucky." I made my voice light and cheery, as though I tackled would-be rapists every day. "I've been taking karate lessons, you see."

"Karate. Right." Swifte started to lean against the side of the building, but thought better of it, given his shimmering white suit. "What you did back there looked like superpowers to me. Some sort of fancy telekinesis or something."

"I don't know what you're talking about." When caught, deny all knowledge.

"Of course you don't," he said.

We stood there in silence. Finally, Swifte spoke again.

"There's been a lot of talk about you lately, Carmen. The incident at the ice cream factory is all that anyone can think about these days."

My mouth dropped open. "How do you know about that?" Nobody in the media had any idea what had really happened at the factory. Even SNN hadn't broken the story. Police officials, including Chief Newman, had blamed the explosion on gas leaks.

"Word gets around. Most of us superheroes know how you saved the Fearless Five and that Malefica was really the one who killed Tornado. You're no longer public enemy number one among the crowd."

"Word gets around? Or just you?"

Swifte smiled, and his greenish eyes glittered. "Both. But it was good of you, saving that woman. Who knows? Maybe I'll see you around again. Your *karate skills* would come in quite handy in certain organizations in Bigtime. I hear the Fearless Five have an opening. But you already know that, don't you, Carmen?"

I opened my mouth to deny once again that I had any sort of superpowers or connection to the Fearless Five, but Swifte sped off before I formed the first syllable. Damn, he was fast.

I did the same. I scurried through the deserted streets to my apartment, shut the door behind me, and locked it. I sank down onto the sofa and stared into space. The enormity of what had just happened hit me. My hands trembled. My knees quivered. I'd just used my power to save someone else. I'd acted like, well, a superhero. Reckless and daring and unconcerned for my own safety. One false move, one lucky shot from those men, and I could have been raped or worse along with that other woman. But I hadn't been thinking about myself. All that had concerned me was saving her. Making sure she didn't get hurt.

It had felt good, right, like what I was supposed to do with my life.

It felt like karma.

My karma had lightened in recent days. It had gone from deep black to a misty shade of gray. Even though Malefica had been the one who had murdered Tornado, I would always feel a deep sense of guilt, of responsibility for his death. After all, if I hadn't exposed him, then Malefica would never have been able to target him. My inner voice whispered a surprising thought to me, one I had never considered before.

Perhaps this was a way to atone for my many sins. To become the very thing I had vowed to destroy—a superhero. I let out a bitter laugh. Karma was funny that way. Just when you thought you had everything worked out, something totally unexpected happened. Like being dropped into a vat of radioactive liquid and getting superpowers.

But did having powers automatically make me a superhero? Was that all it took? I didn't know the answer to that question.

All I knew was that I had to find out. One way or another.

I picked up the phone.

"Talk to me."

I met Lulu the next day in our usual spot by the fountain in the park.

"Sister Carmen, it's good to see you."

"You too, Lulu. You too."

We made small talk for a few moments. I smiled as Lulu gushed about what a great guy Henry was and how thrilled she was I had introduced the two of them.

"I knew you two would like each other," I said in a smug voice.

"Really? How?"

"Oh, it was just a feeling that I had." I wasn't ready to tell Lulu my secret. Maybe someday, but not today. "By the way, I want to thank you for leaking the information about Malefica to the press. Everyone is having a field day with it. Morgana Madison can never show her face in this town again, if she's even still alive."

Lulu grinned. "It was my pleasure. I'm just glad that you're all right. When I didn't hear from you, I was a little concerned. Of course, if I'd known you'd gotten bonked in the head and that the Fearless Five had taken you in, I wouldn't have worried quite so much."

I winced. "Sorry about that. But in my defense, I was unconscious for over a week."

"Just don't let it happen again. Now, down to business. What can I do for you today, Sister Carmen?"

"I need you to find out where the Fearless Five are going to be tonight. Who's on their to-get list."

Lulu arched an eyebrow. "Why do I get a strange sense of déjà vu?"

"It's not like that. I'm not going to expose them. I just want to . . . thank them for everything they've done for me. That's all." I crossed my heart. "I promise."

"All right. Only because it's you, and I need another reminder about the riding program put in the newspaper."

"Consider it done," I said.

Lulu's fingers moved over her keyboard, reminding me of Henry. Documents and files flashed up on the screen and then disappeared just as quickly. I could have called up Henry or the chief and gotten the info myself, but I didn't want them to know I was coming. I needed to be sure before I did anything drastic.

"Looks like the Five aren't too happy with the Westsiders. They're a bunch of gangbangers who run drugs and gambling. They've been trying to muscle in on the Southside crew's turf since that big drug bust a couple of months ago. Some of them have some minor superpowers, but nothing the Fearless Five can't handle. The Westsiders are having a little get-together tonight to elect a new head honcho. The last guy got gunned down last week. The Fearless Five might try to bust up the meeting." Lulu rattled off an address.

I wrote it down. "Thanks, Lulu."

"Anytime, Sister Carmen. Anytime."

Lulu zoomed off to meet Henry for coffee, and I strolled through the thick pines to Bigtime Cemetery. Row 17. Plot 325. I made my way to Travis aka Tornado Teague's grave. Sun bounced off the white marble, which shimmered like a star.

"Well, I suppose you know why I'm here. I've decided to give this superhero thing a whirl. I'll never be as good as you, but I have to try."

A bee buzzed by, and a flock of pigeons cooed nearby. A chipmunk skittered up a tree.

"I'm sorry for what I did to you. For what Malefica did. If I'd known, well, things would have been different. But I'm going to spend the rest of my life trying to make it up to you and the Fearless Five. I'm going to be the best superhero I can be. I swear."

Travis's ghost didn't appear to tell me I was doing the

right thing. No triumphant music played. Lightning didn't crisscross the sky. I didn't even get a warm, fuzzy glow.

But my heart felt a little lighter, my karma a little brighter. It was enough.

I said my goodbyes to Travis and walked back to my apartment to get ready for tonight. I did the usual routine. Shower, clothes, makeup. I stood in front of the dresser in the bedroom and pulled my hair back into a ponytail. My eyes fell on my jewelry box, and my inner voice murmured.

I unlocked the bottom drawer and pulled out the engagement ring Matt had given to me once upon a time. It was a square diamond set in a gold band. I held it up to the light and turned it around. The ring looked smaller than I remembered. Dimmer. It didn't hurt me to look at it, as it once had. Matt and I had had some good times, before the end. I would remember those.

I put the ring back in the drawer, but I didn't lock it away. I didn't need to.

My heart belonged to Sam now. The superhero would take better care of it than Matt had.

I was counting on it.

★ 32 ★

That night, I was once again on Good Intentions Lane, despite my own best intentions. Or rather because of them. I shifted. Something squeaked in the trashcan next to me, and I inched away from it. I didn't want to see the foot-long rat staring at me from the piles of rotting garbage. I could see the waves of energy radiating off its body. That was more than enough.

At the stroke of midnight, the Westsiders appeared, just as Lulu had said they would. The Westsiders were men in their early twenties and thirties dressed in baggy pants and expensive sneakers. They climbed out of black SUVs and low-riders that blared rap music. The men slapped hands and did those complicated handshakes I could never follow.

Suddenly, a silver sword sailed through the air, just as it had so many weeks ago, and planted itself into one of the tires on a particularly large SUV. Striker leapt out onto the hood of a car and launched himself into the crowd. Mo-

ments later, Fiera and Mr. Sage appeared. I even spotted
Hermit in the mix. The superheroes waded through the
gangsters like a chain saw cutting through butter. In less
than a minute, half the gangsters were down. In another
minute, the ones who could still move were running and
crawling away.

My eyes focused on Striker. He punched a Westsider
and lashed out at another one with his booted foot. He
moved with deadly grace, just like always. He looked even
better than I remembered. Even better than in my most
vivid dream. My heart leapt at the sight of him. There was
just something about that tight, black leather suit that
drove me crazy.

Out of the corner of my eye, I spotted someone sneaking up behind Striker. The superhero was busy battling
two other Westsiders. A ball of lightning glimmered in
the hidden man's hand. I reached for the gray waves of energy around him. The ball fizzed out, and I used the ambient energy to throw the man into a nearby wall. He didn't
get up.

Striker finished pummeling his foes. He whirled around,
not quite sure what had happened. I stepped out from the
shadows. He spotted me immediately.

"Carmen." His eyes brightened, burning into me.

Striker opened his mouth to say something, when Hermit came over.

"Carmen! It's good to see you!" He clapped me on the
back.

"You too Hermit."

Fiera and Mr. Sage joined us. Westsiders groaned and
moaned on the ground.

"So what brings you down here? Other than helping us
out again," Hermit asked. His goggles gleamed in the
dark night.

I took a deep breath. "I want to join the team. If you guys will still have me."

"Of course we will. We'd be honored," Striker said in a low, hesitant voice. "If you're sure this is what you really want. We don't want to pressure you into anything."

"I'm sure. This is where I need to be. I can feel it." I gave him a tentative smile, which Striker returned. My heart pounded.

"Excellent. Most excellent," Mr. Sage said, pumping my hand. "Welcome aboard, Carmen."

"Thanks."

Hermit smiled and clapped me on the shoulder. I looked at Fiera.

She stared at me. Finally, she nodded her head. "Welcome to the team."

I let out a breath. "Thanks. I won't let you down. I promise."

"We'll see about that." Fiera stalked around me, her blue eyes hot and thoughtful.

I shifted under her probing gaze. "Why are you looking at me like that?"

"I'm just sizing you up," Fiera said.

"Why?"

She put her hands on her hips. "So I can make your costume, silly."

I rode back to Sublime in the van with the Fearless Five. Once everyone had showered and changed into their regular clothes, we went upstairs to the kitchen. We ate junk food and talked and laughed and joked late into the night. Finally, though, the conversation turned to me and my new job as a superhero.

"There are several things we need to take care of," Chief

Newman said. "First of all, we've got to work on your power. You've got a good grasp on it, but I think you could do more with it."

"I need to plug her into all the computer systems, not to mention get her set up on all the communication equipment," Henry added.

"She needs a costume and a mask," Fiona said. "I've got that covered."

"Carmen needs her own room downstairs too," Sam finished.

The four of them exchanged awkward glances. I knew what they were thinking.

"No," I said. "Tornado will always be with you guys. I can't take his place, and I don't want to. I'll use another room."

Fiona squeezed my hand so hard I thought she was going to break my fingers. Somehow, I managed not to wince at her firm grip. Too much.

Finally, we said good night. I went up to my old suite and sat on the bed, waiting. A knock sounded a few moments later. My inner voice whispered. This was it. The big moment. The one I'd been waiting for all night.

I opened the door. Sam stood outside. For once, the superhero wore a pair of loose jeans and a black T-shirt. Maybe my bad habits were rubbing off on him. He looked as yummy in them as he did everything else, and my hormones kicked into overdrive.

"Hey," I said in what I hoped was a cool, collected voice.

"Hey yourself."

He stood there in front of me. So close. So far away.

I stepped back. "Come in, if you want."

Sam didn't hesitate. He stepped inside, and I closed the door behind him.

"We need to talk," he said, settling on the couch.

"I know." I plopped down on the other end. I didn't trust myself to get any closer to him. Not yet. Not until I knew the answer to my question.

Sam raked his hand through his dark hair. "I don't know how to start."

"Just start," I said. "We'll figure it out."

He nodded. "That day in the garden when you asked me what I wanted, I didn't handle things well. You were going through a lot. I should have understood. I should have been more patient."

I shook my head. "I've been meaning to apologize to you. I was going through a lot, but I shouldn't have flipped out like that. I shouldn't have accused you of just wanting my power. I should have known better."

"No," Sam said. "I'm sorry. I sprang that on you with no warning, without even thinking."

"And what do you want now?" I asked, breathless.

"You, Carmen. Just you."

My heart soared.

"Even if you don't stay with us, even if you decide one day you don't want to be a superhero, I still want to try and figure out what this thing is between us. I care about you, Carmen. More than I've cared about anyone in a long time. I don't want to lose you. Ever." He took a deep breath. "I wanted to die when Malefica dumped you in that vat. I felt like my heart had been ripped out of my chest. For the first time in my life, I didn't want to fight. I only wanted to save you. The truth is, I love you, Carmen. I have for weeks now—"

That was all Sam got out before I threw myself at him. I pressed him down onto the sofa and rained kisses on his mouth, his cheeks, even his eyelids.

He laughed and caught my hands in his. I kept on kissing him. "Well, this wasn't exactly the response I thought

I'd get, but I'll definitely take it. Does this mean that—"

"It means I love you too," I said. "I love you, Sam Striker Sloane."

Our lips met. Happiness swelled my heart until I thought it would burst. Not to mention the liquid fire Sam ignited deep within me.

The kiss ended, and I drew back. "Now that we've gotten those pesky declarations of love out of the way, why don't you carry me over to that big, beautiful bed and make love to me?"

"Why walk all that distance?"

Sam pulled me closer, and I melted in his arms.

Two days later, I sat in the underground library. Swatches of color littered the wooden table in front of me.

"Which do you like better, flamingo or fuchsia?" Fiona asked.

"How about something a little less . . . flamboyant?" I said. "I'm not really an over-the-top sort of girl."

Fiona had kept her word. She was outfitting me with a superhero costume. We'd been looking at color swatches and samples for over an hour, each one more outrageous than the last.

Fiona waved her hand. "Sure you are. You just don't know it yet. Being over-the-top is what being a superhero is all about. Do you have a name picked out for yourself? I was thinking of something bold, something daring, something that looks good in neon pink."

I could barely contain my shudder of revulsion. Neon pink? Ugh! "Actually, I have a name for myself, one I think is quite appropriate."

"Really? What is it?"

I smiled. "Karma Girl."

"Karma Girl? What kind of superhero name is that?" Fiona scoffed. "It doesn't say anything about you. It doesn't even say what your power is."

"You're wrong," I said. "It says everything about me."

After much haggling and some heated words, the two of us agreed on a color—a nice silver that didn't have too many sparkles in it. Now, I could only pray I'd actually fit into the catsuit Fiona was designing for me.

A few hours later, I stared at myself in the mirror. "I look ridiculous. Like a giant snowflake come to life. Or an oversized disco ball."

"You look fine," Fiona snapped. "After all, you're wearing a Fiona Fine original. Put on the mask."

I dutifully pulled on the mask. I barely recognized myself. Silver spandex covered me from head to toe, and the mask obscured the top half of my face. Chunky boots encased my feet and a pair of gloves completed the look. Fiona wanted to add a cape to my new superhero ensemble, but I refused. I wasn't wearing a cape. No way, no how. I might be a superhero, but I had to draw the line somewhere.

"I don't know if I can wear this out in public," I said. "I feel like I'm wearing a Halloween costume."

"Yeah, that's a common reaction at first, but you'll get used to it," Fiona said. "We all did. Soon, you won't want to go anywhere without wearing your superhero suit underneath your clothes or having a backup in your purse."

"Really?"

Fiona nodded. "Trust me. You won't want to leave home without it. After all, you never know when you might have to battle an ubervillain or save some kid who's trapped in a well."

★ Epilogue ★

Two weeks later, Sam and I snuggled together, still blissful from our latest round of passion. We'd both played hooky from work and spent the afternoon making love in his massive bed. I'd never been happier in my entire life. I didn't know what I had done to deserve Sam, but I was damn sure going to do everything in my power to keep him. Bad karma, or no karma.

A loud crackle sounded, startling me out of my dreamy reverie.

"What's that?" I whispered, pulling the sheets up to my chin.

"The intercom." Sam pushed a button on the wall next to the bed.

"Um, guys?" Henry's voice echoed through the room. "I really hate to . . . interrupt, but we've got a bit of a situation."

"What sort of situation?" Sam asked.

"The chief just e-mailed me some information about a

new group of ubervillains in town. They've robbed a couple of museums today, and the police are chasing them. With no success of course. We need to stop them before they level the city."

"We'll be there shortly," Sam said.

"Roger that. Over and out."

Sam flicked off the intercom. "It looks like we'll just have to wait to pick up where we left off later. Unfortunately, untimely interruptions are part of the job."

"I understand." I smiled. "I guess it's time we went to work."

I started to rise, but Sam pulled me back down on top of him. "We still have a few minutes left." His fingers began their familiar route down my body.

I shivered at the wicked, wanton light in his silvery eyes. "Then let's make the most of it," I whispered before lowering my lips to his.

Keep reading for a look at the next novel in
the Bigtime series by Jennifer Estep

Hot Mama

Available now from Berkley Books!

My wedding day.

It was supposed to be the happiest day of my life. A time of joy and celebration and new beginnings. The day every girl dreams of from the time she's old enough to play dress-up in her mother's clothes.

It was exactly that sort of day.

Joy. Hope. New beginnings.

But it wasn't *mine*.

Carmen Cole twirled in front of the full-length mirror. Her white satin wedding dress swung out in an arc then gathered back in on itself. Thousands of Swarovski crystals dotted the fitted bodice and full skirt, giving the dress a shimmering, ethereal air. A matching crystal necklace sparkled like a ring of stars around her neck.

"How do I look, Fiona?" Carmen turned her blue eyes to mine.

I hated to admit it, but Carmen looked fantastic. Absolutely fantastic. A rosy flush tinted her cheeks. Excitement brightened her eyes. Even her auburn hair glistened underneath her simple lace veil.

"You look fabulous. After all, you're wearing a Fiona Fine original."

Carmen frowned at her reflection. "I know it's one of your more subdued designs, but I still think it's a little much."

I crossed my arms over my chest. An errant spark flew from my thumb and landed on the beige carpet. I squashed it with my stiletto. A little much? Please. If Carmen had gotten her way, she would have worn holey jeans, worn-out sneakers, and a ratty T-shirt with some cutesy saying on it to the wedding.

Luckily, hotter heads had prevailed. Mine. Then again, it was easy to get your way when you had the ability to shoot fire out of your fingertips. Getting my way was one of the prime benefits of being a superhero. My favorite benefit.

Just because I moonlight as a superhero doesn't mean I can't be a little selfish—or enjoy the perks of having superpowers. Usually, I'm perfectly happy just being Fiera, one of many superheroes in Bigtime, New York, fighting evil, cracking skulls, and making life miserable for all those pesky ubervillains who want to take over the city, then the world. But every once in a while, I enjoy showing off my fiery skills, especially when it's for the greater good, such as making sure Carmen didn't look like a bag lady at her own wedding.

A knock sounded on the door, the knob turned, and Lulu Lo zipped her motorized wheelchair into the room. A royal blue dress covered the Asian woman's slender form, bringing out the smoothness of her porcelain skin and the cobalt streaks in her spiky black hair. Since we were both bridesmaids, I wore a matching gown, but with a few modifications—a lower bodice, a tighter fit, and a higher slit up the side.

"Nice dress, Sister Carmen." Lulu whistled. "That'll make Sam sit up and take notice."

Carmen grinned. Another spark shot out from my thumb. Sam had already taken plenty of *notice* of Carmen, despite my efforts to the contrary. The two of them were always sneaking off to have wild sex in some corner of the manor house.

"Of course Sam will notice," I snapped. "I designed the dress. Ours too, if you'll remember. They're all fabulous."

"Well, you do look very *hot*, Fiona." Lulu laughed.

I glowered at Lulu. Just because I was a member of the Fearless Five, one of the most esteemed superhero teams in the world, didn't mean that I didn't get snarly from time to time—or that civilians like Lulu had the right to poke fun at me.

Of course, none of this would be happening if Carmen, aka Karma Girl, hadn't insisted we tell Lulu our secret, superhero identities. Carmen had argued that Lulu deserved to know the truth, since she'd helped save us from the Terrible Triad, a group of ubervillains. Lulu was also the main squeeze of Henry Harris, aka Hermit of the Fearless Five, and he'd wanted to tell her the truth as well. The other two members of the Fearless Five, Sam "Striker" Sloane and Sean "Mr. Sage" Newman, had agreed with Carmen.

So the four of them told Lulu everything, despite my protests. Once the shock wore off, Lulu ingratiated herself with the rest of the Fearless Five. Now, everybody else treated her like one of the gang. She even had her own room in the top-secret, underground compound with the rest of us.

I ignored Lulu whenever possible. It was bad enough she knew our real identities. I didn't want to invite her any more into our lives. Lulu was a computer hacker. She did all sorts of highly illegal things, like breaking into the FBI mainframe and swapping corporate secrets, but nobody cared except me. Not even my father, the esteemed police chief of Bigtime as well as a member of the Fearless Five.

In return for my blatant hostility, Lulu zinged me with heat-related puns whenever we crossed paths. *Fiona's hot. Fiona's smokin'. Fiona's on fire.* Like I hadn't heard them all a hundred thousand times before. Ha, ha, ha, ha. Lulu could have at least come up with something original, if she was going to mock me on a daily basis.

My eyes fixed on Lulu's hair. I could turn those blue streaks red in a heartbeat. Heat pulsed through my body. My fingers twitched. Just one little spark . . .

"Fiona," Carmen warned. "There will be no flare-ups today. You promised Sam."

I had promised Sam. And my father. And Henry. And even Carmen. Three times each. I let go of the fire coursing through my veins and banked it deep inside me. It didn't matter anyway. Carmen would have just done her empathy thing and used the ambient energy in the room to buffer Lulu and herself from my heat. Carmen had the ability to tap into other people and use their own energy against them. I hated her power, mainly because I hadn't figured out a way to counteract it yet. Most of the time, I either punched or flambéed my way through danger. But I couldn't do that with Carmen, because she gave just as good as she got.

Lulu smirked at me and motored away. She'd probably max out my credit cards or do some other devious, identity-theft thing as soon as the wedding ended. I didn't know what Henry saw in her. Maybe he was just glad that he'd finally found someone who understood all the techno-babble he spouted on a daily basis.

Lulu left the door open, and classical music drifted in, along with the murmur of distant conversations. I eyed the clock on the wall. Five minutes to go. Good. The sooner this spectacle was over with, the better. I wasn't in the mood for a wedding today. Not any day. Not anymore.

Carmen picked up on my dark thoughts and stared at me in the mirror. "I know this has been hard for you, Fiona. The engagement, the wedding, everything. I'm sorry. I wish things were different. I wish Tornado was still here . . ."

Her soft Southern twang trailed off under my hot gaze. Hard for me? She had no idea.

It'd been over a year since my fiancé, Tornado, had been murdered. Carmen had exposed the superhero's secret identity as Travis Teague to the world, including our arch-enemies, the Terrible Triad. The ubervillains had killed Travis and used Carmen to get to the rest of us. We'd been captured, stuffed in glass tubes, and almost sucked dry of our superpowers, before Carmen had saved us by getting dumped into a vat of radioactive goo and developing superpowers herself.

Sometimes, I couldn't believe the irony of it. Carmen exposing superheroes, becoming one herself, and now marrying one. Things never seemed to turn out the way you thought they would, especially in Bigtime.

Mostly, though, I still couldn't believe Travis was gone. Forever. My heart twisted, and the burning fire inside me flickered and dimmed. My eyes dropped to the square, diamond engagement ring on my finger. Travis had given it to me a week before he'd died. I hadn't taken it off since.

"Fiona? Are you okay?" Carmen asked.

I wasn't. Not even close. But this was Carmen's big day, and I didn't want to ruin it for her.

"I'm fine," I lied. "In fact, I was thinking that it's time for me to get out and start dating again. I've done the men of Bigtime a cruel, heartless injustice, depriving them of my fabulous company all this time." I tossed my long blond hair over my shoulder for effect.

Carmen's face lit up like I'd just hit her with a fireball between the eyes. "That's wonderful, Fiona! Just wonderful!"

Her blue eyes grew cloudy and distant, the way they always did when she was listening to the strange whispers in her head. Carmen called them her inner voice, her instincts. I thought she had more than a few loose rocks rattling around in all that empty space.

"Maybe you'll meet somebody at the reception," she murmured.

I huffed. Please. I'd been active on the social scene ever since I'd moved to Bigtime some fifteen years ago, and I knew everybody invited to the wedding. There wasn't a man among them that I'd date, let alone sleep with.

I twisted the ring on my finger. The silver solidium band heated up on my hot hand, and the diamond glowed like a tiny moon. Still, I would like to find somebody. It'd be nice to be part of a couple again. To laugh and talk and have dinner with someone who wasn't a relative or an employee or a fellow superhero. To find somebody who looked at me the way that Sam looked at Carmen.

Plus, I liked sex. A lot. It sucked to go without.

My hand stilled. Maybe that's what I should do. Get drunk at the reception, have a one-night stand with some anonymous guy to take the edge off, and then start looking for someone suitable. Someone more long-term. The only problem with my plan was that it would take an ocean of champagne to get me drunk, given my fast-burning metabolism. Well, it was a good thing Sam was richer than almost everyone else on the planet put together. He could afford a couple hundred thousand dollars' worth of bubbly if it meant me getting lucky.

The music quickened and swelled, and the conversations faded away. The air hummed with energy and anticipation.

"Time to go." Carmen smoothed down her billowing skirt. Her hand trembled just a bit.

I picked up her long train, careful not to singe the fabric with my fingers. I'd spent too much time sewing the damn thing to ruin it now. Carmen turned and grabbed my arm.

"Do you think this is the right thing to do? Do you think we should go through with it? Do you think we're ready? You know how badly my last wedding turned out." Panic filled her blue eyes.

Badly was the understatement of the century. Right before the wedding, Carmen had found her fiancé boinking her best friend and discovered that the two were her town's resident superhero and ubervillain. That, of course, had set Carmen off on her little mission to expose the identity of every superhero and ubervillain who crossed her path. Which, of course, is how Carmen had met Sam and the rest of us. Karma, she called it. Destiny, kismet, fate. I just thought of it as bad luck on our part.

But I bit back the sarcastic retort I'd been ready to let loose. The nosy reporter had grown on me, despite my best efforts. And she had saved my life and everyone else's. I owed her for that. Plus, it was my solemn duty as a bridesmaid to support the bride—even if Carmen occasionally made me want to put my fist through a wall.

"Do you love Sam?"

Carmen nodded. Some of the tension left her body. "With all my heart."

"Then, it'll be fine," I said. "Sam loves you, and you love him. You're going to have a fabulous wedding, a fantastic honeymoon, and a wonderful life together. Plus, you're wearing a Fiona Fine original couture gown. And what could possibly be better than that?"

Penguin Group (USA) Online

What will you be reading tomorrow?

Tom Clancy, Patricia Cornwell, W.E.B. Griffin,
Nora Roberts, William Gibson, Robin Cook,
Brian Jacques, Catherine Coulter, Stephen King,
Dean Koontz, Ken Follett, Clive Cussler,
Eric Jerome Dickey, John Sandford,
Terry McMillan, Sue Monk Kidd, Amy Tan,
John Berendt…

You'll find them all at
penguin.com

*Read excerpts and newsletters,
find tour schedules and reading group guides,
and enter contests.*

Subscribe to Penguin Group (USA) newsletters
and get an exclusive inside look
at exciting new titles and the authors you love
long before everyone else does.

PENGUIN GROUP (USA)
us.penguingroup.com

M224G1107